CW00496199

TAINAN●
KAOHSIUNG● TAIWAN

●HONG KONG
MACAU
●

CHINA SEA

≡ URBAN AREAS
✦ DETENTION CENTRES

0   5   10   15
KILOMETRES

NEW TERRITORIES

TOLO HARBOUR
✦WHITEHEAD

●SHA TIN

HIGH ISLAND ✦

KOWLOON

MONG KOK● ✦KAI TAK

GREEN ISLAND✦

LANTAU ISLAND

✦ ✦CHEI LING CHAU

HONG KONG

CHI MA WAN

LAMMA ISLAND

PHILIPPINES

AIGON)

400   500

TANIA WILLIS

The Ghost Locust

The Ghost Locust

Heather Stroud

Asia 2000 Limited
Hong Kong

ISBN 962-7160-69-5

Published by Asia 2000 Ltd
302 Seabird House,
22–28 Wyndham Street, Central,
Hong Kong

http://www.asia2000.com.hk/

Typeset with Ventura Publisher in Adobe Garamond by Asia 2000
Printed in Hong Kong by Regal Printing

First printing 1999

Quotes from *Prison Diary* by Ho Chi Minh
are from the translation by Dang The Binh,
Foreign Languages Publishing House,
Hanoi, sixth edition, 1978

After peace is restored, the Vietnamese people will work with might and main to rebuild their motherland. They will turn it into a unified, peaceful, independent, democratic and prosperous country, having friendly relations with all the peaceful people of the world.

HO CHI MINH, NOVEMBER 1966

Dedicated to the indomitable spirit of the people of Vietnam

Contents

Dramatis personae 9

Prologue 11
Hue, Lunar New Year — Tet Mau Than — 25th February 1968

Chapter 1: The bitter taste of salt 15
Quang Ninh Province — North Vietnam, 21st to 24th April 1980

Chapter 2: Struggle, call for noble duty 33
Hong Gai, Quang Ninh Province, Early hours 25th April 1980

Chapter 3: The fates unleashed 57
25th to early hours 26th April 1980

Chapter 4: Failed rendezvous 78
Quang Ninh Province, 26th April 1980

Chapter 5: Before youth has left, old age has come 92
26th to 27th April 1980

Chapter 6: The way north 109
27th April to 7th July 1980

Chapter 7: New Economic Confinement Zone 138
15th July 1980 to 20th January 1981

Chapter 8: Dong Hung Refugee Camp, China 151
10th February to 5th May 1981

Chapter 9: Exit Dong Hung 171
6th August 1983 to 7th May 1984

Chapter 10: Old scores 186
19th June 1984 to 3rd April 1985

Chapter 11: Hoa Lo Central Prison 196
26th July 1985 to 3rd April 1986

Chapter 12: Full circle 217
3rd December 1985 to 17th August 1986

Chapter 13: Thanh Hoa Prison 226
17th June 1986 to 3rd April 1988

Chapter 14: Back to the mercy of the seas 245
29th May to 12th October 1988

Chapter 15: Pearl of the Orient 258
Whitehead Detention Centre for Vietnamese Boat People, Hong Kong
6th September to 12th December 1990

Chapter 16: A switch of identity 273
7th September to 4th October 1990

Chapter 17: Over the fence 299
5th to 7th October 1991

Chapter 18: Hidden cameras 314
20th May to 13th November 1992

Chapter 19: Return to Vietnam 336
22nd March to 3rd April 1993

Chapter 20: To go forward is to go back 357
12th to 29th April 1993

Chapter 21: Returning home 369
Haiphong, 4th to 9th May 1993

Author's note 391

Acknowledgments 393

About the author 396

Dramatis personae

THANH, (pronounced *Tang* with soft *g*) cousin to Nam, wife to Lan and brother-in-law to Minh, Cuong and Tang. Joined the National Liberation Army as a young teenager. Later joined the North Vietnamese Army before being transferred into the Sappers (Special Forces). Worked in intelligence for his Uncle Chau (General Nguyen Tat Chau). Communist Party member and Public Security officer.

GENERAL NGUYEN TAT CHAU, (pronounced *Nwin Tat Chow*) father to Nam and brother to Thanh's father. Former member of the Viet Minh. Served time at the notorious Poulo Condore Island Prison for his communist activities. At the conclusion of the American war he became a Party Member of the Central Committee. Reformist — more on the side of Soviet revisionism than hard-line Chinese policy.

DUNG, (pronounced *Zung*) younger brother of Hien. At the beginning of the novel he is seventeen years old and lives in Cam Pha with his brother Hien. His mother moved to Haiphong, to live with Dung's elder sister and her husband, after the family home was requisitioned during the Chinese border incursion.

HIEN, (pronounced *Hin*) long-time friend of Cuong and Tang. Elder brother to Dung. Former serviceman in the North Vietnamese Army during the American war.

CUONG, (pronounced *Kung*) from the Hmong Hill Tribes in Lao Cai. Married to Minh and brother-in-law to Thanh, Lan and Tang. Fought during the American war with the North Vietnamese Army. Later called back into service during the Chinese border incursion.

MINH, (pronounced *Ming* with soft *g*) youngest sibling of Lan and Tang, mother of three, and sister-in-law to Thanh, wife of Cuong. At the start of the novel lives in Hong Gai. Considered to be from a blacklisted family because parents were Catholic and father worked as a French functionary.

HA, young friend of Dung. Lived in Cam Pha with her elder brother after the death of their parents.

LAN, married to Thanh. Middle child of three, elder brother Tang and younger sister Minh.

HUONG, (pronounced *Hung*) mother to Tuyet. Escaped from Haiphong on the same boat as Hien and Cuong.

KHIEM, (pronounced *Kim*) senior officer in military intelligence. His career path was blocked after Thanh's and Uncle Chau's investigation of the Hue massacre (Tet 1968). Senior officer investigating Cuong's defection from the army.

NIKI, Amerasian camp worker. Born in Vietnam and raised by her aunt after her Vietnamese mother died. Later adopted by an American family and moved to the US.

CHINH, (pronounced *Ching*) Vietnamese camp worker, with Australian passport. Member of Rights for Refugees. Worked with Niki in Whitehead Detention Centre with the asylum-seekers on the camp magazine *Magazine Independence and Liberty*.

Prologue

Hue
Lunar New Year — Tet Mau Than — 25th February 1968

This Tet is different from the others.
It far outshines previous springs.
Of triumphs throughout the land come happy tidings.
Forward, march! Victory is ours.
HO CHI MINH

THE RAIN FELL SOUNDLESSLY, its dampness rising back from the earth in a shroud of haze. The hours, passing without interruption, smudged daytime into night. With shoulders stooped forward, Thanh stood alone. Oblivious to his rain-soaked clothes, he stared fixedly into the growing darkness at the row upon row of ditches stretched out in front of him. The evidence of the impossible was undeniable. The air he breathed was noxious, heavy with the sulphurous odour excreted from the bloated flesh of victims slaughtered during the massacre — their remains thrown carelessly into the ditches, rotted into the ground as though they were of no more value than decaying vegetation. Crushed by horror and shame Thanh tried closing his eyes, but the image imprinted onto his brain refused to go away. Struggling to hold back his revulsion he felt as though it was he who had pulled the trigger which blasted away their breath.

Three weeks ago he had been in Saigon. The surprise Lunar New Year offensive they staged against the Saigon government had been partially successful. Losses were high for the National Liberation Front and the People's Armed Vietnamese Forces, but Thanh, fighting for freedom from foreign masters, had felt proud. Facing superior weaponry his compatriots fought courageously. During the first two days of the offensive in Saigon they penetrated the American Embassy, permanently blowing away the myth that the American's had all but won the war. Although Saigon had been swiftly taken back, the ancient capital city of Hue was still in the midst of a fierce battle. The Citadel was firmly under the control of the National Liberation Front and the North Vietnamese forces. When Thanh picked up a radio message from his uncle, General Nguyen Tat Chau, requesting that he make his way north to Hue to investigate rumours of a civilian massacre reported on a BBC radio broadcast, Thanh had wanted to believe the rumours were untrue. Or if some semblance of truth existed, he prayed they were grossly exaggerated, initiated and perpetuated by his enemies to discredit the revolution.

As Thanh forced himself to absorb the reality of what lay in front of him the words of Thieu, the puppet president of the Americans, crept into his mind. 'Don't listen to what they say. Look at what they do.' He blinked his eyes to press back the tears. Thanh had dedicated his life to fighting for the unification of Vietnam. Their cause was just — of that he was sure, yet this violation against the people of Hue was nothing less than betrayal. Thanh sank his head in despair. He felt degraded, contaminated, his honour stained with the blood of innocent victims. How could he now argue their cause, the people's right to freedom and self-determination?

'We need to go, brother.' Thanh gave a start. The voice came from a few feet behind him. For the first time after years of fighting his defences were down. Having lost all sense of time and place he was oblivious to the dangers around him. Hue was not a secure city. There were fire-fights exploding in every quarter. Thanh had forgotten about Tuyen, the serious, young teenage National Liberation Front soldier who had escorted him to the place of the massacre. 'The Americans will release the illumination flares soon. They will light up the sky like. . . .'

'Why. . . ? How could this happen?' as Thanh spoke he hardly recognised his own voice. Distorted by suppressed rage his words came out choked, uneven.

Tuyen's muscles tightened around his jaw. 'The slaughter occurred on both sides. It wasn't just us.'

'What our enemies do isn't our concern.' Thanh shoved Tuyen toward the ditch. Gripping his left hand around the back of Tuyen's neck he forced his head forward. 'This . . . this . . . was this from both sides?'

Tuyen pulled away. His face blazed red. 'No. These were people we arrested — officials from the puppet government. Lieutenant Khiem ordered the massacre. He was afraid that if we lost they'd take revenge.'

'Lose. Revenge!' Thanh was incredulous. 'We won't lose.' Gesturing toward the carnage he suddenly felt overwhelmed. The effort of holding back his tears was too much and he let them roll freely from his eyes. 'They were our brothers and sisters,' he moaned. 'Given time they would have joined us. We would have celebrated our victory as one people. . . . All men desire liberty.' He wanted to strike out at someone — anyone. For a moment Tuyen seemed the likely target, but Thanh's sense of discipline was too ingrained and he knew Tuyen wasn't the one to blame. 'This man Khiem, how could he have ordered the slaughter? It goes against everything we're trying to achieve.'

Tuyen wiped the beads of sweat from his brow. 'We didn't want. . . .'

The sky suddenly lit up illuminating the terrain in hideous clarity. Frozen in the blast of the magnesium flares, time stopped. Staring up at him from out of the ditch was the face of a woman. Her eyes had been eaten away by vultures, but the empty sockets were more accusing than any living eyes. Thanh felt the blood rush to his head. As his anger surged, mortar fire blasted into the Gia Hoi School yard shaking the ground and hurling soil and debris in all directions. A burning tore through his shoulder, catapulting him backwards. His head struck against a concrete boulder and as waves of nausea swept over him he reeled from the shock. Savouring the pain in his shoulder and the honeyed smell of fresh blood as it soaked through his shirt and spilled into the ground, Thanh no longer cared if he lived or died. The physical injury was preferable to the pain in his heart. He lay still, enjoying the feeling of his lifeblood draining away, his eyes riveted to the spectacular, deadly night show. The sky turning from brilliant white to orange dissolved into a sickly, odorous fog, filling his lungs in a suffocating grasp. His chest tightened as he envisaged the dead woman's fingers, stretching from beyond the ditch, and clawing into the wound in his shoulder.

As they were plunged back into darkness, Tuyen crawled over to Thanh. 'Let's go brother. . . . Oh God! You're hurt? I was supposed to watch out for you.' Tuyen ripped off his shirt and pressed it hard against Thanh's upper chest and shoulder. 'This'll stop the bleeding a little.' Then hooking his arm around Thanh's back and under his arm pit, he tried to pull him upward.

Thanh made no effort to assist him but sank back into the ground. 'Leave me here. It's over.'

'No. You'll die. You have to go to Hanoi, report to Khiem. Believe me, none of us wanted this. We're depending upon you. Please, brother.'

The sudden rapid thump of helicopter motors starting up and the red ribbons of tracers arcing through the sky were disquieting reminders that the fighting would soon be directly overhead. Thanh could hear the exasperation in the boy's voice. If he stayed he would almost certainly die. Perhaps they would both die. Thanh realised Tuyen must be close to breaking point himself. Spurred by his companion's pleas, he allowed himself to be dragged up onto his knees and with Tuyen's help crawl over to the buildings. Taking shelter behind the rubble of a bombed-out classroom, they waited for a lull in the mortar fire.

'My brothers and I will come back here.' Tuyen's voice was heavy with emotion. 'We'll set up joss-sticks. Try to make peace with the dead.' Tuyen suddenly stopped speaking and ducked low as the beam of a helicopter's searchlight swept across the schoolyard. The ribbon of light skimming over their hiding place was enough for Thanh to catch sight of the agonised lines stretched taught across Tuyen's face. He understood the look. He'd seen it too many times before and on boys younger than Tuyen.

Lying down alongside Thanh, Tuyen rewrapped his shirt tightly around Thanh's shoulder then pressed his fist into the wound. 'This isn't good. You're losing buckets of blood. I'll get you back to a safe area where the doctor can look after your injury. You have to leave Hue soon. We can't hold the city much longer, we're already in retreat. Colonel Thiep says he can arrange transport to get you beyond the demilitarised zone to Dong Hoi. From there you'll be able to hitch a ride with the empty convoy trucks returning to Hanoi.'

Tuyen's words penetrated Thanh's consciousness. As the blasts of rocket fire continued to pound the ground, Thanh could feel his dizziness taking hold. Tuyen was right. He couldn't afford to linger. To be careless was self-indulgent. He needed to summon his strength and stay alert just to get out of the school yard. It was too late to achieve justice for victims of the massacre, but at least their suffering need not go unreported. Only the rightness of the contest could bring an honourable victory.

Chapter 1: The bitter taste of salt

Quang Ninh Province — North Vietnam
21st to 24th April 1980

Still darkness covers the earth, but we are forced to set out.
The road is tortuous, as well as rugged and hard.
Stumbling I find I have fallen into a dangerous pit.
PRISON DIARY, HO CHI MINH

THERE IS A VIETNAMESE SAYING that if a father eats salt his children become thirsty, and so it is with this story, the roots of which weave back through several decades. The nineteenth of April, 1980, although not the first day this account could be said to have begun, is, however, the day Thanh's brother-in-law, Cuong, deserted from the army and inadvertently released the karmic forces that catapulted Thanh and Dung onto the path of their destiny. . . .

Dung held his breath. Wiping the drips of rain that splashed down through the leaves onto his face he stared intently as his brother Hien carefully forced a slim iron rod into the ground. They were in Dong Dang, five kilometres from the market town of Lang Son, but dangerously close to the Sino–Vietnamese border. The dense canopy of jungle foliage hanging over the red dirt pathway which wound its way into China, shielded them from the heaviest of the rain.

'It's not booby-trapped!' shouted Hien. Dung let out his breath. Although the worst had passed, the danger was far from over. With muddied fingers Hien clawed his way through the soggy undergrowth to the damp soil. Marking out a circle, he shouted again to his brother. 'Pass the machete.' Dung snatched up the machete and, leaving his place under the heavy-leafed rubber tree, carried it over to Hien. 'Thanks,' said Hien. 'Now shoo.'

Dung reluctantly retreated to his lookout point. The rain, which began in China, was rapidly moving south across the border into the northern provinces of Vietnam. Although it was heavy and might deter many people from their work, there could still be patrols about. If they were to get caught, it was Dung's hope it would be Chinese soldiers and

not Vietnamese who apprehended them. It was safer to be an enemy than
a traitor. Not that Dung regarded either himself or his older brother as
traitors. He saw their actions as necessary for their survival. He no more
liked the government of China than he liked the government of Vietnam.
To his mind there was little to choose between them.

Two years ago his family home had been requisitioned by the government for military use. Dung was fifteen at the time and remembered
their coming with a resentment that still tasted bitter. Hidden behind
the dense leaves of a rubber tree, much like the tree he was taking shelter
under now, he'd watched the jeep spiral its way up the hillside to their
isolated thatched cottage. He'd known from the start that the arrival of
the visitors meant trouble, but it wasn't until later, when he'd dared
himself to climb down from the tree and creep in through the back door,
that he realised how serious the trouble really was.

*With a loud voice and red face his older brother Hien was arguing with the
authorities while his mother sat on the bed weeping. Her shoulders dropped
forward and she seemed to become smaller as she sank more and more into
herself. Dung desperately wanted to go over and put his arms around her, but
afraid to make his presence known he pressed himself behind the half-open
door.*

*'This is our home. What right have you to demand we hand it over?'
shouted Hien.*

*With his eyebrows drawn together the senior of the military officers stared
coldly at Hien. The irritation in his voice was undisguised. 'Your home falls
within a military area. We need to secure the land in the border zone so we
can protect the motherland from the Chinese invaders. If you resist, I shall
have you arrested for treason.'*

*Dung's mother let out a wail. The sound of her cry tore straight into Dung's
heart and without any further concern for himself, he rushed from the kitchen
over to her side and sank down onto the wooden bed. Clasping his arms
around her he felt her sunken frame shake as she gasped out her words in short
jerky breaths. 'Have pity on us. Where can we go if you take our home away?'*

*But there was no pity in the man's eyes, only contempt. His mouth twisted
into a forced smile and when his words came out, they were insulting and
full of mockery. 'What is it you expect, old lady? Are we to provide you with
hotel accommodation until your Chinese brothers withdraw their threats? It
should be an honour to give up your home in defence of the motherland.' The
man turned and drew out a bundle of papers from a worn suitcase. 'I'm
sickened by all this whimpering. Put the blame where it belongs and not on*

us. You will report to the authorities in Lang Son, maybe they can assist you.'
He walked back towards the bed and thrust the papers into her hands. *'Sign here.'*

'Mother, don't!' As Hien moved towards their mother to prevent her from signing the papers two policemen came from behind, grabbed hold of him and, twisting his arms into an arm lock, forced him outside.

'Sign it.' Dung was shaking as the official thrust a pen at her. He wanted more than anything to jump up and slap the man in the face, but he felt powerless to move. It was as though fear paralyzed his arms and legs. He could only watch helplessly as his aged mother reached for the pen. Her gnarled fingers shook as she drew her hand across the sheet of tear stained paper, and scribbled out her name. . . .

When Hien was released from the public gaol after two days of detention, he was beside himself with anger. He paced round the small dwelling like a caged bear throwing papers and clothes into an old leather suitcase. *'Mama, forget about reporting to the authorities. I'll take you to Haiphong where you can stay with Mai's family.'*

'But her husband can't take all of us. There's so little room and he's afraid of the authorities.'

'Dung and I will find our own place to live. I don't trust them. We're not livestock to be herded into a confinement zone.'

Dung had heard people speak of *'Tam Duong Vinh Bao'*. It was rumoured to be a place where the mixed Chinese-Vietnamese were sent when they were forced from the border area out of their homes. No one was certain if it actually existed, but it was thought to be a confinement zone where the inmates were starved and used as slave labour. The threat of its existence was enough to persuade locals not to push the authorities too far in getting them to rehouse them. Dung was ready to do whatever his brother suggested.

Hien, his elder brother by nine years, had become the father Dung never knew. Besides Dung's elder sister, Mai, there had been two brothers in between who died during the American war. Hien had also been a soldier with the People's Armed Forces, but he'd managed to survive. No one knew what had become of their father. His mother said that he'd gone away to war and the jungle had just swallowed him up. It was like that for many families — the number of 'missing in action' was so high they couldn't be counted. With whole families, villages wiped out, there was often no one left to report the absences. If Dung's father was alive, and had ended up in a military hospital for the insane, who would ever know?

The mine was now visible and with the rain splashing onto it, it made the dull vibration of a drum. Dung bit into his lower lip to stop his teeth from chattering. Between them they were making too much noise and the soldiers might come to investigate. He scanned the foliage uneasily for any sign of unnatural movement. Life with Hien was never mundane. Survival constantly drove them to keep seeking ways to earn money. At first they sold blood — but then there was only so much they could spare. With no official papers to seek legal employment they resorted to digging up the anti-tank mines and extracting the TNT to sell to the fishermen back in Hong Gai.

When Hien located the deserted outbuilding at the back of a farm-house in Cam Pha, Dung felt reasonably satisfied with his life. Although they were unlikely to ever be able to loosen their belts or have money to spare, they had food, shelter and there was sufficient adventure to keep them from ever knowing boredom. They gave an occasional gift of money or lumps of coal stolen from the mining yards to the farmer, who happened also to be a prominent member of the people's committee, which persuaded him to turn a blind eye to their illegal occupation of his property and kept the local authorities off their backs. It was, thought Dung, as much as anyone in their position could hope for out of life.

Leaving his sheltered position under the tree he crossed the path noiselessly and, stooping down beside Hien, helped him raise the mine out of its cavity. Taking care not to jolt it, Hien made an umbrella over the mine with his rain cape. 'Go back to where you were,' said Hien. 'This is the most dangerous part. I'm ready to cut the string and remove the kip. I don't want the rain to get in and set it off.'

'I thought I was going to do this one?'

'You're too eager to kill yourself, little brother. Go back and keep a look-out. I need to concentrate.'

Dung reluctantly retreated to a safe distance. He didn't know whether to be relieved or unhappy to be deprived of dismantling the mine. A part of him wanted to prove his manhood, but then the other side of his nature thought, 'Forget it. There's always another one.'

Even though Hien had done this job a hundred times, Dung always remained anxious. While listening for the sound of approaching soldiers, he kept his eyes fixed on the stooped figure of his brother. He leaned forward and watched wide-eyed as Hien slipped the knife and needle from his bag. It occurred to Dung that Hien was so relaxed in his movements that he might just as easily have been preparing to thread one of the fine instruments he liked to make for his friends.

Being careful not to jar the pin, Hien glided the needle into the kip before cutting the string and unscrewing the cylinder. Dung chewed further into his lip as his brother removed the pin slowly, pulled the kip out of the mine and tossed it harmlessly into the bushes. It was done. Hien hurriedly removed the TNT. Wrapping it into an old piece of plastic from a torn rain cape, he slipped it into his bag along with the rest of their bounty.

Looking up at the darkening, heavy sky, Hien slung his rucksack over his shoulders. 'It's time we made our way back. We've enough powder to keep us going for a few more weeks. These heavy rains could swell the streams and turn the gullies into fast running rivers.'

Dung wasn't about to put up an argument. He didn't want to spend another night sleeping outside, serenaded by Hien's rhythmic snores and the ever present low moan of lost souls whispering to him from the hilltops. Besides, he too knew how dangerous the mountains could become when there was a heavy rainfall and, after three weeks of living like a fugitive, he was ready to go home.

Little more than a day's bus ride from Lang Son, Minh stood behind wooden shutters watching the three public security officers let themselves out through the narrow gateway leading from the cottage. She knew the security officers would be back. Once targeted, a family remained subject to their scrutiny for three generations.

Minh tugged at her wet shirt to pull it away from her skin. There was no glass in the cottage window, so the sticky sweetness of the street-fed livestock wafted in. The smell that normally would not have bothered Minh left her feeling sick. Her discomfort was not improved by the cloud of dampness hanging in the air. The public security officers had not said her husband was dead. If it was a simple matter of death, Minh would have received the certificate of the patriot. They might even have treated her nicely. She was not sure whether to be relieved by the absence of the certificate or not. Looking down at her own bare feet, pale and small beside the larger muddy footprints which now discoloured the glossy green tiles, she smudged her feet across the impressions, displacing the mud to make the footprints appear less threatening.

Until today, her cottage with its ochre lime-washed walls had been untouched by the wider troubles surrounding her life. It had been a place of refuge where she felt secure and she took pride in keeping it organised.

Making her way through the courtyard she hauled up the half-full bucket from the well, and swishing her fingers absently through the water, looked around at her home. Besides the tiny stone paved courtyard which led to the dirt-floored kitchen with its brick stove, there were two enclosed living rooms. The downstairs room, with a large wooden bed commanding much of the space, served as both a bedroom and front parlour. Earlier that morning she had pulled back the mosquito netting from the bed and tied it to the ceiling to make the reed matting accessible for mealtimes. Next to the ancestral shrine of red and gold lacquered wood, faded glossy posters torn from last year's calendar decorated the walls, the old and new competing for dominance.

Worn stone steps led from the courtyard to the upstairs bedroom. Grandma and Minh's three small children usually slept there, although since Cuong had been called away to the army the children slept with Minh, and Grandma kept the upstairs room to herself. There was no toilet or bathroom as such, only an open drainpipe running from the next-door cottages through the courtyard. The family drew water from a well and flushed what wasn't needed into the drain to keep it clear.

To an outsider, the cottage nestled comfortably into the neighbouring structures, connected and intertwined in a harmonious embrace. But nothing could have been further from the truth. The trust of earlier generations shattered, Minh feared her neighbours. It was as though the exposed sewer pipe running from cottage to cottage carried with it the waste and lost dreams from one life to the next. Disenchantment contaminated everyone's thoughts, their distrust and bitterness seeping through the drains like a plague.

An agonising thought struck Minh and she let her hand sink into the bucket. Someone might have seen the public security officers entering or leaving her home. If so, it would not be long before Mrs Phuong, chairwoman of the 'People's Committee' would be round. She could cause untold trouble for the family. She might even take the shop away from Minh's brother Tang. His shop was owned by the 'People's Committee' and Tang rented it to sell bicycle parts and do repairs. Because Cuong had worked for Tang before he went away, her brother would now be drawn into their troubles.

Minh drew in her breath. Shooing away the chickens she took a rag from the washing line and rinsed the cloth in the bucket before returning to the living room. The mud on the tiles wiped away easily. Sighing heavily Minh struggled to hold back her tears. They had addressed her in the familiar form of an official addressing a prisoner. They didn't say

Cuong had deserted or done something bad. There were times when he drank too much and voiced his feelings about the present government too publicly. It was also well known in the district he'd been resistant to joining the army, but in the end the authorities left him no choice. No one wanted to be a soldier any more. When Cuong's conscription papers arrived, he'd argued that his wife had just given birth to child number three, and it would be a hardship for him to be away. The officials laughed. Life was a hardship for all families, they said. He should be proud he could tolerate such hardship and had not been softened by a bourgeois existence.

That was twelve months ago. At first the letters were frequent but gradually the length between them increased, until now there were no letters at all. 'Cuong, where are you?' Minh spoke aloud. Staring at the door she listened for the sound of his familiar footsteps slapping against the tiled floor. She hoped he would bounce in, throw his rucksack on the bed, and in his usual unruffled manner, laugh away her fears. But she knew he wouldn't, couldn't come. She was painfully aware of her aloneness. Grandma was at the market with the children selling eggs. The eggs were too much of a luxury item to keep just for themselves and the sale of them helped put rice on the table and an occasional piece of pork fat. Minh frowned and shook her head. Something was seriously wrong.

The outside clatter of bicycle bells and carts intensified the emptiness of the cottage. Her knees trembling, Minh sank down onto the floor. Memories of past troubles flooded into her mind. Because of her father's outspoken Catholic views and his co-operation with the French colonial government, he had been imprisoned and the family branded as outcasts. With no legitimate way of earning a living Minh's mother hawked illegally so they were always moving from place to place to keep ahead of the authorities. There was no time for hugs or sentimentality. Life was survival. The lack of security and hurried moves — often in the middle of the night — left their scars. As the youngest of three siblings, Minh felt she might have been less afraid of life if her childhood had been easier. Minh's older sister Lan was quite the opposite of Minh, but then she could afford to be. She was outstandingly beautiful and consequently had married well; her husband Thanh was a war hero and public security official.

Minh's attention was brought back by the sudden, hurried footsteps along the alleyway. Fearing it might be the police returning, she dropped her floor rag. She barely had time to pull herself to her feet before Grandma appeared at the open doorway with the baby tucked under her arms. Phu and Trinh were following closely at Grandma's heels. 'What's happened?' Losing all resolve to be strong, Minh ran into Grandma's arms. Grandma steadied her, then gently pushed her away so she could look into her face. 'Mrs Viet found me in the market. She said the security police were here. Why?'

'They were from the Hong Gai Public Security Building. They didn't say why. They searched the cottage and asked me when I last saw Cuong. There was no certificate of the patriot. He's not dead. He's not dead.' As Minh blurted out the words she was shaking and frantically twisting strands from her long hair round her fingers. Grandma was looking at her strangely, and Minh realised she needed to get a hold of herself.

'When they searched the cottage, did you go with them?'

Minh hadn't dare follow the two public security officers as they made their search. She had remained submissively beside the third officer who'd stood casually watching her. 'Well no. I couldn't.'

'How do you know they weren't here to steal our savings?'

Minh felt a heavy pounding as the blood rushed to her head. 'I didn't think. . . .'

Setting the baby down on the floor, Grandma rushed out of the room with Minh and the children following in close pursuit. Upon entering the kitchen and seeing that the bricks around the stove were undisturbed she threw her hands up. 'Thank heavens.'

Minh breathed easier. 'The money's still there. They were searching for Cuong so he's still alive, isn't he Grandma?'

'Maybe. I just don't trust them. They're full of tricks.'

Grandma's cynicism increased Minh's fear for Cuong and her feelings of inadequacy. She had been drawn to Cuong and his family because they were not like the other people in the village who seemed to be either bullies or victims like herself. Grandma still wore the indigo robes of the mountain people and, in spite of the low social status of her people, Grandma commanded respect. Cuong's mother had grown up amongst the Hmong hill tribes of Lao Cai and did not tolerate feebleness easily. Minh loved her dearly although she was also a little afraid of her. Her leathery skin, blackened teeth and inquisitive eyes all spoke of a strength and wisdom Minh believed she could never attain. Minh was sure that had Grandma been at home when the officers came they would not have spoken to her as though she were their inferior. Grandma would have questioned them and they might even have told her the truth. Shamed by her failure to ask the obvious question, Minh slunk back into the living room after Grandma.

Dung stopped abruptly as he felt Hien's grasp tighten around his arm. 'There's someone near the out-house.' Hien spoke urgently, his voice close to his ear and Dung could feel his brother's warm breath mingling with the rain on the back of his neck. Trying desperately to suppress his own rising fear, the tingle of his brother's breath was oddly reassuring. Dung couldn't see or hear anything but experience had taught him to trust implicitly in his brother's instincts.

'Police?'

'I don't know. Stay here and hold this, I'm going to creep round to the far side of the yard to get a closer look.' Hien thrust the bag of TNT into Dung's hands. 'At the first sign of trouble clear out. Hide the powder and make your way to Tang's house. I'll meet up with you there.'

As Hien disappeared into the bushes, Dung peered into the darkness. There was now no question in his mind that the noise Hien heard wasn't from an animal. There was someone waiting for them and if it were the police, there wouldn't be just one of them. Crouching down Dung slipped the bag of TNT into the undergrowth then tried to arrange the weeds so that it was not obvious they had been disturbed. Pulling himself up to full height he silently crept forward. If Hien were to be caught in an ambush, he would need help.

As a shadowy figure suddenly took shape from out of the darkness Dung froze, his eyes bulging from their sockets. The figure took a few strides in his direction, stopped, struck a match and lit up a cigarette. For an instant the flame flickered lighting up the man's pockmarked face. Dung had barely time to register his fear, let alone recognition, before Hien sprang out at the intruder.

'Cuong! What in hell. . .?' Startled, Cuong dropped the cigarette and swore. Dung's fear gave way to relief and laughter and it washed over him like a sprinkling of fresh rain. By the time Dung retrieved the TNT from its hiding place, Hien and Cuong were retreating into the kitchen, laughing and slapping each other on the back as they went.

Inside the dwelling, Dung set about lighting a fire in the brick stove while Hien prepared a pot of river spinach. Conscious of the activity of the two brothers Cuong seemed at a loss as to what to do, but as the sparks from Dung's fire leapt into life Cuong pulled up an old milking stool and positioned himself near the oven. Dung stared at him admiringly. Before Cuong had gone away he used to visit them frequently. He was always making deals with people and full of ideas on how to wangle things. There was money to be made by bringing goods in from China so long as one didn't get caught. Once he'd borrowed a boat and taken Dung round the islands of Ha Long Bay to see some of the famous stalactites and stalagmites in the many caves there. There was a cave Dung remembered in particular, which opened out into a secret lake in the middle of the island. It was only accessible at certain times of the year because of the tides. Cuong had said it was one of the best places for fishing since so few people knew of it and consequently the fish were inexperienced. 'They practically leap out of the water onto your lap and you have to fight them off.' He'd also said that it was a good place to bring a girlfriend since they were like the fish, but then he'd laughed at Dung's confusion and changed the subject.

Cuong looked much older than Dung had remembered him. Although he was probably still only in his early thirties, his hair had already started to go grey and sat on his head in silver-peppered tufts. He was also thinner, but there was a toughness to his manner that would have persuaded anyone with a modicum of common sense not to take him on in a fight.

Seeing Dung's scrutiny of him Cuong leaned closer toward the brick oven. As though by way of an apology he said, 'I deserted almost a week ago and have been hanging round your place for three days. I'm wet and cold, and I haven't washed or eaten since God knows when.'

'Well you're in for a pleasant surprise,' said Hien as he put a spoon into the pot and stirred the contents. 'I make the best river spinach soup this side of Haiphong, and with the aid of some garlic and ginger, my little brother Dung, here, fries up a tasty silkworm dish.'

'Ugh shit! What's that smell?' Cuong scraped his stool back from the stove.

Dung grinned. 'Sorry about that. I just threw on some buffalo chip. It was a bit fresher than I realised.'

Laughing, Hien lifted the pot of soup from the stove and raised it above Cuong's head pretending he were ready to tip it. 'I thought you were referring to my cooking for a moment. I was just about to dump the whole lot over you. . . . You weren't were you?'

Eyeing the pot suspended over him Cuong cowered and shook his head. 'No, no. I'll eat anything you can serve up, but the smell of that fire . . . urr.'

Dung hurriedly poked the wet buffalo cakes to the back of the stove before placing on some lumps of coal. 'The coal takes a while to get going and as we don't have a lot we use it sparingly.'

'Why, the whole area's saturated with coal, it gets into our hair and sticks to our bodies like a second skin.'

'Yes, but for us to collect it, even from the roadside or beach is an offence. We don't always have the money to pay the officials to turn a blind eye.'

Cuong shrugged. 'Don't apologise. I know how it is. I was down to my last cigarette when you arrived. I thought this is it. I'll finish smoking it then I'm off. Even if the security police are hanging round my home, I have to risk it.'

'Good job we came back when we did,' interjected Hien. 'Although I have to say you scared us shitless. We've just come back from the border area around Lang Son. After dodging border patrols for two weeks, we're pretty nervy.'

'Three weeks,' corrected Dung. 'We were gone three weeks.'

Cuong raised his brows. 'You were up near the border?'

'Dung and I search for anti-tank mines. We dig them up then sell the TNT to fishermen.'

'You dig up our mines?'

'Yeah. Well we don't cross the border into China,' said Hien giving Dung a wink. 'I'm surprised we didn't come across you.'

Cuong stared at them aghast before dissolving into laughter. 'I don't believe it. So you're the dog farts who kept digging up our mines. Hell! Have you any idea what we'd have done, if we'd caught you? There's a war going on out there.'

'A border skirmish?' proffered Hien. 'So what would you have done?'

Dung gulped and went outside. He didn't want to hear what Cuong had to say. It was better to remain ignorant. The idea of being blown to pieces was enough to disturb his sleep. Hearing about what the soldiers might do if they caught him was madness. But then Hien was mad. He seemed fearless and since coming home from the American war he thrived on things like that. Dismantling explosives and hiding from border guards was just a day's work for him. If he'd had to sit at a desk or work in the rice paddies all day . . . that just wasn't Hien. If there wasn't an element of danger to keep him on his toes he wouldn't have known what to do with himself. And Cuong wasn't any better. They were both mad.

By the time Dung had visited the out-house to empty his bowels and had collected a few scraps of wood along the way back, Cuong was describing his life in the army to Hien. 'You remember how it is? Snakes, mosquitoes, poisonous spiders. Moss growing round your feet because you sit for so long in the rain. Sores . . . sulphamide helps of course, if you can ever get any. Malaria, malnutrition, always hungry and on the look out for food. You know the score, brother. It's a dog's life. And let's not mention ghosts. Shit, the place is crawling with them.'

'Is that why you deserted?' asked Dung.

Cuong looked at him incredulously and for a minute Dung thought he was about to laugh, but then the grin that had spread across his face tightened into a contorted smile holding neither humour nor pleasure. 'Yeah, ghosts,' said Cuong slowly. He sat silent for a moment. Dung could see from the taught lines across his brow that he was in mental anguish. It was as if Cuong were trying to weigh up whether he should tell them his story. When he eventually made up his mind to speak, his voice was flat and unemotional. 'Two weeks ago our unit was on border patrol near the area we call "the murderous mile".'

Dung drew in his breath. The mile which straddled the Sino–Vietnamese border was a place where even the birds refused to nest in the trees. So many soldiers had been killed it was believed that their dead souls outnumbered the trees by a hundred to one. Death was as natural to the place as were the leeches and the marshes. The land itself was said to be able to suck a man's life out of him so that even a soldier's bullet was redundant.

'It was dusk when we picked up the sound of someone ahead of us,' continued Cuong. 'We didn't know who it was so we split up. The idea was to encircle them and to advance from different directions.' Cuong stood up and began pacing the room. 'I was to take up the rear. The foliage was thick so I couldn't see who it was we were pursuing. From the din they created by crashing through the undergrowth, it was obvious they weren't professional soldiers. They were moving into an area we knew was heavily mined. I heard gun shots. The policy in that area is shoot to kill, although on this occasion I could see my compatriots were shooting into the air.' Cuong clasped his hands together into a fist. 'They were refugees. Some of them children. How they even made it so far I'll never know. The area's heavily mined and we were trying to get them to halt, but they scattered in all directions. For all we knew the Chinese could have put them there to ambush us.'

Hien lit up a cigarette and offered it to Cuong. Cuong stopped pacing, took the cigarette and, drawing on it heavily sank back down onto the stool. His shoulders slumped forward and were shaking. Dung thought he might be crying, but in the dim lighting he couldn't be sure. 'It happened so fast there wasn't time to think. This kid, no more than five, was running. She could have been my own daughter Trinh. I leapt

forward and shouted for her to run to me. I don't know why I did it.'
Cuong covered his face. 'All I wanted was to pick her up and get her away
from the chaos. She saw me. God knows why she trusted me, but she
turned in my direction and started to run towards me. I was pushing my
way through the undergrowth when the ground exploded. The blast was
so powerful I thought I'd trodden on it. The noise was deafening. Bits of
tiny limbs hanging hideously from the bushes, blood and flesh splattered
in my eyes, blinding me. Better it had been me.' Cuong crushed his
cigarette into the ground, reached over to the packet Hien had placed
beside him and lit up another one. 'After that I kept dreaming the little
girl was Trinh. That I'd killed my own daughter. I was haunted by the
memory day and night. The nightmares were horrendous. I'd see Trinh
running towards me, arms outstretched. Then I'd see the bits of her
growing from a tree. I just had to leave . . . find out for certain that Trinh
was still alive.' Cuong wiped his brow with his shirt sleeve. He looked
up toward Hien as though seeking his approval. 'You know. I just have
to go home, see my old mother before she dies and check up on my wife
and kids. I miss them so much.'

'Yes, I know brother.'

'When does the misery end? They were probably farmers, peasants,
just trying to get out of this hell hole.'

Hien sat down beside Cuong. 'It's too dangerous for you to go home,
but we can make arrangements to get Minh over here. Not tonight
though. The buses will have stopped running. Right now we should eat
and then get some sleep.'

As the friends sat without speaking, Hien pulled his guitar from its
hook on the wall and began to strum a soft melody, while Dung wrestled
with his feelings. In a place with so many ghosts, where were the spirits
who protected children? Staring at his oversized rubber sandals he
wondered at the endless poverty and hardships experienced by his people.
'Why didn't they escape by boat?' Dung didn't intend speaking aloud.
As soon as he uttered the words he knew it was a foolish statement to
make, but it was too late to take it back. No one responded. There was
nothing to say. Everyone in Quang Ninh Province knew the story of the
estuaries — the Cua Ong through to the Song Trong — where the rivers
emptied out into the open sea. There were dangerous reefs and sand
banks which could cause a boat to sink. A little over a year ago, hundreds
of refugees, trying to escape to the free country had drowned after their
boats became stuck and were beaten to pieces by the waves. The 'sad play'
as it was called, was so well known that for months the fishermen had to

give up fishing. The people would not eat the fish because they were afraid of eating human flesh.

Hien sighed heavily. 'There's no easy escape, is there? Let's face it. We are less precious than the water buffalo.'

It was already dusk when Minh, dressed in a green plastic cape and palm leaf conical hat, set off to see the soothsayer. It had rained all day and was still drizzling as she lifted Cuong's bicycle over the yard wall and wheeled it through the narrow gateway into the alleys behind the cottages. She'd chosen not to leave by the front door because she suspected the police might still be skulking in the café across the street. She couldn't imagine her case warranted the kind of vigil that required their standing out back in the rain, and she reasonably assumed the authorities would only have assigned lower ranking recruits who, being poorly paid, would have little interest in getting wet.

Once out of the village, Minh steadied her pace. She knew that the uneven roads contained potholes lurking beneath the water, poised to swallow her up. Her courage wavered however, as darkness descended and a thick mist rolled in over the fields enveloping her world. First the shadowy branches of a tree took on human shape as its limbs rose up and battered down again under the onslaught of wind and rain. Then the wooden structure of a water dispatcher rose out of the mist as though it were a skeletal human frame. Minh shivered. It was inevitable that after so much war and starvation there would be ghosts roaming the country-side — the souls of warriors searching for goodness knows what, some of them malevolent because they suffered cruel, unjust deaths; others, perhaps only babies, just pitiful and lost. But Minh feared them all. Good or bad, their presence hung round the countryside reminding her of her own mortality. They were everywhere, their low lament carrying across the rice paddies like a chorus of chanting mourners.

As the gloom thickened, Minh pedalled faster. She didn't see the hole until it was too late. Swallowing her bike entirely and catapulting her into a muddy rice stream, the hole was deeper than she'd thought possible. She crawled out of the water gasping, then angrily wiped down her wet clothes and cursed her husband, 'Damn you, Cuong. What have you done?' Bruised and near to tears she would have turned back. It was only shame, her failure to question the security police about Cuong's fate that kept her going. Minh bit into her lower lip, extracted the bike that was totally submerged in the hole, and straightened out its wheels before setting off again.

By the time she covered the six kilometres to the soothsayer's village, she was bruised and bleeding. Her fingernails were caked with mud and her trousers and shirt top were soaking. Her cape had snagged on the bicycle chain and hardly offered any protection from the rain at all. She wondered what the soothsayer would think of her. In her ragged wild state he might even turn her away. 'No,' she muttered. 'The soothsayer's a good man.' Everyone knew that except, of course, the communists. They saw him as competition in gaining influence over the people and preferred to lock him away at the slightest hint of wrongdoing.

Once inside the village, Minh's fears subsided. Peering from under her hat she tried to make out the numbers on the small dwellings. 'Twenty-four, a lucky number. This is it.' It was easier than she'd dare hope. Dismounting her bike she wheeled it towards the shop front. The street was deserted and, with the electricity out, Minh could only imagine the comforting vision of family groups huddled around their oil lamps in the semi-darkness. The only visible sign of life was an emaciated dog crouching under a bench. He gave a low growl as she approached. Minh hesitated, then slipped her hand under her black *ao ba ba* shirt and fingered the pouch tied firmly to her waist to confirm that it was still secure. It was fortunate the police hadn't found their savings. She had no idea how much she would have to pay the soothsayer, so she had taken it all.

Since the dog showed no further inclination toward aggression, she smoothed down her shirt and banged on the door. It was important she waste no more time. One of the children might wake and alert Grandma to her absence. That would be disastrous. Although Grandma believed strongly in the spirit world she would not have approved of Minh's seeking help from the soothsayer. If she found out she would reprimand her severely. Spirits were one thing but money was another. In response to Minh's knock there was a sudden scuttling of feet, but no one approached the door. Summoning up her courage Minh knocked again, only louder this time. At first nothing happened, then she heard footsteps and slowly, as if the person on the other side of the door were experiencing some difficulty, the bar was pulled back from its brackets. The door opened a few inches and a young face peered round. Minh watched his dark eyes expand as he absorbed her wild, bedraggled appearance. 'I've come to see Mr Tam,' she said, 'Is he at home?' The boy nodded and without offering her an invitation to enter, he disappeared leaving Minh standing at the doorway. However, he was back within less than a minute and opened the door wider in a gesture of invitation.

Although Minh was anxious to be inside, she hesitated. The street appeared to be deserted, but she did not want to leave Cuong's bike unattended. There were too many beggars who didn't even have shirts on their backs. The bike, left outside, would be a huge temptation if anyone saw it. Seeing her concern, the boy pointed to the two bikes already resting against the wall in the front parlour. Minh heaved a sigh and wheeled her bicycle into the house. She let it rest against the wall beside the others before bending over to remove her sandals. Swiftly crouching down beside her the boy motioned for her to leave her sandals on.

The room was dimly lit by an oil lamp and as Minh ventured further in, it was a minute before she could make out the black shadowy shapes of a group of old women sitting cross-legged on a wooden bed in the corner. Huddled over a large, black tureen of some steamy concoction, they could almost have been witches. As Minh slowed her pace the boy grasped her hand and ignoring the women led her out through a back door to an outbuilding.

As they approached the broken down shed Minh felt a pang of sadness. In the old days the soothsayer would have been rich and well respected. The whole house would have been his, whereas now, it seemed that he didn't even have a proper door to his home. All that existed was a piece of jute cloth tied over the entrance. The boy guided her inside. Although the flooring was made out of compacted earth much like Minh's own kitchen, it was dry and looked as though it had been recently swept. With horror she noticed the muddying of her wet sandals on the floor and wondered if she shouldn't take them off.

'Your sandals are fine. Please, it is not necessary to remove them. I apologise for the humbleness of my dwelling.' The speaker, whom she presumed to be Mr Tam, materialised out of nowhere and was standing alongside her. His honeyed voice, however, immediately put her at ease. 'Come, sit down by the stove, child. Dry yourself off.'

Minh obeyed. She wanted to say something about his home although she wasn't sure what. To have contradicted him and told him it was splendid would have sounded like an obvious lie and embarrassed him, yet there was indeed something splendid about his home. An oil painting of the Messiah hung from the unplastered wall dominating the room with its richness of colour. All she could think to say was, 'You believe in Christ?'

'You sound surprised my dear. Christ was the divine prophet of all spiritualists,' he said.

Minh looked at him with astonishment. She had never heard Christ referred to as a spiritualist and wasn't sure if it was an appropriate statement for him to make. Her knowledge of Catholicism was limited because of the prohibition on religion and she was unsure of her ideas. But, had it not been that she sensed an essential goodness in the soothsayer, she would have thought his statement blasphemous.

'Chinh will bring us some tea in a minute. You're wet. Dry yourself.' Minh moved her stool closer to the stove. She had forgotten how desperate she looked. Taking off her hat and cape, she ran her fingers through her wet hair in an effort to remove the tangles.

Within minutes the boy, Chinh, nudged his way through the jute doorway with a flask of boiling water and set about making the tea. When he finished he handed Mr Tam his tea before passing a small badly chipped cup to Minh. Bowing toward the soothsayer he then quietly extricated himself from the room. Minh wrapped her fingers around the cup and sipped the hot liquid gratefully. It warmed her insides, so she emptied the cup before setting it down.

During the whole of this process she was conscious of Mr Tam's scrutiny. She hadn't dared look at him, but she'd felt the intensity of his glare. However, when she did look him full in the face, she discovered that his earlier expression of concern had changed to one of .... almost fear. 'You're here because of your husband. I don't think I can help you.'

Minh sat up straight. She was stunned. 'Why not? Is he dead?' Her words tumbled out in shocked, angry sobs. 'There was no certificate of the patriot.'

'Let me study your hands.' Minh's hands were trembling as she offered them to him. Mr Tam clasped them into his own, then closing his eyes as though he were praying he seemed to slip into a trance-like state. Several minutes elapsed before he opened his eyes. Turning her hands over he studied her palms. 'It is as I thought. He is worse than dead. There is a dark cloud descending over all of us. Please drink your tea and leave. I don't want your money. You bring grave trouble to yourself and to me by coming here.'

'I came to you for help. You can't turn me away.'

'I'm sorry. Your coming here was a mistake.' Mr Tam stood up and started to leave the room, muttering and shaking his head. 'You should never have come. Never have come.' He stopped suddenly and turning back to face Minh said excitedly, 'Go quickly. Maybe, even now, we can cheat the fates.'

Minh sat staring after him. Her eyes misted over and tears rolled down her cheeks. Paralyzed with indecision, she couldn't comprehend what she was hearing. She'd believed the soothsayer to be a good man. His turning her away, especially when it had taken so much courage to come out at night and find him, didn't make any sense. It wasn't fair. Then, what he'd said about Cuong being worse than dead. . . . A chill ran down her spine. If Cuong was in the half-world of spirits, lingering between a state of heaven and hell. . . ? No, it was too awful to contemplate, and then why had the security police come? She gulped in the air, stood up and reaching for the bed frame tried to steady herself as her vision clouded. Perhaps he'd done something wrong and couldn't enter heaven. Minh had heard of such things in her Catholic religion, and in her own Vietnamese folklore there were also such beliefs. To find peace, the body and soul of the dead needed to return to the home of his ancestors. It was the responsibility of the living to take care of the dead. Perhaps it still wasn't too late to free his soul. She would pay atonement for his sins whether Mr Tam liked it or not. Cuong wasn't perfect, she knew that as well as anyone, but his soul needed to be tended. What use was all the gold in the world if her beloved Cuong was suffering? The gold belonged to Cuong and not to her. Even in his death she would not deny him his rightful inheritance.

Minh felt her sanity wavering. Snatching up her cape, she unstrapped the money pouch from her waist and rushed into the main house. Mr Tam was nowhere to be seen. In desperation Minh thrust the money at the old women. The five gold pieces clattered onto the wooden bed bouncing into the soup bowl and splattering hot liquid over the women's faces. They squealed in shock but as the glint of gold registered on their lined faces they pounced on the soup bowl and overturned it. 'Tell Mr Tam he has to help my husband make it to the good spirit world. This is all the money we have.' The roles reversed. The old women, although excited by the gold, now feared her. They stared, wide eyed, at the mad spectacle of Minh as she yanked Cuong's bike away from the wall, dragged the bar from across the door and let it crash to the brick floor. Forcing the bike through the half-open door, she fled from the house.

Chapter 2: Struggle, call for noble duty

Hong Gai, Quang Ninh Province
Early hours 25th April 1980

Our brothers of the South are citizens of Vietnam. Rivers may dry up,
mountains crumble, but that truth will remain forever. . . .
Let him who owns a rifle use his rifle, let him who has a sabre use his
sabre, let those who have neither sabre nor rifle use spades, shovels, sticks!
Let us all rise to oppose colonialism and defend the fatherland. . . .
PRISON DIARY, HO CHI MINH

THANH STOOD UP from his desk at the Hong Gai Public Security Office
in Quang Ninh Province. Snatching his jacket from a peg on the
door he pulled it carelessly over his shoulders. It was past midnight.
Having completed his work, he should have gone home hours ago, yet
he'd hung around the office as though there was something he still needed
to do. Lan would already be in bed although probably not asleep. She
would be cursing him for putting his work before their marriage. Thanh
wondered what explanation he might give — certainly not the truth. The
news of the desertion of her sister's husband and the telephone call from
his uncle warning him he was to stay out of the affair, troubled him more
than he'd expected.

Outside, the night air was fresh with a cool breeze blowing in from
the sea. Avoiding the deep puddles, Thanh wheeled his bike away from
the village residences. By twenty to one, most people would have retired.
Their sleep would be disturbed soon enough because in five hours the
loudhailers would blast out songs celebrating early rising, exercising, and
the rewards of another day's toil. The slumbering streets would wake up
as the local authorities drummed out their messages of self-praise reminding everyone how well they lived and how the economy was thriving.
There would be warnings to be alert for dissenters. The generals pushed
the message that enemies were coming at them from all directions and
that if the people weren't constantly vigilant for signs of subversion, they
risked losing their newly found independence.

It seemed to Thanh they had been defending their homeland from
foreign invaders for an eternity. During the past century they had fought

the French, the Japanese, the Americans, Pol Pot's Khmer Rouge, and now they were fighting their ancient enemy China. The wars rolled unmercifully into each other. Tensions were high, especially among the border provinces of Lang Son and Quang Ninh. Tired of war and poverty, the people turned their anger on the government. No one was immune or unhurt. Suspicion, disillusionment and unrest were viruses that invaded everyone's brain. The communist government had failed to establish a thriving economy, but its detailed record-keeping on the activities and attitudes of the people surpassed that of most sovereignties.

Suspicion had now cast its dark shadow over his sister-in-law's husband. Thanh had always liked Cuong and saw Cuong's disillusionment as mirroring his own. His belief that the legitimate fears of the new revolutionary government were tearing the country apart had deepened in him to a serious despondency. Instead of protecting the people from outside aggressors, the government was extracting a heavy toll by turning their fears inward. Cuong was a victim of the times, just as Vietnam, in losing sight of her revolutionary objective — liberty, equality and happiness — was becoming a victim of her own tumultuous history.

Thanh mounted his bike at the edge of the village. Splintering the tranquillity of the night air, he accelerated to top speed and rode headlong into the thickening darkness. The breeze brushing over his face felt good as it swept away his fatigue allowing new thoughts to rush in with brilliant clarity. Turning the bike away from the road home, he decided to find some isolated place where he could think. Memories, long since buried, kept resurfacing and he needed to relive them to gain perspective on his life. The villages he sped through were not so unlike his own childhood hamlet. The trail of smoke rising from the chimney of a small cottage could be his parents' home in the central coastal area south of Qui Nhon. Following the flow of smoke as it meandered skyward, Thanh let his thoughts rise, away from the disillusionment of the present to a time when life held the promise of something better. The trail took him back to Uncle Chau's first visit in the spring of 1962.

At that time, it had seemed to Thanh that the whole country was prickling under the surface with anxious anticipation. At the age of fourteen Thanh was on the threshold of manhood. Impressionable, idealistic, he was ready — eager even, to give his life for his country. Like a seed, sensing the change of season, he foresaw the new life and was ready. Better to die in battle than remain cowering. . . .

'This is a time for celebration,' announced Thanh's father. 'It has been twenty years since I was last with my brother. And since it is bad luck for the hand that fed the pig to slaughter it, I'm sure my brother Chau will do us the honours.' Uncle Chau looked apologetically in the direction of the pig which was contentedly scrounging around the yard for scraps. 'But first, wife,' continued his father, 'fetch a bottle of rice wine to the table so my brother can prepare himself for the heinous deed.' Thanh's mother obediently rushed into the store house and retrieved a bottle of wine. The visit of Uncle Chau with his son Nam was an honour, and in keeping with Vietnamese custom to save the finest for guests, she sent her two youngest boys, Vinh and Hau, to select the best quality rice from the bins.

After sampling the wine to see that it was up to the job, Thanh's father turned toward him. 'Son, collect the bucket and go stand next to your Uncle Chau. After he slits the pig's throat, it's your job to collect the blood as it spills out. We'll want to mix it with the intestines when we make blood pudding.' As Uncle Chau whacked the pig over the head then jerked it up and swiftly drew his blade across its throat, Thanh closed his mind to the pig's squeals and ran forward with the bucket to stop any of the blood pouring wastefully to the ground. The belief that to be born a pig, the creature must have committed some wrongdoing in an earlier life and was now paying penance for it, didn't convince Thanh that the pig's agony was any less painful and it was only as the last of the blood dripped into the bucket that Thanh was able to make an honourable retreat. After pouring boiling water into the bucket of pig's blood, Thanh's mother spilled the remaining water over the carcass. Clouds of steam, shroud-like, enveloped the redeemed creature. The pig sizzled as the repugnant odour of scalding flesh rose in the air. . . .

The odour of scalding flesh. . . . Other memories interrupted his flow of thought and tumbled over each other, throwing things out of order. Thanh pushed the bike to full throttle. He wasn't ready to remember the destruction of his unit and his friend Anh's death. The meeting with Uncle Chau and Nam, the celebration . . . it was important to see events in their historical context. To understand his youthful passion and optimism. Maybe even to regain his faith in humanity. Faith in himself, in Uncle Chau and in their struggle for freedom.

Working as a synchronised team, Thanh moved in to help his father cut the fatty flank away from the pig's rib cage. Once the fat was removed Thanh's father shaved off the meat from under the flank and tossed it into the giant granite mortar. Thanh then set about the laborious process of pounding the meat into a doughy consistency. The job required substantial muscle power, and after some minutes Thanh was feeling the strain in his arms. His cousin, Nam, came over, and taking the pestle from him,, took a turn at grinding the meat. Both of them were sweating by the time Thanh's mother decided the meat was pasty enough to add to the other ingredients. First she added pepper, then fish sauce and finally a little gluten. The aroma of the dish started to come alive. While Thanh stood watching, she laid out some freshly washed banana leaves. Nga, Thanh's younger sister by two years, came over to help her roll the best of the sticky pork onto the leaves. They would select the less tender pork to make pancakes which they would steam in a basket.

After the initial preparations for the pig were completed, Thanh's father picked up the bottle of rice wine and invited Uncle Chau to join him in the kitchen. Before following him inside, Uncle Chau hesitated at the door, then, turning, he told Nam and Thanh to get to know each other. It was more of an order than a request. Thanh, already in awe of his cousin Nam, said nothing but looked helplessly toward him. Two years Thanh's senior, Nam appeared much older than his sixteen years. His face, although strikingly handsome with his broad cheeks and finely pronounced classical Vietnamese bone structure, bore a hard and determined expression. His eyes, fierce and impassioned, darted around as though he expected to have to defend himself at any instant.

Absorbing all of Thanh's scrutiny, Nam stared back. Then shrugging his shoulders and pursing his lips into a quizzical smile, he said, 'Shall we go for a walk? I won't shoot you.' Thanh felt the heat rise in his cheeks. 'You can show me round your hamlet, comrade.'

Thanh relaxed. 'If you like.' He admired Nam and considered it an honour to be a guide to this worthy young recruit of the freedom fighters. As they wandered around the cottages, Thanh was impressed by his cousin's intelligence and quickness to absorb the family names and relationships of those who lived in the hamlet. They discussed who lived where and who owned what, what work a person did and how he behaved toward the Saigon government forces.

As they left the hamlet and wandered along the dyke, Nam asked if there was anyone within the community whom Thanh thought might be loyal to the Saigon government. Thanh knew of some families whose sons had gone south to join the Republican troops, but he preferred to keep quiet about them. They were his neighbours and while some sons went south others went north. Even within one family brothers were divided in their loyalties. His own mother, fearful of who might be listening, used to whisper to him at night of the brutal atrocities conducted during the implementation of the land reform policy of the fifties. She spoke to Thanh of the plague on both houses. There was no right cause she could fully support since there was guilt on both sides.

Evading the question he said, 'By day all of us pretend to co-operate with the Saigon Republican forces. To do otherwise would invite being taken away and tortured. But at night . . .' Thanh grinned, 'at night we welcome in the freedom fighters. When they come into our hamlet, we supply them with food and medicine. In return they give us talks on the political situation, and we share in their victory celebrations.'

Nam nodded. 'The villages are our homes. Without your support we couldn't sustain ourselves. There would be no safe hiding place from the puppet's security forces.'

Thanh was relieved Nam accepted his evasive response and didn't push the question. If he had done so, Thanh wasn't sure how he would respond. He didn't want to put Nam's father in danger, but he also didn't want to create unnecessary trouble for his mother or neighbours. President Diem's brother Nhu, head of the Cong An, the internal security agents, had offered a reward of one million piastres for information leading to the capture of Uncle Chau. 'It's no more than our duty,' said Thanh continuing on his elusive tract.

Thanh scuffed his sandals in the soft dirt and changed the subject yet again. 'You won't believe this.' Nam stopped and looked at him. 'Several months ago the puppet Diem made a visit to our hamlet.' Thanh couldn't suppress his laughter at the absurdity of the story he was about to share with Nam. 'The day before the planned visit, three officials came from Saigon. They closed our school and forced us children to go round the countryside cutting down small trees. They then stuck the trees in the ground round our hamlet to make it look as though they were growing there.' He looked into Nam's face then raised his brow. 'When Diem came, we heard the Saigon officials boasting to him about how well the programmes that offer support to the hamlets were going.'

'And I suppose Diem went away believing that his development programme, was winning the hearts and minds of the people.' Nam shook his head and laughed along with Thanh.

They were already several miles out of the village when Thanh asked Nam the question he'd been itching to ask. 'Being a freedom fighter must be exciting?'

'It is exciting in many ways, but . . .' Nam hesitated as though uncertain whether to go on. Thanh noticed Nam's face looked pained. 'It can be frustrating . . .' Nam scuffed his hand through his hair, 'and lonely, too. You see this isn't a proper war as such. We're in a period of waiting.'

Thanh was intrigued. 'I know we're waiting. I feel it, but, waiting for what? What's going to happen?'

'It's complicated. In all likelihood there'll be a full war, but it's not what we want. Although my father's job is to recruit new members to our cause, Uncle Ho asks that he counsel the revolutionary groups against acts of sabotage and violence. My father's relationship with Uncle Ho goes back a long way.' Nam paused. 'You see there was an agreement in Geneva which promised an election for the whole country. If such an election were ever to take place Uncle Ho would win.'

Thanh's eyes lit up. 'I would vote for Uncle Ho . . . if I was old enough. But I don't see how we can remain submissive. Just a month ago our teacher was complaining about the puppet Diem's high taxes. Someone informed on him and a day later Nhu's secret police arrested him.' Thanh stopped speaking for a moment. He'd loved his teacher and the loss still upset him. The level of education the children received in the villages was high and teachers were amongst the most respected members of the community. When he spoke, his voice rasped. 'We heard he'd been tortured to death. They tied him to a post and poured honey over him. The ants bit him unmercifully, then because he still wouldn't admit to being communist and inform on his comrades, the Cong An strung him upside down and smashed open his skull like a coconut.' Thanh's throat knotted up. 'Now my sister and I walk nine miles to a school in one of the neighbouring villages. We live in fear. No one dares say anything. Why shouldn't we retaliate?'

Nam clenched his fists. 'That's what the revolutionaries say too, but Uncle Ho wants to maintain peace. He hangs onto the hope that the international community will one day see reason. Many Southerners claim Ho and the North are abandoning them.' The muscles in Nam's cheeks knotted as a pained look spread across his face. He mumbled something almost unintelligible. 'Sometimes I feel ashamed of. . . .'

Thanh shuffled his feet uncomfortably. 'Do you think there'll be an election where we can vote for Ho and not just Diem?'

Nam shrugged. 'The Americans will never go for it.'

'What has it to do with them?'

'It seems the American's think everything has to do with them.'

'Why?'

'I don't know. It has to do with them not trusting the Soviets.'

'So how does that relate to our elections?'

'It doesn't.'

Thanh shook his head in disbelief. 'Do the freedom fighters see you and Uncle Chau as Northerners? What do they say when you urge restraint?'

*'Mostly they treat us as brothers, but they're disappointed.' Nam picked up
a stick and flung it into the trees. 'You know if we can't have real peace, I'd
rather we go to war. This in between is the worst.'*

Thanh gulped in the night air. His disbelief, and anger were still with
him and had become no less intense during the passing years. He was
driving the bike too hard, he knew it, but his anger needed to be vent
and the recklessness of his speed felt oddly satisfying. Buried in the roots
of Nam's frustration Thanh could see the beginnings of his nation's
anguish. The war was unwinnable because of the terms on which it was
fought. By turning brother against brother, North against South,
America could claim her victory. The mess she left behind went far
beyond the destruction of the land.

*Dusk was falling when Thanh returned to the hamlet with Nam. His mother
and sister had finished cooking the rice and were setting out the dishes on the
bamboo matting. Thanh sat on the floor next to Nam. Before putting any
food in his own bowl, he selected the best of the pork slices from the dish of
cabbage and pork dipped in crushed peanuts, and put them into Nam's bowl.
Today we eat like Mandarins, thought Thanh, tomorrow we starve. It was
the way it was, and Thanh couldn't imagine it being any different. The
contrast between famine and feast made the celebrations more poignant.*

*When they had eaten their fill, Thanh's father produced the bottle of rice
wine and for the first time in his life Thanh was invited to drink with the
men. As the wine slipped down his throat, he felt as though his larynx were
suddenly on fire. His eyes watered and he could feel, rather than see, the faces
turned toward him to observe his reaction. Fighting the urge to cough the
burning liquid out of his mouth, Thanh forced a grin. In a rasping,
spluttering voice he said, 'It's pretty good, eh.'*

*The evening wore on and as the conversation grew animated, Thanh's
younger brothers and sister went over to their corner of the room and sprawled
out on the floor. Having lost all feeling in his throat Thanh was persuaded
to take more sips of the rice wine. By the third and fourth sips the liquid was
sliding down easily and he was totally into the hang of it. The warmth of the
lamps and the wine glowing in his stomach, left him drowsy, but he was
determined to stay awake to hear the stories his father and uncle had to tell.
Tonight was a special occasion and Thanh was anxious not to miss a second
of it. Since Uncle Chau had risen to the position of general and was an
important person in the new revolutionary government, Nhu's secret police*

were constantly trying to track him down, so there were few times when he could fully relax.

Thanh's father casually waved his hand in front of Thanh. 'Son, you are now of an age to understand more about your family.' Thanh leaned toward his father and gave him his full attention. 'Your grandfather was a teacher in the northern province of Ha Tinh and was highly respected in our community. When he challenged the French over their abuse of the people, he was robbed of his teaching status and forced to work on a rubber plantation.' A grin spread across his face. 'They couldn't keep him down though. He escaped, went south, and changed his name. Your great-grandparent's family took him on as a labourer. They didn't know what a fine man they'd hired. But, of course they soon discovered he was no illiterate and so when he asked to marry your grandmother, they were delighted. Such a fine son-in-law they said would be welcome in any family.' Thanh's father drank back his wine before pouring himself and Uncle Chau another glass.

'Chau and I were inspired by him. Having heard of the anti-French movement that sought to gain nationalist independence for Vietnam, we formed our own secret youth organization — Sons and Daughters of the Justice Seekers. Your Uncle Chau . . .' Thanh's father put his arm around his brother's shoulder, 'was not the eldest of our group, but he soon emerged as our natural leader.' His face glowed as he surveyed his brother. 'Our group gained strength. We found ways to link up with other groups forming in the neighbouring areas. Ah but. . . .' he shook his head. The scorched creases across his brow were inflamed by both the conversation and the wine; his eyes glittered in the lamp light. 'Central Vietnam was a beehive of anti-French activity. The depression of 1929 forced the price of rice to drop so drastically we were all hungry. In some areas there was starvation. Like the rice wine we are drinking, the mood for rebellion fermented with each passing month. No one was untouched by what was happening. The French were on full security alert. When a series of strikes and uprisings in the plantations took place, they arrested our compatriots by the hundreds. Madame Guillotine hungered for our heads. She was never satisfied.' Thanh's father tightened his fist. 'Anyone suspected of being a dissident could be put in prison without a trial and with little or no evidence. Friends just disappeared.'

Thanh's father paused and sipped his rice wine. Sitting with wide eyed anticipation, Thanh, wondered what he would say next. The evening was closing in. Total blackness surrounded the small farmhouse, leaving them suspended in time and space. The air was electric. 'I was thirteen when the police stopped me. Hidden inside the handlebars of my bicycle were pages of anti-French literature. The secret police must have been wise to our tricks, or maybe an informer tipped them off, but the first thing they did after searching me was to dismantle the bike. When the police found the literature they wasted no time in hauling me off to the police station.' He turned to his brother and smiled. 'Hearing of my arrest, Chau dashed over to the public offices to try to obtain my release. He told the Sûreté Générale the literature was his.'

Filling Uncle Chau's and Nam's glass his father sought to fill Thanh's glass. Thanh shook his head, but ignoring the protest his father filled his glass anyway. 'I propose a toast to my elder brother, Chau.' Thanh sat up and raised his glass along with the men. 'May you know peace in your life-time, brother.' Thanh nodded and, in one gulp, threw the fiery water back down his throat. His head spun, but he felt more alive than at any other time in his life.

'Chau confessed to having written and printed the material on the school premises,' said Thanh's father. 'He insisted I was an illiterate with no idea what I was carrying. He told them he'd only let me carry the papers because he thought the police wouldn't search a child. Some hope, yeah?' Thanh's father gave a grim laugh. 'They sentenced me to twelve months imprisonment.' Thanh moved his stool closer to his father.

'You went to prison! I didn't know. What was it like father?'

'Pretty dismal, but it was nothing compared to what your uncle experienced.'

Thanh looked over toward his uncle. It was hard to read his expression. Although Uncle Chau was smiling, there was also a deep sadness in his expression which he hadn't been fully able to hide.

'Your Uncle Chau, already under the eye of the Sûreté, was brought before a tribunal as an adult and sentenced to seven years on the penal colony of Poulo Condore.' Thanh gasped. Poulo Condore was the worst place in the world. 'What Chau didn't know,' continued Thanh's father, 'was that the literature he was passing off as his had already been widely distributed around the country. The French concluded that Chau must be connected with the wider network of anti-French revolutionary groups. Young though he was, they suspected him of being a dangerous enemy.' Thanh's father laughed heartily. 'Which of course he is.'

Uncle Chau nodded. 'More dangerous to them than they dare suspect.' Turning to Thanh and Nam he reached forward and took hold of their hands. He seemed about to say something then paused. He tried to smile but his lips quivered. Thanh, embarrassed by his uncle's effort to hide his emotion, lowered his eyes. When Uncle Chau did eventually speak, however, his voiced came out steady. 'I'm getting old. I can't fight like a guerrilla as I used to. My contribution to our motherland comes from the information I can share around the villages and pass on to Vietnam's children. And it is our children they should fear.' Thanh looked full into his uncle's face. Uncle Chau's eyes reddened by the rice wine, smouldered. 'In 1930 and '31, ten thousand of our patriots were executed, tortured to death, or died from bombs and bayonet guns. They were the bloodiest years.' In the lamplight Thanh thought he saw tears glistening in his uncle's eyes. 'Perhaps. . . .' There was a prolonged silence as Uncle Chau absorbed the full weight of his words, then he nodded as though satisfied with what he was about to say. 'Those of us who survived the cages of Poulo Condore were the lucky ones. It was there I joined the Indochina Communist Party. There could not have been a better recruiting place. The atrocities we were subjected to at Poulo Condore . . . the caged tiger in our hearts, strengthened our resolve to keep fighting.'

Letting go of their hands Uncle Chau pulled himself up to his feet and paced round the room. Although a little drunk, he remained dignified and controlled. Thanh harboured no doubts that had Nhu's security forces rushed into the house at that moment, Uncle Chau could have cut them down in seconds. He turned back toward them. 'Our motherland cries out to every man, woman and child to make whatever sacrifice he can to gain our country's freedom.' Clenching his hand into a fist he struck at the air. 'And Vietnam will be free one day. That I promise you.'

Guiding his bike over to the side of the road Thanh dismounted and breathing in the tangy, seaweed air blown in from the Gulf of Tonkin, filled his lungs with its therapeutic qualities. The distant steady rhythm as the waves lapped against the muddied sand and then withdrew, allowed his pain to ease a little. His thoughts were jumbled, but there was something about the vast expanse of the ocean which he believed could help him to gain perspective on his life.

Despite all the conflicts which had later arisen between himself and the new revolutionary government, Thanh still loved his uncle just as he loved his country, but in the aftermath of the American war, poverty, corruption and fear had led them off course. He knew it and everyone else knew it, but it was a matter not to be spoken of. He felt a tinge of regret that he could not be more like his colleagues who were less analytical. They probably harboured as many doubts as he did, but they had the sense to bury their feelings and keep from banging their heads against the system.

Before venturing along the beach, Thanh concealed his bike behind a leafy hibiscus bush. From the evidence of dry sand at the water's edge, he judged the tide to be on its way in. The cold water lapping around his ankles was invigorating. Rolling his trousers above his knees, he waded in further. The protection his Uncle Chau offered had served him well and had placed him on a fast rising career path for which any other person would be grateful. Thanh was grateful. Being a revolutionary — then later protecting his country's newly gained independence was what he wanted. Still wanted, and yet....

Thanh waited every evening, contemplating the arrival of the freedom fighters with eager anticipation. Sitting on the steps of the old village school, he planned what he would say when they arrived.

'You're waiting for them, aren't you?'

Thanh gave a start. Taken aback by his sister's sudden appearance, he looked at her quizzically. 'Waiting for who?'

'I'm waiting for them as well. Uncle Chau told me that the women in Ben Tre staged an uprising. They pretended to be the Viet Minh returned from the North.'

Thanh laughed. 'What's this?'

'Yes it's true. The women put dirt on their faces. They made fake guns out of wood then pretended to attack the Saigon troops as though they were the Viet Minh returned.'

'Why would the soldiers think that women with sticks were Viet Minh?'

'Because they let off fire crackers. They sprinted around in the darkness as though they were firing off weapons. The Saigon troops ran away so the women collected up the soldiers' real weapons. Clever, ha?'

'That sounds ridiculous.'

'It isn't ridiculous. After they did this the troops and police came into the village searching for the soldiers. The women said the Viet Minh had come back from the North and were hiding in the countryside.'

'Uncle Chau told you this?'

'Yes. The women liberated Ben Tre Province. He also told me the women were the spies. They carried messages and supplies to the markets and between villages. Uncle Chau said that without the help of the women and children we couldn't hope to win our freedom.'

'Why are you waiting for them?' asked Thanh. He knew the answer but he needed to ask the question so he could argue with her.

'Because I'm going to join them, just the same as you are. It's why Uncle Chau came here, isn't it?'

Thanh knew his sister was right. One of the reasons for his uncle's visit had been to recruit them into his cause. His sister's understanding surprised him. 'Little sister, Uncle Chau didn't mean you. Our parents will be sad to

see me go away. If you go away as well, it will break their hearts. Stay here
and do your fighting in our village. Anyway you're too young. You're only
twelve so they won't take you.'

'Fourteen's young. Why do you think they'll take you?'

'I can join the Youth Brigade and carry messages for them. There are lots
of things a boy can do.'

Nga looked steadily at Thanh. 'A girl can carry messages. After we go our
parents will have Vinh and Hau. They're very young so it'll be ages before they
can go.'

'If both of us leave together they'll be really sad.' Nga fixed her eyes angrily
on Thanh. Ignoring her defiant gesture he continued speaking. 'And I'm the
eldest. It's only fair I go first.'

Her eyes continued to shine fervently. 'I'll stay one more year, then I must
go.' Thanh shrugged and then nodded his agreement.

When the freedom fighters came, they came with stealth. Clad in their peasant
pyjamas with their Ho Chi Minh rubber sandals, they stole into the hamlet,
materialising out of the darkness like black shadows. Thanh could hardly
contain his excitement. Sitting around the fireside with Huynh Van Phat,
the political commissar, he expressed his desire to become a freedom fighter.

'Life with us is not an adventure,' reiterated Phat for the seventh time that
evening. 'It is serious warfare.'

'I know. My uncle is. . . . He told me. . . .'

'Yes, your uncle. He's a good man, one of our great revolutionary leaders.'
Phat ran his hands across his chin as though brushing the soft hairs of his
beard. 'We rise before dawn and don't bivouac until late in the evening.
Although discipline is hard, our camaraderie is good. We operate like one
large family. From the oldest to the youngest, everyone is treated with respect.
The seven rules of a revolutionary are simple, you must memorise them:

    Be polite — don't swear.

    Be fair and honest.

    Return everything borrowed.

    Cause no damage, especially to the crops, and if damage is caused then
pay for it.

    Do not bully our compatriots or mistreat prisoners.

    Do not fraternise with women — they are our sisters in arms. Treat
them with respect.

    Love the people and when possible help harvest the rice.'

Thanh nodded his head. He didn't need to memorise them — they were the rules he'd been taught to live his life by and he'd heard this political speech many times before. He was ready to face hardship and put his strength to the test. At fourteen he knew what was expected of him. The liberation of his country was all that mattered.

Young though he was Thanh was accepted into the revolutionary brotherhood. His youthful face allowed him to be chosen as the scout to accompany the women when they smuggled arms up the river. He would meet the women at the market and accompany them to the place where his compatriots were waiting. The place would not be decided too far in advance — circumstances could change rapidly and the freedom fighters, although poorly equipped, made up for it with their ingenuity and flexibility. If the first meeting place had to be aborted Thanh would know of a second place and a third.

Thanh was on one such assignment when their small boat was stopped by an Army of the Republic of Vietnam launch. They saw the patrol boat approaching them from a distance but there was no way to outrun it. The best they could hope for was to bluff their way out of the situation. Thanh smiled at Mrs Mai to assure her he wasn't about to panic, then placed himself next to the stinking dried fish and nuoc mam *(fish oil) where the guns were hidden.*

Among the soldiers was an American. It was the first time Thanh had seen an American up close and the tall, handsome man, with yellow cropped hair, looked like an ancient god figure. As the launch drew level and the American stepped onto their boat, Thanh found he couldn't take his eyes off him.

'Where are you going?' demanded the ARVN *commander.*

'We're taking our fish to sell at the market,' said Mrs Mai.

'The market's in the other direction.'

'We are going all the way to Vinh Binh where we can get a better price.'

The American pulled out a handkerchief and covered his nose. 'This stuff stinks. We aren't supposed to be fighting women and children are we? Forget them.' The ARVN *commander was about to say something, but the American climbed back onto the patrol boat and seemed anxious to be on his way.*

As the boat pulled away Thanh grinned at Mrs Mai. 'The American didn't like the smell of the nuoc mam, *did he?' said Thanh.*

'You're right, child. But he was also fooled by your angelic face and my white ao ba ba *shirt. If I'd been wearing black, he might have assumed we were Viet Cong.' She nodded knowingly. 'It was lucky for us, child, the American was on board. Without him the commander would have demanded a search. This is not a game.' She looked at Thanh seriously as though weighing*

up his boyhood naïveté. Her old eyes glittered in the sunlight. 'If they had found the guns, we would have been lucky if all they did was shoot us.'

During those trips Mrs Mai taught Thanh more about the game of bluffing, which for the women in the South was much of what the war really represented. An individual's dress, manner and confidence were all tools for creating an image. These skills became particularly relevant when Thanh was assigned to linger around the ARVN military base at My Tho and collect information from the women cleaners as they left the base. Thanh's job was to memorise the information they gave him and then make the fifteen kilometre trek back to his own unit. Thanh's genuine friendliness and interest to learn about everything convinced the ARVN soldiers he was going to join them as soon as he was seventeen. He became such a familiar face that he was able to walk past the guards and enter the base without anyone thinking too much about it.

There were American advisors at the military base, and since Thanh had such an excellent memory and was a fast learner, it was not long before he was learning English from them. His father had taught all his children French and Mandarin since they were small, so learning another language came easily to Thanh. He set himself the task of learning twenty new words a day. His determination to learn English caught the attention of Captain James Turner, an American from Wisconsin. Turner, as almost everyone seemed to call him, would often sit with Thanh talking in English.

At first Thanh found it hard to understand everything he said, but slowly he began to put the pieces of Turner's life together. Turner had three sons, the youngest being the same age as Thanh. As Turner spoke about his life on the dairy farm in Wisconsin and of his high hopes for his sons, Thanh could almost imagine his own father talking. Their lives were so different, yet in some ways they were the same. Turner was eager to learn Vietnamese and also seemed genuinely interested to understand how the Vietnamese farmers felt about the American presence. Thanh gave him honest answers. He was careful not to couch his words in slogans, but in the best English he could muster, he described the simple values of his people.

'The people want peace. No one really want to fight. We have our own way and the people not like being forced into the spike wire compound away from the graves of their ancestors. For us the land is part of us. It protect and feed us just as we care for it. The bones of our ancestors feed the ground so we become inseparable. In America you own land. Here the land own us. It is right that the Vietnamese people clean their own house — not the foreign master.'

'Do the people see us as foreign masters?'

Thanh shrugged. 'In our village we only have so much food and water. If one man were to become very rich while we are poor, then it mean he is robbing us of our share of the . . .'

'Resources,' interjected Turner.

'Correct,' said Thanh. 'He rob us of resources. Maybe it because his land is better. The rich man sees the upset balance of the village so he put money back. He pay the wages of the school teacher. Or he might have someone work his land with him and share the crop. No one tell him what to do; he know because it is the way our village been for hundred and more years. If he disobey common sense it destroy the village and he become lonely because the poor people go away and live somewhere else.'

'I like that,' said Turner. 'It's like our social security — an umbrella for the people — but it sounds more effective. It's more personal and spontaneous. In my country no one likes to pay taxes, but if we didn't we would have to go to prison.'

'Oh, to go to prison is bad. Better the man become lonely because he not take care of his neighbours.'

Turner laughed. 'I don't think the threat of being lonely would deter my countrymen from avoiding payment of taxes. So what else is important to you?'

'Beside our land and our family, we value education. To study hard is to honour our parents.'

'I shall tell that to my sons.'

Turner surprised Thanh one day by giving him a dictionary and a book of English grammar, which his youngest son, John, had specially purchased for Thanh in the States. Thanh was initially embarrassed, although when pressed by Turner to accept the books, he was grateful. When Thanh put in his nightly report to Phat and informed him of the gift, the commissar expressed unease and immediately called a meeting of several members of the unit. Thanh was young, he said, and might easily be influenced by the American. Accepting a gift from the enemy could compromise him. Thanh understood his reasoning although it sorrowed him to have to part with the books.

'Your ability to absorb languages is impressive,' said Phat. 'If we were a rich country like America, we could reward your hard work by giving you many, many books, but we are a poor country Thanh; our strength is in our bodies and our minds. We cannot afford to befriend our enemy. If we accept the foreigner's gifts and submit to his will then we sacrifice our own freedom.

We must hate him until our land is free. Only in peace time can we become friends.'

When Thanh returned the books Turner expressed his disappointment, but since Thanh was adamant about not keeping them there was little he could do other than take them back. Thanh quickly realised that his fears, that Turner would be insulted by his refusal to accept the gift, were unjustified. It was barely perceptible, but as the months passed Thanh sensed that Turner now regarded him in a different light. If anything, their relationship seemed to have deepened and, although nothing was said directly, Thanh felt Turner understood some of the inner turmoil going on within his head.

When Thanh learned that Turner was to drive with several Saigon Republican officers to Can Tho, he was in a quandary as to what to do. Thanh knew the road to Can Tho had just been taken over by the freedom fighters and would be impassable to the enemy by the morning, and was sure that if Turner went, he would either be blown up by a landmine or killed in an ambush. Thanh knew his duty to the revolution was to allow events to take their natural course — it was as Phat had said, to like one's enemy weakened the fighter's resolve to win — but, Thanh also felt the sense of duty that a son owed his father. He lay awake all night worrying what he should do.

By morning his mind was made up. Before going to the base, Thanh stopped at the market and made inquiries of an old woman who sold ancient herbal remedies. He told her he was looking to purchase the root his mother used when any of the family were ill. He couldn't remember its name, but his mother would crush the root and mix it into a drink. This special concoction of the medicinal root mixed with fruit juice, would induce vomiting and cause a cold sweat to bring the fever out. Thanh was in luck. The old women understood what he wanted and he left the market with an armload of mother's milk fruit and a small packet of the ancient root powder.

Turner was beginning to lose some of his hair so it wasn't difficult for Thanh to persuade him to try the special potion the Vietnamese used to prevent hair loss.

'You're kidding me. Does this stuff really work?'

'Of course. Besides the monk, you ever see a bald Vietnamese?'

'No.' Turner sniffed at the potion. 'It smells good. Do I rub it on my head?'

'No, you have to drink it, then Turner have plenty hair. Maybe when you go home, your wife think you are girl.'

'My wife will think I am a girl, Thanh, not are girl.'

'Your wife think you am a girl?' said Thanh shaking his head in disbelief at Turner's correction. Turner laughed and flipped through Thanh's returned grammar book to illustrate what he meant.

Within fifteen minutes of drinking the potion, Turner's interest in the conversation rapidly dissolved. His mouth turned a yellow greenish colour and without excusing himself, he suddenly stood up and dashed headlong toward the latrine. He didn't make it. As Turner emptied the contents of his stomach into a flower bed, Thanh skulked around the base. He wanted to be sure Turner was not about to make a quick recovery. But it was only after the jeep with the ARVN *officers had left for Can Tho without Turner that Thanh knew it was safe to leave.*

As Thanh slipped out of the base unobserved and made his way towards the market, he couldn't believe how smoothly his plan had worked. He'd expected Turner to make more of a protest over drinking the potion. Since his own people were so suspicious, Turner's gullibility struck him as strange and it struck him that it was Turner who was the innocent while he, Thanh, was the devious old man. It was, however, a role reversal Thanh was uncomfortable with and since Turner was his friend he couldn't help feeling bad for having been forced to betray his trust.

Thanh had gone only a short distance when a military jeep hurtled past and came screeching to a halt a few yards in front of him. He turned to run but two Republican officers came from behind and after grabbing him in an arm lock they tossed him into the jeep as though he weighed nothing. . . .

Thanh broke into a run. The resistance of the sea against his ankles, the cold stab of water as it splashed against his face, made him feel as though he wanted to run forever. But even as he ran he knew he could never outrun the bad memories. His life had always been complicated. Looking back on it, Thanh wondered at his own ability to stand up to his interrogators for so long. He didn't pretend to himself that it would have lasted forever. Another day, or maybe just another hour and he could have folded under their interrogation. . . .

Thanh felt the blood drain from his face as he was led through the hallways of the Police Interrogation Headquarters. Stretched out along the narrow corridors, battered, bleeding prisoners lay side by side, their ankles and wrists chained together like some grotesque charm bracelet. Thanh tried to look away but their eyes, sunken deep into their sockets, held his gaze. His legs weakened as the thread of their low moans resonated through the hall taking on a life of its own, but with a guard either side of him dragging his arms, he was forced to push forward. He knew instinctively that to display any sign of fear would give his accusers an additional advantage over him.

But the feeling was escalating within him, mixed with an overwhelming sorrow which he experienced from seeing his compatriots in such misery, so that Thanh was hardly conscious of being steered away from the main hallway, down a short passageway and into a side room. 'Sit down.' Before Thanh had a chance to focus his thoughts and obey, he felt himself forced into a chair. Biting back his tears and summoning up all of his courage Thanh stared squarely into his interrogator's face.

'If you tell us what we need to know it will not be necessary for us to hurt you.' The man smiled. 'You understand?'

Thanh tried unsuccessfully now, to blink away his tears. 'Yes.'

'Good. You are a communist, yes?'

'No.'

'Then why did you poison the American advisor?'

Thanh thought back to his lessons from Mrs Mai. He knew his only hope of survival was to stick firmly to his story. Any deviation from it would be fatal. 'I was tricked. I was sold the potion in the market.' A smile crept across his interrogator's face, but Thanh ignored the look and continued. 'I believed it would help my friend regain his hair.'

'Rubbish. You take me for a fool. There's no such potion. You're a communist. Admit it and I'll let you go home. You either confess to us or I shall turn you over to the Americans.'

Thanh kept his gaze direct. 'I've told you the truth.'

'What a shame. You're so young, yet you have to learn the hard way. Isn't that the way it always is with youth.' He nodded toward the man standing behind Thanh. 'Very well. Let's show our young friend how we can lubricate his tongue.'

Thanh was yanked from his seat and hauled down the passageway to another room where he was forced onto a wooden table. Pearls of sweat broke out from his temples. He was shaking uncontrollably as the second guard dragged straps across his body pinning him firmly down. It was all happening so fast he had barely time to register his protest.

A cloth was pressed over his nose and his mouth was forced open. He struggled and tried to cough as a soapy liquid was poured down his throat. Some of it spilled out of his mouth but most drained right into his stomach. Then more liquid. Thanh couldn't breath. As the nausea rose in his stomach the liquid kept coming. Even as Thanh's body tried to eject it, the liquid came. He was suffocating. He tried to push against his restraints but a foggy, black dampness pressed into his head and he lapsed into unconsciousness.

When Thanh came to he was lying flat on his back in the hallway and was vaguely aware of someone pressing against his stomach. He tried to strike out but a wave of nausea swept over him and as he rolled onto his side the soapy liquid gushed out of his mouth all over his assailant. It was only then that Thanh saw that the man responsible for making him vomit was not one of the interrogators but a fellow prisoner chained securely to him by the ankle. 'I'm sorry,' moaned Thanh.

'Best to get it out child. The detergent kills all the bacteria in your stomach. It's bad stuff.'

Thanh had barely time to register his gratitude when he felt a sudden yanking to his ankle as one of the guards struck his companion's head and sent him sprawling across the floor. 'Shut up. Talking's not allowed.'

It was more than Thanh could take. His eyes filled with water as he saw the blood drip from the prisoner's ear. He tried to mouth out a sorry but even his jaw locked and he was unable to register a simple offer of thanks to this brave man.

By the fourth day of his interrogation, Thanh was not sure how long he could hold out. He was becoming physically and emotionally weaker by the hour. There were moments when he considered giving in to their request and confessing to be a communist. If he could have been sure that they would have just killed him, it would have been worth it, but that was naïve. Mrs Mai's words hammered onto the floor like a lead weight dropped from a loving hand. 'Stick to your story,' she had said, over and over again. 'Don't confess. They will never be satisfied with just a confession. They will want more and more until they are certain they have extracted every morsel of information from you. By the time they have finished they will know the colour of your mother's undergarments.'

A day later when a healthy Captain Turner arrived at the Police Interrogation Centre, Thanh could hardly believe his good fortune. As an American advisor, Thanh suspected that Turner must have some authority over the Saigon security police. Turner's verification of his innocence was accepted, if not believed, and after an exchange of money Thanh was handed over into his custody.

On the four-hour journey back towards My Tho neither Turner nor Thanh exchanged any words. Thanh sat with his head forward not knowing what he could possibly say that would come close to expressing his love for Turner and his complex turmoil of emotions. It was Turner who eventually broke the silence. Before entering the town he pulled over to the side of the *road. 'I know what's going on. You saved my life. There was an attack on the jeep going to Can Tho, two* ARVN *officers were killed.' Turner hesitated before going on. Thanh could feel more than hear the suppressed anguish in his voice. 'They were both fine men. Tran Thai was the father of three. . . .' He paused and touched Thanh lightly on his chin so that Thanh felt compelled to make eye contact with him. 'You are like a son to me. I don't hold you responsible for their deaths, but you cannot come back to the base. You know that?'*

Thanh hung his head forward in shame. 'Hey, you saved my life. It's probably as much as you could do. Is it your fault my government chooses to support the wrong side?' Thanh lifted his head and stared back at him in amazement as Turner, seemingly oblivious of the full significance of what he had said, reached over and unlatched the door. 'You will probably be in trouble from your own side . . . I'm sorry.'

As Thanh got out of the jeep Turner caught his arm, 'I suppose there is no such thing here as a potion to stop balding.' With tears gleaming in his eyes Thanh grinned and shook his head. 'Just one that makes you sick, right?' laughed Turner. 'Go on, beat it, kid.'

The account of Thanh's arrest had not escaped Huynh Van Phat's notice. With his loyalty now in question Thanh was brought before a committee where his breach of security was evaluated. . . .

'You know you put your compatriots at risk?' said the political commissar. 'I didn't give them any information.'

'We know that. Had you done so, you would not be here. The point is anyone can be broken by torture. Your actions and your being captured put the lives of all of our spies on the base at risk. Would you like to be responsible for their deaths?'

Thanh hung his head. 'I'm sorry for my mistake. There is something within me that causes me to act willfully. If you wish to shoot me for treason . . . I accept my fate.'

Phat laughed. 'It would not be your fate. It would be your punishment.' He raised his brows as he stared at Thanh. 'You understand the difference?'

Thanh hesitated before answering, 'Yes.'

'There are four attributes we consider make a good revolutionary: moral character, revolutionary spirit, personality and loyalty. You have all the attributes of the first three. However, you display too much independent thought. To quote Uncle Ho's teachings, "individualism runs counter to revolutionary morality. It is both deceitful and perfidious. Revolutionary morality consists in absolute loyalty to the Party and the people. If the Party's interests contradict those of the individual, the latter must give way to the

former." *Wittingly or unwittingly your actions risked the work of the Party and could have impeded the revolution, but . . . your mistaken thinking can be changed by your willingness to study. If you seriously and sincerely practice self-criticism then. . . . We all hold high hopes for you.' Phat paused. 'I share some of the responsibility. When I knew about the gift from the American, I should have insisted we remove you from your duty at the base.'*

'It's not your fault. You guided me well. The blame is all mine. I knew what I was doing and am ready to be punished for my mistake.'

Phat looked across at the unit commander as though seeking agreement for the timing of what he was about to say. The unit commander nodded. 'In view of your earlier good character,' continued Phat. 'and your young age, we prefer not to treat your misconduct as treachery. We know you didn't intend to harm the revolution. A young mind can be molded. Maybe one day you will be a worthy revolutionary. I have great faith in you.' The political commissar stood up as though preparing to leave. Then he turned. 'We are not barbarians. We are capable of forgiveness. The hand from the fist that beats you can also rub you better. You will not be punished for this offence. Instead you will spend two days reading To Win the Heart. *I hope then you will appreciate how much the success of our revolution depends upon us all working together.'*

'Thank you, uncle.' Thanh bowed his head toward Phat. He knew he'd done wrong. In saving Turner's life he'd risked the lives of many. It was a choice he'd no right to have made. Yet, he knew, that given the same circumstances he would repeat his mistake. It seemed as though there was some badness within him that made it impossible for him to submit to another's will.

The political commissar nodded his acceptance before leaving the room to cross the jungle clearing to his own hut. Thanh could see the pained, tired look on his face. Phat was a good man and Thanh cared for him as deeply as he cared for Turner. They were both honourable men conducting themselves according to their own beliefs. It saddened Thanh to realise that circumstances, and his own strong will, had led him into a situation where he'd betrayed the trust of both men.

'We are sending you to Hanoi,' said the unit commander. 'Your father's elder brother General Nguyen Tat Chau, has put in a special request that we take an interest in you and see that your teaching is adequately supervised.' The unit commander stared sternly at Thanh. 'You should understand that brother Phat has been severely criticised over this, as have we all. You have done us a grave disservice — brought shame not only upon yourself, but upon us. It is lucky for you there are people in Hanoi who are of the thinking that

it is not in our national interest for American advisors be killed.' He stopped speaking. Then almost as an afterthought he added. 'None of us wishes to do anything which will encourage the Americans to further enter this war. Our aim is to free our country of foreign interference and bring peace into our lives.'

The sweat poured from Thanh's body as he slowed his pace to a walk. He was out of breath. He'd loved Turner, and through his friendship he felt he'd glimpsed what the ordinary American people might be like as individuals when seen separately from their government's policy of aggression toward Vietnam. But with the full force of American intervention in Vietnam, any hope of an election or peaceful settlement had been shattered. The war had left his country in ruins with little hope of finding an easy peace. Thanh looked at his watch. He felt nauseous with fatigue and knew it was time to retrace his steps. He'd been walking along the beach for two hours. He sighed. He was thirty two years old. The thought struck him that in another world he might still be a young man with a young man's aspirations. Fate could even have landed him as one of Turner's sons. Who would he have been then, a young American soldier fighting against the Vietnamese? The idea highlighted the absurdity of it all — men killing men simply because of an accident of birth.

But was destiny an accident or was he born right where he was supposed to be, the challenges peculiar to his life meant only for him? He pondered the thought. What of the choices he'd made — individualism versus community? These were the challenges which he lived with day in day out, and by accepting them he knew he was on his own. There was no tradition in his country for internal dissent. After decades of fighting foreign invaders they had learned as a people to band together and to make whatever sacrifices were necessary to expel the invaders. To rebel against this tradition was to betray the motherland.

Thanh had remembered life at fourteen or fifteen to be simpler, but was it really? Weren't the signs of his individuality — his inability to accept guidance from his elders — already showing? And wasn't his marriage to Lan a symptom of this same expression of individualism, or perhaps more likely, a symptom of rebellion against his uncle's benevolent guidance?

Thanh took a deep breath. How honest was he prepared to be with himself? He'd met Lan two years ago when he was first assigned to the public security office in Hong Gai. The American war had ended and after studying languages and political science for three years at the university in Hanoi, Thanh's uncle arranged for him to temporarily take the position in Hong Gai to further his career. It was a good job, he said, and would put Thanh in a strategic position to keep a pulse on the developing tensions between the ethnic Chinese community and the authorities. Uncle Chau was keenly aware of abuses carried out by some of his unethical comrades: by fueling unrest amongst the wealthy Chinese, they were able to make personal financial gain by increasing the numbers of those seeking escape.

Thanh had been drawn to Lan from the beginning although perhaps for the wrong reasons. Uncle Chau was very much against the relationship and was ready to make arrangements to transfer Thanh back to Hanoi, but Thanh had resisted his interference. Lan's beauty was enough to attract any man, but more than that it was her having been labelled as coming from a family who owed a blood debt to society, which made her even more attractive in Thanh's eyes. But hadn't his uncle understood that — perhaps seen better than Thanh that his motives for marrying her were wrong?

Thanh set off at a brisk pace to walk the nine miles back to where he'd left his bike. Lan would have fallen asleep by now, but if she woke to find herself alone in the bed, her jealous nature would get the better of her. She had no reason to be jealous. Although other women offered opportunities for Thanh to digress, he ignored them and remained faithful to her. It wasn't infidelity she needed to fear. He kicked the rocks out of his pathway. It was his inability to deal with his inner turmoil, to show her the normal expressions of companionship a husband owed his wife. He was secretive. A spy almost against himself. Looking in, looking out he felt lost. Trapped by his own ideas of how things should be, but were not.

On the other hand, his brother-in-law, Cuong, who'd married Lan's sister Minh, was very much a family man. Although not a member of the elite Communist Party, with three young children and a devoted wife he was a more successful man than Thanh. Cuong had taken the chance to desert. In one passionate act of heroism, he'd abandoned the war with China in the northern provinces and fled.

Where would Cuong go — not home? Although desperate, Cuong was not a stupid man. He'd know that they would be watching his home. Earlier that morning Thanh's colleagues from the Hong Gai Public Security had visited Minh. She hadn't understood what was happening, but they had questioned her and searched her house for the stored bags of extra rice, maps, compasses — all tell-tale signs of her collusion in a planned escape. There was nothing he could do for Minh to warn her — not yet anyway. He needed to get his own thoughts in order; to decide where he stood — where his loyalties lay. Was he really such a different person from the boy of fourteen who, inspired by his uncle's stories, had joined the revolutionaries? Here he was, once again, preparing to oppose his uncle because — wasn't Cuong as worthy a man as Uncle Chau's chosen dissidents?

Chapter 3: The fates unleashed

25th to early hours 26th April 1980

In the cells how nice it is to doze.
For hours we lie about in deep repose,
Dreaming of riding a dragon up to heaven.
But upon waking, I find myself still pining here in prison.
PRISON DIARY, HO CHI MINH

THE BUS WHICH HAD PICKED UP PASSENGERS from the Haiphong ferry terminal in Hong Gai was already overloaded when it reached Minh's village. Although originally designed to hold twenty-five passengers, the bus held over forty. Bags, bicycles, baskets of chickens, ducks, rubber tyres, anything that could be lifted to the roof was strapped on. To compensate for the lack of seating some passengers sat on the window ledges, half in and half out of the bus.

Along with the bus conductor and one other passenger, Dung clung desperately to a rail as he hung out of the open doorway. The intermittent rain of the past three days had stopped, but it would be several more days before the puddles could be expected to drain away. As the bus pitched, swaying dangerously from left to right while the driver tried to avoid the deeper holes, the shallow puddles splattered into Dung's face. He tried wiping his eyes, but after a couple of jolts from the passenger next to him — which nearly sent him flying headlong into the street — he decided it was safer to keep both hands gripped firmly to the door rail.

The metal-gated shop fronts of busy Hong Gai slowly disappeared giving way to littered broken-down cottages with unkempt yards of tethered emaciated livestock and ragged banana trees. As the bus sped past the cottages Dung caught glimpses of Ha Long Bay. He never tired of seeing its dramatic landscape. The eighth wonder of the world, the French had called it. Scissor-sharp mountains jutting out from the sea bed like crooked, broken teeth. According to legend, in ancient times a dragon descended from heaven swinging his tail and imprinting his giant feet into the earth. When he dived into the sea, the water splashed and filled the valleys creating Ha Long Bay, named after the descending dragon. For Dung, entrenched since childhood in the stories of his country's folklore, its hidden enclaves were also the meeting places of Ngoc Hoang, the Jade Emperor, and Hai Long Vuong, the Dragon King of the Sea. Only the most courageous would venture there, in search of princesses, because should their lives become entangled with the immortals they risked the wrath of the thunder spirit, Thien Loi.

Turning his head away from the door, Dung glanced across at Minh sitting squashed between two old ladies. With her soft almond-shaped eyes and long dark lashes, she was uncommonly pretty. He had always secretly suspected that she and her sister Lan, might have French blood from some distant ancestor. Minh didn't have the classical Asian grace of Lan, but there was definitely a gentleness to her face which he found appealing. Looking at her now with her red, swollen eyes, he wondered about her behaviour. She had cried when he arrived at her home and told her Cuong wanted to see her and was waiting for her in Cam Pha. Her eagerness to meet with him was clearly apparent, yet now her face looked sullen — fearful even. Somehow he'd imagined a different response although he wasn't sure what. She had every reason to be upset, yet he sensed something else was wrong, something deeper.

They were now approaching the end of their bus ride. In contrast to the splendor of Ha Long Bay, Cam Pha was considered one of the dreariest and most polluted places on earth. For years it had been an open coal-mining town where the black coal dust, having been crudely dragged out of the ground, was left to blow freely around before descending back over everything. On a rainy day, such as this was, coal dust hung heavy on the trees, dripped from the leaves and ran headlong down the streets in black inky streams. Yet beyond the town's ugly exterior Dung perceived its comeliness. A black despairing kind of beauty, yes, but beauty all the same. There was something honest and unpretentious about the blue and yellow, black stained, lime-washed walls of the cottages, which Dung loved. He liked the way the sea channels, bearing burnt-umber-sailed junks, carried the craft right into the back yards of the houses.

As the bus approached their stop, Dung caught Minh's attention and nodded to let her know that this was where they needed to alight. Without registering the exchange Minh stood up and excused her way through the layers of people. The bus had stopped right next to a large puddle, so Dung offered his hand to help her climb down. Ignoring his gesture Minh took a huge leap and cleared the puddles easily. But as they walked up the alley to Dung's home, she fell back several paces behind him. It was only when they reached the open doorway, and she heard Cuong's voice, that Minh's sullenness suddenly gave way to joy. She rushed headlong into Cuong's arms knocking him off balance. He staggered back laughing. 'My God, what a welcome. I've missed you, so, so much.'

Exhausted and dirty from his travels, Dung paid marginal attention to Cuong and Minh as he slipped past them and entered the kitchen. Lifting a pot of warm water from the stove, he set about washing his hands and face. There were clumps of black dried mud glued to his hair so he dipped his head in the bowl of water and ran his fingers through the wet mud to release it.

'Hien and I've been talking,' said Cuong. His voice was excited and it was obvious he was still keyed up after their night of heavy drinking. 'Hien has an elder sister in Haiphong. For five taels he thinks he can arrange to get us out of Vietnam. Grandma, the kids, all of us.' Cuong drew in his breath waiting for a response from Minh, but nothing came. 'It's a great future. After Hong Kong we could live anywhere in the free world — imagine that.' All the while Cuong was speaking he paced the room, incapable of sitting down. 'I'm done for here. You know that.' Dung noticed Minh wasn't smiling. Her face had become sullen again and she fidgeted nervously with her hands. As Dung wiped his head with a cloth he pondered why Minh should be so desperately unhappy. The opportunity Cuong was offering her was better than their miserable lives in Vietnam. From where Cuong was standing he couldn't see her face, but something in her manner must have alerted him to her petulance. Cuong's face hardened. He turned towards her and yanked her up from her chair so that he could look directly into her face. 'What's the matter with you? Don't you want to come with me?'

Trying to avoid his stare, Minh pulled away. 'I do want to come, but we can't.'

'We? I just told you I'm going. You're my wife, you'll do. . . ?'

'I'm sorry, but. . . .'

'You have a lover,' he yelled. 'There's someone else.'

Minh's body jerked at the accusation. 'No. You have no right to say that.'

'Then what's wrong? Why do you say you can't go away?' Cuong's voice was harsh. He grabbed her by the shoulders and shook her.

Minh was trembling. Keeping her head low to avoid looking at him, she mumbled something. Dung was suddenly all ears. It wasn't that he was deliberately eavesdropping, but his interest in trying to understand Minh was roused.

'I said we can't go. None of us can go. The security police came to our cottage two days ago,' said Minh. 'We knew you were in trouble, but then we thought you were dead.'

Dung watched as Cuong gently lifted Minh's chin up. 'Go on, what else?'

Minh hesitated. She wiped a strand of hair from her face before speaking. 'I took our savings to the soothsayer. He said you were worse than dead.' Her voice was flat as though she were afraid to give the words life. 'I paid him to make it right for you in the spirit world.'

Cuong froze. His eyes widened and he stared hard at Minh. When he spoke there was a forced calmness to his tone. 'How much did you pay him?'

'All of it.'

'What. . . ! You idiot! How could you?' Angrily Cuong pushed Minh away. Dung hoped the push was maybe more than he'd intended because Minh lost her balance and toppled to the floor. 'We're trapped without money. Even if they released me from prison, the shame on our family would be enormous. I'd never be able to earn a living.' Cuong was breathing heavily. His eyes darted round as though he were a trapped animal. His face burning with rage, he turned on her in a frenzy. 'I know where the magician lives. The robber. You let him steal our money?' Dung stooped over to help Minh from the floor as Cuong slammed his fist against the door. 'Damn you, woman.' With that final remark he stumbled through the doorway.

'Hey, hey. I'm coming with you.' Hien leapt over the stools and disappeared after Cuong.

'Cuong, don't,' screamed Minh. She was now up on her feet and ran to the door, then she stopped, frozen, and stood staring into the empty space. 'Oh God, what have I done? It's like the old man said.' She spun round so that she was facing Dung, her face wild with panic. 'We have to stop him. He'll kill him.'

'Oh, I don't think so. Cuong's not a murderer, a bit wild sometimes, but not a murderer.' Dung shrugged. Then almost as an afterthought he said, 'Hien wouldn't let him kill him anyway.' He gave a giggle. 'It would be bad luck to kill a soothsayer, right?'

'Stop it. Stop it.'

Dung had thought Minh's behaviour incredible, but now he was certain she was like some hysterical younger sister who wasn't capable of taking care of things in her husband's absence. The women he knew were tough and always very careful with their money. He couldn't imagine what the soothsayer could have said to persuade her to hand over all of their savings. He must have known Cuong wasn't dead so why would he trick her? Still it wasn't his business. 'Are you hungry? I can heat up some soup.'

Minh was shaking. 'Cuong was so angry. It isn't like you think it is. He's changed. I don't know him any more.' Minh was crying. 'Besides the soothsayer's a good man. He didn't want to take the money. Oh God, he knew this would happen, but I ignored the warning and thrust it at him. I thought Cuong was trapped in a world of earthbound souls. I did it for Cuong. Doesn't Cuong understand how much I love him?' Snatching hold of Dung's arm she looked pleadingly into his face. 'We have to stop Cuong harming the soothsayer.'

'We!' thought Dung. It wasn't 'we' she was talking about, it was him. 'That won't be so easy,' he said. He would have liked to add that he didn't want to go chasing off again. He was hungry. He'd barely just got back from fetching her. The plan had been for Hien to escort her home after they had eaten something and Minh and Cuong had had time to plan their escape.

'Cuong's a deserter. It's dangerous for him to be outside. If there's a fight, it'll attract the police.'

It was the first sensible thing Minh had said. Dung hadn't quite admitted it, but although inwardly he was trying to argue it wasn't his responsibility to put right Minh's mistakes, he was also beginning to feel uneasy. Hien didn't need to draw the attention of the police to himself either since the authorities would grab at any excuse to create trouble for him.

'Look, I don't want to leave you here alone. If there is trouble the security police might go back to your house and they'll wonder at your absence.' Dung's mind was racing as he tried to figure out what to do. 'My friend Ha lives near here. Her brother has a Honda motorbike.' Dung moved the pot away from the stove. With some agitation in his voice that he found hard to disguise, he said, 'Put your cape on. We'll go and find her.'

Minh had barely time to throw the plastic over her shoulders before Dung caught hold of her hand and pulled her through the open door. 'Come on.'

It had started raining again as they ran out into the street and headed toward Ha's home. The gullies were aflow with black streams, but Dung knew his way around the potholes. Leaping here and there he managed to get Minh to Ha's cottage without either of them stepping into the drain or tumbling into one of the deeper holes. Dung banged urgently on the door. 'Ha can take you home on the bike while I see what I can do to stop a fight.'

'I can take the bus home,' said Minh adamantly. 'You take the Honda.'

Ha opened the door. She was several years younger than Minh, yet she carried herself with a confidence that defied her young age. Upon recognising her visitor, a smile danced across her face. 'You're back. Come inside,' she said, still grinning.

Dung hung back. 'I don't have time. Look, this is Minh,' he said, pushing her forward. 'Ha, she's in trouble. She's the wife of my brother's friend. It's important she get back to her home in Hong Gai. The security police might start looking for her if she's away too long. I'll leave Minh to explain as much of her situation as she wants, but can you borrow Tuan's Honda and take her home?'

Ha looked bewildered. 'Of course.' Snatching her cape from the table she stepped outside.

While Dung bent over to roll up his trousers, Minh hurried after Ha as she walked down the back alley to the kitchen where the bike was stored. 'I can go on the bus, little sister,' said Minh. 'It isn't necessary for you to take me home.'

Ha stopped and stared at her. 'Dung asked me to take care of you. That makes you my responsibility. It insults me if you refuse my hospitality.'

'I'm my own responsibility, not Dung's. This has nothing to do with any of you,' said Minh.

'Please, don't take offence. It's so easy for me to take you and I can be there and back in no time.'

Having secured his trousers, Dung hurried after them. He grabbed hold of Minh's arm. 'Look, I want Ha to get you home safely, understand? This is no time for pride. Besides it will take a long time to go by bus, and if the security police come back to your cottage and you're not there, it'll make the situation worse for Cuong. They'll ask around and someone will almost certainly have seen you on the bus. Going with Ha just minimises the risk.' Minh looked wretched and for a moment Dung regretted speaking so harshly. He hadn't liked the way Cuong treated her and now he was doing almost the same thing. It wasn't like him to get agitated, but he was as anxious as she was to stop a fight taking place between Cuong and the soothsayer. In a softer tone he said, 'We're your friends, Minh. How can we not get involved?'

As Dung neared the village he slowed his pace. He'd been running for more than an hour and still hadn't managed to catch up with his brother. Exhausted and out of breath, he greedily gulped in the air. It frustrated him not being able to catch up with them. He didn't imagine for one minute that Cuong would kill the magician, but Minh's manner disturbed him more than he cared to admit. It was something she said although he could no longer recall exactly what it was that had triggered his uneasiness.

It was only after his breathing eased that he felt comfortable enough to approach the village. It was already dusk. His idea was to slink in unnoticed and blend in with the shadows as though he belonged. Setting off at a steady pace he made his way down the sloped mud track which wound its way to the edge of the village. The swaying lanterns, shimmering in the early evening murkiness, gave an eerie outline to the hoards of people gathered in the street. There was now no question in Dung's mind that Hien and Cuong had already been there and that he was too late to prevent anything bad happening. His late arrival might only have been by a matter of five or ten minutes, but that was enough for fate to have entered upon her own course.

Mingling discreetly into the crowd, Dung tried to gather what information he could. It wasn't necessary for him to ask questions, everyone had something to say. Chatting amongst themselves like excited school children, some blamed the soothsayer, whereas others spoke of two robbers who'd entered his house and beaten him up before escaping. As the villagers competed with one another in raised voices as to what they'd just witnessed, Dung pushed his way closer to the soothsayer's front door. The crowd separated to reveal an old man sitting submissively on a bench between two policemen. blood was dripping from his jaw, forming a stained puddle at his feet. Dung drew in his breath. The man was Mr Tam, the magician, and although Dung was relieved that he wasn't seriously hurt, it nevertheless shocked him to see him sitting there in such a pitiful state.

A young boy standing beside Mr Tam offered him a cloth to wipe his face, but Mr Tam, seemingly unaware of the boy's presence, looked defeated and sat staring with glazed, vacant eyes into the distance. The child went frantic when a public security jeep arrived and the two policemen, linking their arms under Mr Tam's armpits, pulled him from the bench towards the jeep. Leaping forward the boy grabbed at one of the policemen's arms and bit savagely into it. The policeman yanked his arm away, sending him spinning. 'Damn you, you little brat.' He tried taking a swipe at the boy, but missed. Before he could grab hold of him, an old widow woman hurtled from the open doorway, snatched the boy roughly by his arm and pushed him back into the house. The policeman inspected the red welts rising up on his arm and scowled after the old woman and the boy. 'You nasty little runt. I won't forget this.'

As the jeep pulled away, the woman appeared back in the doorway. 'You'll pay for this,' she yelled. 'All of you will pay dearly. The spirits will pluck out your eyes when you're asleep, tear out your tongues and rip off your balls.' The public security were already halfway up the road, but Dung, hearing her words felt a shudder. He shook his head in frustration as he reinstated his early thought that Minh was an idiot and should never have gone to see the soothsayer, let alone given him all their savings. It was a bad situation that could so easily have been avoided and since Hien and Cuong were nowhere to be seen, the police were bound to accuse the old soothsayer of some wrongdoing.

Since there was nothing he could do in Khe Lang, Dung began the journey home. It was a miserable trek and by the time the glow of his village came into sight Dung was tired and hungry and felt as though he'd been walking for an eternity. The day seemed like it had been a disaster beginning with the bus ride to Hong Gai when a baby had urinated over his feet, and then finally the race along the rough track to Khe Lang and the added frustration of having missed them by a few minutes. Still, he reasoned, compared to others his life wasn't so bad and he certainly wouldn't want to be in Cuong's shoes or Mr Tam's.

After almost two hours of gentle walking it was a relief to be home, however, as he approached the building and saw it was all in darkness, he stopped in his tracks and stood puzzled, gazing at the window. Disappointment flooded through his body. He'd expected Hien and Cuong to be waiting up for him, perhaps sitting with their feet up on a stool and puffing on Hien's old water pipe, or maybe even having another slug at Hien's homemade rice wine. It was out of habit, rather than serious alarm, that Dung began his approach with caution. He'd covered only a short distance when the urge to laugh crept over him. It was late. Goodness knows what the time was. The journey back from Khe Lang had taken him much longer than going there and it was ridiculous to expect Hien and Cuong to wait up for him. They were both probably exhausted after the fight and after last night's celebrations. In all likelihood they had fallen asleep where they sat and the candles had burnt themselves down to the wick.

Dung sensed the danger, heard the whisper of movement as his assailants leapt from out of the shadows, too late. He'd barely time to confront them or think about taking off at breakneck speed, when an arm grasped him in a savage strangle hold. If his windpipe hadn't been restricted he would have yelled out, maybe even summoned some help from someone. Who, he didn't know because only his brother or Cuong would have come to his aid. In the struggle to break free, Dung tried to swing his leg back, but his aggressor, anticipating the move, kicked his legs from under him and forced him face down onto the ground. Before he had time to push himself onto his knees, his arms were wrenched back and he felt the cold metal of handcuffs snap onto his wrists. The attack had barely lasted seconds. Dung lay stunned.

Next moment he was wrenched to his feet, hauled through the alley and thrown headfirst into the back of a jeep. Cracking his shoulder against the metal flooring he let out a groan. Two men jumped in the jeep behind him and snatched hold of his head. The sudden brightness of a torch shining on his face caused Dung to screw up his eyes. 'He's the brother.'

There was a minute of confusion as the men, frustrated by having grabbed the wrong man, whispered among themselves. Then a voice snapped out of the darkness. 'Arrest him anyway, but get him away from here.' The door slammed shut. As Dung tried to raise himself into a sitting position the jeep lurched forward throwing him off balance. Laughter came from his two assailants.

Dung was shaking uncontrollably but his anger and fear eased a little when, after rattling over bumpy roads for no more than five or ten minutes, the vehicle pulled into a cobbled courtyard. Even without the advantage of seeing where he was, he knew instinctively it was the local police station. Had they taken him further it would have meant that the police considered his crime more serious so he tried to regain his composure by assuring himself that the police must know about the fight with the magician and just wanted to keep him out of the way for a while. Their arresting him meant they didn't have Hien or Cuong.

But as the door of the jeep crashed open Dung gave an involuntary start. Trying desperately to pull himself together so as not to appear so jumpy he attempted to focus his mind on something pleasant. Gathering all of his concentration he stared into the darkness beyond the jeep and scanned the tree-tops for a glimpse of the moon. It was there as he'd known it would be, bright and glowing. It was more than three-quarters full and he could just about make out the mythical figure of Cuoi and his magical banyan tree. Their images, although scarcely visible, were enough to help him feel less alone.

As one of the policemen jumped out, the other forced Dung from the jeep and hauled him towards the back door of the police station. He hadn't registered his injury before, but as they hurried him forward his knee kept giving way and through his bloodied, torn trousers, he now noticed that his knee was swollen and badly bruised. Limping across the courtyard he tried to keep his thoughts focused on Uncle Cuoi. Cuoi, the simple wood cutter, whose luck changed when he rescued the tiger cub from a trap. Startled by the mother tiger's appearance, Cuoi had put the wounded cub down and backed away, then peering at the mother from behind a bush, he'd watched as she stripped leaves from the banyan tree with her jaw and carefully wrapped them around the cub's leg. The wound healed instantly. It was this discovery of the magic healing tree which changed Cuoi's life. He'd gone from poor woodcutter to fame, fortune and eventual immortality. Dung visualised the magic working on him as he mentally wrapped Cuoi's banyan leaves around his own knee. Silly though the image was, it pleased him. It wasn't only his knee felt better, but his confidence increased — with Cuoi looking down on him there was nothing they could do to harm him. Armed with this new insight he straightened his back and walked with barely a limp into the darkened building.

Inside the interrogation room the officers removed the hand cuffs and shoved him into a chair. Dung cautiously looked around him. Apart from a low table and two chairs the room was empty. The walls were bare and a fluorescent light strip, hanging loosely from the ceiling, gave off intermittent spurts of light. Cursing the inadequacy of modern inventions, the taller of the officers flicked off the light switch and turned his attention to fiddling with the wick of an oil lamp until it flared into life. Drawing back into his chair Dung decided that he preferred the softness of the evening darkness to this eerie combination of dim lighting which cast ominous shadows on the walls, and distorted the policemen's faces until they took on inhuman qualities.

By the time a third official entered the room Dung was feeling nauseous. Perspiration was pouring freely from the nape of his neck and from the creases behind his knees. He imagined great pools of water collecting at his feet and worried that the officers might think he'd wet his pants. Lowering his eyes he glanced down at his feet. He could smell the dank odour of his sweat as it glued his clothes to his body, and he wondered if the others could smell it too.

Pulling up a chair an official placed himself in front of Dung so that they were at eye level, then leisurely letting his back rest against the chair, he scrutinised Dung's face. It was a threatening gesture which, from the curved smile at the edge of his lips, he clearly took pleasure in. Dung was at a loss as to what to do. He was afraid to stare back in case his look be misinterpreted as defiant, but then he was also afraid to lower his eyes. The officer was searching for signs of guilt and lowering his eyes might make it appear that he was trying to hide something. Affecting a glazed look Dung averted his eyes, and it was only as his interrogator began questioning him that he dared refocus his eyes and make his own examination of the man's face.

'What's your name?'

Looking his interrogator full in the face didn't inspire Dung with confidence. The man staring at him had cold hard eyes which held no hint of sympathy. Trying to suppress his rising panic and keep his voice steady Dung replied hesitantly to the question. 'Tran Van Dung.'

'Age?'

'Seventeen.'

'Where were you this evening?'

'I went to visit some friends, but they weren't at home.'

'What are the names of these friends?'

'I don't know them very well. I call them brothers Do and Duyen.'

The officer scowled and leaned forward. Dung could almost taste the smell of stale cigarettes on his breath and see the blackened coal dust embedded in the creases on his face.

'What's their family name?'

'I don't know.' Dung tried to lean away, but the officer behind him forced his shoulders forward. 'Honestly, that's all I've ever heard them called.'

'Where do they live?'

'I'm not sure. The house I went to was empty. I think I made a mistake.'

The officer eased back a bit. 'You made a mistake all right. It was a mistake your being born. Where's your elder brother?'

'I expected him to be at home. I don't know where he is. I thought you'd arrested him.' At this last statement the officer's eyes opened wide, a smile spread over his face and Dung knew he'd made a mistake.

'Oh yes. Why would we arrest him? What's he done wrong?'

'You arrested me. Neither of us has done anything wrong. It doesn't stop us being arrested.'

'Are you making a complaint about the way the people's security forces conduct their inquiries?'

Dung shook his head. He knew he was getting into dangerous ground. He needed to change the course of the questioning and quickly. 'Please, can I have a drink of water?'

The officer looked surprised for a moment then laughed. 'Do you think this is a hotel? That we brought you here to make life pleasant?' Then, as though suddenly tiring of his own banter he stood up, snatched Dung by his shirt and pulled him to his feet. 'Enough of this. Where's your brother?'

'I don't know. Really, I don't know.'

'We'll hold you until you tell us. It's him or you. Think about it.'

'Then you'll hold me forever, because I don't. . . .'

The officer went red in the face and seemed ready to strike him, but then for no reason that Dung could fathom he restrained the impulse. Still hanging onto Dung's shirt, he yelled through the door. 'Sergeant Vu.' As the duty officer entered, the official pushed Dung into the man's arms. 'Lock him up. The boy's an idiot. We're wasting time with him.'

Wrapping his long arms around his slender frame, Dung sat in the corner of his cell trying to nurse his sore knee and ward off his anxiety. His sweat had soaked through his clothes and he couldn't stop himself shivering. Every ten minutes or so it seemed as though his energy would surge up and then suddenly expire into a huge sigh he'd feel compelled to shake off. The urge to do it came in waves. He tried to relax by telling himself that the questioning had been easy, it hadn't lasted long and no one had struck him. But this involuntary sighing and shaking kept coming back of its own accord. It was the most ridiculous thing he'd ever experienced. Leaning back against the cell wall Dung decided to allow himself one last sigh. He reminded himself over and over that the police didn't suspect him of any crime and that his only wrong doing, in their eyes, was that he was the younger brother of Hien. Tomorrow or the next day, they'd release him. In a week he'd be laughing the incident off with his friends. Ha might scold him for being arrested but secretly she would think of him as a hero. The younger boys in Cam Pha would certainly regard him as a hero. He'd stood up to his interrogator very well. He hadn't told them where Hien was.

The sighing stopped and Dung chuckled. What a conman he was. Here he was lying to himself. How could he have told them where Hien was? He didn't know. Suggesting that they might have arrested his brother was a truthful answer. His laughter, however, eased his fears and he shook his head in wonderment at his own conceit. The best and only thing he could really say in his defence, as to how well he'd stood up to police interrogation, was that he hadn't messed in his pants.

Here he was worrying over his own skin when it was his brother and Cuong he should be thinking about. If the police were to arrest them they would be in serious trouble. Cuong would go to prison for certain, but then so would Hien. Hadn't the villagers accused them both of robbing the old magician and beating him up. These were serious offences and it could escalate as things always did. As an awful thought struck him Dung let out a moan. 'Oh, hell!' The blood drained from his head and he felt as though he were going to pass out. Up until now he'd given no thought as to where he'd hidden the bag of TNT. Everything had happened so fast he'd just been swept along in its tide. He closed his eyes as frightening images of them searching his home flicked through his brain. 'Where? Where in hell did I put it?'

Burying his head in his hands Dung tried to stop his panic taking hold. His breathing was coming in heavy quick successive waves. The duty officer might hear him, might come to his cell to investigate. He would become suspicious of him, read the guilt in his face. With conscious deliberation Dung slowed his breathing. It might still be all right. They might not search his home. They were looking for Hien and Cuong, that was all and if they had already found the TNT his interrogation wouldn't have been so easy. In fact, they must already have been inside because they knew Hien and Cuong weren't there. They didn't know about the TNT, so he must have set it down in a place that didn't command their attention.

Dung forced himself to think logically. He'd go through what happened step by step. Cuong's arrival had thrown them out of their usual routine, and although Hien was normally always insistent that before he did anything else — go to the toilet even — Dung climb up into the rafters and hide the dynamite, he knew that hadn't happened. He closed his eyes to try to blot out the image of the cell and focus on each area of space of their home. The green lime-washed outbuilding they lived in was small, not even house size. It comprised the stable area which had once stalled the old farmer's water buffalo, but was now Hien's bedroom. In it was Hien's bed which consisted of a generous layer of straw covered with jute sacking, his guitar, and apart from his old brown suitcase which he used to set a kerosene lamp on, there was nothing else. Dung slept in the kitchen next to the wooden milk stools and the brick stove. There were two tall clay pots, one of which was filled with rice when they could afford it and the other was for fresh water. On top of the pots lay a short wooden plank which served as a place to keep their bowls and chopsticks. Suspended over the stove were a few saucepans, above which was a makeshift chimney channelled through the wall. Then there was the hay loft above Hien's bed, but Dung already knew with a horrible certainty he hadn't climbed up there. He leaned back against the wall. He could see the room clearly but, defeated by his own state of shock, he could not visualise where he'd put the bag of TNT.

Pulling himself up to his feet Dung paced the cell. He wondered what his chances were of escape. When they were up in the mountains searching for the anti-tank landmines, Hien used to speculate on what they should do if they were ever caught. He'd warned Dung that he must try to escape as early on in his arrest as possible. The earlier one made an escape attempt, the more likely it was to be successful. Were the police to find the TNT and transfer him to Hanoi or Thanh Hoa, he would never be able to escape. Each successive prison he went to would be more secure than the last. The local police were often lazy and incompetent, but further down the line they would be more professional.

For a moment Dung stopped his pacing and surveyed his surroundings. Besides a piece of threadbare rush matting for his bed, there was a bucket in the corner. A single lightbulb hung from the ceiling, but other than that the cell was empty. Dung was disappointed to note the absence of a window as it seemed that almost everyone he knew who claimed to have escaped from gaol, said they climbed through a window. There was one friend of Hien's who regularly salted the bars in his cell and after three months the metal rotted sufficiently for him to be able to yank the bars away and climb out. Another friend had told him how he tore apart the rush roofing and climbed out through the rafters. In Dung's cell there was no barred window, no food from which to extract salt and no rush roofing to break out from. The only way out was the way he'd come in.

Tired and hungry, a feeling of despair drenched over him. There was nothing to do except resign himself to fate. Almost mechanically and with little hope of actually sleeping, Dung pulled the matting away from the toilet bucket and settled himself down by the door where the smell of urine seemed weakest. Fate — that's what Minh had been talking about. And there was something else, something the magician had said to her. She'd been sullen because she'd had some inkling of the trouble. . . . Dung suddenly sat up. He'd remembered. Before going to fetch Minh he'd pushed the bag of TNT under his jute bed. 'Phu!' Giving a huge sigh of relief he breathed out heavily. Well, at least it was hidden, not as securely as he would have liked, but wedged into the straw bedding was better than on top of it. He cursed himself for not climbing up into the rafters and hiding it properly.

The lightbulb dimmed then suddenly came bright again. Dung sat up startled. Then as another power cut robbed Cam Pha of its electricity the bulb went black. Dung lay back down and stared unseeing into the enveloping darkness as slowly the magnitude of his crime began to take on apocalyptic proportions. If the police did look through his bed and find the TNT and if they didn't shoot him for the sheer audacity of his crime, he could expect be in prison for a long time. His youth would slip away and he'd be an old man before he came out. Dung shivered. Better to be shot. With the threat of another Chinese invasion, they'd say, digging up the mines was like welcoming the enemy into the mother-land's back garden. They were never going to accept that Dung and Hien were not terrorists and that collecting the TNT was just a means of making a living. And who was it they sold the dynamite to, they would ask? As often as not the fishermen Hien and Dung traded with were Chinese so how could he claim the fishermen were not spies and that he wasn't working for the Chinese government. He was half-Chinese himself so which country did he owe his allegiance to?

Dung closed his eyes. Fatigue was, at that moment, a stronger emotion in him than fear and as he pressed his nose against the door crack, to breath in the fresher air, he wondered how many other wretched pri-soners around the country were doing the same thing. It was only in that sense he knew himself not to be alone.

Despite the lateness of the hour word of the arrests spread quickly. When Ha returned from Hong Gai and learned from her neighbour that Dung had been taken to the police station in Cam Pha, she was initially outraged. However, as the realization of all the facts sank in, Ha's outrage turned to anxiety. Like almost everyone else, she knew enough to fear the police. People privately said that justice in Vietnam was like the wild forest — there was no system to it. Many times the lower-ranking police officers arrested people they didn't like just to intimidate them and to get money from their families. Trouble could escalate out of nothing. Ha knew something of Dung's illegal residence status and of his activities on the border so it would be dangerous for Dung if the police looked deeply into his life.

Wheeling her brother's Honda back out of the kitchen again Ha made her way to the police station. It was a short distance and within a few minutes she was hammering on the door with all the force she could muster. The place looked deserted but after several minutes of persistent knocking, she heard footsteps. The duty officer opened the door and glared at her in disbelief. His trousers were creased and his shirt was open exposing his oversized beer gut. From the way he leaned unsteadily against the door, Ha suspected he might have just woken from a deep sleep.

'What is it you want?'

When the light fell fully across the duty officer's face Ha recognised him as Sergeant Vu. Alcoholic and close to retirement Sergeant Vu was never going to move up higher in the ranks. His reputation for being brutal and easily corrupted was well known in the town. 'You're detaining a friend of mine,' said Ha. 'His name is Tran Van Dung. He's not a criminal. What can be done to obtain his release?'

Vu was about to slam the door, but then hesitated. Looking her up and down and with a lecherous smile tickling the corners of his mouth, he made no pretence to disguise his approval of her small breasts and gently rounded figure. 'Come in. Let's talk about it. You've already disturbed my sleep, you may as well keep me company.' Ha felt uneasy and her instinct was to get as far away from the man as possible, but as she turned to leave, Sergeant Vu called to her, 'You're leaving. What about your friend?'

Ha grit her teeth and turned back toward him. As she wheeled the Honda into the police station, Sergeant Vu secured the door behind her, then followed her down the hallway. Pushing past her he opened a side door and pointed into a dimly lit room for her to enter.

'What is it you are offering me, little lady?'

'You can have this bike.'

Vu burst into laughter. 'The bike belongs to your brother Tuan. Everyone in Cam Pha knows that so how am I going to explain to people when I'm riding around on it? Oh, no little darling, that's not what I had in mind at all. This arrangement has to be our secret. You know that. We could never keep the exchange of the Honda secret.'

'I can obtain money.'

'How much?'

'Tell me how much you want. I can sell the bike to someone else then bring you the cash. If you just let my friend go I promise I'll keep my word.'

'Why should I trust you? It's better we consummate our deal here and now, then you will not be beholden to me.'

'I will keep my word.'

'No. We consummate our deal here and now or your friend will rot in gaol forever. If there was any doubt about that before, it's a certainty now.'

Ha felt her skin creep. She looked over to the door and wondered if she should not insist he open it and let her leave. But even though she was trembling and a mountain of hatred was rising up in her stomach, she knew she could never leave. Dung was her whole life. In the daily drudgery of her existence there was nothing else to look forward to. The idea of one day being Dung's wife was what helped her cope with losing her parents. She had always imagined Dung would be the first and last and that love making would be something beautiful, ethereal. Not something dirty and sordid. She looked round hoping she might get a glimpse of where he was. He must be somewhere close, locked up in a cell. If he knew what was happening, he'd break his way free, punch the sergeant in the face, and they could both ride off on Tuan's bike laughing. She thought about calling to him, but she knew that wouldn't be how it was. It was all pretence. They weren't mythical creatures, and the strength of a cell door and the power of the police was real.

Ha's hesitation was only momentary. She loved Dung so what could she lose that was more valuable than him? He need never know. Sergeant Vu had said it would be their secret. He had his reputation and his wife to consider and if this were known, he wouldn't even make it to retirement but would lose his job instantly. She would close her eyes and pretend this liaison never took place, will it out of existence. The longer Dung was in prison the greater the chance they would find out about his border activities, and besides, Ha knew well enough that Sergeant Vu was vindictive and would do everything in his power to find a way to keep his threat. If she didn't take action now she risked Dung being transferred to a prison where she might never see him again. It seemed almost certain the old sergeant thought he had someone worthless in his custody, otherwise he would not have invited her in.

'What's your decision? Do you want your friend to rot his life away in one of my cells?' Sergeant Vu extended his hand.

Ha's vision was beginning to blur, tears welled in her eyes and soaked her dark lashes. 'Let me take my own clothes off.'

'Oh, by all means. I'd like that, but you have to stand in front of me. No cowering behind the desk, little spring flower.'

Pale and vulnerable Ha stood in front of him and unfastening her clothes let them slip limply to the floor. As Vu advanced toward her she pressed her eyes closed tight. She did not watch him as he wrestled with his own trousers, then, falling toward her, pushed her onto the floor. His hands groping across her body were hard and calloused, not like Dung's would have been. His breath smelt of rice wine and stale cigarettes. She wanted to throw up.

Ha was at least grateful for his greed. In his eagerness to release his sexual lust he didn't bother to kiss her, or make any pretence at its being love. He'd bought her and he was taking what he thought was his. The pain seared through her groin as he thrust into her, again and again slamming his body against her while his heavy breath came in bursts. His sweat dripped over her nakedness like the blood oozing onto her thighs. Not soon enough the darkness closed around and Ha felt as though she were passing out.

When Ha wheeled the Honda out of the police station she wondered if she could ever cleanse herself of the dead ache between her legs. All she could think of was to get home and wash her body clean. Dung would come to her and it would be all right. Nothing had happened.

A few miles away in Hong Gai, Trinh Thu Tam, locally known as the soothsayer, was being interrogated. He'd been awakened from a fitful sleep and escorted down to the interrogation room during the early hours of the morning. As a clairvoyant and spiritualist who dedicated his life to helping people avoid trouble, he was liked and respected by the local people. This, he knew, put him in conflict with the Communist Party. Superstitions were outlawed by the government, so anyone who profited by telling fortunes and making contact with their dead relatives was seen as an enemy. Mr Tam had spent many years in prison paying for his crimes of exploitation and since his last release he'd tried hard to keep a low profile. He'd even insisted that he live in the outside kitchen shed so as to dispel any jealousy toward him, but he was a generous man by nature and he found it difficult to turn people away.

'If you didn't know her, why did Nguyen Cao Cuong's wife visit you in the first place?

When Minh visited him Mr Tam had sensed her desperation, but he'd also read the danger in her hand. The danger was both to her, her family and to himself. Had he understood the nature of the danger more precisely it might have been possible for him to avert it; however, his gift brought him only veiled information. 'I have a reputation for being able to help people. She came seeking information about her husband but I was unable to help.'

'You took gold from her?'

'No. I have no idea about any gold.' Mr Tam was telling the truth. When Cuong and Hien turned up at his house he only knew danger threatened all of them. He tried to warn Cuong, but Cuong was so crazed in his head, he was incapable of listening. He kept yelling and demanding his gold back but Mr Tam had no idea what he was talking about. When he tried to calm Cuong in order to unravel the reasons for his anger, Cuong had grown impatient and struck him in the face. It was at about that time his widowed sisters-in-law must have alerted the police because within minutes of the fracas the police made an appearance. In the ensuing chaos Cuong and his friend escaped, exiting the house through the rear yard and across the stream to the rice paddies. If Mr Tam had been a younger man he'd have been inclined to follow them, but he was too old and too worn down by his earlier prison experiences to make an escape. Partially blind and a little deaf, his defences were all gone. To his mind he'd done nothing wrong, but then, he thought, what did that ever count for?

'If there was no gold involved, then why did these men come to your home demanding it? Your story doesn't make sense. There's something deeper here. These men were your friends. Perhaps you crossed them in some way.'

'Colonel, it isn't true. I don't know them,' said Mr Tam. 'The wife came to me seeking help. I turned her away. Why the husband came back, asking for his money, I don't know. Maybe she told him a lie, or he thinks I insulted her by turning her away.'

As Mr Tam pleaded his ignorance a knock came on the door and a young man entered and whispered a message into the ear of the most senior of the public security officers. Mr Tam watched as the officer's previously calm expression, became suddenly alarmed. Standing up he hurried out of the room with the messenger and it was a full fifteen minutes before he returned and then it was only to call the other officer from the room. Sitting silently as the two guards behind him remained watching, Mr Tam sensed the interruption was not to his advantage.

When the two officers returned their questioning seemed to take on a greater urgency. 'Where are your friends.'

'My friends?'

'Nguyen Cao Cuong and Tran Van Hien.'

'Since they are not my friends, I have no idea where they are.'

'Your denials won't help you, Mr Tam. We will get your friends, have no fears about that.'

'I just told you, they are not my friends. The man beat me. A friend doesn't break your jaw. It's nonsense for you to bring me here. I'm the victim of a crime, not the perpetrator.'

'What do you know of their activities?'

'I don't. I know nothing about them.'

'That won't do, Mr Tam. I've just been informed that explosives were being stored at your friend's home. We are not simply investigating a village brawl. We know who you are, and of your past offences against the state. We are not amateurs who can be messed around with.' Mr Tam felt the blood drain from his head. He knew that his fears, which had first been awakened when Minh came seeking his help, were being realised. 'Your friends must be terrorists. Why else would they keep explosives? If you confess your crimes and tell us all you know we're prepared to deal leniently with you.'

'Why are you saying this? You know these people are not my friends.'

'Don't take me for a fool. It's very much in your interests to co-operate with us.'

'I have been co-operating.'

Mr Tam's interrogator leaned over him. His eyes were steady and hard. When he spoke his voice was unemotional. 'And the matter of the child. Your sexual conduct with him is against the law.'

This was too much. Mr Tam sprang up from his chair and with his eyes blazing glared into his accuser's face. 'The child! I am like a father to Chinh.'

'Which makes your crime even the more odious.'

Mr Tam could no longer contain himself. The accusations were vile. It was worse than anything they had ever thrown at him in the past. He wasn't a violent man, but if the two officers hadn't drawn his arms back in a vice-like grip, he would have grabbed his provocateur by the throat. 'He's a deaf, defenceless orphan,' he yelled. 'I took him in and adopted him as my own.'

'As your own slave, Mr Tam. Your own sexual slave.'

'No . . . no.' Mr Tam was weeping. The officers released his arms as he became limp, letting him collapse onto the floor. 'Don't do this to me. Don't hurt my child. You'll ruin his reputation and he'll never survive. I'll say whatever you want about these men. They're nothing to me.' Mr Tam was on his knees. 'Don't hurt my child. I beg you. He's all I have left in the world.'

Chapter 4: Failed rendezvous

Quang Ninh Province
26th April 1980

Every morning the sun, rising over the wall,
Beams on the gate, but the gate is not open.
Inside the prisoner lingers a gloomy pall.
Night still tarries in the depths of the prison,
But, the prisoner knows that outside the sun has risen.
PRISON DIARY, HO CHI MINH

IT WAS FIVE O'CLOCK in the morning when the old police guard opened the cell door and Dung sprang to his feet. For several minutes Sergeant Vu stood scowling at him without saying anything, then stepping aside he said, 'Go on, get away.' Dung was barely awake and didn't quite register what it was the sergeant was saying. 'Go, I said. Get out of here.' This time his message was clear. Dung didn't wait to be told a third time and slamming his feet into his oversized sandals, he took off from the police station as fast as he dared. His first thought was they hadn't found the bag of TNT and there was still time for him to run home and hide it properly, but as he hurried along the empty street towards his home, doubts crept into his mind. He was certain Hien and Cuong hadn't been brought into the police station during the night so the police would still be watching the house. Dung slowed his pace as it occurred to him that they might be setting him up. He didn't want to risk being arrested a second time but was unsure what he should do or where he should go.

At the corner of Cam Thuy, Dung turned away from his home and headed towards Ha's house. The streets had dried out a little from the night's rain and he skipped over the black puddles easily. He knew Ha's brother Tuan would be annoyed with him for calling, but he didn't know where else to go. If he were to leave Cam Pha for good he needed to first say goodbye to Ha. There was a time when their parents had been friends and discussed their betrothal. The family connections, although not always apparent, were still buried there threading back through several generations and it was for this reason Hien had been drawn to find a place to live in Cam Pha. Since childhood Dung had always assumed that he would marry Ha. There never had been anyone else and so far as he was concerned there never would be.

When Tuan opened the door and saw Dung standing in the doorway his face paled. It seemed as though he were about to say something, perhaps tell Dung to clear off, but then as though suddenly changing his mind he grabbed at Dung's shirt and yanked him inside. Slamming the door behind them Tuan quickly pulled the bolt across and hurried away to find Ha. While waiting in the parlour Dung regretted having gone there. He'd always taken Ha's friendship for granted, but perhaps under such circumstances as these, he had no right to. Being in her home could bring trouble to her family. His arrest alone was bad enough, but his relationship with Hien and the deserter Cuong now almost guaranteed his being labelled as a marked man.

At the sound of Tuan and Ha's approaching sandals slapping in unison against the brick floor Dung looked anxiously towards the door. Their whispered voices were barely audible, but he sensed, rather than heard, Tuan's words were not to his advantage. Sidling closer to the door he strained his ears to hear what they were saying. 'I'm going back to bed,' said Tuan. 'It's dangerous for us if he stays here and you shame yourself by your continuing association with him. Get rid of him quickly and make sure he knows not to come back. If the neighbours saw him come I could lose my job at the coal mining company.'

'Stop it, Tuan. Dung's family has been friends with ours for decades. Your words are hateful and you dishonour the memory of our parents.'

'Well, things change. If he had any real regard for you he'd stay away.' Tuan sighed. 'Okay. Offer him food if you like, but then he must go. That's just how it is.'

As the door opened Dung quickly stepped away from the passageway so that they would not know he'd overheard part of their conversation. Ha entered the room alone looking flushed and Dung could see she'd recently finished bathing. Her hair hung damp on her shoulders giving off the fragrance of boiled *bo-ket* leaves. The smell was intoxicating and it took all of Dung's will-power to stop himself rushing over and embracing her. He was proud of her for standing up to her brother and yet as she stood shivering in the cold room dressed only in a white shirt and sleeping shorts she suddenly seemed terribly fragile.

'I'm sorry,' he stammered. 'I know I shouldn't have come here. I was just . . . I was afraid I would never see you again. Last night I had the most awful. . . .'

Ha interrupted him. 'I know.' She then hesitated, as though torn between propriety and instinct, then dropping all pretences of correct behaviour she ran sobbing into Dung's arms. Dung was both delighted and overwhelmed by her open show of affection. He clasped her to him tightly. 'It's not safe for you to go home,' she whispered. 'The police are watching your house. We have to find a place for you to stay and my place won't be safe enough, and anyway my brother. . . .' Her eyes darted from the window to the door as though she expected the police to push their way in.

'It's all right. I was released. I didn't escape.'

'No.' Ha was shaking her head. 'It's not all right. Sergeant . . . the policeman maybe made a mistake releasing you. It's all over the neighbourhood that the security police are looking for your brother. They arrested the soothsayer and took him to Hong Gai. Please, you have to hide.'

Dung was confused. It was less than thirty minutes since he'd been released. All he had done was walk the distance between the police station and Ha's house. Events couldn't change so fast. And if they did how would Ha know any more than he did. She was clearly distressed, irrational even. 'It's all right, I wasn't planning on staying here. I just wanted to see you before I make my way over to Tien Yen.'

Ha pulled away from him. 'Why Tien Yen?'

'Hien's friend Tang has a shop there.'

'Tran Thu Tang's sister married a public security officer. Why would you go there?' Ha looked clearly disturbed.

'Tang's an old friend. He's not going to report us to his brother-in-law. Besides Major Thanh is also a relative of Cuong. He wouldn't turn him in.'

'Of course he would. He's communist. They're not like us. The Party comes first, remember. He'd turn his own mother in if that was what expected of him.'

'I think you're wrong Ha. Family loyalty still exists in this country.'

'Not amongst communists.'

'Look, I'm sure Hien went to Tang's. I have to go there.' As Dung spoke he convinced himself more and more that that would be where Hien was hiding. 'I'll go now. I didn't want to cause any trouble, I just came here to say goodbye.'

Ha looked frantic. 'No. We have to think about this. You can't just go.' She ran her finger nervously through her wet hair as though trying to give herself space to think. 'When did you eat last?'

Dung shrugged. 'Oh sometime yesterday, I suppose.'

'I'll cook us breakfast.'

'No, it's better I leave now. Your brother. . . .'

'Forget my brother. This house . . . it belonged to my parents. He acts as though it were just his. Dung stay. It won't take me long.'

Dung followed her through to the kitchen and out into the courtyard. He helped pull a pail of fresh water up from the well then carried it inside and poured some into a saucepan. While Ha chopped garlic and ginger Dung threw some charcoal into the clay stove and struck a match to get it going. He was hungry, starving in fact. He had forgotten how much, but hunger he could cope with. It was saying goodbye to Ha that was going to be difficult and he was glad to be doing something constructive while forestalling the inevitable. If he didn't find Hien at Tang's he had no idea what he was going to do. Filling his stomach, he hoped, would at least help ease the gnawing feeling of emptiness growing inside him.

Sergeant Vu dashed out of the room into the compound just before a gushing stream of vomit rose out of his stomach and splattered over his feet. He'd drunk whiskey during his night duty and the effects of the home-brewed alcohol soured his stomach. Still feeling a little light-headed he wiped his mouth with his shirt sleeve as he struggled to get his thoughts together. If the officials from Hanoi knew he was drunk there would be even more trouble to face. His rushing out during their questioning of him didn't help his situation either, but then that couldn't be helped. When he'd released the prisoner Tran Van Dung he'd no idea the boy was wanted for anything more serious than being the brother of the street brawler Tran Van Hien. It was outrageous no one had warned him that he was suspected of being involved in terrorist activities. How was he supposed to know the brothers kept explosives in their home? It just wasn't fair for them to hold him responsible for the prisoner's escape. Kicking at a stone, Sergeant Vu cursed them. These were difficult times and no one knew what was expected of them. The fact that he was just a rural official didn't mean he didn't do his job well. Tucking his shirt into his trousers Vu lifted his head up and walked back into the police station. Well, they would soon learn, even the likes of him had his pride.

Back in front of his superiors, Vu attempted to defend his position. 'If everyone else knew the prisoner was dangerous, then I should have been told. They let me think we were just holding him for the night to keep him from warning his brother — that's what I understood. If anyone's to blame for his escape, it's them. Besides there was a power cut last night and the oil lamp has a limited range.'

Senior Colonel Khiem eased back into his chair and smiled. 'Whiskey's a good sedative. You were asleep weren't you?'

'I didn't sleep,' protested Vu, but as the officer kept his gaze fixed on Vu's face he lost his nerve and decided to temper his denial. 'Well, maybe in the early hours I might have dozed a little. If someone had told me the prisoner was important I'd have sat outside his cell all night. No one said anything about his being a terrorist.' Vu was sweating. He wasn't used to being the one being interrogated. It was a lot better to be sitting at the other side of the desk. These people from Hanoi were different from the people in Quang Ninh; they were arrogant. They dangled their authority in front of him, like a naked lightbulb penetrating his private thoughts and leaving him exposed. 'I told you I thought the boy was arrested because of his brother. Just a minor fight with the old magician. Nothing serious.' Vu knew he was protesting too much yet once he'd got started he seemed unable to stop himself from blabbering on. 'After a night in the cells we'd planned to release him anyway. How could I know things had changed?'

'You lying incompetent. You took a bribe. It's written all over your face.'

'No. That's not true.'

'What was it? Money?'

'No.'

'No, it wasn't money. We'd have found it.' He leaned forward. 'Sex. It was sex, wasn't it?' Khiem stood up and walked over to Vu. Standing behind him he rested his hands on his shoulders and leaned toward his ear. In a whispered voice he said, 'Brother Vu, A pretty girl. I know about these things. Who of us can ever say we've never been tempted?' He straightened up then moved back in front of Vu so he could look at him full in the face. 'Taking a sexual bribe is a punishable offence, but assisting an enemy of the motherland is a much more serious matter. Any information you can give which assists us in tracking down this man and his accomplices will be to your advantage. If they escape arrest and commit further terrorist offences you will be held accountable. I might think differently, but there will be others who would say you are a traitor. Think about it.' Vu lowered his head. His stomach was turning somersaults and he suspected that if the interrogation were to go on much longer he would need to vomit again. 'They'll say you helped the prisoner escape because you were one of his accomplices.' Khiem smiled sympathetically. 'I can help you, brother, but only if you help me.'

Vu wiped his shirt sleeve back across his face. Pearls of sweat were dripping down from his brow. They were not going to give up. They would keep on at him, day after day, until he confessed. The official Khiem was relatively friendly now, but later he would approach him differently. It was all part of the technique.

'Who was it visited you during the night? She was pretty, wasn't she? She used you, brother. Don't you see that?' Vu felt incensed. The girl had tricked him. Khiem was right. She'd come to him all innocent and virgin, but underneath she was a cold vixen. She must have known what activities her boyfriend was involved in, otherwise, why come?

'What's her name?'

Sergeant Vu raised his head. If he was going down so was she. 'Her name is Ha. Her parents are dead but she lives with her brother, Pham Van Tuan and his family.'

Khiem looked excited. 'Address?'

'They live just a few miles from here. I can show you.'

Dung sipped his tea as he watched Ha scurrying round the kitchen collecting up odd items of food. 'We can take a picnic with us. I've packed up bread and bananas, cucumbers, some pork rolls.'

Dung registered the word 'we'. Setting down his cup he stood up and catching hold of Ha's hands he stopped her in her tracks and turned her to face him. 'Thanks for the food, but Ha, it's better I go on my own. I don't want you drawn into this. This won't be a picnic.'

Ha looked up at him, the tears glistening in her eyes. 'I know better than you, it's not a picnic.' Her voice was beginning to break up. 'I'm already drawn in. Please don't leave me. If you're going to Hong Kong, so am I.'

'Hong Kong!' Dung pulled back and laughed. 'Who ever said I was going to Hong Kong?'

'Minh talked about it.'

'Minh! Oh, I might have known. Minh's sweet but she's a real idiot. Besides their situation is different. My plan is just to lie low for a while. I need to speak to Hien and find out what's what, then maybe we'll set up our home in another village. When things quiet down, I'll contact you.'

'Dung, I don't care what risks there are. I want to be with you.'

Dung knew he hadn't the strength to refuse her request. The loneliness of his night in the cell left him feeling vulnerable and uncertain. Being in Ha's company always made him feel good. She wasn't just beautiful, she was strong. It would tear his heart open to separate from her permanently, but once he'd spoken to Hien he'd know what to do. 'You can come as far as Tang's. After that I'm not sure, but if the situation becomes serious you have to promise me you'll come back home quickly.'

Ha's expression relaxed. She put her hand lightly on Dung's shoulder. 'Sit down and finish your *pho*. I'll run upstairs and change my clothes, then we can be on our way.'

As Ha disappeared from the room Dung considered sneaking out of the back door. Even her coming as far as Tang's might ruin her reputation. If he were to just leave quietly. . . . She wouldn't like it but, after a while she would understand. She'd know that he did it for. . . .

As Dung weighed up these thoughts Ha rushed into the room. Her shirt wasn't properly buttoned and her cheeks were crimson. Shocked and embarrassed Dung jumped up to his feet. 'What!'

'Public security jeeps . . . there are two coming down the street.' She was halfway out the back door before Dung caught the meaning of what she'd said and snatching the basket, took off after her.

After his disappointment at not finding the prisoner and his accomplice, Khiem set a watch on the Pham household and then drove straight over to the Public Security building in Hong Gai. He knew the PSO would have extensive records on the citizens within the local community and he wanted to check out the names and addresses of other family members. Although the prisoner had not been at the girl's home when Khiem and his men arrived there, they had interviewed the girl's brother, a woman and two small children. Little came out of it. The man protested they'd been unaware of any visitors as they were sleeping upstairs and, as to where his sister might have gone, he could only presume she'd set off early for the market in Mong Cai which was something she did about once a month. Further inquiries in the neighbourhood, however, unearthed a woman from two doors away, who confirmed that she'd seen Dung entering the house a half-hour or so before the public security jeeps arrived. The realization that Khiem probably only missed capturing them by minutes had stuck at the back of his throat all the way to Hong Gai. Sergeant Vu's incompetence was intolerable. He wouldn't do anything to him right away since the man might still be useful in helping them identify the prisoner and the girl Ha, but later, when he didn't need him any more, he'd see that he paid dearly for his crimes.

The paper search in Hong Gai had so far only served to frustrate him further. Both Tran Van Hien and Tran Van Dung were not officially registered anywhere although local information from villagers confirmed they had been be living in Cam Pha, at the place where the police unearthed the TNT. After exhausting the information on the Tran brothers, Khiem turned to the files on Nguyen Cao Cuong. As a senior ranking officer from military intelligence it was because of Nguyen Cao Cuong's involvement and the potential seriousness of the crimes with the Tran suspects that he'd been drawn in. Flipping through the pages of registration and military background he turned to the section on historical family background.

Nguyen Cao Cuong born 1953 at Ba San, Lang Son Province. Only surviving child of six siblings. Other siblings starved during the occupation of the Japanese Armies.

Father: Nguyen Van Thai born 1918. Fought with the resistance group against the French Imperialists. Later worked with resistance fighters defending the motherland and aiding the Americans against the Japanese invaders. Died of tuberculosis 1956.

Mother: Vu Hai born 1923 in Lao Cai Province. . . .

'If you want to know more about Nguyen Cao Cuong, why not ask Major Thanh. He's not in right now since he spends part of his time in Hanoi at the legal training centre, but he married the sister of the wife.'

'The wife?' Irritated, Khiem looked up from his papers to see a young officer looking over him.

'Major Thanh is Nguyen Cao Cuong's brother-in-law.'

Suddenly interested in what the young officer might have to say Khiem gave him his full attention. 'Who is this Major Thanh?'

'Nguyen Chau Thanh is a public security officer here.'

Khiem froze. He couldn't believe what he was hearing. 'Is he the nephew of General Nguyen Tat Chau?' As Khiem asked the question he hardly dared believe it possible he would get the answer he wanted. General Nguyen Tat Chau was retired but he was still a Party Central Committee Member which placed him too high within the government for Khiem to be able to attack him directly, but his nephew Thanh was accessible. Besides, it was Thanh who first muddied his name.

'Yes. His uncle is General Chau.'

Khiem felt his heart racing. He couldn't believe it was a coincidence that their paths had crossed again. This was fate. He'd waited years to get his revenge against Nguyen Chau Thanh, and now here was his chance to do it. He stood up and walked over to the window. Gazing out over the arched driveway to the street beyond he wondered how he could play this situation to its best advantage. After some minutes of pondering he asked, 'Who else is in this family of Cuong's wife?'

'Besides Major Thanh's wife and the wife of Cuong, there's another brother-in-law who lives in Tien Yen.'

Dung didn't stop running until they were several miles from the village. In his panic he hadn't given much thought as to which way to go, but as he slowed to catch his breath he realised that heading out cross-country actually made sound sense. If the police had taken off after them, the rice paddies offered a good advantage over the roads since the ox paths were too narrow for their jeeps to follow.

Ha caught hold of Dung's arm. She was breathless and holding her chest. 'Please, I have to sit down a minute.'

Dung could see she was exhausted. He was tired himself and scanned the horizon for a secure place to rest. In the distance he could see the hump of a dyke and pointed it out to Ha. 'That looks like a good place. We need to be sure to stay well below the skyline since they're likely to have binoculars.' Then noticing the worried look on Ha's face he asked, 'Can you make it that far?' Ha nodded her agreement and linking her arm into Dung's prepared to trudge the half-mile over to the dyke.

When they reached the dyke they found that the steeped path was waterlogged from where the buffalo had trodden into the soft soil and in her tiredness Ha tripped. Dung was quick to react and catching hold of her hand he kept a couple of steps ahead of her as they eased their way down the slope toward the water. 'We're safe for a minute. We can rest while we think about what to do next.'

Although the sun was still low in the sky they could already feel its warmth, and after all the heavy rains, Dung felt grateful that it looked as though the day would be pleasant. He'd been sitting on the bank for only a few minutes when the thought struck him as to how absurd their situation was. It was as though the tension of the last few hours just evaporated and the compulsion to laugh washing through him was so refreshing and consuming that he collapsed back onto the soft earth in a fit of giggles. Catching the look of disapproval on Ha's face he tried to control his laughter. 'Look Ha, don't you see the craziness of our situation. Firstly, I haven't done anything wrong, and secondly, they already released me for the thing that I didn't do wrong. We've run all this way and we don't even know for certain they were after me. That's a laugh, isn't it?'

Ha glared at him sternly. 'They are after us.' She seemed close to tears. 'What about your activities on the border? How do you know they aren't going to lock you up for that?'

Dung looked shocked. 'What do you know of my activities on the border?'

Tossing her arms back in frustration, Ha looked totally exasperated with him. 'When you sell dynamite, people hear about it. Of course I know why you and your brother keep taking off for the mountains. And the authorities know about it as well. It was inevitable that one day you'd be caught.'

Ha's words hit with a sobering blow. She was probably right although Dung had not wanted to admit it before. He should have known that one day they'd be caught, and to dismiss her concerns was foolish, especially when the smell of a prison cell was still fresh in his nostrils. Dung breathed in a sigh and while using the long fingernail on his little finger to pick at the soil wedged between his other finger nails he tried to plan out the best way for them to get to Tang's without being observed. He was certain that once he could locate Hien everything would be all right. Hien would probably suggest they go into hiding while Tang made discreet inquiries as to what was going on.

Dung glanced toward Ha. Since her breathing was steady and she looked as though she had recovered from their run, he scrambled up the bank and peered around. He could see a distant farmer with a young boy riding on his water buffalo, but other than that there was no one around. Sliding his way down the bank towards Ha, he reached over and hesitantly touched her hand. 'I'm really sorry to have dragged you into this, but if what you say is right we shouldn't hang around here for too much longer. It's a long way to Tien Yen, even if we risk taking the bus.' Dung scrambled back onto his feet and offered Ha his free hand. 'We need to be making tracks.'

Ha took Dung's hand and pulled herself up. 'I chose to be involved. I wouldn't have it any other way. I'm okay.' Her face brightened. 'We can set off again. I'm not afraid of anything so long as I'm with you.'

As the jeep bounced over the rough track towards Tien Yen, Khiem sat on the front passenger seat hanging on to the partially opened window. He was irritated by the slowness of their pace. They had already collided with an oxcart when it veered to get out of their way and spilled the contents of its load in front of them. Now the road seemed to be packed with more idiots, who, ambling along at their mid-morning pace, held no regard for his need to hurry. As they approached a further obstacle Khiem yelled across to the driver, 'Put the siren on and get these morons moved out the way.' When the siren blared into action the road magically cleared. 'Keep it on.'

'Sir.'

'Keep the siren on until we get closer to Tien Yen. I've already lost the prisoner because of one man's incompetence. Don't let me lose him again.'

The siren remained on for a further half-hour until they reached the outskirts of the village, when Khiem ordered it to be turned off. He didn't expect to track down the suspects so easily, but checking out Tran Thu Tang's house was the only lead they had. Khiem never liked to hear of any wrong-doer escaping justice, but catching this particular man Cuong, the brother-in-law of Major Thanh, would bring him more than usual satisfaction. If he could find some evidence or somehow make it appear that Major Thanh was involved with these men so much the better. Khiem had absolutely no doubts in his mind that at some point in the near future the score between them would be settled.

Before going to Tang's house, Khiem made a detour across the estuary to pick up Mr Vien from the local People's Committee. He wanted local knowledge and to put the word out among trusted locals that a watch was to be kept on Tran Thu Tang's bicycle shop. He also wanted to use the presence of the cadre to further intimidate Tang. They wouldn't have to say anything, but Tang would know that if he didn't co-operate with them fully, he could lose not only his reputation, but also his bicycle shop. With his livelihood removed he could expect to live no better than a beggar.

When they arrived at Tang's bicycle shop, Khiem noticed that the wire-grated security door was open by only a couple of feet. He peered into the dark enclosure to see a young man sitting cross-legged on the floor with a bike resting on his knees. Littered around him was an assortment of tools and bicycle parts. At the sound of their footsteps the man lifted his head and stared at them wide eyed.

'Tran Thu Tang?' asked Khiem.

Tang disengaged himself from the bicycle and stood up quickly. 'Yes.'

'You mind if my men take a look around while Mr Vien and I have a little word together with you? I believe you can be of help to us.' Khiem posed his order as a request, knowing full well that Tang would never dare to refuse him. In fact, even before he finished speaking, his men had anticipated his wishes and pushed the grating back and rushed through the shop into the interior of the house.

Tang inclined his head deferentially, then pulled out three stools. 'Please, sit down, brothers.'

'We thought you might be able to help us. We're looking for some friends of yours and have every reason to believe they came here.' Tang looked uneasy. Recognising the look of a man who knew something but didn't want to say, Khiem prepared himself for a lie.

'I haven't seen anyone all morning. Who is it you're looking for?'

Khiem smiled. The man was clearly scared of him, yet he wasn't so feeble that he didn't know how to couch his answer sensibly.

'We are looking for your brother-in-law Nguyen Cao Cuong and two friends of his, maybe even a woman. I believe you know the brothers Tran Van Hien and Tran Van Dung.'

'I haven't seen my brother-in-law in over a year, not since he was recalled for military service. As for Tran Van Hien, I spend so much time working I have little time to keep up with old friends.'

'Tran Van Hien is your friend then?'

'We were in the military together, I don't deny it.'

'What about his younger brother Dung. We believe he might be travelling separately with a young girl. Have you seen them?'

Tang shook his head. 'I told you I haven't seen anyone.'

As Tang was speaking, one of Khiem's officers came into the room. 'There's no one here. Do you want me to take a look around the village and ask questions, prod a few memories?'

Khiem nodded toward the officer before turning back to Tang. 'These men have acted against the Socialist Republic of Vietnam, maybe even in collusion with a foreign power. Anyone who assists them will be

brought to trial. You know if you help us apprehend these men it will be
to your advantage. The People's Committee of your district will honour
you as a hero. On the other hand, if you hold back on any information. . . .' Khiem raised his brows and stopped speaking while weighing
up the full impact of his words on the man sitting opposite him.

Dung knew well enough not to approach Tang's house directly. Grabbing
hold of Ha's wrist he pulled her from the bus two stops outside of the
town. 'This is as far as you go.' The smooth lines on Ha's youthful face
creased into a frown. 'I'm not leaving you permanently,' he assured. 'I
just want you to wait here while I check the town out. Sit down with the
basket.'

'Just for a few minutes. If you're gone a long time, I'm coming to look
for you.'

Dung laughed. He knew she wasn't kidding. If he was gone too long
that's exactly what she would do. 'Just twenty minutes or so, I promise
you. Sit over by the tree so it looks like you're a farm girl taking a rest
before going into the town to make your purchases.'

Dung hurried along the path as fast as he could without attracting
attention. He was almost into the town when he spotted the public
security officers walking out of Tang's shop and the jeep parked a street
away. He froze. In spite of his arrest and everything Ha had said to him,
he still couldn't totally get it into his head that he might be a wanted
man. He quickly ducked into a garment shop and fingered bolts of
material as though he were interested in making a purchase. When the
shop owner hurried over to him thinking she might have a sale he
apologised and made a rapid retreat. It wasn't until he was certain he was
well out of sight of the public security officials that he broke into a run.

By the time he neared the tree where he'd left Ha he was sweating.
Seeing him she jumped up and ran toward him. 'What's wrong?'

Dung grabbed her arm and pulled her back behind the trees. 'We can't
stay here. There are security police everywhere. They really are after us.'

'I told you. What are we going to do? Minh said Cuong wanted to go
to Hong Kong. Do you think that's where they've gone?'

Dung was shaking. Up until now he hadn't realised how much he was
relying on being able to find Hien. Now they were truly on their own.
He was the one in charge and it was for him to protect Ha. If it was him
they were after, then it probably wasn't even safe for her to go home any

more. He was trying to think quickly. At Tien Yen they were already a good part of the way toward the Chinese border. Perhaps that was where Hien had gone? He had felt sure they hadn't arrested him, but maybe they had. Maybe they just arrested him at Tang's shop which was why they were hanging round there.

Dung put his arm around Ha. He felt her stiffen. Maybe she felt shame for having run off with him. But she was his responsibility now and he wouldn't abuse her trust. He would always treat her honourably. He looked at her full in the face. 'I love you, you know that. I've just never said it before.'

Ha looked pained. 'I know that. Maybe women know these things before men do.'

'Rubbish. I've known it for years, I just never said so before.' He looked at her seriously. 'You want to be my wife and come with me to Hong Kong?'

He'd half expected her to laugh at the outrageousness of his proposal, but instead the pained look intensified on her face. Tears sprang into her eyes and for one dreadful moment Dung thought she was going to refuse him. Then her face softened and her mouth spread slowly into a shy smile. Gripping his hand she nodded and gave a barely audible, 'Yes'.

Dung pulled her into his arms. 'That was a yes, wasn't it?'

Ha looked up, the tears glistening in her eyes. She nodded again, but more assertively this time. 'Yes, yes. I'll be your wife.' Dung felt a rush of love and pride. Let the public security hunt him. He had beside him the girl he loved, the girl he'd always loved, and for the first time he understood that she loved him as much as he loved her. She was willing to give up her security, everything just to be with him. Whatever challenges lay ahead of them they would face together.

'How are we going to get to Hong Kong?'

Dung shrugged. 'We'll walk.'

Chapter 5: Before youth has left, old age has come

26th to 27th April 1980

Strive at the front and at the rear.
All compatriots together in one will.
Production and combat are one thrust,
Our struggle will end in triumph!
HO CHI MINH

THANH SQUARED HIS CAP as he surveyed himself in the mirror. He looked impressive with his green freshly ironed public security officer's uniform, creased trousers and jacket with the yellow stars and red lappet stitched neatly on the shoulders. It wasn't normally his intention to intimidate people, but today it was. Besides the warnings from his uncle, he had specifically been instructed by his superior officer to stay out of his brother-in-law's affairs. Having come to the decision to help Cuong escape from Vietnam, Thanh was determined to see it through. He had some ideas about where Cuong might go, but he wanted to first speak to Minh to glean some information about Cuong's friend Hien. Before he could speak to Minh, however, he had to get past the three public security officers watching her house. They would be lower in rank than he, hence his idea to use, or as the case might be, abuse his power.

Thanh approached Minh's cottage without any hesitation. He was about to knock on the door when a young officer lightly touched his shoulder before nudging his way between Thanh and the door. 'I'm sorry, Major Thanh, but I can't allow you to enter.'

Thanh immediately recognised the officer but acted as though he'd never met him before. 'What! I think you fail to comprehend the situation. You are telling me, a senior officer, that I cannot enter?'

'It's our instructions. No one is to enter, except Colonel Nhieu.'

'It was Colonel Nhieu who sent me here to question the suspect's wife.' Thanh pushed his way past the officer. 'Out of my way.'

The officer snatched at Thanh's sleeve. Thanh abruptly stopped and stared hard at him. 'You challenge my authority? What's your name?'

The officer was trembling. 'Sergeant Ngo Van Lat. I'm sorry sir. I didn't mean. . . .'

Thanh pushed the door open. 'Make sure I'm not disturbed.'

'Yes, sir.'

When Minh saw Thanh enter the cottage her face reddened and as he strode across the room towards her she seemed uncertain as to whether to greet him or respond to his authority. 'It's okay, younger sister.' He took her arm. 'Come, let's sit down. I'm not supposed to be here, but I need to speak to you urgently.' At that moment Cuong's mother entered the room with Minh's three young children. Seeing Thanh she nodded her head, smiled, then quickly departed from the room shooing the children ahead of her. Minh sat on the wooden bed while Thanh pulled up a stool opposite her. By her posture Thanh suspected she was still uncertain how to react to his visit. 'Minh, I'm not here officially. In fact, as I said, I'm not supposed to be here at all. That's why I had to wear my uniform. It was the only way I could gain entry.'

Minh eyed him cautiously. 'How do I know that. You are . . . all of you are full of tricks. Why should I trust you.'

'Because I'm your brother-in-law.'

Minh threw her head back defiantly. 'Yes, and what does that count for these days?'

'It counts for a lot. Cuong and I are not enemies. I was a soldier too, for more than ten years, remember? You think I can't understand how he might feel?'

Minh lowered her head. 'I don't know.'

'If you don't trust me, who can you trust? I'm probably the only person who can help Cuong.'

Minh raised her head again. 'Why would you risk your job to help us?'

'I like Cuong.' Thanh paused, 'And maybe I can pay Lan back for my neglect of her.'

Minh opened her eyes wide. Scrutinising Thanh's face for a further five seconds she seemed hesitant to speak her mind. 'So, if I do trust you. . . ?'

'Cuong must leave Vietnam. If I can find him, I have a little money. I know the snake-heads and can help him make the arrangements to escape.'

'I don't know where he is. Everything happened so fast. There was no time for us to plan anything.'

'What happened fast, Minh? Have you seen him since he deserted?'

Minh was visibly shaking. 'It was all my fault. I gave all our savings away to Mr Tam, the soothsayer. Cuong didn't understand. He was angry and thought Mr Tam tricked me.'

Thanh was puzzled. He couldn't fathom what would have prompted Minh to give Mr Tam all their money. 'I can see why he might have been angry. Why did you do that?'

'When the public security officers came here they didn't tell me anything. They were threatening.' Minh hesitated. 'Not by what they did, but how they acted.' Thanh smiled at Minh's choice of words. He understood exactly what she meant. 'It wasn't that they hit me or anything, but it was what they didn't say that was really frightening. I thought Cuong was dead.' Thanh nodded. 'Mr Tam didn't want to talk to me. He said there was nothing he could do to help me and that I should leave quickly. That panicked me even more. I know what I did was outrageous. If I'd stopped to think about it then maybe I wouldn't have been so rash, but I thought Cuong was in the spirit world, trapped between ... trapped somewhere. I left the gold pieces with the old women to pay Mr Tam to release him.'

Thanh raised his brows. 'But you didn't tell all this to Cuong? He only understood that the soothsayer had tricked you out of your money?'

'He was too angry to listen. He just ran off.'

'Where did you see Cuong? Did he come here ... send someone to fetch you?'

'He went to his friend Hien's house. They sent Dung, Hien's younger brother to fetch me. If I hadn't gone to the soothsayer we could have escaped to Hong Kong.'

'Maybe you still can, sister.' Thanh leaned toward her. Experience warned him that the timing of what he wanted to say next was too fast, but since he didn't have the luxury of time he decided he had to risk upsetting her. 'Why did Mr Hien keep explosives in his house?'

Minh shrank away from him. 'I thought I could trust you. What's this about? I know nothing about explosives. Are you tricking me?'

'Listen to me Minh. I'm not tricking you. I'm in deadly earnest. They found explosives in Hien's shack. Do you think the public security officers would still be waiting around your house if this were a simple case of desertion?'

'But, I thought ... maybe Cuong hurt Mr Tam. Maybe he hurt him seriously.'

'Cuong didn't physically hurt Mr Tam, not seriously anyway. A bloody jaw, that's all.' He could have added that Mr Tam was in serious trouble because of Cuong's visit, but it would have done nothing to alleviate Minh's distress.

'I don't know about explosives. Hien is a long time friend of Cuong. He's a good man.'

'They think he's some kind of terrorist.'

Minh froze. 'And Cuong too. Do they think Cuong's a terrorist?'

'It's important I find him first, Minh. Where is he likely to be?'

Minh stood up and paced around wringing her hands. After a few moments she came back to Thanh. 'My brother Tang is a friend of Hien as well as Cuong. Have you spoken with him? Could they have gone there?'

'I wanted to speak to you first, sister.'

Lan scrambled off the back of the Honda as Thanh prepared to wheel it into Tang's shop. Upon seeing them Tang's face turned crimson. He let go of the bicycle he was holding and it went crashing to the floor. He breathed in rather too quickly which sent him into a fit of coughing. 'Why have you come?' spluttered Tang.

Lan rushed past Thanh and grabbing Tang's arm asked him, 'Have you seen Cuong?'

Tang's whole body jerked, his eyes darting from Thanh's face to the door as though he expected someone else to enter. 'No. Why would he come here?'

'Let's go inside and sit down. It's foolish to talk in the open,' said Thanh. He deliberated the words calmly hoping to level off some of the panic his appearance had inadvertently created. 'I haven't come here to cause trouble for you.' Tang still looked uneasy but obediently led them inside. Lifting the bike out of the way, he then dragged out some stools from beside a cupboard. He waited until they were seated before sitting down himself. 'You know Cuong's in trouble?' Tang didn't respond. 'If he doesn't get out of Vietnam it could be very serious for him. Lan and I would like to speak to him. It may be that I can help.'

'We can trust Thanh. He's family before he's a public security officer,' said Lan. Despite Lan's assurance it was clear that Tang still didn't trust Thanh. 'Please, brother,' coaxed Lan. 'Tell us what you know about Cuong's whereabouts.'

Tang wiped away the sweat gleaming from his brow and turned to face Thanh. 'Your colleagues were here earlier. How do I know that they haven't sent you?'

'Believe me, they haven't.'

'Thanh's telling the truth,' pleaded Lan. 'He wants to help Cuong.'

'Was Cuong here?' asked Thanh.

Tang leaned forward. 'They were here. But I couldn't help them. I let them sleep the night but then I sent them away.' Turning to his sister, 'I'm sorry Lan. I wanted to help more, but. . . .'

'I understand. No one blames you for their trouble.'

'Where did they go?' asked Thanh

'Truly, I don't know. I think they weren't sure themselves what to do. Besides, the less I know the better for them.'

'You did right to advise them not to stay. Where do you think they might have gone?' said Thanh. Tang shook his head. 'What about relatives? His friend Hien, what relatives does he have?'

Tang pursed his lips. 'They may have gone to Haiphong. Hien's mother and married sister live there,' said Tang.

'Haiphong's a big city. Do you have any idea where in Haiphong?' Thanh tried to keep the urgency out of his voice. He spoke slowly and quietly. He didn't want Tang to feel he was being interrogated, but he was aware that time might not be on their side. If they had been seen entering Tang's shop their conversation could soon be interrupted.

'Hien's mother is Chinese. They were all supposed to be living in a confining zone, but you know how it is. They preferred to live illegally. I heard she lives somewhere in one of the back alleys off Chinese Street.'

Thanh nodded his head. He knew of the street where many of the Chinese lived. 'Hien's mother . . . what's her name, or the sister's name. Do you know?'

'His mother's name is Duong Kim Dao.'

Thanh stood up and was about to leave when a further question occurred to him. He hesitated. 'What do you know about Cuong's friend Hien? What kind of person is he?'

Tang's eyes lit up in puzzlement. 'Hien! I've known Hien for years. He's not a trouble maker if that's what you're thinking. He just tries to make a living like everyone else. You don't have to worry about Hien. He might not like the government, but then what's new? He's not a traitor.'

Thanh pressed Tang's hand. 'Thanks, brother.' Lan jumped up from her seat. 'If anyone asks you, I simply brought your sister over for a visit as I sometimes do. They can make what they want of the coincidence. The rest of our conversation you must forget.' Thanh turned and wheeled his bike out of the shop. Before getting astride he glanced round to see if he could pick up the signs of their being watched. An old woman, with a collection of young children round her, was sitting across the street selling rice cakes. Further down the road a group of young men were hanging round a lemonade stand and laughing. They looked harmless enough, but Thanh couldn't be sure.

As they made their way south down the coast road Lan put her arms tightly round Thanh. It had been a long time since she had held him like that. In recent months when they rode on the bike together she would sit proud, putting her hand on the metal grid of the seat to keep her balance and remain separated from him. Thanh felt exhilarated. Going against the system gave him back his sense of freedom. Freedom from his disillusionment, from his uncle's good advice and careful nurturing of his career.

It wasn't that it had escaped him that Cuong's desertion from the army was a crime. By rights he should be working with his comrades to track him down and bring him to justice. But Thanh understood Cuong's desertion. There were times when he would have liked to have deserted from the army himself. It was as though Cuong's desertion was now his own. Looking back he wondered why he hadn't deserted from the military himself. There were opportunities when he could have. . . . At the main road Thanh turned the bike south. Yes, there had been opportunities. . . .

It had been more than three years since Thanh first joined the Front. He was still only eighteen, yet he felt as though he'd aged a decade in the past few years. Unable to sleep he lay in his hammock and let the night-time hum of the jungle crowd into his thoughts. It seemed that with each progressive month the jungle and darkness closed in on him more and more. The branches above his head knitted together in an exotic canopy, blocked out the sky. Darkness was everywhere — above and below. The fungoid rotting odour rising from the undergrowth acted as a constant reminder that everything had an end. He longed for it to come quickly, even if the end meant his own death. But then he longed for home — to hear the sweetness of his mother's voice, just once before he died. He knew of the thousands of patriotic certificates delivered to mothers around the countryside. The weeping mother would be told how brave her son was, how valiantly he had fought — his deep sacrifice for the motherland. Many of the lost sons were young boys who, like himself, were too young to have known the ecstasy of a woman's body. It seemed a cruel injustice that they were forced to be old men before they knew manhood.

For the third night in a row his mother had come to him in his dreams.
As noiselessly as a ghost, she had stooped over his hammock, urging him to
come home. Woken by he wasn't sure what, Thanh lay brooding in the stillness
unable to shake off her words. There seemed to be an urgency to her pleas.
The gift of sleep having deserted him, Thanh composed a letter in his head.
Even though he would never send it he would write his thoughts down in his
journal when daylight came.

My Dearest Mother,
*   You are like our motherland who suffers the pains of birth and*
separation so that her children might know liberty and independence.
I know you wish more than anything for my safe return. I try to carry
your love with me like a shield, protecting me from the bullets and the
endless rain. I meet thousands of mothers on my journey and when
their searching eyes meet mine, maybe in hopes of finding their own
son, I look into their faces and think of you.
*   If only this war were like the northern winter giving way to spring.*
But we are locked in an endless tribulation of losing land and
reclaiming it. Sometimes I fear there will never be an end. Our dreams
of living a good life are illusions. There are no better days for us to look
forward to. I will die here. Twenty years, or more — if that is what it
takes — is a long time to expect to survive. But, so long as our country
remains divided I shall continue fighting in the struggle for us to become
a single nation. I am resigned to death, but the thought of never seeing
you again, or my father bending over his rice field, my sister embroider-
ing pictures and my young brothers riding on the back of the water
buffalo — this is too painful for me to contemplate. If only there were
someone I could give this letter to. . . .

'Thanh, are you awake?' Thanh sat up. It was Tuan. 'Anh is sick. He has
malaria again. You're to replace him and come with us on scout patrol.' Thanh
raised himself from his hammock. He would write in his journal later.
Packing up his few possessions in the dim light, he prepared to follow his
companions out of their temporary camp.
    As he nudged his way silently through the forest, Thanh savoured the
beauty of the early morning. The moon, glistening and reflecting from the
silvered cobwebs, gave the morning a magical, almost ethereal quality. Thanh
breathed in the moist air. He was alive. So long as he remained alive there
was hope of seeing his family, of working the land again with his father. He
wondered, was it so wrong to wish to go home — to wipe the war from his

memory and bring normality to his existence? He was old enough now to marry a young village girl, raise children and look after his aging parents.

They wound their way through the dense foliage to the mountain's summit. The heat of the coming day was already beginning to make itself felt and after the cold wintry nights in the mountains it was a relief to know spring was coming. The climb was strenuous, so after rolling up his shirt sleeves and trouser bottoms, Thanh strode forth with determination.

'Did you know that the American troops are given ice-cream?' announced Loc.

Thanh laughed. 'I don't believe it.'

'It's true. They even have water flown into their bases so they can have showers.'

Thanh took note of his own sweaty appearance. He washed whenever he could. He'd quickly washed himself in the stream that morning, but often as not there was no stream, only a muddy water hole suitable for the buffalo.

'They can never win,' interjected Tuan. 'Even with their superior weaponry we will win in the end.' As Tuan spoke his eyes blazed. He'd been a former school teacher and member of the Viet Minh for many years so was well respected in the unit for his intelligence and quick wit. Thanh and Loc looked at him with an inspired reverence. They could feel the truth of his words bearing into their skulls. 'We are fighting for the independence of our country. We will make any sacrifice for freedom. Look how the motherland protects her children with her dense jungle coat. How can the Americans win? These young men don't know why they're here. Ice cream, hot showers — it's tragic many of them will die without ever understanding the absurdity of their sacrifice.'

They had covered less than three kilometres when the roar of the low-flying planes suddenly shattered the peace of the early morning sky. Thanh understood the danger even before he could visually register what was happening. Following the flight of the planes he looked back down the mountain to where they had just climbed up from. As the first plane sent out a wave of fire engulfing his division camped far below, the three scouts stood paralyzed. Shock rooted them into the ground, while their compatriots far below, silhouetted against the surge of yellow light, ran disorientated into the wall of bullets sent out by the second plane. Shreds of scorched flesh flew in all directions as the bullets rained into them.

After the initial dizziness of shock lifted, Thanh and his two companions tore down the mountainside. Oblivious to the possibility of further assault from the enemy, they crashed headlong through the undergrowth. The noise of their descent sent birds flying and wild animals running for cover. Barbed cacti tore their clothes, ripping through to their flesh, as the vines tripped them and bruised their skin.

Thanh was first to arrive at the division base. He stared aghast, unable to take in the scene before him. Littered bodies, contorted by the agony of their death, blended into the charred soil and blackened, desecrated landscape. The charcoal skeletal trees rising starkly from the ground were barely distinguishable from the mass of human bones. Reeling in shock at his own narrow escape, Thanh felt an even greater horror grip his soul. The heat of dying embers burned his cheeks. Rage tore at his heart. He lifted his gun upward preparing to fire into the empty sky. 'Curse you.'

'Thanh, no.' Tuan pushed his gun to the ground. 'It'll bring them back. When the heat dissipates we'll bury our dead. We're the only ones to do it.'

As Thanh stood at the edge of the carnage, he felt as if he were unravelling. Tears streamed openly down his face. He wanted to scream out his rage, strike out at someone, or something. Where was there any justice, any higher power to prevent the world cascading into the chasm from which they could never climb out? The sight of Anh — a lone survivor — staggering from out of the burning undergrowth brought his reason back to reality. Thanh dashed across the glowing undergrowth, unconcerned about the scorching charcoal biting into his sandalled feet. Wrapping Anh in his jute cape to stifle the flames, he attempted to guide him away from the heat. Tuan and Loc were beside him. They guided Anh over to the stream and gently lowered him into to the cooling water. As the water hissed around the scorched wounds the repugnant odour of scalded flesh rose into the air. Anh's whole body convulsed and twisted, violently rising out of the stream as though possessed by demons. Tuan gently pushed him back under. 'Sorry, brother. It's the only way to stop you cooking further.' Anh's resistance left him and he lay exhausted while the water slowly calmed the heat from his burning flesh.

Thanh knelt down in the water. 'Anh, I'm here. Forgive me taking your place.' Anh's eyes seemed to roll in his head, then focusing on some distant point he suddenly laughed, not his usual laugh, but a laugh that belonged to something not quite human. Thanh shrank back. Then as strangely as the laughter started, it changed. In a final act of defiance against his agonised death throes Anh gripped Thanh's hand and smiled. His eyes held Thanh's in a moment of recognition, then his body slumped into a relaxed heap. Thanh sat silently beside him. Unable to pull himself away, his thoughts froze into stunned oblivion.

After burying their dead, Thanh and his two companions bathed their hands and feet in the stream while contemplating what they should do next.

Everyone was thinking the same thing, but it was Loc who eventually put their thoughts into words. 'We could desert,' said Loc. 'Who's to say we didn't die with our unit in the assault?'

Thanh was certainly sick of war. The temptation to go back to his village and visit his family tugged at him. He wouldn't need to write letters in his journal, letters he never posted, he could just look into his mother's old woman eyes and she would know what was in his heart without there being any written or spoken words. Desertion was tempting.

Tuan sighed. 'If you two want to make your own way, I'll never tell. I'll say I was the only survivor. As the oldest of our group it's my duty to report the names of our dead comrades and the location we buried them. If I had died I'd want to be sure my family knew where I was buried.'

Thanh recalled the words of a poem his uncle Chau had recited to him a long time ago. He spoke the words softly, as much to himself as to his two companions.

'Pity them, the souls of those lost thousands
They must set forth for unknown shores
They are the ones for whom no incense burns
Desolate they wander, night after night.'

Tuan and Loc looked across at him, clearly moved by the words Thanh recited. 'They're the words from "Call to the Wandering Souls",' said Thanh quickly, trying to get a grip on his own shattered emotions. 'Written by Nguyen Du.' The muscles on Tuan's face tightened. He looked down at his hands, turning them upward as though it was suddenly important he contemplate the rough scorched calluses on his palms. 'Until there's peace for everyone,' continued Thanh, 'there's peace for no-one. I'm with you. We fight till the end.'

Loc shrugged his shoulders. 'We're brothers. One stays, we all stay.'

Tuan nodded his head to acknowledge their solidarity. 'Since your own three-man cell was wiped out, Thanh, I'll put in a special request for you to join us when we reunite with our main force unit. For now, at least, you're part of our cell.' Thanh tried to express his thanks with a smile, but instead of being able to relax his mouth, he felt his jaw contort into an uncontrollable quiver while the tears built up behind his eyes.

Tuan stood up and kicked at the charred soil. 'God, I hate this war. What does America want our country for anyway? Their own country is big enough. All we want is independence. How can they see that as a threat? Surely if the whole country had risen up in support of Uncle Ho in the promised elections of '56, what objections could the Americans have? Isn't that democracy? And if we do choose communism above capitalism, why shouldn't we?'

Thanh swung his bike over to the left hand fork leading toward Haiphong. Even after all the years of fighting, followed by the years of uneasy peace, Tuan's words had stayed with him. In many ways they reflected his own thinking. The American war should never have taken place, but thousands of deaths later what was there to be done about it? It was his country's fate to defend herself against invaders. And now the economic embargo was devastating Vietnam's economic revival. He wondered if things would have been different if the new revolutionary government hadn't had to face such crippling problems. The devastation of the land after chemical spraying and the continued threats at their western and northern borders, all pushed them toward imminent failure. Would the internal suspicion, which aroused such fear and animosity among the people, have existed if the new government could have established itself without these crises to contend with?

Now Cuong was the enemy of the motherland. Maybe even he was himself? Thanh opened the bike up to full throttle. Lan gripped his waist tighter. As an official of the state and decorated war hero, he would almost certainly be considered by his colleagues to be a traitor if they discovered he was seeking to aid an enemy of the people. But was he really a traitor? Was Cuong? Wasn't it life that betrayed them, the Vietnamese people?

'Don't drive so fast Thanh. The road's full of potholes. I don't want us to tumble off the bike.'

Lan's voice broke momentarily into his thoughts. Hearing her concern Thanh eased back. 'We need to get to Haiphong before nightfall. It might not be so easy locating Hien's mother.'

As Lan fell back into silence, Thanh slipped back into his own thoughts. He felt as scarred by Anh's death as though the flames had devoured his own skin. . . .

After joining up with the new unit Thanh felt as though he was a seasoned soldier. Now nothing could touch him. In cheating death, his youth had slipped so far away that life no longer held any meaning. He took idiotic risks which were interpreted as heroic. His selfless deeds and willingness to put his life at risk to save others caught the attention of the unit's political commissar. Although Thanh was young, the political commissar recommended he be

transferred out of the unit and undergo special training for one of the Sapper (Special Forces) units. There were some initial objections thrown up in view of Thanh's age and past mistakes as a young revolutionary in My Tho. But since General Chau, Thanh's blood relation, was willing to vouch for his integrity, Thanh's case was viewed favourably. It was agreed that despite the traits of individuality Thanh displayed in his teenage years, he had learned his lessons thoroughly and was a true revolutionary. With the blessings of the party he could be given the opportunity of proving himself in the Sapper unit.

It was while Thanh was in training in the North that his uncle paid him a visit and gave him the news that was to further haunt his dreams.

'*Thanh, you know that I regard you as my own son. I felt it only right that I be the one to give you the tragic news of your parents' death.*' *Thanh felt his body go rigid as he waited for his uncle to continue speaking.* '*Their hamlet, thought to be a Viet Cong stronghold by the Americans, was bombed with napalm.*'

Thanh stopped breathing. '*When?*'

'*It was a month after your own unit was wiped out.*' *The words hit Thanh like a bullet. Recoiling in horror at his own narrow escape, Thanh closed his eyes. Anh's laugh resounded through his head.* '*I would have told you sooner but this information did not reach me until recently.*'

The news Uncle Chau spoke of was too awful to comprehend. Thanh felt his head reel. It wasn't true. It had to be a mistake. '*My sister Nga and little brothers?*' *he mumbled.*

'*Nga and your young brothers Vinh and Hau rest peacefully with your parents. They are with the souls of the innocent victims of this war. I have seen to it that they had a proper burial. An ancestral shrine has been erected in your hamlet. The crimes of our enemies have been written in stone.*'

'*Thank you for coming to Son Tay, Uncle.*' *Sickness was rising in his stomach. The saliva built up in his mouth.* '*Thank you for taking time to see me.*' *Thanh's vision was blurring.* '*Giving me this news yourself.*' *Making every effort to be dignified he stood up. His knees felt weak and he grabbed at the table edge to steady himself. He gave a half bow to his Uncle then quickly excused himself. After closing the door carefully behind him, Thanh dashed toward the bushes. The vomit rushed from his stomach and splashed haphazardly against the wall of the building. Sinking to the ground Thanh made no effort to stop the tears pouring from his eyes.* '*It was me that was supposed to die. Me. I could have deserted and been with them. Damn this wretched, miserable world.*'

Thanh envied Cuong. Cuong had deserted. In one crazy disobedient act he'd freed himself from their power and grabbed at the opportunity to see his family again. If it were possible to arrange for Cuong and his family to get safely to Hong Kong, he would do it. Uncle Chau would not approve, there was no point even discussing it with him. Thanh had some money saved and knew the procedures for smuggling someone out of the country, but first he had to locate Cuong. He would have preferred to drop Lan off in Hong Gai, after their visit with her brother Tang, but she had insisted he needed her. Regrettably Thanh knew she was right. If Thanh approached Cuong's hideout without invitation, Cuong would panic. Although half-crazed by his own disillusionment, Thanh knew he was still seen as part of the establishment. As far as they were concerned he was simply a public security officer and Party member: one of the feared elite. It was his own fault that he'd never developed a closer relationship with his in-laws. Retreating into his private thoughts, he'd become a loner even amongst his colleagues.

The traffic increased as they neared Vietnam's major port city of Haiphong. Everything had narrowed down to a tight bottleneck leading toward the hollowed steel car ferry. Bikes, cyclos, overloaded buses, battered cars and pedestrians all pushed their way forward. A war veteran, with one leg missing, blew into a mouth organ and strummed an electric guitar rigged up to a microphone, as he hobbled towards Lan with his hat outstretched. Thanh thought his music, high pitched and whiny was both haunting and beautiful. Seeing the man's pained expression as Lan dismounted the bike and turned her head away, Thanh reached into his pocket and pulled out some notes. 'Our country has failed you. You served well and deserve better than this, brother. Good luck to you.'

The man's eyes lit up and he gripped his hand. 'Thank you, comrade. Your words mean as much to me as your money.'

Lan glanced at them disdainfully. 'What a fool you are, Thanh. There are hundreds of beggars in Haiphong. You don't even know he fought on your side.'

'It doesn't matter which side he fought on. He was a soldier.'

'If you give money to them all, there will be nothing left to help our own family.'

Ignoring her comments, Thanh dismounted the bike and pushed it through the throng of pedestrians. Once on board, Thanh allowed his feelings of mental exhaustion to surface. Leaving Lan to sit on the bike he crouched down in the narrow space between the rails and the vehicles and letting his head slump between his legs he sank back into his memories. The individual versus the state. The issues were always the same. In keeping honour with his country, he'd failed his parents, his young brothers and sister Nga. By not deserting he'd robbed himself of the opportunity of going home, of maybe seeing them one last time. Perhaps even burning with them in the fire, as should have been his fate. Now there was no village home to go to. He was the only one left.

He looked across at Lan. Some young men had gathered round her and were trying to get her to flirt with them. She tossed her head and looked away, but Thanh could see from the expression on her face that she enjoyed the attention. If he could just give more freely of himself, explain what was wrong, then perhaps their relationship might improve.

Darkness was already falling as Thanh wheeled his motorbike off the ferry. Even though the hour was late the streets teemed with activity. Thanh drove the bike expertly, weaving in and out the traffic easily. However, as he turned from the bridge into Chinese Street a man with a cart-load of pigs rushed toward him. Thanh swerved. The man with the pigs also swerved but as one of the wheels of his cart hit a large cobble stone, the cart tipped, catapulting the terrified pigs across the road. Lan dug her finger nails into Thanh's chest and shuddered. 'Ugh! What disgusting creatures.' Thanh was shocked by her words. He could see nothing disgusting about the pigs, only their fear.

Thanh dismounted and walked over to the pig man to help collect up his cargo of pigs and secure them back in the cart. Thanh knew the error had been on the pigman's part, but slipped him some money for the inconvenience he had caused him. Thanh then explained that he was looking for a relative whom he believed was now living in Chinese Street. The pigman didn't know Hien's mother but was eager to make inquiries of other passersby he knew to be local. After a few wrong leads the pigman established that Mrs Dao lived along a gully which ran round the back of a group of houses and offered to lead Thanh over to it.

Lan hurried to Thanh's side and whispered to him. 'It's best I go in alone. Cuong won't panic if he sees me.'

'If he's there. We don't really know who is in that house.'

'Don't be so ridiculous. His sister and old mother are in the house.'

Thanh reluctantly let her go but paced the street anxiously while he waited for her to return. He wasn't comfortable with involving Lan but he couldn't see any other way. Keeping his feelings in a tight knot had kept almost everyone, including his family, at a distance. His cousin Nam was the only one who came close to knowing him. When Thanh had completed his Sapper training in Son Tay, he was sent south to join the same unit as Nam. They became part of the same three-man cell where their intimacy and reliance on one another was essential to their survival. Thanh enjoyed the challenges of being in one of the Sapper units since it left little room for grieving. When they carried out a mission they were swift and effective. They were on the front line. The first to rush in and plant their explosives before the enemy even realised they were under attack.

It was only much later when the buzz of being with the Sappers was becoming routine that Thanh was moved with Nam to more clandestine activities. Thanh's loyalty to the revolution was now considered beyond question, and his uncle thought it time to maximise his strengths. His language skills, his ability to work alone and make intelligent decisions were useful assets the generals would be foolish not to exploit. Thanh spent six months in the Soviet Union learning about Soviet weaponry while also grasping the basics of the Russian language. Uncle Chau being a purist was passionate about where his country was headed. He was determined to work from within to see that Vietnam did not lose its independence and fall under the all pervasive control of their more powerful allies. When the People's Armed Forces captured weapons which displayed evidence of the latest in American technology, Thanh found ways to sabotage and frustrate his Soviet allies' attempts to ship the weapons to the Soviet Union. It was a game he found both challenging and not without humour.

When Thanh saw Lan smiling and beckoning to him from across the road, he felt a rush of relief. Pushing his way through the pedestrian traffic he entered the dark alley behind Lan to where a toothless old woman was waiting at a side door. Inviting them to follow her she led them through a honey comb of passages to a staircase. The stairs were narrow and as they ascended the stairway and the candle which the old woman was carrying flickered menacingly off the peeling lime-washed walls, Lan gripped the back of Thanh's trouser legs. It was hard to imagine what the building had once been. The rank smell of decaying fish and the moss growing over the walls and stone steps suggested it might once have been a factory for storing fish. Now it was a residential building and as to how many people lived in it and who they were, Thanh didn't want to imagine. When they reached the highest landing the old woman led them into a room. It was several minutes before his eyes adjusted to the dim lighting, but he sensed the two figures of Cuong and Hien sitting on stools in the centre of the room. One of the figures stood up and walked over to him and as the cast of light from the candle fell across his face, Thanh recognised Cuong.

'Why have you come here, Thanh?'

'Let's sit down, brother. We need to talk. I hope you will believe me when I tell you that I place my loyalty to family above the considerations of our government.'

Cuong nodded. 'Please sit down. Perhaps Hien's mother will make us some tea while we talk. Have you eaten?'

'We don't need food. We can get something out in the street after we've had time to talk.'

Hien walked up to him and shook his hand. 'I won't hear of it. You've come a long way to help us. It's only right we offer you our best hospitality.'

When Thanh and Lan arrived at their home in Hong Gai the following morning, they found Thanh's cousin, Nam, waiting for them. He had driven down from Hanoi in a jeep and having let himself in through an upstairs shuttered window, he was busy making chicken noodle soup when they entered the kitchen.

'I was wondering when you two would get back. I thought you might be hungry so I went ahead and made something for us to eat. It seems to me you've been away all night.'

Thanh grinned at him. 'Well, brother, you were right. We are hungry.'

'And were you out all night?'

Thanh laughed. 'I was with my wife, honestly.'

Lan nodded a greeting toward Nam. 'You haven't come to question us have you, Nam? Let me see what you have put into the *pho.*' Lan put a chop stick into the soup and stirred it round. 'It looks good.' She cleared the table and set the food out so that they could sit down and eat.

For a while they sat round the table eating in a companionable silence. It was Nam who was the first to speak. 'I was concerned about you. This business with your brother-in-law isn't good. I heard that you went to see his wife, then later went to her brother's shop.' Thanh raised his brows. He was certain he hadn't been followed when leaving Tien Yen. He wondered how much more they knew. 'Where did you go after that?'

So Nam didn't know where they'd been. Perhaps that meant the authorities didn't know either. Thanh had intended visiting Minh later that day but decided it would be better to stay away for a while. 'Would you believe me if I said we went to Hanoi to see you?' said Thanh.

Nam laughed. 'No.' He stirred his chop sticks round his soup. 'I know this is a family matter. I understand your wanting to get involved, but the fact is this other fellow Tran Van Hien and his brother have been hoarding explosives at their place. That's serious business. Why would they be doing that?'

'The first thing that comes to my mind is that they use the dynamite for illegal fishing.'

Nam laughed. 'So that's it. You have been speaking to them.'

'Or it's simply that I have a better imagination than most of my compatriots.'

'That is almost certainly true. The fact remains, however, the dynamite they collected comes from the landmines set to repress the Chinese invasion. Your brother-in-law Cuong was with a unit in the border area. It seems likely that he was involved in helping them defuse the landmines.'

'That's speculation, Nam. Just as it's speculation that the old magician was having a sexual relationship with the deaf child.'

'I don't like the charges against the old man any more than you do, but it doesn't change things regarding your brother-in-law. I came here to warn you. Our relationship goes back too far for us to quarrel. If it was just me that was suspicious of your activities, it wouldn't matter. The fact is there are people who don't like you and who are also jealous of my father. Getting at you would be a way to get at him.' As Lan began to clear the empty dishes from the table, Nam stood up. 'Let's go outside and smoke.'

Thanh hadn't smoked in years. Nam knew that, but his suggestion to have a smoke was an excuse for them to speak privately. Quietly he stood up and followed Nam outside.

'They've been watching you for a while. Maybe they even have some suspicion as to what we do.'

'Was it Uncle Chau sent you?'

'My father's not worried about himself, you understand. His concern is for our work. Sometimes, it seems to me that you deliberately invite their criticism. In our position we can't afford to make any slips.'

Chapter 6: The way north

27th April to 7th July 1980

That day you went with me to the edge of the river:
'When will you be back?' — 'When you see the rice ripen.'
But now that the fields have been ploughed for the next season.
In a foreign land I shall remain a prisoner.

PRISON DIARY, HO CHI MINH

HIEN PEDALLED HIS WAY through the throng of people who daily crowded the narrow, bustling streets of Haiphong. He'd borrowed the bicycle from his brother-in-law Hau and was relieved to be taking charge of his life again. The last two days of cowering behind closed doors was beginning to grate on his nerves. Weaving his way between the cyclos and Honda bikes he breathed deeply and filled his nostrils with the spiced aromas of the street. Wafts of stagnant seaweed drifted in from the nearby docks. The smell was not altogether pleasant, but he savoured its salty rancidity with the appetite of a hungry man. It was better than the damp sulphuric stench of urine emanating from the alleyway leading to his sister's home. Hien found the dingy city rooms in which they lived to be more depressing than the rugged, leaky farm building in Cam Pha he and Dung called home.

Keeping the bike steady with one hand, Hien pulled out the scrap of paper from the package tied to his waist and studied it carefully. The information and money Thanh had given them last night came as a total surprise. Hien knew of Cuong's brother-in-law, the distant Public Security officer with the powerful uncle, but he'd never met him and never envisaged becoming acquainted with him under such strange circumstances. When Lan arrived at the house unexpectedly with the message that Thanh was waiting outside and wanted to speak to them, Hien was ready to flee into the back streets. Only at Cuong's insistence and after long reassurance that Thanh could be trusted did Hien agree to stay and listen to what he had to say. But it wasn't until later that evening, when Thanh accepted the offer to spend the night in Haiphong and they'd eaten their fill and drunk a few glasses of rice wine together that Hien really warmed to his dry humour and felt secure in his company. The rest of the evening sealed their friendship, and as they gathered round a low table talking and drinking, it seemed as though none could have claimed a care in the world.

Hien was relieved that locating the snake-head was easier than he'd dared hope. Although he felt relatively safe in the busy streets of Hai-phong for the moment, he would not have risked asking directions and identifying himself as a stranger, especially round the dock area where it was not unusual for people in trouble with the authorities to be searching out the snake-heads to help them escape illegally from the country.

After paying a young boy who was employed to watch bikes at a dock-side café, Hien clambered up the worn stone steps to the snake-head's office. It was just as Thanh described, a small yellow door leading off an iron platform to the left of the stairs. As he knocked and waited for a response, Hien pondered just what kind of man would exploit another man's misery for his own profit. When the door opened, however, it revealed a small grey-haired man in drab oversized trousers with small wizened, sun-baked features. At the sight of Hien his thin lips expanded into a toothless grin. Hien wasn't sure why he felt such a sense of relief, but as he thought about it, he realised the snake-head was not at all the sophisticated, leather shoed and dark sun-glassed type he'd expected to find. In fact he was surprisingly unimpressive, even feeble looking. Laughing back his fears Hien addressed the man with some confidence. 'Mr Tien sent me. He said I was to ask to speak to Mr Luyen.'

'Yes. I am Mr Luyen.'

'He said you could help me with a package I have to send to Hong Kong.' Hien hoped he'd said the message correctly. Mr Luyen, if that indeed was his name, took a quick look down onto the docks then beckoned him to come in quickly. Hien stepped inside. The room was cluttered with a mass of boxes and packages piled high against the wall. Seeing the boxes Hien felt a sudden wave of panic as the thought struck him that the trader might have taken his words literally.

'We send many packages to Hong Kong. Just what size parcel were you thinking of?'

Hien gritted his teeth. If they were to understand one another, there was nothing for it but to be direct. He trusted Thanh now and couldn't believe he'd have sent him into a trap or given him incorrect information. Thanh wasn't a careless man and the directions, so far, had been quite precise. 'There are two of us,' he began. The man didn't seemed surprised by his confession, so Hien continued. 'But I also have a younger brother.

If he doesn't contact me soon I want to leave money and travel plans for him to follow.'

'The cost for one person is two taels of gold or the equivalent in foreign currency. Dong are no good to me — the inflation causes too many problems. New hundred-US-dollar notes are okay.'

'Two taels per person! That's expensive. I have gold, but only enough for two people. It's important I leave an escape route for my brother.'

Mr Luyen nodded his head while listening. 'I'm only a contact man. Often I wonder why I take the risk to help people; I could go to prison for just talking to you. You must understand that I make very little money for my effort. There is a fixed rate on the boats going direct to Hong Kong, places on them are precious.' Mr Luyen shook his head. 'I'm sorry there's no room for negotiation.'

'But there must be room to negotiate. I'm offering you four taels of gold for three people. It's just one extra person that's all. How much space can he take up?'

'I told you, I do not negotiate. These places are precious. You're offering me little more than half the rate. I can't do it.'

Hien felt desperate. Only pride had prevented him from asking Thanh for more money to include Dung in the trip. He'd just assumed that with the quantity of gold Thanh gave them there would be room for negotiation. 'We have to leave here. All three of us. Where's your humanity, brother?'

The snake-head pulled a tattered note book from his pocket and scribbled out an address on a blank sheet of paper. 'Look, I have a friend who's a helmsman. He ran into some trouble recently and wants to get out of Vietnam. He doesn't have enough money for all the fuel and food supplies he needs, so he's looking for others to make the journey with him.' Mr Luyen turned the paper over and scribbled out a rough map. 'If you offer him two taels of gold for the two of you, I'm sure he'll agree to take you and your friend. That will still leave enough for your brother to take one of my boats to Hong Kong.'

Finding the helmsman was not as easy as finding Mr Luyen. Hien wandered down several streets before it dawned on him he was heading in the wrong direction. Reflecting on his interaction with the snake-head Hien realised that the information Mr Luyen had given him seemed unnecessarily vague and nothing like the clear instructions given to him by Thanh. There wasn't even a code with which he could use to approach the helmsman in safety. It was almost as though Mr Luyen had written down the first thing which came to mind just to get rid of him. Hien's initial instinct was to return to Mr Luyen's office and confront him, but he quickly realised the idea was foolhardy and dismissed it. If Mr Luyen were really determined to be rid of him he could already have informed the police of his whereabouts.

Hien sat down on the sea wall and lit a cigarette. If his situation were not so desperate he would have given up and gone back to his hiding place in defeat. He envisaged Cuong's face as he presented him with his failure. Cuong wouldn't berate him, but his silence and quiet acceptance of his fate would be more excruciating than Hien could bear. Cuong's situation was far more desperate than his own. Drawing on the last two long puffs of his cigarette, Hien stood up and crushed the stub out with the heel of his sandal. Failure simply wasn't an option. He'd try for a little longer, but if there was no Mr Kim Bang he would have to openly ask around the docks for names of other helmsmen, who might be interested in the trip to Hong Kong, even if those inquiries put him at risk.

It took another thirty minutes of winding his way through alleyways before Hien found himself in an area similar to that which Mr Luyen described. When he spotted the boat tugging against her anchorage and bouncing freely with the flow of the tide, he could barely control his excitement. The *Sea Dragon,* although horribly shabby and decidedly smaller than most of the other fishing vessels around her, existed.

Hien noticed a thin, middle aged man, perhaps ten fifteen years his senior, standing in the water and sorting through a fishing net which he'd draped over the front of his vessel. The description seemed to fit Kim Bang so without further hesitation Hien tossed his bike onto the beach and jumped down from the five foot sea wall. Wheeling his bike through the soft sand he forced himself to stride past the boat and continue on along the beach. Although there were other fishermen, they all seemed to be busy with their own boats and none paid him any particular attention. After satisfying himself that he was not being watched, Hien could no longer contain his impatience and sidled back toward the boatman.

'Excuse me, Mr Luyen sent me.' The helmsman didn't respond. On the assumption that the man might not have heard him Hien spoke again, introducing a little more force into his voice. 'Actually Mr Tien sent me as well as Mr Luyen. I'm looking for Mr Kim Bang.'

The boatman raised his head. 'That sounds like quite a mouthful. I know who you are, brother. Mr Luyen already told me you were looking for me. You took a long time.'

Hien shrugged his shoulders. 'I was lost. I'm sorry. It was hard finding you. The instructions. . . .'

'Never mind. Help me with these nets. It looks more natural if we talk while we're working. How is it I can help you?'

'My friend and I need to leave Vietnam. We're looking for a passage to Hong Kong, leaving as soon as possible.'

Kim Bang smiled. 'Do you have money?'

'I have gold. One tael.'

The smile on Kim Bang's face broadened to reveal his decayed broken teeth. His eyes glittered. 'It would take two taels to persuade me.'

Of course thought Hien, Mr Luyen had already spoken to Kim Bang. 'Very well, I'll pay two.'

'Then I think we can help each other. I have this fine boat you see, but no money for fuel and provisions.' Kim Bang waded out of the sea. 'And you're a friend of Mr Tien?'

'Um, I'm not sure if I know him.'

'Of course, I understand.' Kim Bang nodded his head. 'It doesn't matter.' He lifted up some netting. 'See these holes, you need to restring them while we make our plan.' Hien took the netting and began knotting together some of the holes. 'You said you're in a hurry to leave.' Hien nodded. 'Good, that's suits both of us. The longer a man plans, the more time he gives the authorities to uncover them. We leave tonight.'

Hien opened his eyes wide. 'Tonight!'

'Is that a problem?'

'No, no. It's great. My friend will be delighted. It's best we leave as soon as possible.'

'Then it's decided.'

Eager to leave Vietnam before the security police tracked them down, Cuong applauded Hien's decision to arrange cheaper passage on the smaller boat. It was only after their third day out at sea, as they tried to navigate their way beyond the land point of Mui Tra Co towards the peninsula of Pai Lung, that Cuong began to question his wisdom in agreeing to the hurried deal Hien negotiated with Kim Bang. For the past hour Cuong had watched alarm spread amongst the other passengers as it slowly became evident that Kim Bang was not the experienced helmsman they had all taken him to be. Since entering Chinese waters the swell of the sea had become stronger and the tide was forcing them closer and closer to the shore. Huge sandbanks regularly reshaped themselves below the surface and only the most canny of sailors, or those with local knowledge, could have anticipated them. It seemed that no sooner had they managed to avoid one sandbank than they were in danger of running into another. Further out to sea Cuong could see the water was clearer, but close to shore the rougher waves churned the sea into the consistency of a thick yellow soup. With visibility almost negligible it was impossible for them to see where the sandbanks were hidden.

'Can't we stay further out to sea?'

Kim Bang gave him a harried look. 'That's what I've been trying to do for the last four hours. The current here is simply too strong for the *Sea Dragon*.'

Cuong urgently scanned the faces of the passengers. There were fifteen people in all. Besides the helmsman's attractive young wife, whom Hien seemed unable to take his eyes off, and small daughter, there was another young family. As their father leaned over the boat searching out the sandbanks, his two boys clung anxiously to him. An aging couple, whom Cuong presumed to be relatives of Kim Bang's, sat with frozen faces as they stared fixedly toward the horizon: their thin bones which protruded through their clothes, appeared increasingly fragile as they braced themselves against each new rising swell of the sea. The remaining passengers, whom Cuong judged to be single men of military age, were of more interest to him. In a crisis it would be to them he would turn for assistance in forming a rescue plan.

The *Sea Dragon* was too small for such a load and was riding dangerously low in the water. When Hien first spoke with Kim Bang, the helmsman had said there were only going to be seven passengers in the boat, including himself and Hien. Cuong shook his head as he wondered where the other people could have materialised from at such short notice. In addition to having taken on water the boat was heavily laden with luggage. The whole venture seemed suddenly too absurd to be comprehensible, and he wondered how he'd managed to be so relaxed for the past three days.

Snatching hold of the cabin roof, Cuong pulled himself to his feet and yelled above the roar of the wind, 'You can all see the danger. If we don't dump our possessions and ride higher in the water none of us are going to make it to Hong Kong.' Kim Bang, looking close to exhaustion as he was frantically trying to keep a grip on the helm, shot Cuong a grateful glance.

'These bags contain everything we own,' shouted Kim Bang's old relative. 'If we throw them overboard, we'll have nothing.'

'And if we don't,' retorted Cuong, 'We'll be dead. Then what'll you have?'

Kim Bang's wife pulled her young daughter protectively into her arms. 'We have nothing here except rice and fuel. We must hang on to these till the last.' She turned to the old man who had spoken to Hien. 'Uncle Thai can we throw Aunt Mai's sewing machine overboard?' Uncle Thai looked aghast, then as though taking in the seriousness of their situation his expression changed and he glanced across at his wife. Her old sad face creased up in dismay, then with slow resignation she nodded her agreement. As the old man tried to free up the sewing machine from the bundle of bags Hien clambered over to help him. The machine splashed heavy in the water then quickly disappeared. Passively the other passengers untangled themselves from the mass of bodies cramped on the deck and began sifting through their own belongings. As the volume of bags bobbed away with the tide, the boat eased up higher in the water.

Someone sighed, 'It's going to be all right.'

The young man's optimism hit the boat like a curse. No sooner had he spoken than the vessel ran hard into a sandbank. With a definitive thud the boat lurched upward, forcing everyone to tumble backward, and then buried itself into the bank. Despite Kim Bang's effort to free her, the vessel held fast. In desperation several passengers tossed more of their possessions over the side, but despite the sacrifice, the boat only buried itself further into the sand.

With sweat pouring from the open pores in his brow, Kim Bang looked close to panic. 'I'm sorry, I'm sorry. I'll get us free, I promise.' Before any of the others could dissuade him he'd ripped off his shirt and dived into the sea.

'Bang, no.' Kim Bang's young wife leapt to her feet, letting her daughter tumble ungraciously to the floor, then leaning over the edge of the boat she peered into the water after him. Hien lifted the child to his lap as Cuong nudged his way over to the boat's rim and stared into the gloomy water. When Kim Bang resurfaced for air it was evident he was fatigued. Without further thought Cuong threw off his shirt and jumped into the water beside him. For an instant the sea's coldness gripped his muscles, but as he sank below its surface and struggled against the rudder, all he could think of was setting the boat free. The *Sea Dragon's* freedom and his freedom were now intertwined. If he could just release her maybe several of the them could swim together and tow her clear of the other sandbanks. It was something he should have thought to do sooner.

In spite of both Cuong's and Kim Bang's repeated efforts, the rudder held fast. Hien urged the passengers to shift their weight and create a rocking motion within the boat while Cuong and Kim Bang clung to her side. For a moment it seemed as though the boat was going to break loose. Its stern lurched upward and swung around, but as it came full round again, the rudder sank into the sand. Kim Bang dived down as the boat shifted violently to the left. Cuong immediately dived after him, but it was several seconds of staring through the clouded water before Cuong realised that the rudder had stuck fast again trapping Kim Bang's arm as it turned. Pushing desperately against the rudder Cuong tried to force it upward. In an instant Hien and several of the other young men joined him. They tried shouldering the boat in a concerted effort to shift it out of the sand, but it lurched violently embedding the rudder even more firmly in the sand. Cuong's lungs were bursting and his head reeled, but he reasoned Kim Bang must be needing air even more desperately than he and was reluctant to leave him. He must have been close to passing out when he realised Hien was beside him and forcing him to the surface. Cuong didn't have the strength to resist and when his face broke through the surface he clung to the boat and gulped in the air gratefully. As the pounding in his head eased he became aware that Hien was shouting at him. 'We're all taking it in turns down there, okay. No one's to be a hero. We stay down only as long as we can.' Before Cuong could express his thanks, Hien disappeared below the surface. Waiting a moment to clear the dizziness from his head, Cuong filled his lungs and dived after him.

Even through the murky waters Cuong could see Kim Bang wasn't going to make it. He was no longer working frantically with the other young men to release himself. His body was floating and his mouth gaped open and then closed with the current. Hien was shaking his head as he urged the others to resurface. Defeated, Cuong reluctantly rose with them. As he clambered over the side of the boat he saw Kim Bang's wife looking at them, searching everyone's eyes for some acknowledgment that her husband was going to be all right, that maybe there were still others down there who were right at that moment carrying him safely to the surface. Hien was the last to resurface. As he pulled himself up over the side of the boat Mrs Kim Bang reached toward him. Seeing her expression Hien turned his face away and pulling himself over the side rolled exhausted into the boat. 'We should have axed his arm off,' moaned Hien. 'I'm sorry. . . .'

As the night wore on bringing with it a cold northerly wind, the passengers drew closer to one another. Mrs Kim Bang wrapped her arms tightly around her daughter and wept silently. Only the odd stifled sob betrayed her distress. Hien nudged closer to Cuong and after sorting through his shirt pocket he produced a packet of damp cigarettes. After selecting the one which looked to be the driest, he tried lighting it up. 'Want to share a cigarette, brother?'

'You've little hope of getting that to light. Besides smoking is bad for your health. Didn't anyone ever tell you that?'

A grin spread over Hien's face. 'That has to be the voice of a hypocrite. And I suppose spending the night on a leaky, unseaworthy vessel wedged into the sand and likely to break up at any moment isn't bad for the health?' Against all odds Hien's lighter actually worked and the cigarette smoldered into life. After drawing heavily on it until the end glowed red, Hien passed it over to Cuong. 'Our last cigarette. It's what they give you before they stand you in front of the firing squad.' Cuong accepted the cigarette without further comment.

So this is how it would end, he thought. They were not the first of his people to drown in the sea, and end up as fish fodder after a failed attempt to escape from their homeland, nor would they be the last. Thousands had perished in the same way. It was too dark to venture back into the water and besides it was pointless; the rudder was held fast. If they tried swimming to shore there was the risk of being attacked by sharks. It seemed the sharks usually fed at night or early morning. The best they could hope for was that the boat would hold together long enough for the tide to turn and the increased water level would raise them up enough to let them break loose.

Time passed slowly and as the water level dropped the boat wedged further into its sandy grave. With each wave the boat creaked and groaned as it threatened to break up. The woman with the two boys held them close to her. Rocking them in her arms she appealed for Buddha's intervention. Cuong found her wailing distressing and, suspecting that the other passengers might feel the same, wanted to tell her to shut up, but he hadn't the heart. He stared into the darkness wondering how far they were from shore. If the boat could last till morning some of them could probably make it. They could tie themselves together and swim to shore in a human chain, the weakest linked between the strongest.

At around 4 AM, Cuong judged the tide to be on the turn and the sea at its shallowest. The waves continued to lash out at them with a vengeance which offered little hope of respite. Even the tiniest of the children must have known the end was coming. There was nothing anyone could do to prevent it. 'Who among us can swim?'

Three male voices rang out in the darkness. 'We can. We'll help those who can't.'

'Uncle Thai, you and I have lived a full life. We've no need of anyone's help.'

'Of course not. The children must be protected first, then the two young mothers.' Uncle Thai leaned toward his wife and grasped her hand. 'We'll just look after each other.' He put his thin arm around her frame and looking her in the face he said, 'Like we've always done, my dearest. Like we've always done.'

Their calm resignation was more than Cuong could bear. 'Don't we have any rope on board, for pity's sake?' Kim Bang's wife shook her head. Cuong felt a lump rise in his throat as he turned to address the old couple. 'Try to hang onto something. When the boat breaks up there will be plenty of driftwood.'

Less than fifteen minutes later the boat groaned and entered into its final shuddering dance with death. Little by little, pieces began to break away until there was no more pretending the body could hold together any longer. Cuong knew it was time for them to make their move. If they waited any longer they risked being battered to death by the larger pieces of the boat as she was torn apart. 'It's time to go, brothers.'

Grabbing hold of Kim Bang's daughter he leapt as far as he could from what remained of the boat and splashed feet first into the sea. The shock of cold water flooded over their heads as they sank below the surface. Blinded by the churned up water, Cuong felt the child dig her fingers into his ribs. Then she was struggling and trying to break free of him. He snatched her tighter. Without the free use of his arms he could feel the current dragging them down under the force of the waves. He was fighting his own panic as he pulled the child in front of him and clawed their way to the surface. When they broke through he gulped the air in greedily. The child's face looked terrified as the waves continued to smash against them and hurtle them up into the air before dragging them down. He'd hoped to somehow supervise the other passengers in their escape, but the waves were too strong and very quickly they were all separated, each fighting for his own survival. He was a strong swimmer, well used to swimming in the sea, but even for him the conditions presented too much of a challenge. He had no idea how Hien or the others fared. All he could do was look to his own and the child's survival.

Summoning up the last reserves of his energy Cuong pitted his strength against the flow of the tide. Through the darkness he could barely make out the hazy twinkle of a distant light and it was toward this he set his course. But it wasn't until his legs were scraping against sand that Cuong could really believe they'd made it. With the child still in his grasp he pulled up onto his knees and dragged himself out of the shallow water to the beach. Collapsing on the firm sand he lay exhausted until he felt able to sit up and examine the situation. With his faculties restored, he glanced anxiously at the child. Even in the faint moonlight he could detect the paleness of her face. Her eyes were open and although she was still breathing, the life seemed to have drained out of her. Cuong gently wiped her face with his hand, but her pained dulled gaze remained fixed as her eyes focused beyond him to some distant point in the sea. Kissing her small face, Cuong cradled her limp body into his own. 'We're alive, little one. We'll find your mama for you and everything will be all right.'

Lifting her frail body into his arms he hurried along the beach calling into the darkness. 'Hien, Hien. Answer me. Anyone. . . .' The rocks tore savagely at his feet, but Cuong paid them little attention. 'Please God, let them be alive.' Then, out of the gloom, he saw a small group of bedraggled survivors walking towards him. He cried out and raced across the beach to join them. 'Hien, are you there?'

A woman ran from out of the shadowy figures and snatching the child from out of Cuong's arms sank down on to the beach. 'My baby, my baby. . . .'

'We were looking for you.' Cuong, still in shock from Mrs Kim Bang's emotional reunion with her child, barely registered Hien's words. Tears ran down his cheek as he stood watching mother and child search out each other's faces. 'You must have arrived at the shore much further down than the rest of us. I thought. . . .' Hien flung his arms round Cuong. 'Thank God you're alive.'

Cuong embraced him, then drew back. 'How many of us survived?'

Hien pointed to the bedraggled group. 'We're it. We were hoping to find Tyan Yu's family with you, but there are no more survivors, I'm sure.' He turned toward the sea. 'It's my fault. If I'd followed Thanh's instructions we would have been safely on our way to Hong Kong. How can you forgive me?' He sank back down onto the sand. 'My God, what a disaster.'

Cuong felt his rage boiling up inside him. His anger wasn't toward Hien, nor toward anyone in particular. He didn't even blame the gods. His rage was directed toward all the injustices suffered by his people. Hien's words reflected his own feelings of despair. They had to find something to hang on to, otherwise what was left for them? 'Look around you, brother,' he yelled. 'Look at this mother weeping over her child. It was fate placed us on this boat. Fate in all her colours of cruelty and redemption. If we hadn't been here you think they would have survived? There's a reason for our being here.' Hien, visibly shaken by Cuong's harsh tone, glanced down at Kim Bang's wife and daughter. 'Don't fall apart on me, Hien. If we were separated, there could still be others.'

While Kim Bang's wife sat with the two children, Cuong, Hien and the other remaining survivor Long, scoured the beach. After an hour they were all ready to give up. Cuong realised that with the tide against them it would be at least another day before the returning tide would carry any bodies back to the shore. It was even doubtful they would ever retrieve all the bodies because some would have drifted out to sea to be eaten by fish. Cuong shivered. Suddenly conscious of the cold wind penetrating through his wet clothing he wrapped his arms around his body. 'We're too exposed on the beach. Let's seek shelter in the dunes.'

It was not long before the Chinese authorities heard of their arrival on the beach. Tuyet, Kim Bang's daughter, was the first to spot them. 'Soldiers! Soldiers are coming.' She seemed fearful. Hien quickly stood up and looked toward the horizon where the troop of green uniformed men came striding over the ridge toward them.

'They're not soldiers, it's the police,' shouted Long. 'What can we do? If we run, we've no money or food to look after ourselves.'

Hien looked across at Cuong wondering if they should make a dash for it. Cuong was clearly tired and just shrugged his shoulders resignedly. 'We're not seriously going to outrun them. Not with two kids.' He paused, 'Unless we try to make it on our own.'

Wide eyed, Kim Bang's wife, Huong, shot her head up toward Hien. Her face paled as if she anticipated his running off and leaving her. The look riveted him to the spot. 'You're right,' said Hien. 'With two kids we wouldn't make it.' Hien couldn't explain it, but right from the time they were on the boat together, he'd been aware of Huong. He'd known many attractive women, but there was something about her coal black eyes, her long silken hair, the graceful way she moved. Perhaps it was her inaccessibility. Now with her looking at him like that, he experienced guilt for the feelings her vulnerability aroused in him. He shrugged his shoulders, resigned to whatever else fate threw at them, and sat back down on the sand waiting for the police to approach.

The Chinese police captain who came to arrest them, was immediately sympathetic to their plight. Placing them under guard, he went back down to the beach. Along with curious villagers, who meandered down to inspect the wretched flotsam the sea had thrown up onto their shore-line, the captain and his men scoured the area looking for more survivors. With his knees huddled into his chest as a barrier against the cold and his own misery, Hien wished them success. He was not surprised, however, when after a further hour they gave up their search, and the police captain shepherded them the three miles to the police station.

In the warmth of a communal police cell Hien stripped out of his wet clothes, wrapped himself up in a dry blanket and gratefully drank down the bowl of hot soup given to him by the Police captain's wife. His earlier despondency at not being safely on his way to Hong Kong dissipated as the warmth of the soup left his body glowing. He was alive and he was out of Vietnam. It was pointless to harbour regrets, and besides, maybe Cuong was right, he was where he was supposed to be. Several of their compatriots were dead, Kim Bang included, but the helmsman's wife and daughter were alive. He glanced over at Huong who was coaxing Tuyet to drink down the warm soup. Huong looked up and catching his glance smiled shyly. Embarrassed by the feelings her smile aroused in him, Hien quickly turned his head away. It was only as he processed his thoughts that he regretted his impulsive action to turn away. He cringed. His behaviour was inexcusable and adolescent. How could he have failed to recognise that in her state of bewilderment and shock Huong was not smiling at him as a young village girl might smile at a young man, she was desperately seeking the comfort and support one might expect from a fellow human being who had just rescued her from the sea. They were in an alien land where their future was as uncertain as it had been in Vietnam. They were all scared. Hien pulled himself up to his feet and walked over to Huong. 'How are you?'

Huong let her hair fall across her face as she tried to discreetly wipe the tears from her eyes. 'We're fine.'

'Look, I'm sorry about just now.' Hien tugged at his fingers and, one by one cracked the joints until his hands felt more comfortable. He was ill at ease in talking to Huong. She was a handsome woman in every respect and it was hard for him not to be aware of it. 'Sometimes I behave like an awkward school boy. It's inexcusable, I know. But really, I'm here if you need me.' With her lips tightly closed together Huong forced her mouth into a smile.

'Don't criticise yourself. You owe me nothing. It is me who is beholden to you for saving my life.'

'We are all facing the same unknown future. I promise you that so long as our paths remain together I shall do everything I can to protect you and your daughter.'

They were awakened at six the following morning by a young police sergeant who brought in some small boy's clothes which he said were from the captain's wife and were to be given to the orphan child. A second guard entered the communal cell and produced a bucket of rice soup which he spooned out into small bowls. There seemed to be no shortage of soup and after finishing the first bowl, which Hien gulped down in gratitude fearing that it might be his last for a while, they were all allowed to receive a second and, even third, helping. Tyan Yu was the only one indifferent to the food. Hien tried to persuade him to eat, but he turned his face away and drawing his knees up under his chin stared vacantly into the distance.

Hien looked toward Huong hoping for assistance, but she only shrugged. 'I can't get him to respond to anything. I tried cuddling him last night, but when I touch him his little body just stiffens. He needs time. We can't force him to accept us. I suspect he'll eat when he gets hungry enough.'

Hien felt uncomfortable with the idea of not being able to do anything and reaching his hands toward Tyan Yu offered him the bowl again. 'Eat something, child. It'll help fill the emptiness.' A glimmer of acknowledgment showed in the boy's eyes before he sank his head to his knees.

'We've all tried,' said Cuong. 'Long sat up half the night stroking his hair. It's probably shock. Maybe we can persuade the captain to let him see a doctor.'

It was not long before the opportunity to speak with the authorities presented itself. As Hien was still pondering the question of what they should do for Tyan Yu, two policeman came in and informed them they were to meet with the police captain for individual interviews. Cuong was first to be called to the captain's office. As Hien sat on his seat in the narrow corridor and waited his turn beside Long, he glanced up at the two policemen guarding them. Their faces were expressionless and when the younger of the guards eventually looked down at Long, to signal that it was his turn to go into the interview room, his blank indifference seemed more threatening than the impassioned hatred Hien had observed on the faces of his enemy during the war years.

When it was his turn to be interrogated Hien braced himself for a difficult time. He was surprised therefore, by the non-interrogative approach of the police captain. The captain presented each question as though he were a concerned relative asking for details of a family disaster. He was particularly interested in the orphan child so Hien relaxed and took the opportunity to speak of his concerns for Tyan Yu. 'We were thinking that perhaps the child is sick and needs a doctor.'

'A prison cell is not a good place for a child in the best of circumstances. Let me think about it.' The captain pulled a sheet of paper from his desk file. 'Now, since you have come into our country illegally, it is important I pass on your names to the Red Cross. Your two compatriots have been helpful in supplying the names of the people on your boat, but there are gaps. It is important the information I pass on to them is as accurate as possible.'

After giving details and listing the names of those he knew on the boat Hien described the events which led to the *Sea Dragon* breaking up. When he finished speaking the police captain nodded his head knowingly. 'Yes, our sand banks claim many lives.'

It was only when the captain questioned him about the border area; how many units were stationed there and had he been in the army, that Hien began to feel his nervousness returning and broached his answers with more caution. He saw no reason not to admit to having served in the army during the American war, but denied having knowledge of the border area. It was a prohibited area, he claimed, that he knew nothing about. After a further twenty minutes of quizzing, the captain seemed satisfied Hien had no further information to give and arranged for him to be escorted back to the holding cell.

As Hien entered the cell he saw that Cuong and Long had both returned. Cuong was sitting beside the barred window and gazing seaward. Hien wandered over and squatted down beside him. 'We need to go back there, see what bodies have been washed up on the shore,' said Hien. Cuong nodded, but said nothing. Hien carried on speaking. 'I've been thinking. So far the Chinese have been reasonable. I'd say the interrogations have been fact finding rather than intimidating.' Cuong looked at him waiting for him to continue. 'It's because we're travelling with a woman and children. If we'd been three men travelling alone, I'm sure our treatment would have been different. They would think we were spies.'

'I'm sure you're right,' said Cuong. 'The captain's wife certainly pays a lot of attention to Tyan Yu.'

'Yes, exactly. The two-year-old Tyan Yu gives us respectability. We need to bury our dead. My thinking is that since Tyan Yu's parents were Chinese and amongst those who died, we might persuade the police captain to allow us to go back to the beach and search for bodies.'

'Good approach, Hien. And when we've seen to the dead, you and I could make a quick disappearance.'

Hien looked at Cuong aghast. 'No! That's not what I'm suggesting. What you said yesterday about fate putting us on that boat. I took it seriously. Our lives are now meshed with these people. We have to stay with them and see what happens.' He leaned toward Cuong. 'I wasn't thinking about escape . . . not yet anyway.'

Cuong laughed out loud. Glancing across the room, toward Huong who was sitting cross-legged and combing out her daughter's hair, he leaned toward Hien and whispered, 'I've seen the way you look at her.'

Hien turned crimson. 'It's nothing like that. I just think we should hang around a little longer.' With his cheeks still glowing, Hien stood up and pushed his way past Cuong. Hammering on the door he tried to attract the guard's attention. Several seconds passed before the guard ambled over and peered through the barred door slot. Hien pressed his mouth toward the opening. 'Can you obtain permission for me to speak to the captain of police again?'

The guard shrugged. 'I'll see if he's busy.' Hien hovered near the door for a full twenty minutes, waiting to see if his request would be granted. By the time the guard returned and ordered him to follow, Hien was beginning to regret his impulsive act. He had no idea how he might best present his request.

The police captain was sitting at his desk leafing through the accounts given to him by the illegals when Hien entered the room. 'Sit down, please.'

As the captain looked at him expectantly, Hien realised he needed to say something. Without further thought he sprang into a garbled speech about Tyan Yu's parents. 'You see, they're Chinese. All of us are anxious to try to help retrieve the bodies of our dead friends and relatives. We were thinking that perhaps you might release us for a few hours.'

The police captain smiled. 'Vietnamese bodies or Chinese bodies, they are all the same to me. I dispatched several of my men earlier this morning. I know the tides, so I've a pretty good idea where they might turn up.' He paused and shuffled the notes on his desk. 'Of course I can't release you, but your offer of help appeals to me. I'm interested in locating the body of this man Kim Bang, the helmsman. The body may still be trapped under the rudder of your boat so getting an approximate location of where you hit the sand bank would help us.'

Hien nodded. 'I think we could help you. And if it means we can bury all of our dead we will be glad to do whatever it requires.'

Later that afternoon the captain of police arranged for Hien, Cuong and the third man in their group Long, to be taken back to the beach where they joined the police in their search for the bodies. It was a gruesome search but in total they succeeded in retrieving seven bodies, including the body of Kim Bang. It was only as the light faded that the captain of police ended the search for the two remaining bodies.

Hien was reluctant to stop searching. 'There are two more bodies, an old couple. It's only right we find them and bury them along with the others.'

The captain of police looked toward him sympathetically. 'Seven bodies is more than I expected to find.'

'Then there could be more.'

'No. I know these waters. We've looked in all the places where they would come ashore. I have a responsibility to return you men to the police station.'

As Hien reluctantly moved to begin his climb back into the police van Cuong leaned toward him and gave him a pull up. 'You heard what Uncle Thai said when the boat was breaking up. I doubt they even tried to swim to shore. They would have just sunk in each others arms.'

The captain shook his head. 'Many people drown in these waters. It serves as a constant reminder to our community that nature is stronger than us. I've done the best I can. I will make arrangements for you to bury your dead in the morning. Our community is poor and wooden coffins are a luxury most people cannot afford for their own relatives, but we can provide you with thinly padded mattress quilts. You can stitch your dead into these.'

After the bodies had been carefully stitched into their cloth wrappings the men laid them out on the prison floor for the night's vigil. Although

there was an unpleasant odour emanating from them, when Tyan Yu
snuggled down beside the tiny bundle which contained the body of his
younger brother, no one had the heart to pull him away. It was the first
time since the tragedy that the child had slept soundly. While Long sat
watching over the sleeping Tyan Yu, his back rigid, his eyes red and
swollen with tears, Hien sat by the barred window listening to the crickets
and the hypnotic rhythm of the sea. It was a long night that he wished
would soon pass. It haunted him that he'd abandoned Uncle Thai and
his parched, bent old wife, Aunt Mai, to a watery grave. Those who
faithfully lived out their lives never harming another living being and
honouring the land, were always the ones to suffer.

When morning eventually arrived and they were ready to set off with the
carts a heavy mist hung low over the ground, hugging the gently sloping
contours in pockets of dense vapour. In contrast to the barrenness of the
landscape a few scattered thistle flowers pierced the horizon in a blaze of
purple. As the three wooden carts, pulled by oxen, trudged slowly
through the villages in the early morning hours, a small group of villagers
looked up from their work of restringing fishing nets, to watch the sad
procession. Two scrawny village dogs ran from a thatched cottage yap-
ping at their ankles, but the five small children standing in the doorway,
seeing the wrapped bodies, hung back shyly.

   Although the sea was close to a mile away the air savoured a sour tang
of seaweed and rotting fish. Hien drew his arms around his chest to protect
himself from its salty bitterness. He felt disoriented, lost. He could have
been in a coastal village in Vietnam. There was the same poverty to be
seen in the ragged clothes of the villagers, the same farm cottages with
their simple farm instruments and the same washing lines of salted fish
hung up to dry. But despite the likeness of the villages the oxcarts with
their bundled cargo were real and there was no willing them away.

   The sun made its appearance for a few brief seconds as Tyan Yu's
four-year-old elder brother was placed in the gritty, yellow soil next to
the bodies of his mother and father. Standing behind Tyan Yu, who was
held protectively in the arms of the captain's wife, Hien could observe
the boy's tiny expressionless face and wonder how much the child
understood. Only when Kim Bang's body was lowered into the ground
and Huong fell to her knees weeping, did a single tear drop roll down
the child's cheek. Hien moved forward a step wanting desperately to offer
Huong some comfort, but propriety stopped him in his tracks and he
remained a few inches from her.

It was the morning before their proposed transfer to the Dong Hung Refugee Camp and Hien was preparing his mind for the move. When the police captain called him and Cuong to his office, Hien felt a wave of panic. He was certain the captain must have heard of their border activities, otherwise why not include Long? News of what they had done would have reached the Vietnamese newspapers by now. Maybe there were even old military photographs of them published alongside a description of their crimes against the people. There was little doubt in Hien's mind that the Chinese authorities would scan the Vietnamese media as closely as the Vietnamese scrutinised theirs.

As they were escorted along the corridor, Hien deliberately hung back and, tugging at Cuong's shirt sleeve, whispered in his ear. 'He knows about us. Maybe he'll stop us going to the Refugee Camp.'

Cuong scowled and shook his head. 'How could he know?'

'They might have mentioned our names in the newspapers or on Hanoi radio.'

'Didn't you give a false name?'

'How could I have done? You were first out for the interview. There was no time for us to agree on what our names were.'

'I gave a false name. You could have simply made one up.'

They were almost entering the captain's office and there was no time for Hien to explain to Cuong that besides being asked his own name he'd been asked to give the names of everyone else in the boat. He'd been vague, claiming he barely knew the people, but he had given their single given names so far as he knew them to be correct.

After dismissing the guard, the captain invited them to sit down. Hien puzzled over this polite treatment because he was certain now that the captain must know they were wanted by the Vietnamese public security. As the captain pulled a sheet of paper in front of him and prepared to speak, Hien held his breath. 'The Camp you are going to is for Vietnamese,' began the captain. 'As you know, besides Vietnamese nationals many ethnic Chinese have also crossed over the border from Vietnam. Many thousands in fact. They are our own people so we welcome them back home. We have set up plantations where they can work and establish a new life. Your situation is different. You came to this country by accident.'

'Our hope is to be allowed to continue our journey to Hong Kong,' said Cuong.

'I understand that. Unfortunately, I cannot release you so easily. Our law demands that you be interned in Dong Hung for further investigation. You must understand that with the existing tension between our two countries, your coming here, by accident or on purpose, is of great concern to us.'

'How long we will be in Dong Hung?' asked Cuong.

'That I cannot say. It may be months or it may be years.'

Hien gasped. 'Years!'

'It is for that reason I wanted to speak with you. Tyan Yu is not Vietnamese — we must look at his situation differently.' Hien relaxed as he caught the drift of the conversation. 'Besides that the boy is very young,' continued the captain. 'He has no parents. No one to take care of him.'

'Of course, we'll take care of him,' interjected Cuong.

'Of course you would, but what life can you offer him in Dong Hung?' He hesitated. 'You see, my wife cannot have children. She has become attached to Tyan Yu and we would like to adopt him.'

Hien looked across at Cuong. Looking back on how things had gone, he should not have been entirely surprised by the proposal, but he was unsure what their responsibility might be toward the child's dead parents. He also suspected that whatever they said, they didn't really have any choice in the matter anyway. The captain was merely trying to avoid a fuss. His words were spoken more as a formality than an actual request. After a moment's hesitation Hien said, 'We would like to discuss this with the rest of our group.'

The captain smiled and nodded. 'Of course. That is the correct thing to do. I'll await your response.'

When Hien and Cuong explained the situation to Huong and Long, their overwhelming concern was what would be right for Tyan Yu. 'We don't know what our future is. If he were my child and I were the one to drown in the sea,' said Huong, 'I would only care about what was best for him. It doesn't matter what is right or wrong in the legal sense. If there was any real justice in the world, we wouldn't be here.'

'You saved his life, Long,' said Cuong. 'What do you think we should do?'

'I agree with Huong. We do what's best for him. But what is best? He's too young to decide for himself.'

'I think Tyan Yu has already decided,' said Huong. 'I tried many times to comfort him but he doesn't respond. Tyan Yu has become as attached to the captain's wife as she to him. No one knew his family really well.

In fact, I don't actually think he understands our language very well. I'm sure his parents just spoke Cantonese with him.'

Hien nodded. 'We're facing an unknown future in the Dong Hung Refugee Camp. I think if it's possible to place Tyan Yu in a loving home then we have no right not to do so. The treatment we've received from the captain and his wife has been good. There's no reason to believe they will not treat Tyan Yu well.'

Huong looked across at Tyan Yu who was sitting alone by the window. 'Every child needs loving parents. Let him stay here.' She shrugged. 'What can we offer him?'

'Good,' said Cuong. 'We agree then.' Nudging Hien he stood up as though preparing for them to make their report back to the captain. 'It's just as well we agree because I don't actually think we had any real choice in the matter.'

Climbing out of the cramped police truck, Hien stretched his legs before looking up and gaining his first view of Dong Hung Refugee Camp. He shuddered. Dong Hung could hardly be considered a camp at all. It was an old prison fortress with high stone walls around it, crowned with rusted barbed wire. Glancing toward the fifteen-foot iron gate which barred their exit to the outside world, it was not the first time that day that Hien wondered how long the Chinese authorities would detain them before allowing them to continue their journey.

As they marched towards the centre compound, Hien raised his eyes to the stone turret and gloomily took note of the three guards posted on top and the machine gun pointing down into the courtyard. Hien searched the thin curious faces of the inmates who silently emerged from the thatched buildings. He did not expect to recognise anyone but he examined each face all the same. As his pace slowed, one of the guards prodded him in the back. 'You will mix later. First, you register.' Although the guard had spoken to him in a strange dialect of Cantonese, Hien understood him well enough.

They were marched inside a long barracks shed where they were told to register their names, addresses and details of military service to the three officers seated at a desk. Since Hien's confession to Cuong of having given all of their single names to the Captain of police, it was agreed that, at least as far as that information was concerned, they should tell the truth. Any other information was only limited by their own imagination.

Hien gritted his teeth to prevent a smile creeping across his face as he listened to Cuong describe to the guards how he had been excluded from military service because he suffered from a congenital heart defect. 'You lie to us. First your name is Dong Vien Tung, then you say it's Dong Vien Cuong. This thing with your heart. Why should we believe you? You're a soldier, I can tell. We will find out these things eventually and then you will regret having insulted us with these untruths.' Cuong shrugged. 'Go sit on the floor by the window. The commandant is away from the camp but he will want to inspect you after his walk.'

Cuong pursed his lips. 'I'm sorry about my name. Since childhood some people called me Cuong others called me Tung.

'I said sit down. Your lack of co-operation has already been noted. This is just an initial interview, and I am not interested in your games. Later we will investigate your case in more detail.'

After giving the briefest account of his own military service during the American war, Hien was dismissed and followed Cuong over to their allocated place on the floor. 'So much for it being a refugee camp,' whispered Hien. 'It's a bloody prison.'

Cuong nodded his head. 'Let's just hope we don't have to stay here long.'

'No. It really wouldn't do your heart much good. I don't suppose they keep a resident doctor on hand.'

Hearing their conversation Huong shuffled on her bottom across the floor. 'Are you sick?'

'No.' Cuong grinned. 'My brother here just has a misguided sense of humour. First he drops me in it, then he torments me. It's called rubbing salt into the wound.'

'How long do you think we might be here?' inquired Huong.

'It's anyone's guess,' said Cuong. 'But don't worry. Hien and I will look out for you.' Cuong raised his eyebrows as he glanced at Hien. 'Right, old friend?' Ignoring the deliberate provocation, Hien turned toward Tuyet and engaged her in a children's game of finger rhymes.

It was almost an hour before the commandant arrived for the inspection. He walked into the room with three huge dogs lurching at the lead in front of him. If it had been the commandant's intention to get their immediate attention and leave them feeling intimidated by his obvious strength, then he succeeded. Prior to his entrance, Hien had considered asking him about the length of their stay, however, after looking at the saliva dripping from the dogs open jaws, he decided that it was better to remain silent and just listen to what the commandant might have to say.

A young man, whom Hien suspected to be of mixed Vietnamese and Chinese blood stood beside the commandant and translated from Cantonese to Vietnamese. 'My name is Pac Che. I am commandant of this camp. This is a good refugee camp and we do not treat you as our enemy even though your soldiers kill our brothers just a few miles from here. We know you have reason to dislike your country so . . . you are our guests. If you behave well and co-operate there will be no trouble for you. You will be instructed as to the areas where you can go freely. If however, you attempt to go anywhere that you are not permitted, then of course, you will be punished.' He waved his hand, sweeping the air in an impersonal gesture. 'But, we are friends, and I expect your full co-operation in all matters.' Hien dipped his head to hide his smile at the reference to friendship in such an obviously dictatorial relationship. 'The rules here are simple. Obey them and you will have a good stay.' He paused. 'Any questions?' It was no surprise to Hien that neither Cuong or Long said anything. 'Good then, it means you are all happy. Later my men will ask you more questions. Depending on how you answer them may lead to your time here being shortened.'

After the cramped journey over to Dong Hung, the commandant's speech and the tour of the camp with instructions as to where they were and were not allowed to go, Hien was relieved to be shown his personal living space in the single men's dormitory. Stretching out on his wooden bunk in the semi-darkness, he prepared to take a nap. He'd barely drifted into sleep when two hands roughly shook him into wakefulness. 'What the. . . !'

'I might have known you'd find your way here. What took you so long?'

At the sound of his younger brother's voice Hien sprang off the bunk to his feet. 'Dung, you . . . thank God you're alive.' Flinging his arms round his brother he hugged him for a full minute before pulling back and smiling. His heart was pounding and questions tumbled over themselves to be answered. 'How did you get here? Did you go to Haiphong?' Hien kept shaking his head in disbelief. 'This is just incredible. Cuong was right, fate's brought us together. It has to be.'

Cuong's bunk was just three sleeping places along. The disturbance must have awakened him. Slinging his legs over the side of his bunk, he advanced toward Dung with arms outstretched. 'It's good to see you. In between fussing over a certain pretty widow, your brother's been worrying himself to death over you.'

'Pretty widow!' said Dung. 'That sounds like an interesting story.'

'It's a sad story,' interjected Hien, 'But first tell us what's been happening to you.'

Sitting cross-legged Hien arranged himself on his bunk so as to make room for Dung and Cuong. Dong Hung suddenly didn't seem so bad. Looking into his brother's eyes Hien marvelled at the good fortune which brought them together. 'Thanh told me about your arrest,' said Hien. 'It seems our bad luck has been balanced by good luck. If the police had found that powder a little earlier you would never have escaped. You'd be at Hoa Lo Central Prison.'

Dung grimaced. 'I know. It was only Ha's insistence that I was still in danger which stopped me from walking straight back into their arms.'

'Is Ha with you?' asked Hien.

'Ha was determined not to be left behind.' Dung's face coloured and he looked down at his hands. 'I should tell you brother, I proposed to her, and we consider ourselves to be married.'

Hien patted his shoulder and nodded. 'That is as it should be. In another situation I might be scolding you for rushing into such a relationship, but since none of us know our future and we're forced to make decisions quickly, it's only proper you consider making some kind of commitment to your young umh. . . .'

'Bride.' Encouraged by Hien's approval, Dung's face glowed. 'That was my thinking exactly, brother. In fact when we arrived in Dong Hung I told the authorities we were married. Ha and I live in the family quarters.'

Hien burst into raucous laughter. 'I'm not sure I believe what I'm hearing. My little brother sleeping . . . well, it's just as well our mother isn't here.'

'She needed protection,' protested Dung. 'And besides we couldn't risk being separated. Ha thinks she may be pregnant.' Shocked by Dung's words, Hien broke into a fit of choked coughing. Before he could say anything Dung continued speaking. 'I remembered you told me to meet you at Tang's should there be trouble. After making our way to his shop and seeing all the security police, we panicked and made our way cross country to the border.'

'You didn't go to Haiphong?' interjected Cuong.

'We travelled north, mostly on foot, although we did manage to get a couple of rides from tradesmen. We were almost at the border when it occurred to me you might have taken refuge in our sister's home with our mother. But Haiphong is in the opposite direction.' Dung laughed. 'Anyway, by that time we were committed to going north. It would have been too dangerous to turn round.'

Cuong raised his brows. 'It would have been disastrous.'

'We hemmed the border for twelve hours in hopes of finding a safe crossing place. The area was teeming with army patrols. The "murderous mile", right! We tried criss-crossing the streams to make our way north-west. Each time we left a stream we had to scour our bodies for leeches. Ha almost went hysterical when she saw the leeches, but somehow she managed to grit her teeth and keep going.'

'What did you do about food and water?' asked Cuong

'We had some food to begin with. Later when it was gone we couldn't risk lighting a fire so we ate raw fish, raw lizard. I made a cross bow with some willow bark. Short of eating the leeches, we ate everything we could find. If we hadn't been picked up by the Chinese after we crossed the border, we would have eaten the leeches as well.' Dung suddenly laughed. 'Not that the food here is good. They practically starve you to death. We get served a bowl of soupy rice twice a day. Sometimes we get a bit of vegetable or pork fat, but it's never enough.'

Hien managed to suppress his coughing and regain control over the conversation. 'You said Ha might be pregnant. Since when might she be pregnant?'

'Oh, it's very recent,' stammered Dung. 'We never . . . um did anything when I was in Cam Pha. A week, two weeks. That's all.'

Hien sighed. 'Well, maybe she isn't pregnant. This isn't really a place to bring a baby into. Let's hope she isn't.'

Cuong had been in Dong Hung barely a week when he was ordered to report to the commandant's office. The request alone was unsettling, but when he was blindfolded and pushed forcibly into a car, his defences leapt to full alert. As the car left the camp and bumped over rough track for several miles, Cuong's imagination ran circles around him. His first thought was they were going to take him to some deserted place and shoot him, but then why bother with the blindfold and why travel so far? There were areas around Dong Hung which were deserted. Cuong was certain that they must know he'd been a soldier, who just weeks ago, had been pitted against them along Vietnam's northern border.

After what seemed to Cuong to be about thirty kilometres, the car pulled off the road and came to an abrupt standstill. Cuong felt the grip on his arms tighten as he was wrenched from the car and led into a building. He tumbled up several stairs before managing to adjust his step correctly to the climb. When he reached the top he was led along a narrow passage to a room where he was pushed into a chair and told to wait. Cuong would have liked to rip the bandage from his eyes, but since there were no departing footsteps he concluded his escorts had not left the room. The riddle of why they had blindfolded him still worried him. He could only presume they did not want him to be able to recognise either the people he was to meet with or remember the location he'd been brought to.

It was almost a relief when after over an hour of waiting two or more men entered the room and the questioning began. 'What is your name?'

Cuong spoke some Cantonese and had expected to have to answer questions in that language. He was surprised, therefore, when the official addressed him in fluent Vietnamese. 'Dong Vien Cuong.'

The official sneered. 'Dong Vien Cuong, not Dong Vien Tung? Or could it be your name is Nguyen Cao Cuong?' Cuong clasped his hands together and wondered if this was just the prelude to torture. 'Which is it?'

Cuong shrugged. There seemed little point in lying further since they obviously knew who he was. 'My name is Nguyen Cao Cuong. Although why that should be of such importance to you, I fail to see. It wasn't my intention to come to China, and I'd be happy to leave.'

'You don't need to be afraid of us. We're here to help you. You were in the army, weren't you, Cuong?'

Cuong forced a smile. He wondered if they also knew of his trouble with the Vietnamese authorities. He could feel the sweat itching his hair round the nape of his neck. He wasn't going to be fooled by the man's silky snake tongue. There were over a hundred asylum-seekers being detained at Dong Hung, so he supposed that one of them must have known who he was and passed this information to the Chinese. 'I was conscripted into the army during the American war.'

'And called up a second time during the disputes over our border with your government?'

'My choice would have been for our countries to find a peaceful settlement.'

'Very good. I think we are of the same understanding. If more of your compatriots thought like you, maybe we wouldn't be fighting one another.'

Cuong wasn't comfortable with this cozy, congenial chat, but since they hadn't done anything to physically harm him, he decided it was better to go along with them rather than risk raising their antagonism. He wasn't giving away any military secrets, not that he had any to give, and the conversation seemed harmless enough. Not being able to see the face of his inquisitor, however, left him feeling at a distinct disadvantage.

'What made you desert from the army? Was it your conscience that told you this war is wrong?'

So they did know quite a bit about him. Cuong hesitated before answering. 'I think all war is wrong.'

'That doesn't quite answer my question. Your country has done some wrong things, yes? Maybe they have even done some wrong things to you, Cuong.'

'I haven't been treated any differently from other people. May we remove the blindfold?'

'If they did nothing bad to you, then why did you desert?'

They were clearly not going to allow him to remove the blindfold. 'I didn't want to be a soldier any more.'

'That's it. . . ? I don't think so. Why did you desert?'

Cuong hesitated before answering. Oh, what the hell he thought. 'My patrol herded some civilians into an area of landmines. It resulted in a child being blown up. I was in a state of shock and ran away.'

'That is a terrible thing for Vietnamese soldiers to do. It's all right that you ran away, Cuong. We understand.' The speaker paused before continuing. 'You see how well our officials treated you. When your boat became stuck in the sandbanks, we helped you. It is sad that the Vietnamese government should treat its people with such little humanity, is it not?'

'Yes.'

'And have the commandant and his officers treated you and your people humanely at Dong Hung?'

Cuong wondered if the commandant were not sitting in the same room just waiting to pounce on him if he made any complaint. 'Yes.'

'Do you not agree that our government is good and that your government is behaving rather badly?'

Cuong preferred not to say anything. He wasn't fooled for one minute into thinking that the Chinese government treated their people any better than his own. In fact, he knew from Chinese friends in Vietnam that the Cultural Revolution had been far more devastating than anything his country had done. As the silence mounted Cuong felt pressured to respond in some way, so slowly he nodded his head. What did it hurt to play along with them if feeding their own egos was what they were after?

'You nod your head, Cuong. Does this mean that you agree that your government is not behaving so well.'

'Yes.'

'Yes, you agree.'

'Yes, I agree.'

'And you deserted from the Vietnamese military because you did not like what the soldiers were doing. You were unhappy after a child was murdered when she was driven into a mine field?'

'It wasn't exactly that. The soldiers behaved quite reasonably. It was my. . . .'

'The child died after running into a mine field?'

'Yes.'

'And that's why you deserted?'

'Yes, I suppose.'

'Not suppose, Cuong. That is how it was. Yes?'

Cuong responded hesitantly. 'Yes.'

'Then say that, Cuong. Stop dancing around us.' The official made no effort to hide the annoyance in his voice. Straining his ears so as not to miss any of the signals which might give warning of his predicament, Cuong stiffened when the official suddenly scraped his seat along the floor. There were approaching footsteps, then warm breath as the man, clearly very close now, spoke urgently into his ear. 'Say it again, Cuong.' Cuong felt the man's fingers dig into his shoulder muscles. 'Say it, Cuong.'

Cuong hesitated. He couldn't see the point of the conversation. What did it really matter to them why he deserted? Surely the child wasn't Chinese? 'I deserted because of the child running into a mine field.'

'You're doing very well. It was because of the Vietnamese soldiers the child ran into the minefield.'

Cuong didn't want to lie. He knew if anyone was to blame it was himself. He should never have called her without first establishing that the path was clear. 'It was when I called to her. It was me that was responsible for her death.'

'And of course you are a Vietnamese soldier. It is as I have said. Vietnamese soldiers were responsible for the death of an innocent child.'

Cuong felt his throat tighten into a knot. 'It wasn't what we intended.'

'Then are we to conclude that the Vietnamese soldiers are incompetent?'

'Things happen during war time. Of course we're not infallible.'

'No one flees from China into Vietnam, but isn't it correct to say that many thousands of Vietnamese refugees have lost their lives while trying to escape from their homeland? They must be desperate people to take such risks, don't you think?' Cuong remained silent. 'Answer me, Cuong. Is what I say correct?'

Cuong sighed. He was suddenly tired of their games. Many people were desperate in Vietnam. Uncle Thai, his wife, Tyan Yu's four-year-old brother, his parents and the young men. All of them must have been desperate to venture onto Kim Bang's unseaworthy boat. It would be a betrayal to their spirits to deny it. Cuong lowered his head. 'It's true many thousands have fled from Vietnam, many thousands also left. . . .'

'Thank you. That is all.'

Cuong was about to force his words upon them, but managed to bite his lips together. The officials stood up and left. The interview ended. Still blindfolded Cuong was escorted back down the stairs to the waiting car. On the drive back to Dong Hung, he pondered over the point of the whole exercise. He hadn't told them anything particularly important, but he didn't feel happy. The experience left an unpleasant taste in his mouth.

Chapter 7: New Economic Confinement Zone

15th July 1980 to 20th January 1981

That day, never to come back, you went away,
Leaving me alone, weighed down with sadness.
The authorities, in pity of my loneliness,
Invited me to prison for a temporary stay.
PRISON DIARY, HO CHI MINH

As THANH DISMOUNTED his bike and wheeled it in through the alleyway to the kitchen, Lan came running out to meet him. Her eyes looked red as though she'd been crying and Thanh was taken aback by her apparent distress. 'What's wrong?'

'It's Minh. Oh Thanh, you have to do something. It was so terrible.'

Thanh bounced the bike up the step and tilted it against the kitchen wall before guiding Lan over to the table. 'Sit down. Now, tell me slowly. What's happened to Minh?'

'I was over there today. I know you told me to be careful and only speak to Minh in the market, and I intended to do that except Minh was weepy when she saw me so we went back to her cottage to chat privately. We had been there just a short time — the children and Cuong's mother were there — when some men from Hanoi arrived with a truck.'

Thanh was puzzled. 'Hanoi! Are you sure? How do you know they were from Hanoi?'

'I heard them say so. Anyway, if they'd been from Hong Gai I would probably have recognised them and they would have known who I was. They had papers for Minh to sign. At first she refused, but they started to empty the house and put her things on the truck anyway. Minh went hysterical. I didn't know what to do. One of the men said I should leave, but I didn't. I helped Grandma with the children. The baby was crying, and then I think because Minh was acting so strange they forgot about me.'

'You say Minh was acting strange. . . .'

'Minh is normally timid. Today she wasn't. She was shouting at one of the men. I saw him pull her into the courtyard. The shutter was open so I could still watch them. He was telling Minh she had to sign the paper. That's when Minh went to hit him — she was really serious . . . anyway he was too quick and grabbed her wrists. He then spun her round so he was holding her tight and she couldn't move. I could hardly believe her behaviour. I wanted to go and help her, but I knew if I did they would just send me away.

'They would either have arrested you or sent you off, that's for certain.'

'Well, yes. That's what the man said to Minh. "You're forcing me to arrest you, and it won't be Dong Cuong Yen Bai you'll be going to with your family — it'll be prison." "What's the difference?" Minh screamed back. "Believe me, there is a difference," he said. "You want your children to have no mother to care for them?" That seemed to calm Minh, so after a few minutes when it seemed like she wasn't going to hit him any more, he let go of her. Then he said, "Your husband has acted against the Socialist Republic of Vietnam. He not only deserted from the army, but he's linked to a terrorist group who were found to have explosives in their possession. So we ask ourselves what did they intend doing with the explosives?" Minh just stared at him. Of course I'd already heard of some of this so I wasn't surprised. The man then sat her down on the little wall in the courtyard. He seemed to be genuinely concerned about her. He said he'd forget about what just happened, you know, her trying to hit him, and then he said he believed that she was not involved in her husband's activities, but that there were others who thought differently.'

As Lan described the scene and said almost word for word what she remembered of the dialogue, Thanh could see it taking place. But Cuong had already been gone over two months. He'd been waiting for a letter or some communication from him, so he'd know how to help Minh escape and join him. He wondered what had prompted the authorities to suddenly arrest her. 'Is that all the man said?'

'No, I'm coming to that. After he sat her down his tone sounded, um . . . almost conspiratorial. He leaned toward her but I could still hear. Then he said, "I shouldn't tell you, but your husband escaped into China."'

'He's in China?'

'I don't know, but I promise you that's what he said. Do you think he was lying?'

'No, maybe not. Go on.'

'He looked her full in the face, then said, "We monitor all Chinese radio broadcasts. Last week New China Radio broadcast Nguyen Cao Cuong, making public criticisms of the Vietnamese government and the military."' Lan looked down. 'Oh, then he said if Minh signed the order, he'd try to make things easier for her.'

Thanh sat back. So that was it. Something had obviously gone wrong in Cuong's escape, and he'd ended up in China. It wouldn't be difficult to obtain the details of the actual broadcast and hear what Cuong said. The Chinese had either bribed, tortured or tricked him into speaking on the radio. Thanh wasn't sure why, but he hoped Cuong hadn't accepted a bribe, although given the circumstances of Cuong's hurried departure from Vietnam, he felt it was hardly his right to judge him either way. His plan to help Minh and her family join him in Hong Kong would have to wait. 'Where's Minh now?'

'Dong Cuong Yen Bai, the new economic zone, I suppose. After they packed up Minh's household possessions, they noticed me and told me to leave. I thought of hanging around, but then I realised what the time was and wanted to get back here to tell you. What can we do?'

Thanh was still trying to take everything in. Cuong should have been in Hong Kong. The snake-head he'd introduced him to wasn't an amateur. There were good, reliable boats leaving Haiphong for Hong Kong every day. 'You do nothing,' he said, turning his attention back to Lan. 'I'll make some inquiries as to what happened. Then I'll visit Minh at Dong Cuong Yen Bai myself.'

'She's *my* sister.'

Thanh was feeling irritated that Cuong hadn't successfully made it to Hong Kong. His detour into China could escalate into something really dangerous. Lan would just have to listen to him for once. 'No. I shouldn't have taken you with me to Haiphong. You have no idea about these matters, and you shouldn't really have gone back to Minh's house.'

Lan stood up from the table. 'Well, thank you, Mr Know-it-all. If I hadn't gone, you wouldn't know anything about the conversation she'd had with the Hanoi official.'

'Lan, sit back down. It's just. . . .'

'Forget it. I'm sick of the way you think you should handle everything, and I'm sick of your secret conversations with Nam.'

'Nam! How does this have anything to do with Nam?'

'Oh, you think I don't notice. You talk to Nam all the time, and when anything's wrong he appears like magic. I'm sick of your secret ways. And your trips to Hanoi. For all I know you could have a wife in Hanoi . . . and in every other province for that matter.'

Thanh stood up and tried to pull her toward him, but she backed away. 'Lan. I have one wife. Don't let jealousy spoil our relationship.'

'Relationship. A husband is supposed to speak to his wife, not just have sex with her. We don't have a relationship for me to spoil. And if I decide one day to visit my sister, then it has nothing to do with you.'

Exhaustion washed over Minh as she stretched out on the rush matting. Conditions in the confinement zone were harsher than she imagined possible and she wondered how much longer she could keep going. Every day she was expected to strip the bark off five cinnamon trees, but with Grandma's failing health, Minh had been stripping three of Grandma's trees beside her own. She'd known she wasn't doing a thorough job, but when Comrade Nhung hauled her up before the workers' committee and accused her of laziness, Minh had been unable to keep the tone of resentment and irritation out of her voice. So now she was being punished for both her sloppiness and her poor attitude. Just at the time when she would normally be able to lie down with her children and grab a few precious hours of sleep before they were all forced to rise to attend the morning indoctrination session at five, Minh had to take herself off to the evening sessions. It was unfair. The treatment she received was definitely harsher than that received by other detainees, but if they thought it could break her spirit or turn her against Cuong, they were wrong. She could see through their game and she would fight them until her last breath.

Minh lay back and closed her eyes. What if she didn't go, but just stayed there and slept? The idea was tempting. Tempting but not realistic. If she didn't go, they would say she was not co-operating or pulling her weight, and they would probably cut back on the family food ration. The children would go hungry and the deprivation of food could cause permanent damage to their health. As Minh weighed up these thoughts a small hand touched her arm. 'Mama, are you going to stay with us tonight? Won't you be in trouble if you don't go?'

Forcing her eyes back open Minh gazed up into the face of her young daughter. Trinh was such a blessing to her. In contrast to all the horrors of her life, Trinh's loyalty and love shone through like the warm sun encouraging her to keep going and to believe in a better future. The knowledge of how the camp teachers tried to turn the children against their own father troubled her, and she could see that forcing her to attend the extra indoctrination sessions served their purpose well by lessening her time with them. Trinh always closed her ears to criticisms of her parents, but the boys she wasn't sure of. They were so little and open to what other people said. How could she expect them to know better?

Minh let out an exhausted sigh and pulled herself up. Kissing Trinh on the forehead she said, 'No, little mouse. I just needed to close my eyes one minute. Grandma's a bit sick tonight, so you take care of things while I'm gone.'

'I will, mama.'

When Minh arrived at the classroom and saw that everyone was already gathered and sitting cross-legged on the floor, she realised that she would pay dearly for those few minutes of relaxation. 'Ah, Comrade Minh, you have decided to join us at last, thank you. Will you stand before the class.' Minh felt her face redden as the rows of upturned heads looked toward her. 'Comrade Minh,' continued Comrade Nhung, 'is by far the most rotten apple in the barrel. If we are not careful her rottenness will spread and contaminate the high ideals of all of us. Not only is her work shoddy, but when the workers' committee confront her with this, and offer her extra classes to help change her attitude, she is ungrateful. Her late arrival just gives us another opportunity to see what happens to a society when it lets discipline lapse.'

Nhung heaved out her chest and breathed in deeply. Her eyes narrowed and her thin lips spread out as a smile prowled stealthily across her face. 'But comrades, we should also congratulate Comrade Minh for demonstrating to us this fine example of tardiness, without which we would not have been able to contemplate the root cause of Western degeneracy.'

Minh's face burned as she stood rigid in front of her class mates while they, already compromised by their invitation to the sessions, were compelled to clap and jeer. She felt humiliated beyond endurance. The quota of ten trees for her family was outrageously unfair. Comrade Nhung knew her mother-in-law was sick and old and that Minh had been taking on the extra load herself. She was neither lazy nor ungrateful, but to have tried to defend herself would have only given more ammunition to Comrade Nhung to humiliate her further. Determined to hold back her tears, Minh bit into the inside of her lip. She swallowed hard as a trickle of warm blood oozed around her tongue and teeth.

It was late afternoon when Thanh arrived at the dock yard in Haiphong and made his way toward Mr Luyen's office. He had decided that before visiting Minh at Dong Cuong Yen Bai, he would try to find out what had gone wrong with Cuong's escape and learn why he was in China. His visit with Hien's sister and brother-in-law had not revealed anything. They were definitely holding something back, but to have pushed them would have made the situation become ugly and Thanh could not afford to draw attention to their meeting. The only thing left for him to do was to approach the snake-head directly, even though the risks were high. It wasn't just to satisfy his own curiosity that he needed to seek out the truth. Since the late seventies Thanh and Nam had worked with Uncle Chau to assist several of his prominent friends to escape from Vietnam. Mostly they were writers and reformists, who having become disillusioned, had fallen out of favour with the new revolutionary government. It was essential to Uncle Chau that the escapes went smoothly and safely. If their involvement in the escapes were ever to become known, it would mean disgrace for all of them. Uncle Chau's high position in the government would be no protection and his fall from grace would be made harder because of his high position.

The streets were beginning to wake up again as people roused themselves from their siesta and began preparing for business. For the past hour Thanh had sat in the café across the street from Mr Luyen's office waiting for the crowds to come back, and watching. Watching nothing in particular, just noting the movement of the people and the details of everything around him.

When he knocked on the yellow door, he waited a few minutes before the door was opened and the face of a middle aged man peered round. Although Thanh had never met the snake-head, he knew immediately that the man was Mr Luyen.

'Yes, how can I help you?'

'Mr Tien sent me, may I speak to you?'

'Come in quickly.' Mr Luyen shut the door behind him. 'Well, how is it that I can help you?'

'I have a package I need to send to Hong Kong. Can you help me?'

'Yes, I have many other packages that need to get to Hong Kong. How urgent is your need?'

'Then let's talk straight. I'm in trouble with the authorities and need to leave for Hong Kong on the next available boat.'

'That can be arranged.'

'I have two taels of gold. That is all I can offer to pay you.'

'Since you are a friend of Mr Tien that will be sufficient, brother.'

'I have a question for you. Two friends of mine recently left on one of your boats for Hong Kong, but they ended up in China. How is that possible?'

Mr Luyen's face drained of colour and he made a sudden bolt for the door. Thanh, anticipating the move, was quicker and placed himself in Mr Luyen's pathway. Sweat broke out on his brow and Thanh could see he was trembling. 'Who are you? What do you want with me?'

'I haven't come to do you any harm. After I leave, you can forget you ever saw me, but I want information about my friends.'

'I don't know about your friends. The passages I arrange are reliable. No one goes to China.'

'My friends did. They approached you about two months ago. Just one of them met with you perhaps. He was about five foot eight, broad shoulders, mid twenties. His eyes, more Chinese looking than Vietnamese. Good complexion, good teeth.'

'Their mishap was nothing to do with me,' said Mr Luyen. 'There was a third one, a brother. The man wanted to arrange passage for all three of them, but only had enough money for two. I could have just sent him away, refused to help, but he seemed desperate. I introduced him to an acquaintance of mine who had a boat and was wanting to escape himself. Your friend seemed satisfied with that. He was going to leave gold with his family for his brother's passage and take the cheaper passage himself with his friend.'

Thanh stared at Mr Luyen. No wonder Hien's sister had been nervous. If Dung hadn't contacted them they might have pocketed the money themselves. It was such a simple explanation. He wondered why he hadn't anticipated Hien's concern over his younger brother and given them the additional gold. It wasn't that Thanh was wealthy, the money was from his own savings, but to have allowed the situation to develop as it did, just because of money, could have been avoided.

'Look, what happened wasn't my fault. I have this agreement. I don't make any money on Mr Tien's friends. Then people leave me alone. If you hurt me. . . .'

Thanh moved away from the door. 'I have no intention of hurting you. You can forget I ever came here. There will be no repercussions from this visit.'

Mr Luyen relaxed and sank back into a chair. 'The boat your friends left on — do you know what happened? You see the helmsman was my cousin.'

Thanh shrugged. 'I'm sorry. All I know is that they ended up in China.'

Since her argument with Thanh several months ago, Lan noticed that her relationship had been even more strained than usual. Thanh was always busy with his own affairs. She knew he'd visited Minh and taken her some medicine and food because he'd spoken of it, but whenever he'd raised the subject of Minh, she'd felt jealous and made it clear she wasn't interested in hearing him speak about her. For weeks she had wondered how she could visit her sister herself without his knowing. The opportunity came when Thanh was called to Hanoi for a few days. Lan hadn't inquired why he was going and he hadn't offered an explanation. All morning she'd waited in brooding silence until he'd left the house. It was only when he turned his bike toward the main road that she stopped moping and rushed into action. Running up stairs she dragged out the packages she had stored for Minh under the bed, then, after a quick glance along the road to make sure that Thanh had really left, she set off at a brisk pace for the bus station.

The journey to Dong Cuong Yen Bai involved two bus rides over rough potholed tracks. By the time Lan reached her destination, she was exhausted. The dust from the roads had flown in through the windows and settled in her eyes and hair. She blew her nose into her handkerchief and curled her lips up in disgust at the traces of red soil. Even though Lan knew that Minh wouldn't have the resources — good clothes, make up — to make herself presentable, Lan couldn't help but dress herself up for the visit. Before leaving the house she had been indecisive what to wear, but in the end it was her vanity which had won over. As she tried to brush the dust from her pants, she felt irritated that the journey should have been so difficult.

When Lan entered the camp facility she was totally unprepared for the gruelling questions thrown at her by the camp superintendent Mr Thao. At first she thought he wasn't going to allow her to see Minh, that she'd made the awful journey for nothing, but then after he'd made some private phone calls his attitude changed. He informed her that it would take a while for her to see Minh, since they would have to find her, but if she didn't mind waiting about an hour, the visit could be arranged. Lan did mind waiting, but since she'd come such a long way and there was no other choice, she settled herself down under the shady branches of a tamarind tree and prepared to wait out the hour in relative comfort.

An hour-and-a-half passed and Lan was beginning to grow impatient. She wondered how large the plantation could be that it would take so long to find Minh. She was considering walking over to Mr Thao's office when a government car pulled up. The arrival of the car was of little interest to her, but since its male occupants were also interested in speaking to the superintendent, she thought she had better wait. Her patience, however, was soon rewarded. Fifteen minutes after the arrival of the car, Lan was escorted by Mr Thao into a waiting room for visitors.

It was not long before Minh entered the room. When Lan saw how thin she'd become, she forgot all about her own discomforts and jumping up from her seat she rushed over and drew Minh into her arms. 'Oh little sister, whatever have they done to you?'

Minh clung to Lan for several minutes before pulling back. 'I'm doing fine, sister. It was hard at first but really I'm okay now. Let's sit down and enjoy our time together.' They moved over to the bench and sat down. 'How was your journey?'

'Oh, it was nothing. I'm afraid my shirt has dirt on it, and I must look an awful sight.' Lan pulled her shirt away from her waist to show Minh the stains. 'But you know how it is on the buses.'

'You look beautiful, sister. No one here would notice the dirt on your clothes.'

'Yes, of course it's nothing. What do you do all day here? It must be boring.'

'No, boring isn't how I would describe it. I work on the cinnamon plantation.'

'Oh.' Lan knew nothing of what working on the cinnamon plantation might entail.

'How is your husband, elder sister?'

'Much the same. He works hard and spends much of his time in Hanoi or Haiphong.'

'And Tang, have you seen our brother lately?'

'Tang is fine. Well, actually he moved to Cam Pha and is working for the coal mining company.'

'Why? His business was good. Coal mining is a harder job with probably less money.'

'It was silly nonsense, really. The People's Committee took his shop away because he didn't have a picture of Ho Chi Minh hanging up.'

'Oh, that's so unfair. They use Uncle Ho as a weapon against us. That's not what he'd have wanted.' Minh hesitated. 'It's because of Cuong, isn't it?'

Lan shrugged her shoulders. 'How about my niece and nephews? Are they well?'

'They're fine.' Minh drew in her breath. 'Grandma died a little over a month ago.' Her voice was flat as she spoke. It was as though she'd already resigned herself to whatever fate might throw her way.

'Oh Minh, I'm sorry. You must think me awful. I wanted to come and see you sooner, but Thanh forbade it. Sometimes I hate him. He's so arrogant and self-composed. I can never tell what he's thinking.'

'Don't say that. Thanh came to visit me twice. He brought food and medicines. If he hadn't done that, Grandma could never have lived as long as she did.'

Lan forced a smile. 'Here I am telling you of my troubles. The old lady's death must have been awful for you.'

'No. In a way it was a relief. Her life was terrible here. She tried to keep up with her allocation of work but. . . .' Minh slipped her hand under her shirt and pulled an envelope from her trouser waist band. 'I wrote this letter just after she died. I've kept it on me because I thought Thanh might come back.' She thrust the envelope into Lan's hands. 'This is a letter for Cuong. It's important he gets news of his mother's death. I don't know how to find him. Maybe your husband or our brother has some news?'

Lan hesitated before slipping the letter into her bag. 'None of us have heard from him. I'll keep the letter in case we do, but right now I really don't know how to get it to him.' Lan looked around. The room was empty and they were sitting far away from any of the windows and door. She leaned forward. 'I never told you before because Thanh swore me to secrecy, but now I'm finished with doing what he tells me. I hate the role of being a dutiful wife, I deserve better than that. After Cuong's fight with the soothsayer, Thanh and I went to see Tang. He didn't know where Cuong was, but suggested they might have gone into hiding in Haiphong. Hien's mother and married sister live there.' Lan stopped speaking for a moment and looked around. 'We didn't know the address exactly, but anyway Thanh made inquiries and we found them.'

Minh's eyes lit up. 'You spoke to Cuong?'

'Yes.'

'How was he? What did he say?'

'He was fine. Thanh gave them some gold and information to seek out a snake-head.'

'Snake-head!'

'Yes, he's the man that arranges for people to escape on boats out of Vietnam. Once Cuong was settled in Hong Kong, he was going to write and then Thanh was going to make the arrangements to get the rest of you out.' Lan sat back. 'I've no idea what went wrong. How he ended up in China.'

'The explosive powder. Why were his friend's hoarding it? They say that Cuong's a traitor. That he and his friends intended to do harm to our country.'

Lan shook her head. 'That was nothing. Hien and his brother stole the TNT from the anti-tank mines to sell to the fishermen. The TNT makes an explosion in the water and the stunned fish float to the surface. The fishermen scoop them up. What can I say? It's a lazy way of fishing, I suppose, but when people are desperate and their children are hungry, what do they care?'

'He wasn't a traitor then?'

'No. He was upset because a child was blown up by a land-mine. He obsessed about the child being Trinh and ran away from his division just so he could come home and see you.' Lan sat up straight. 'If I believed Thanh would do that for me, I could love him. You're so lucky, sister. Anyway, that's all he did wrong. If they'd caught him straight away they'd have returned him to his unit. He would have been punished, but nothing as serious as now.'

Minh breathed in. 'It's because I went to the soothsayer. He said I was bringing danger to everyone.'

'How could you have known? You were trying to help Cuong.'

'The soothsayer knew.'

Lan grinned. 'Well, yes. He's a soothsayer. He's supposed to know. That's his job.' Lan could see immediately that Minh didn't appreciate her joke.

'Did anything bad happen to him?'

Lan hesitated. She was about to say that Mr Tam had been accused of sexual misconduct and was in prison, but then it occurred to her that Minh was burdened with enough guilt. 'So far as I know his life goes on much as before. I should forget about him if I were you.'

Lan almost jumped out of her skin as she heard someone turn the door latch. Minh heard it too and grasped Lan's hands. 'You'll find a way to get the letter to Cuong?'

'Yes, I promise.'

As Lan left the visitor's room and prepared to leave the confinement zone, the camp administrator ran after her and asked her to step into his office for a minute. Lan suspected he was going to ask her for some money for the favour of allowing her to visit Minh, but since she didn't expect to be coming back she decided she wasn't going to pay him. 'I'm sorry but I really can't stop. I already wasted an hour-and-a-half sitting round and if I don't get the bus to Haiphong from here soon I'll miss my last bus back home.' Smiling seductively she said, 'You can understand that it would be bad for a woman to be alone at night in Haiphong.'

The superintendent was unmoved. 'That won't happen,' he said catching hold of her arm with a politeness to the touch but a firmness also. Lan suspected that if she challenged him further he might physically force her to come to his office. 'This won't take long. When a visitor comes to the centre we have to debrief them before they leave.'

Lan almost laughed at his use of terminology. 'I'm not a soldier. What absurd rule is this?'

'Please, just come with me first. Then if nothing's wrong you'll be free to go on your way.'

His words 'if nothing's wrong' made her feel suddenly uneasy. When she entered the office and saw that it wasn't just the superintendent she was going to meet with, but the three men who'd arrived in the car, her unease rose to panic. The men were sitting drinking tea. Upon seeing her one of them stood up and walked over. 'Please, sit down, Mrs Lan. This won't take a minute of your time. How is your husband?' Lan was too surprised to speak. 'I trust he's well.'

Trying her best to appear composed, Lan sat down, then slowly and deliberately arranged her clothes so it might appear as though she was indifferent to their presence and simply preoccupied with her appearance. She knew her lipstick would have smudged off long ago and her clothes probably stank of poultry from the bus journey, but she sat with her head held high in keeping with someone who had an important uncle in the government. She could feel her hands trembling so to keep them steady she clasped them over her bag.

'I'll take that, if you don't mind.' Before Lan had time to protest, the man reached over and snatched her bag from her hands. For a second Lan thought she was being robbed. She felt incensed, but not personally threatened. No . . . they knew who she was, they wouldn't dare. This had to be something serious. The officer walked over to the table and emptied out the contents of her bag. Lan jumped as a lipstick rattled across the desk and landed on the floor. Her thoughts raced through her head. Then she watched in stunned silence as the officer pushed the money aside with the rest of the bag's contents and digging deeper pulled out the crumpled envelope Minh had given to her minutes earlier.

Stooping down the official picked up the lipstick, placed it back into her purse with the money and handed it back to her. He then ironed out the envelope with his hand before passing it to the older of the men for his inspection.

The senior man looked at her. 'Why did Mrs Minh pass this letter to you? It has the traitor Nguyen Cao Cuong's name written on the envelope.'

Lan felt a sickening weight in her stomach. 'Her mother-in-law just died. My sister thought I might be able to get the letter to him.'

'Why would she think that?'

'Because she was desperate. I don't know where Cuong is, but there was no one else for her to give the letter to. I'm her sister. When someone is grieving they do things that don't make sense.'

'You're not in a state of grief and appear to have all of your senses together, so why accept the letter knowing, as you say, you could not deliver it? Wasn't that deceptive?'

'I told my sister I couldn't deliver it. I accepted it only because I thought it would bring her some comfort. What else was I supposed to do?'

'Did you know that Nguyen Cao Cuong is a traitor to our country? It was very foolish of you to accept this letter.' He wandered over to the telephone. 'I'm very sorry, but it will be necessary for me to arrange to have you accompany us back to Hanoi. We will notify your husband of the matter. Maybe he can throw some light on your behaviour. Maybe you were here to collect the letter at his request?'

Lan felt as though her head were ready to explode. Did she imagine it or was the older man smiling as he sat reading Minh's letter? She had to steady herself as she stood up. She couldn't believe how stupid she'd been. Now they would involve Thanh. He would know about her deceit, and worse — her stupidity. It wasn't just the letter — she'd spoken to Minh about Thanh helping Cuong escape. She didn't see that they could have heard, but how could she really know? They would almost certainly question Minh about their conversation. Maybe they would even threaten or hurt her. She felt sick. Thanh had been right in telling her to stay away. It was insulting to have him come and collect her from Hanoi. But as the thoughts flooded in Lan's head, what frightened her most was the sudden realization that it wasn't her or Minh they were really interested in. It was Thanh.

Chapter 8: Dong Hung Refugee Camp, China

10th February to 5th May 1981

Each morning the sun emerges from behind the mountain
Bathing the country in a rosy glow.
But over the prison remains a shadow,
Sunlight cannot yet reach the warder's domain.
PRISON DIARY, HO CHI MINH

DUNG COULD HARDLY CONTAIN his excitement as the creature inside his cupped hands fluttered its wings trying to escape. He'd let it go soon enough, but first the children must see it. They would be in rapture at the sight of it. However, it wasn't just the find of the locust which was making Dung's spirit soar; he'd been in the camp eight long, dreary months when, just last week, the Chinese authorities brought round application forms for them to fill out for emigration to Australia, Canada or Britain. With the promise of freedom in the air everyone was ecstatic. Even the most cynical couldn't keep a smile from their lips. The camp was buzzing with talk about where everyone wanted to go. Some favoured Canada while others preferred Australia. Dung didn't care where he went; so long as he was with Ha and his brother, anywhere had to be better than where they were.

Watching Ha through the fence, Dung enjoyed her moment of liberation. For several months now the commandant had allowed her to go out with the children to a nearby stream. Since she was heavily laden with child, he must have considered the risk of her escaping minimal. Dung smiled as he observed her finish washing up the last of the children then dash off into the scrub. It happened the same every day. First Ha would help the mothers, then in those few precious minutes before they were ordered back to camp, she'd scurry round with the older children as they scanned the bushes for spiders. The children kept spiders as pets which they housed in folded pineapple leaves, and with nothing more exciting to do, the competition to see whose spider was the biggest and strongest was the focal activity of every day.

They had barely entered through the camp gate before Dung bounded over to meet them. 'See what I've caught.' Excited squeals rang out as several of the children ran toward him, then leaping as far into the air as they could manage, the taller ones tried to make a grab for his hands. 'Oh no you don't. You wait.' Dung kept his hands stretched up until Ha and the younger ones joined him. 'Look at this creature. It's the oddest thing. . . .'

Ha stood up on her toes laughing. 'Whatever is it, to cause so much excitement?' Lowering his arms, Dung carefully opened his hands so that even the littlest could peer down at the exotic insect fluttering frantically between his fingers. With its shadowy green body and translucent wings peppered with brown spots, it was the strangest locust any of them had ever seen. 'It's so beautiful. Where did you find it?'

'Well, unlike some of us who have the luxury of going outside, my hunting ground is limited to here. . . . It flew in through the fence.'

The children's excitement spread to the adults and within minutes a large crowd formed round Dung. One of the women was Mrs Kieu, who pushed her way to the centre of the spectacle. Out of respect for her seniority, Dung spread his hands out so she could see what he was holding. When the old woman saw the locust she screamed and leapt backward. 'Oh, heavens save us. Get it out of here. . . .'

The sound of the woman's torment was so unexpected and terrifying it took Dung completely by surprise. He'd barely time to register his shock when Ha, clasping her womb, crumpled forward to the ground. As the locust flew into the crowd, Dung dropped to his knees and took her into his arms. 'What happened?' Ha could not utter a word. She just stared at the panicked insect beating its wings while the hysterical Mrs Kieu wildly batted at the air to prevent the locust landing on any of them.

'It's the ghost locust — *chau chau ma,*' screamed Mrs Kieu. Then looking down on Dung she seemed ready to strike him. 'You've released an evil spirit into our midst. Get rid of it. Get it out.' With his arms still round Ha, Dung paid her little attention.

The commotion drew the attention of the guards and one of them rushed over with his gun already drawn from his holster. 'Break it up. Go back to your huts. We can't have crowds gathering in the compound so close to the gate. What's wrong with you people?' Then turning on Mrs Kieu, he advanced threateningly toward her. 'Go back to your hut, you stupid old grandmother. Why did you scream like that? I could have shot you.'

Mrs Kieu looked ready to direct her anger toward the guard, but thinking better of it she turned and scurried away. Dung watched her go then helped Ha to her feet. She was still unsteady as Dung helped her over to the family hut.

'What happened to the insect?'

Dung was totally nonplused. 'I don't know. I suppose it flew away.'

'Mrs Kieu called it a ghost locust. When she screamed it was as though something was trying to drag our baby out of me. It was terrible, Dung.' Cradling her stomach she pulled herself onto the bunk and slowly rocked back and forth. 'How could something like that happen? Oh, my baby, my poor baby.'

Dung felt helpless against such superstition. This was a woman's thing — the strange stirring in her womb of their baby being dragged out — and he didn't understand any of it. Climbing next to her he wrapped his arms around her and rocked with her for a while. Then a thought came to him as to what might be wrong. He stopped rocking. 'Ha, my darling I know what's wrong. You feel vulnerable because I haven't protected you. It's my fault. This pretending to be married, it isn't good enough. We'll have our own marriage ceremony, among our own people. We don't need a government certificate. Our love and God's blessing will bind us together.' Ha was looking at him and the fear seemed to have gone out of her face. 'The old woman's words are just silly superstition. When you're my wife you'll feel safe.'

Burying her head into Dung's shoulder Ha seemed to take comfort from his words. 'Perhaps you're right. Being properly married might make a difference. Then there will be no question in anyone's mind as to who our baby's father is.'

Dung suddenly sat back and laughed. 'Of course there's no question as to who his father is. You silly duckling, what ever made you say a thing like that?'

When Dung broached the subject of the wedding, Hien thought it an excellent idea and determined that in spite of the deprivation of their environment he would organise a splendid celebration for his younger brother and wife-to-be. The incident with the ghost locust was ridiculous, but it had spooked everyone. A wedding would be just the thing to lift their spirits, and since Ha's baby was due in a matter of weeks, the arrangements for it needed to be put into place fast.

For several months Hien had been aware that the commandant kept a pig in the restricted area of the camp. It grieved him to see the guards carrying buckets of left over rice from the guard house to the pig pen when the camp inmates barely had enough to eat to keep themselves alive. On the day before the wedding Hien decided that he'd take positive action to set the scales to balance. Seeing Cuong ambling across the compound from the wash house, Hien hurried after him. 'Brother, wait up.' Cuong stopped in mid-stride. Catching him up Hien said, 'I've an idea.'

'What's on your mind?'

'For some time now I've suspected that the commandant has not been giving us our full allocation of food. The guards get much more than us. So much that they daily carry buckets of left-over rice and vegetables over to the pig house. It's obscene that the commandant's pig should eat better than us.'

Cuong shrugged. 'I'm sure you're right, but what can we do about it?'

'I've been trying to think of a way to make Dung's wedding ceremony more like a real celebration. Think on it brother. What do we normally do in preparation for a wedding?'

Cuong puckered his brow. 'We butcher a pig.'

'Not *a* pig, *the* pig.'

Hien watched as Cuong's mouth gave a faint quiver then slowly spread into a broad grin. 'You know I really fancy a bowlful of pork slices with a chunk of crispy fat. I haven't eaten a full meal since the night we celebrated with Thanh and Lan at your sister's house.'

'We'll need help, but I don't want to involve Dung. I thought if you and I tackle the business of the pig we could ask Long to keep a watch for us.'

As Ha slipped the pants of her bridal *ao dai* over her rounded tummy, a feeling of sadness overwhelmed her. Huong must have noticed the change in her expression because she rushed over and put her arms around her. 'What is it, little sister?' Ha tried to force a smile but her lips only quivered as tear drops rolled down her cheeks.

She'd come close to telling Dung that the child inside her might not be his, but always as she was about to speak something warned her to stay quiet. She wondered now if her silence wasn't cowardly and dishonest. If he knew, Dung might regard her as contaminated and not the worthy bride he considered her to be. Until that moment she'd always felt there was no one she could confide in. Her own parents had died several years ago and she had been largely left to raise herself. Although she admired her brother's ability to get on well within the communist system, he had never taken much notice of her. The loneliness and hurt had been so deep that she had always kept her feelings hidden. It was only in Dung's presence that her loneliness lifted and she felt a lightness of spirit. If she lost him she couldn't imagine how she would survive.

Huong brushed the hair away from Ha's face. 'Oh, child, whatever could be wrong?'

'Can I trust you . . . share something so terrible?' Eyes brimming with tears, Ha lurched forward. Wrapping her arms tightly around Huong's shoulders, she clung to Huong as though she were her own dear mother come back to be with her on her wedding day.

'Oh my dear. It pains my heart to see you so unhappy, today of all days. What's wrong, my love?'

It was several minutes before Ha felt able to speak. Looking round anxiously to make sure they were alone, she leaned back towards Huong. 'No one knows about this.' Ha lowered her eyes and fixed her attention on her clasped hands, her knuckles shining white through her stretched pale skin. 'When Dung was arrested I went to the police station. I thought I could trade my brother's Honda for Dung's release. My brother would have been furious to find his Honda gone, but I promised myself I would find a way to earn the money to pay him back.' Ha hesitated. Even admitting her intention to steal her brother's bike now seemed despicable. Closing her eyes as though to pull a shutter down on the shame, she sighed deeply before continuing. 'The situation was desperate, you see. I knew it was only a matter of time before the police would look into Dung's activities on the border. Maybe Hien told you, but the two of them regularly took trips to the border to dig up landmines to sell the gunpowder to the fishermen.' From the puzzled expression on Huong's face it was obvious Hien hadn't told her. 'What they did was very dangerous and if the authorities ever found out their lives wouldn't be worth living. Because in the end the communists always find out about everything.'

Huong nodded. 'Yes. It would not have taken them long to investigate Dung's life history. When they start asking questions there's always someone who can be bribed or threatened into giving information. But, what prompted them to arrest him in the first place?'

'When Cuong deserted and fled to Hien's home he was desperate to make contact with his wife so Dung went to fetch her. She'd barely arrived when she told Cuong that she'd given all of their savings to an old soothsayer. Cuong went crazy and took off with Hien to the soothsayer's village to get the money. Dung went after them to calm things down but he was too late. There was a fight, but when Dung arrived Hien and Cuong had already fled. Dung didn't know where they were so he went back home. That's when they arrested him. Of course they just wanted to stop him warning his brother.' Ha looked directly into Huong's eyes. 'You do see I had no choice?'

'You were right to get Dung out. And now you feel guilty toward your brother?'

Ha opened her eyes wide. Then it dawned on her that Huong had misunderstood. She shook her head slowly. 'I think I could live with the thought of being a thief because my intention was to pay my brother back tenfold.' The tears began to roll more urgently down her face. 'The old policeman didn't want the bike. He said everyone knew the Honda belonged to Tuan.' Ha hesitated. To speak the words of what she had done. . . .

Huong grasped her hands. Her eyes glistened. 'We're sisters, little one. My own marriage was not a happy one . . . it was a marriage of convenience, although I came to care about my husband after a manner, but if Hien . . . of course since I am a widow I would never dare express my feelings toward him, but if Hien were to be in prison I would gladly give my body to save him.'

Ha felt a sudden surge of blood rush to her head. 'You understand. You don't think I'm a street girl?'

A gentle smile spread over Huong's face. Taking out her handkerchief she wiped the tears from Ha's cheeks. 'What a ridiculous thought. You're as innocent and lovely as the new blossoms on the trees.'

Ha sniffed back the tears. 'But it's more than my virginity I lost. What if . . . what if?' The awful possibility that the baby growing inside her might be from the seed of Sergeant Vu repulsed her. Then the shame of having deliberately encouraged intimacy with Dung so as to protect herself and her child. . . .

'The baby inside you is Dung's.'

'But, it might not be.'

Huong suddenly looked stern. 'The old man's sperm has dried up. Dung is young and virile. The chances of it being the policeman's are so slim and besides, this child is innocent of any crime. You must never think of it that way.'

'I thought of telling Dung.'

'Why? To make him feel guilty?'

Ha was aghast. 'No.'

'If you tell Dung of your sacrifice, he will have to live with the guilt of what the beast did to you. It will cause him endless suffering. Can't you see that?' Placing her fingers under Ha's chin Huong raised her face so their eyes were level. 'Child, be proud of your courage in taking action to save the one you love. If you had done otherwise, Dung would almost certainly be in prison. Casting doubt on the baby's ancestry serves no one. Our Creator gave you this child. Trust in Him.' Ha relaxed. What Huong was saying made sense. 'Now wash your face and let me rub some red die into your cheeks. When I'm finished, you'll look like a goddess'

Pushing his way through the crowd of well-wishers who'd gathered in the compound, Dung could no longer stand the tension. Half an hour had passed since the time they had agreed on. It wasn't that time was normally of importance to him, but Ha had seemed so strange since Mrs Kieu's outburst that he worried she might have changed her mind.

Snatching hold of his shirt sleeve, Hien pulled him back into the shade. 'You're working up a sweat, little brother. It makes people anxious. It makes me anxious. Just stand still. They'll be here in a minute.'

'But I am anxious.'

'Then join us in our game of poker?'

'Why's she taking so long? Do you think she's changed her mind? Can you go and find out from Huong what the matter is?'

Hien laughed. 'Nothing's the matter. It's not like she's run away or eloped with someone else. This is a special day and she'll want to look her best.'

Dung turned to face Hien. 'She can't look her best in here.'

'Don't be so sure. A lot of things can be obtained when one has a mind for it.'

'Nice clothes, make-up. The sort of things a woman expects when she gets married. I don't think so. Even the grass round the commandant's hut struggles to show itself and when it does appear, it's never a lush green colour. Everything. . . .' Just as Dung was speaking, Ha walked out of the long family hut. She was radiant. Forgetting what he was about to say, Dung caught his breath.

Dressed in a pale silk *ao dai*, with threads of gold spun through it, Ha looked everything a bride should be. The sunlight shimmering off her shirt, shone like ripples across a golden pond. Dung let his jaw drop. He was so overcome by his feelings that all he could do was smile gormlessly. His fears of the past week vanished into the pool of sunlight. He couldn't imagine anything evil ever touching them again. Walking towards her he extended his arms and drew her to him. 'How is it possible that such beauty can blossom in a place like this?'

Smiling, Ha briefly turned her face toward Huong. 'The *ao dai* was a gift from the women of Dong Hung. Huong arranged for one of the guards wives to purchase the silk from Nan Ning market and made the garment up herself.'

'The *ao dai* is stunning, but it's your beauty which leaves me speechless. Yesterday you looked so pale and drawn and I cursed myself for ever having brought you here. Today. . . .'

'Today . . .' smiled Ha, 'I'm no longer the pitiful creature I was before, running into hysterics because of some silly ghost locust. Today I'm worthy to be your wife. If you still want me.'

Dung gulped. 'Want you! I want you more than anything else in the world. Even the prospect of freedom pales in comparison for my wanting you. You will be my wife today and always.'

Without any of the formal requirements of the fulfillment of a long-standing contract between two families, the ceremonial service was performed by Mr Kien. He was neither a priest nor a government official, but as the oldest member of the community and considered by many to be the wisest, he was the natural choice. When people wished to voice their troubles it was to him they turned. The son of a mandarin, he'd once been a reputable doctor, who after treating the sick child of a blacklisted family at the expense of ignoring a call from a senior cadre, fell foul of the authorities.

'This is a happy day for Dung and Ha to get married,' said Mr Kien. 'We are prisoners in a foreign land and although we do not have all the trappings for a wedding as we would in our motherland, we do have an abundance of love and friendship. We have dignity and despite the harshness of our living conditions our integrity remains intact.' Mr Kien turned toward Hien. 'Hien, as the representative of Dung's family I invite you to speak on his behalf.'

Hien stepped forward. 'Since the loss of our father during the American war I have taken on a father's responsibility toward Dung. I have always felt proud of him. He has the qualities of the poet I never possessed. This ceremony quite simply and honestly recognises the union of love which has long existed between Dung and Ha.'

'Since neither of Ha's parents are living I invite Huong to be her representative,' said Mr Kien.

Huong stood beside Ha. 'It is an honour for me to be Ha's representative and to take my place with this family. Dung and Ha are both special people within our community. Ha is not only gentle, but in all truthfulness I can say that Ha is the most courageous and loyal human being that I have ever known. I wish Dung and Ha the greatest happiness known to man.'

'Let us exchange the betel-nut,' said Mr Kien. There was no precious betel-nut — the bitter sweet nut traditionally chewed at weddings — only coconut, but the substitution wasn't noticed by anyone, least of all Dung. It was the most magical moment in his life. When the frenzied clapping reached the crescendo of a thousand fire-crackers shattering the stillness of the air, Dung drew Ha into his arms and kissed her. He couldn't imagine a better wedding.

After the noise abated Dung and Ha turned first toward Mr Kien and bowing their heads expressed their thanks. They then turned toward Hien and Huong. 'Thank-you, elder brother and elder sister.' Turning once again Dung clasped Ha's hands and raised them up. 'We both especially want to thank you all for making this dangerous journey into China just so that you could share this special day with us.' Laughter spread through the gathering of well-wishers. Hien picked up the guitar he'd borrowed from one of the young men and as he strummed out the melodic threads of an old Vietnamese love song, Dung swung Ha away from the crowds and danced around the compound with her. The children were the first to join them. Then as the music became infectious, it seemed that everyone joined in. Even the guards from the watchtower relaxed as they clapped and cheered whenever Dung and Ha came into their sight.

By late afternoon, the dancers thinned. Seeing that Ha was tiring, Dung led her over to the shade. 'You must take a rest. I don't want my wife to ever say I don't take of her.'

'Your wife will never have cause to say that. You are the best husband ever.' As they sat underneath the overhang of the thatched roofing Ha looked around her. 'Where's everyone gone?'

'We outlasted them.'

'And me with child to.'

'Huong was right. You may look delicate, but underneath you have the strength and courage of a Sumo wrestler.'

'A Sumo wrestler!'

'Underneath. On top you are as beautiful as the immortal mother of our people. She laid all of the eggs from which our ancestors hatched.'

Ha burst into laughter. 'Stop before you say another word. First I'm a big fat man with a protruding belly, then I'm a chicken only good for laying eggs.' Dung ran his fingers over Ha's silk *ao dai.* It was such a rare occurrence to find themselves alone. Gently slipping his hand under the shirt he felt to see if their son was kicking. Ha slipped her hand on top of his. 'Dung, we are going to have such a good life together. This child will be just the first of our children. After him there will be sons and daughters until our house is so full of laughter that there won't be room for any of the past bad things. Our memories of Dong Hung will shrink down to this one wonderful day.'

When Dung noticed Hien beckoning to them from the family dormitory he withdrew his hand quickly and stood up. 'We'd better see what Hien wants.'

As they entered the dormitory a chorus of cheers rang out. Seeing the surprise and happiness shining through Ha's eyes Dung wondered why the idea to arrange a marriage ceremony hadn't come to him sooner. The dreary days at Dong Hung had seemed endless and now, suddenly, there was so much to look forward to that he felt overwhelmed with joy. Pushing his way forward Hien thrust a bowl into each of their hands. Dung was amazed. 'What!' The bowl was full of huge chunks of roast pig. 'Where did all this come from?'

Hien laughed. 'Look over at the table. There's rice, salad, fish sauce. Everything the palate desires. And that's not all. Here, take a swig of this.' Hien stuck a mug into Dung's free hand. 'Go on. Drink it.'

As Dung let the scorching liquid slip down his gullet tears sprang to his eyes. 'I can't believe any of this. My brother, my friends, how can I express my. . . .'

'Think nothing of it. We brewed the wine ourselves out of fermented rice. The pig, by the way, is a gift from the commandant. He says he hopes you will be very happy and have many children.'

Ha opened her eyes wide. 'Really!'

'Well, I wouldn't say "really" exactly, but enjoy — the day is yours.'

The gift from the commandant did not go unnoticed. Within two days of the ceremony, the camp inmates were ordered into the compound. Putting his arm protectively around Ha's waist Dung watched the commandant as he paraded up and down with his dogs, waiting for everyone to assemble.

When all of the inmates were assembled and the whispers had died down, a morbid silence descended over the group. 'I am not pleased. I have treated you fairly.' At his remarks a rumble of discontent rose up, hardly perceptible at first, but which gained in momentum. 'I have treated you fairly,' repeated the commandant with greater force.

Dung watched anxiously as Mr Kien stepped out of the crowd and approached the commandant. 'You say you have treated us fairly, yet you steal the food from our mouths. We have all grown thin since we came here. Look at our broken teeth because of lack of calcium, look at the sunken figures of our old people. Our children frequently have dysentery because the water is dirty. You promised to make arrangements for us to go to the free country, yet we hear nothing of our fate. We wait here in this prison, day in day out, wasting our lives away.' The quiet authority with which Mr Kien spoke was evident to everyone, including, Dung suspected, the commandant. Hushed murmurs of approval rolled through the crowd as they anticipated the commandant's response.

'Nguyen Son Kien, I have known you to be a trouble-maker for a long time, but I have been tolerant. I can be tolerant no longer. As the representative of your group, I hold you responsible for the theft of my pig.' Dung gasped and threw a hurried look toward Hien. At a nod from the commandant two of the guards walked toward Mr Kien as though to arrest him. Several of the young men near Mr Kien came to his defence and blocked the guards from approaching. A piercing, deafening bang split the air as the commandant fired his gun, stunning the crowd into sudden stillness. 'Any more trouble and I shall order my men to fire into you, not above you as I have done. I cannot promise that your children will not accidentally be in the line of fire. If they die, it is you who are responsible.'

Mr Kien waved the young men away and gave himself over to the guards' custody. As they were about to lead him away Hien pushed his way toward the commandant. 'I stole your pig. You have no reason to arrest the old man.' Before the commandant had time to respond, Cuong and Long had also come forward and stood resolutely beside Hien.

'The three of us stole the pig together. Nguyen Son Kien knew nothing about it,' protested Cuong.

As Dung gripped Ha's hand he swallowed hard. There was little doubt that Hien and the others had stolen the pig, but they had done it for him.

Dung let go of Ha's hand and rushed forward. 'They didn't steal the pig. I did.'

The commandant stared at him. Then Loc stepped forward, followed by Duyen. Within minutes all the young men of the camp were claiming to have stolen the pig. Ha stepped in front of Dung. 'It was me stole the pig. I need to eat protein for my baby.'

In an impromptu chorus the children jumped up and began to chant. 'We stole the pig. We stole the pig.'

The commandant's face looked ready to explode. 'Have it your way. If you wish me to punish you I will, but don't imagine you can humiliate me. You are dependent on my good will until the time when China and Vietnam repair their relationships. Australia, Canada, Britain have all rejected your applications for refugee status. They no more want you than I do. You will all be returned to Vietnam as soon as negotiations between our two countries can be resumed. Regrettably for all of us, that may take years.' The commandant's words hit like a bombshell.

'Take the three men and Nguyen Son Kien to the lock up. The rest of you can go back to the dormitories and ponder your own fates. There will be no outside activities today. And for anyone who has thoughts of stealing from me again, the special punishment I intend giving out to these three thieves will stand as an example for you.' At his words Dung felt the happiness and confidence of the last two days evaporate and in its place a sense of dread descended.

There were no obvious signs of Ha being ready to give birth for several weeks more. Dung could almost have been happy — it was only the knowledge that his brother and friends were still caged in the monkey houses that dampened his relief at the late arrival of the child. Dung didn't know what had triggered it or when the idea had first come to him, but for some weeks he'd known that maybe, just maybe the baby inside Ha wasn't his own. The information had collected in his head in little pieces. Then as the puzzle fitted together, he'd began to see the pattern of it. Slowly, because when the initial trickles of it entered his consciousness he'd not wanted to believe, but then as the pieces fell in to place it had become increasingly hard for him to deny it.

First there had been the morning of his release from the police station. He'd accepted it so easily at the time, but looking back wasn't it an unlikely event? Then when he'd gone to her home, Tuan was in his sleeping shorts, but Ha was already showered. With her wet hair dangling from her shoulders she'd been so vulnerable. He'd felt it in every fibre of his body. There was no reason for her to be up so early and she'd known better than any of them that the danger wasn't gone. It was only her insistence of danger that had panicked him when the police jeeps came. And why would the police let him go only to try to re-arrest him? A game of cat and mouse? No, it was a matter of missed communication. Sergeant Vu had acted of his own volition.

Sergeant Vu . . . the memory of him made Dung want to vomit. It was too painful to think he might have touched her. But that's how it must have been. At the border, before crossing into Vietnam, they'd made love. It was his first time. He'd believed it was Ha's first time. He wouldn't have done it — he had too much respect for her, but Ha had insisted. She said if she were to die crossing into China she wanted to know him first. To know him so intimately that their souls would be forever bound to each other as ghost lovers. He'd been aroused by her touching him. There was no way he could have cautioned her — to have even suggested that maybe what they were doing was dangerous because soldiers could come upon them any moment. It was the danger which stimulated their passion. He'd loved her so much it was frightening to bear the intensity of it. Still loved her — the tears trickled down Dung's face — loved her even more because of her sacrifice. How could he ever repay her, protect her from anything bad ever happening again?

He closed his eyes hoping to see something bright in their future. The baby was his. He knew it. It was enough to keep him going. To be a father was one of the greatest joys a man could know. And soon, today or tomorrow maybe, Hien would be released from the monkey house. The beatings, their ordeal of being penned up in the small cages with no place to defecate except their own space was an indescribable humiliation. Dung was also inclined to believe the rumours that Mr Kien had been pushed back across the Vietnamese border at gun point. Since the time of the arrests, he'd seen that the commandant was far more disturbed by Mr Kien's criticisms of his running of the camp, than by the loss of his pig.

Seeing Ha approaching, Dung jumped up to greet her. 'How's our baby today?'

'He's fine.'

'He?'

'Yes, he. Really, I'm not that big yet so maybe I wasn't pregnant as early as I thought I was.'

'He'll come when he's ready.' Dung drew her toward him. 'And I'll love him whenever he comes. I'll love him as I love you. Forget about the superstitions, the ghost locust. One day we'll escape from this place. We'll put Vietnam, China, all of this behind us. We'll make a good life for ourselves and. . . .'

Huong rushed into the dormitory. 'Dung, quickly. The guards have released them. They need your help because they can't walk properly.' Dung planted a kiss on Ha's face and ran out of the hut after Huong.

Outside, several young men had already gathered and were half-lifting, half-dragging Hien, Cuong and Long over to the single men's dormitory. Dung pushed his way through and drew Hien's arm over his shoulder. 'Let me help you, brother.' Hien's weight was negligible and it worried Dung that after a month they could have become so skeletal. 'Several of us have been talking and we've agreed to give up part of our food ration to get you back into shape.'

'Just make sure you don't feed us pig,' said Cuong. 'I'm a little bit off eating pig right now.'

Hien stopped as Ha rushed toward him. She looked like she wanted to fling her arms around him but then her shyness clouded her face, and she stopped just short of him. 'Little sister, I expected to be an uncle by now. Why is my nephew taking so long?'

Ha beamed at him and patted her belly. 'Not yet elder brother. I miscalculated. See how small I still am. There's at least another month to go.'

Ha screamed and sat bolt upright in her bunk. Dung realised it was the shots which had woken her. At the first sound of the siren and the dogs barking he'd awakened and known instantly that Long must have chosen tonight as his time to escape. Since being released from the monkey house, Long had told of his intention to escape. He'd wanted Hien and Cuong to go with him, but Hien had argued that they were not in good enough shape to contemplate an escape, and he wouldn't escape until Ha and the baby were strong enough to accompany them.

Ha was now fully awake, wide eyed and trembling. Pulling her to him, Dung kissed her eye lids. 'Go back to sleep, darling. It's nothing.'

'I heard shots.' Then as the realization dawned across her face, 'Long. Oh my God.'

'Long was stupid. To escape, you have to have a plan. He wouldn't even wait for a moonless night. When we go Ha, we'll do it properly.' Dung was as shaken by the shots as was Ha, and the confidence he spoke with was faked. Long's had been the first escape attempt in the camp: his failure had probably cost him his life and jeopardised any further attempts by the others. The guards would now be prepared for them to follow. There was nothing to keep them any more. Since the announcement of their return to Vietnam, the commandant must have known there would be escape attempts; maybe it was even his plan to have them try. A single man on his own, with the element of surprise, probably had as good a chance as any of success. What chance had he, with a wife and baby?

Pulling the blanket over them, Dung coaxed Ha to lie back down. 'Lie down, darling. We must sleep.' He was glad of the darkness in the long hut. There were tears in his eyes that he didn't want his wife to see.

<hr>

Ha gave birth to her son, Tran Van Diep, five weeks after the night of Long's escape. The child looked so much like Dung, even down to the crooked slant of his little fingers, that the thrill of being a father for the first time occupied most of his thoughts. It wasn't until Huong pointed out that Ha's bleeding was going on for too long, and she wasn't making the kind of recovery one could expect after a normal delivery, that Dung took note of the dark rings round Ha's eyes and the hollowness of her cheeks.

'You look tired, my sweet. Huong says you must rest more. Let us take care of little Diep while you sleep.'

Although weakened by the birth, Ha was reluctant to pass Diep over and pulled him closer to her. 'No. I must keep him near my breast otherwise he won't get enough nourishment.' Her eyes looked wild and frightened. 'My milk is running dry and little Diep doesn't even cry any more to complain.'

Dung was at a loss as to what to do or say. He regretted that Mr Kien was no longer in the camp and looked over towards Huong for support. Huong immediately pulled herself from her bunk and came over. 'Sister, it's not so unusual for a mother's milk to dry up. Your body's not making enough milk because you're tired. Dung's right. Let us hold Diep while you get some rest.'

Reluctantly Ha passed Diep over to Huong as Dung placed himself beside her and stroked her hair. 'You sleep now, darling. Diep is in safe hands. I'll stay beside you.'

Several days passed with little sign of Ha showing any recovery. On the fourth day, standing out of earshot of where Ha was sleeping, Huong beckoned Dung over to him. 'This isn't normal. You must go to the commandant and demand he send for a doctor.' Huong hesitated. The lines on her face looked strained making her appear older than her twenty four years. 'I'm afraid for her, Dung. Really afraid.'

The commandant was reluctant to call in a doctor, but after Dung threatened to find a way to inform the Red Cross of conditions in the camp, the commandant adopted a more congenial tone and promised he would send for someone. But as the days passed without any sign of a doctor, Dung doubted that he intended keeping his word. Each day he marched into his office and demanded to know when the doctor was coming. The commandant was clearly irritated but the reply was always the same. 'The doctor's busy. She'll come when she can.'

By the third week it was clear that unless the commandant acceded to Dung's request, Ha was not going to recover. Dung marched into his office. He no longer cared what happened to him. If Ha died, his life was ended anyway. Marching round the commandant's desk he snatched hold of his shirt and pulled the commandant to his feet. 'My wife is dying, and it's your fault.' Dung had barely time to register the surprise on the commandant's face before he found himself in an arm lock, but as the two guards attempted to hoist him out of the office Hien, Cuong and a party of about thirty or forty inmates began pushing their way through the door.

'We demand proper medical care,' said Hien. 'If Mrs Ha isn't seen by a doctor this morning then not only will we force our way out of here and take her to a hospital ourselves, but we'll also see to it that the International Red Cross and United Nations hear of the way you treat asylum-seekers. Even your own men are ashamed. If Mrs Ha dies all the newspapers around the world will know about it.'

The commandant looked momentarily confused, but then deciding that it was probably better not to let the situation escalate, he signalled to his guards to release Dung. 'It isn't my fault that the doctor's busy. I see now that Mrs Ha must be very ill, so of course she will receive medical care. In fact this morning I already sent one of my men to fetch her. She will be here within the hour. Go back to your dormitory quietly.'

When the doctor finally arrived, Dung viewed her with suspicion. Although she made a cursory examination of Ha, Dung felt she was at a loss as to what she should do next. After several minutes of looking at the faces anxiously scrutinising her, she took a syringe from her bag and proceeded to give Ha an injection.

'What's wrong with her?' asked Huong.

'She probably has an infection in her womb. I can't tell exactly, but you can give her two of these tablets, every six hours for ten days. Either she'll recover or she won't.'

Dung was upon her in seconds. Shaking her by the shoulders he shouted, 'Is that it, you stupid old vet. Is that all you're going to do? Isn't it obvious she needs to go to the hospital?'

Hien quickly pulled Dung away from the doctor as one of the guards, alerted by the shouting, strode purposefully towards the dormitory. The doctor glared at him. 'There are sick people in the hospital. She's so vulnerable to disease that if I took her there, just how long do you think she'd survive? I've given her the best antibiotic medicine there is. These are expensive drugs, so count yourself lucky I can even supply them to you. Keep bathing her face with a wet cloth to get her temperature down.'

Dung still wanted to tear her throat out. Only Hien's restraining hand on his arm and the presence of the guard persuaded him it was better to stay calm than to risk being locked up in one of the monkey houses where he wouldn't be able to nurse Ha.

No one seemed to know why Ha died, least of all Dung. He could not shake the feeling that maybe the old woman was right and that he had been responsible for her death by capturing the bad luck of the ghost locust. During the night she had slipped as silently into death as she had borne the treachery of her sacrifice for him without complaint or accusation.

When the commandant gave instructions to the guards to place Ha's body on a stone slab a few feet outside of the camp because he did not know if she was diseased, Dung set up his lonely vigil by the fence. With a pile of stones at his feet he sat staring through the wire mesh as though he were a corpse himself. It was only when stray dogs ventured near to Ha's body that he leapt up and began screaming obscenities while barraging them with stones. His aim was good, and as the dogs scattered in wild panic, several were yelping.

Even though the fence was a restricted area the guards did not approach Dung and when evening curfew came, they went about their duty as though he was not there. It was only when Huong came out with some food and a blanket that they showed some concern. However, after some discussion amongst themselves they agreed that she could stay with him for half an hour.

'Dung, Hien sent me out with some food. You have to eat. Ha wouldn't want you to suffer.' Dung heard her words and didn't hear them. It was as though the voice was far away and somehow not connected with him. 'You're a father now. For Diep's sake, if not your own, you must eat and keep your strength up. One day all of us will escape from here and you will bring your son up to be a fine young man.'

At the sound of Diep's name Dung lifted his head. 'He was my son, you know. Ha and I both knew that.'

'He is your son. Dung, your son is alive and there is absolutely no doubt as to who his father is. Look at the timing of his birth. And he even looks like you.'

'I feel him slipping away. She'll take him with her because this world isn't good enough for him. It isn't good enough for either of them.'

Huong let out an anguished sob. 'Oh, Dung.' Tears streamed down her face. His own dry eyes felt parched, and he wished he could release some of the emotion trapped inside him. It was as though he was dead too. 'Please eat some food. Fight for your son. Fight for your survival. What else is there to do? The world isn't all bad. We just have to find a place where we can all be together and know peace.'

'Is there really such a place, sister?'

'Oh yes. Ha knew that. She was so strong and brave. If she were here she wouldn't let you think so negatively. Please Dung, I beg you, eat some food for Ha and little Diep. You have to keep your vision of freedom for them.'

On the day of the funeral, it was raining. The dampness seemed to penetrate into Dung's heart as though the heavens were crying out in shame at Ha's untimely death. Three days had passed before the wood for the coffin had been delivered, and having slept very little during that time, Dung was beside himself with grief and fatigue. He could barely register that less than two months ago he had sworn his undying love to Ha and guided her around the compound as they danced to the melody of a love song.

The commandant had said that only Dung and a small group of women and children were to be allowed up the mountain to bury Ha's body. Since Long's escape he was wary, and to allow any more than that, he said, constituted a security risk. Hien in any event would not have been allowed out. His own guards would assist Dung in carrying the coffin.

Before raising the coffin, Dung helped Huong wrap a waterproof cape, given to him by one of the guards, around Diep. 'Keep him dry for me, Huong.'

'He's as precious to me as my own child Tuyet.'

Everyone took great care negotiating the path up the mountain, for the steps carved into the red soil had partially disintegrated with the rain. It was a steep climb even for a man who was fit and of their small party of ten, only the three guards were in good health. As the guards assisted him with the coffin they could not have been more considerate. Since Ha's death, Dung could feel that their mood had changed towards him. It was as though they experienced Dung's loss as their own. When Dung lost his footing they quickly shifted the weight of the coffin to their own shoulders.

Tuyet and her two friends trailed after Huong and Mrs Yen in sombre silence. On any other day, leaving the camp and climbing the mountain would have been a journey into freedom which all of them would have experienced with the profound joy only the prisoner can truly know, but today there was no joy, only a sense of dread as to what else was to come.

Before the coffin was laid into the ground, Huong asked the guards if they might place a banana plant into Ha's arms. None among them needed to ask the meaning of her request. It was on all of their minds that Ha should not be buried without anything to cradle. When the senior guard granted permission, Dung took the spade over to a nearby shrub and dug it out by its roots.

Kneeling down beside Ha, Dung placed the plant into her arms. 'Here you are, young spirit. Embrace this plant as you would your own child. I know of this world's wrongdoing to you and your fears for our child, but please leave Diep for me to love.'

Overcome by emotion, Dung stepped back as one of the guards nailed the lid back on and lowered the coffin into the ground. With Diep held protectively in his arms, Dung stood beside the grave and gratefully accepted Huong's offer to speak some words for Ha. 'Ha brought beauty into all of our lives. She enriched the lives of the camp children with her gentleness and sense of fun. For me she was the little sister I left behind in our motherland. When I felt lonely and homesick, it was Ha who lifted my spirits by her cheery words of comfort.' With tears glistening in her eyes Huong glanced toward Dung. 'And I know for Dung she was the love of his life. We shall all miss her by no small measure. We cannot bring her back, but maybe we can take encouragement from the time we shared together and be inspired by her courage and generosity of spirit.' Huong set her hands as though in prayer and bowed her head. 'Good-bye sister.'

Dung was shaking when the guard gently coaxed him away from the grave side. 'I'm sorry brother, but the clouds are darkening. Heavy rain could come and I have a responsibility to return you safely to camp.' As the guards threw soil over the coffin, Dung stood desolate unable to contemplate a future without Ha. It was only when he felt his young son's breath warm against his chin that he dared pray for their future.

It was as they feared. In spite of constant nursing and the baby food supplied by the commandant, Diep died two days after Ha was buried. Dung believed his son's spirit had departed with his mother and that it was only his body which lingered on. From the time of Ha's death the baby had shown no interest in food and had lain listless — neither asleep nor properly awake. Dung wondered if Ha, having lost sight of their hope of a bright future, had foreseen that a baby of such innocence could not thrive in a cruel world and that she had forfeited her own life in order to go ahead and prepare his entry into the spirit world.

The second excursion up the mountain was even more painful than the first. Since Ha's death, a constant rain had drizzled over the camp and the paths were treacherous. This time, only Dung and Huong, besides two guards, were allowed up the mountain to bury Diep. Dung cradled the tiny child in his arms as he ascended the steep slope. He felt the lightness of the linen wrapped body contrasting starkly with the enormous weight bearing down into his heart. The red soil running between his toes was like his life blood draining away. Gone was his joy of adventure and story telling. All that remained of the seventeen-year-old boy who fell in love with the girl from his village, was guilt and regret.

At the grave, Dung stooped and removed the banana plant and placed Diep into Ha's arms. 'Here, my lovely wife. Take our son. You are both free, free of this world's wrongdoings. Fly away, little spirits. Fly free for all of us.'

Chapter 9: Exit Dong Hung

6th August 1983 to 7th May 1984

A rose blossoms, and then fades.
It blooms and withers heedlessly.
But its sweetness the prison cell pervades
To arouse our deep-felt bitterness.
All the world's injustices
Shriek within the prisoner's heart.

PRISON DIARY, HO CHI MINH

DUNG STIRRED INTO WAKEFULNESS. The night felt unusually heavy, so he swung his legs over the side of his bunk and took himself outside. It was rare for him to sleep through the night, and since Ha's death almost two-and-a-half years ago he had taken to roaming the camp at nights. Other than Hien and his close friends, the camp inmates referred to him behind his back as the 'Ghost Locust'. The name didn't bother Dung. His grief was beyond their whisperings, and he knew that the name was not spoken out of malice but from their pity and fear of him. His gaunt appearance and night-time wanderings did little to change their opinion that Dung, now half-alive and half-dead, was indeed mad. Even the guards ignored his blatant indifference to the curfew laws imposed on the rest of the camp inmates.

Dung was not, however, indifferent to Hien's wish to include him in their escape plans. He hated to contest him, but he just couldn't contemplate leaving Dong Hung. Several other young men had made their escapes, although whether they had been successful or not, no one was sure. It bothered him most that Hien was probably delaying his escape because he hoped one day to persuade Dung to go with them. The endless drudgery of their daily life would persuade any sane person that the risks were worth it.

Dung didn't know what compelled him to stay or what compelled him to wander. He thought maybe the whisperings that rolled down the mountain every evening and early morning possessed him. The murmuring hushed voices that he could not quite hear. And there were other ghosts besides Ha and Diep. He could feel them all around him. The things people said of him were true. He was partially immersed in the world of spirits and if he could just take that extra step he'd gladly join them.

Outside the dormitory the air was less heavy. It blew around in gusty onslaughts whipping its way under the thatched roofs and lifting the straw from its anchorage. Dung knew that the storm coming would be no ordinary storm and anticipated its arrival eagerly. The ghosts were revolting against the continuous onslaught of injustice. They were lashing out at Dong Hung in anger — tearing into the buildings and tugging at the wire fencing with the full hatred of their imprisonment. Because that's what it was about. The sacrifice of Ha and Diep hadn't been enough to bring about any real sympathy from the commandant, so while the agony of the camp inmates deepened, the ghosts felt ordained to the earth in a holy tryst.

The new arrival of asylum-seekers who, having failed in their bid to get to Hong Kong, were sent to Dong Hung, told of reports in the Vietnamese newspapers of the separate arrests of Nguyen Son Kien and Pham Van Long on charges of spying for China. The trials had received much publicity. Nguyen Son Kien had been sentenced to ten years, while Pham Van Long, who had been implicated in more serious acts of espionage, had been given a sentence of fifteen years. The Vietnamese authorities now knew of the Dong Hung camp and regarded it as a training base for spies. While there was no way forward there was also no way back, and the ghosts grew ever more restless.

As the sky darkened bringing with it a blanket of rain, Dung could feel his excitement overwhelm him. Running into the rain he let its wetness wash him. The graves were opening as the spirits rose out of them and in huge white swirling mists yelled and shouted as they pounded into the compound. Dung called out to Ha and Diep. He hadn't cried for over two years but as he felt their love soak into him he fell down to his knees and sobbed. 'I've waited for so long and now you are here.'

Huong woke to the sound of rain pounding into the thatched roof. A sweet musky smell of weeds hung in the air, and despite the high humidity she shivered. She pulled herself onto her knees and searched round the bunk to understand the reason for her discomfort. Her clothes were soaking and when she ran her hands over the rush matting, she found it was sodden with the rain. Tuyet was still sleeping soundly, but even in the dim lighting Huong could see that the rain was dripping through the roof straight onto her body. She tried to shift Tuyet away from drips but there was nowhere large enough that was any drier.

'She can sleep on my bunk. There's plenty of space and it's reasonably dry over here.' Huong looked up. It was her neighbour old Mrs Trinh.

'I'm sorry. Did I wake you?'

Mrs Trinh laughed. 'I hardly think so, daughter. Listen to this wind and rain. It's enough to wake the dead. Bring little Tuyet over here.'

Huong lifted the sleeping Tuyet over to Mrs Trinh's bed. 'Thank you.'

'Now where are you going to sleep? There's a dry spot here. Not much, I'm afraid,' said Mrs Trinh.

'I think a typhoon is heading our way.'

'Well we probably have a few hours before we really need to start worrying. Come and sit here. It'll be a squash but we'll manage. We might be grateful later on for these few extra hours of sleep.'

With her back pressed up against the wall, Huong let herself drift in and out of sleep. She was actually in quite a sound sleep when Hien's voice broke into her consciousness. 'There's a typhoon coming. We need to rouse everyone and get them to take proper shelter. The roofs on the dormitories are not going to hold, and if they collapse while anyone's underneath it could be fatal.' Huong forced her eyes to open as she took in the seriousness of Hien's words. Looking around, she wondered how she had ever managed to fall back to sleep. The wind was screaming around the dormitories and sounded ready to tear the place apart. Several children were crying as their parents dashed round in a state of confusion trying to tie down the shutters. The rain blasting in through gaps in the roofing had turned the impacted dirt floor into slime and collected in puddles in the low spots.

Cuong ran into the dormitory. 'We've okayed it with the guards — everyone's to gather in the kitchen. It's the only building of any substance. No one is to go alone. We must go in groups, holding on to one another and keeping as close to the buildings as possible. The children are to be carried by their fathers or one of the single men. And if anyone has dry blankets, they are to take them along as well.'

'Come on, let's get you and Tuyet out of here,' said Hien. He snatched Tuyet into his arms. Grinning he uttered a few remarks almost under his breath, 'It's as Cuong says, the fathers must carry their little ones.'

Huong wasn't quite sure that she really heard what he said. Over the years she and Hien had become close friends and he was always a wonderful uncle to Tuyet, but even though she sensed his strong attraction towards her, he'd never actually spoken romantically or suggested there could be anything more than friendship between them. As Hien carried Tuyet toward the doorway Huong clambered from the bunk ready to follow, but seeing the alarm in Mrs Trinh's face she stopped and reached out her hand. 'Come on, Mrs Trinh. You heard what they said, no one's to go alone. We must stay together and look after one another. We're all family in this place.'

Cuong took the lead, accompanied by several other families. Hien followed them with Tuyet clinging like a young monkey to his chest, while Huong positioned between him and Mrs Trinh, linked her arms tightly round both of them. With the rain battering against their bodies they edged their way along the buildings toward the kitchen. The distance wasn't far but the danger was still present. It wasn't the constant pressure of wind bearing into them which they were most afraid of; it was the sudden swirling gusts, with the strength to uproot a full grown tree, that threatened to hurtle them to their deaths should it pluck them from their course.

As the wind snatched at a shuttered window, and ripping it from its brackets hurtled it into the air, Huong screamed and loosened her grip on Hien's arm. Hien was swift to react and while still keeping hold of Tuyet he managed to get a firm hold on Huong's arm. Fortunately for Mrs Trinh she'd kept her grip on Huong's arm and the four of them stayed locked together as they braced themselves against further onslaughts from the wind. Keeping their heads bent forward they pushed their way through the torrential rain until they came to the side door of the kitchen building.

After the wildness outside, the kitchen seemed dry and secure, and as the crowds of wet, bedraggled bodies pushed their way in, Huong found a space near the wood kitchen stoves. 'We can all sit round here. It's quite cozy and there's plenty of space to stretch out.' However, it wasn't until they were comfortably seated that it occurred to Huong that Dung wasn't with them. She looked fruitlessly among the familiar faces to find him but he was no where to be seen.

Hien was settling Tuyet down with a dry blanket, when Huong walked over to him. 'Hien, I've been looking for your brother. Have you seen him?'

'No. He wasn't in the single men's dormitory earlier either. I assumed he was herding people over here with the rest of the single men, but as I look around, it seems like the bulk of our people are here now. I'll take another look before I check outside.'

Dung was sitting against the wire fencing when Hien ran over to him. 'For God's sake, brother. I've been looking everywhere for you. It's dangerous out here so everyone else has gathered in the kitchen.'

As he gripped the fencing, Dung partially registered the look of alarm on Hien's face, but he was feeling too preoccupied with his own world to give it much attention. 'They're here, brother. Don't you see them. They are going to tear this place right down to its foundation so that the misery of our lives will end.'

Hien snatched at the fence to stop himself being blown away. 'Who's here?'

'Ha, little Diep. I've seen them, felt their love swirling around me. But there are others, too. They speak to me of their sorrow. This storm isn't like other storms. It's theirs. Normally they only talk in whispers so you have to listen really hard, but today it's different. They have gathered up all of their anger and will pound it into the ground until our Chinese gaolers also hear them. Dong Hung is a prison built over a burial ground. This ground was sacred until they came with their guns and wire fences. It needs to be cleansed. Don't you see?'

'Yes, I see. But Ha doesn't want you to stay out here while the cleansing takes place. She wants you to take shelter with me.' Bracing himself against the wind, Hien reached his hand toward Dung. 'Please come, brother.'

'The storm won't hurt me.'

'Maybe not, but it might hurt me.'

Dung took one last look toward the mountain before pulling himself up to his feet. 'Yes. Soon she'll tell me what I have to do. In the meantime you and I can be together brother.' Grasping Hien's hand, he added 'Let's go brother. You shouldn't be out here. You'll get wet.'

'Get wet! I'm already soaked to the skin. What's left to get wet?'

When they entered the kitchen Huong ran up to meet them. 'Oh little brother, I was so worried about you. You look terrible.'

Dung was surprised by her concern. 'I'm fine sister. In fact I feel better than I've felt in years.'

'Both of you wrap yourselves up in a blanket and discard those wet clothes. Some of the women gained permission from the guards to organise soup. It's a bit on the thin side but it's hot. I'll fetch some for you while you change.'

Hien pulled Dung over to the wood stove where Cuong and Tuyet had saved a couple of old worn blankets for them. Picking up a blanket Hien shoved it into Dung's arms. 'Here pull off those wet things and put this around you. It's going to be a long noisy night so I doubt we'll get any sleep.'

When Huong arrived with the soup Dung accepted it from her and drank it down gratefully. Cuong magically conjured up a pack of playing cards and invited Hien and several other young men to join him in a game of poker. Declining their invitation Dung settled himself down against the brick stove. The chatter of young mothers as they soothed their children, the wind battering against the building were strangely comforting sounds and within half an hour he was fast asleep.

Huong sat outside the long hut and splashed water over Tuyet's small buttocks. It had been a over a month since the typhoon and one by one all the children had suffered from dysentery to some degree or other. Severe diarrhoea could cause them to become dehydrated very rapidly, and though no one wanted to speak openly about the possibility of further deaths, it was a becoming increasingly likely.

'How's our little peach flower this morning?' Tuyet was standing naked with beads of water running down her tanned skin. She grinned as Hien scooped up a handful of water from the bucket and splashed it onto her face.

'Mummy says I stink like a durian fruit.'

'Not any more you don't.' Huong straightened herself up. 'I'm angry. All the kids are having problems. Even me. We can't be expected to drink water like this. I've tried everything. Sieving it through stones and muslin, boiling it, nothing works.' Huong didn't usually like to complain, especially to Hien, but she was scared. Although it had been well over two years since Ha's and little Diep's death, it was always on her mind that the only way out of Dung Hung was in a box. 'I hate this place. Sometimes I think Dung is the only sane one among us.' Huong shook her head. 'Better to dream than to face this reality.'

'Then we escape.'

'How?'

'Cuong and I have been talking about it. Maybe there's a way.'

'Dung won't leave here.'

Hien sighed. 'Dung. Well that's really what's been holding us up. Maybe you can work on him, he listens to you as much as anyone.'

Huong felt a wave of despair. Even if it were that easy to escape, which she was sure it wasn't, she understood why Dung stayed. To ask him to move away from Ha's mountain would be like ripping out his soul. 'I'm not sure he really listens to what I say. Often I think he just humours me.' Huong regarded Dung's madness as a spiritual superiority. While they busied themselves with their daily drudgery, Dung roamed in another sphere. If he sprouted wings one day, and flew up into the clouds, it wouldn't have really surprised her. 'I couldn't ask him to leave. It has to come from him.'

'I know. We'll never mind that just now. Look what I have.' Hien produced a piece of tubing from his pocket, which Huong looked at, perplexed. 'There are all sorts of amazing things one can do with a tube.'

'Like what?'

'Like boiling water from one bucket, then letting it evaporate up the tube and drain into another bucket.'

It was all Huong could do to stop herself laughing outloud. 'This is so desperate that if I don't laugh I'll cry. It'll take ages to get clean water through that and what will you do for fuel? You'd need a forest.'

'Just look at all the debris around us.'

'That debris is our shelter.' Huong was exasperated. 'We're all going to die in this God-forsaken place aren't we?'

Hien looked serious. 'Some of the young men and I were talking about approaching the commandant this afternoon.'

'No. Let the others go. The commandant hates you.'

'I hate him, so that makes two of us. I can begin the conversation by saying, "We both agree we hate each other, so what else is there we can agree upon? How about us agreeing that the camp inmates need clean water."'

'Hien, stop it. The commandant is dangerous: we're powerless to go against him, you of all people should know that.' Seeing the lines deepen across Hien's forehead, Huong knew immediately that she had said the wrong thing. He was already turning away as she tried to cushion the harshness of her words. 'Your idea with the tube . . . I think it's a good one. How about I help you collect some debris for a fire?'

Hien stopped in mid-stride and briefly caught hold of her hands. 'I told you once that I would protect you and Tuyet. They weren't just words. The situation may look impossible, but I promise you I'll find a way for us all to be free. If it means whacking my brother over the head with a two by four and kidnapping him from this prison against his will, I'll do it.'

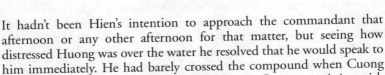

It hadn't been Hien's intention to approach the commandant that afternoon or any other afternoon for that matter, but seeing how distressed Huong was over the water he resolved that he would speak to him immediately. He had barely crossed the compound when Cuong called to him from outside the old guard house. Cuong was sitting with three of the single men, Tien, Lap and Duyen, under the shade of the building. 'Join us in a game of cards.'

Hien changed direction and walked over to them. 'You know all the kids are going down with dysentery. If this situation with the water continues, one if not all could be dead soon.'

Duyen looked up. 'It's that serious?'

'Yes. It's that serious. I was on my way to the commandant's office. We have to make some protest over this, it just isn't right.'

Cuong breathed in deeply. 'You're walking yourself straight into the monkey house. Have you thought this thing over.'

'What's to think over. Are we to let our children and old folk die. It's them who have no tolerance for this.'

Pulling himself up to his feet Cuong ran his fingers through his hair as though to straighten it up for an important encounter. 'Ah, what the hell. We survived it once: we can do it again.'

Tien shook his head. 'You're idiots. You can't reason with the commandant. You'll achieve nothing. Besides the water's fine, I don't have the runs.' Tien looked toward Duyen and Lap. 'Do you? This is all a fuss about nothing.'

Duyen pulled himself up to his feet. 'As it happens I do have the runs,' said Duyen. 'What about you Lap? Having any toilet problems?'

'All the time.'

Tien picked up the cards and shuffled them before spreading out a game of patience on the compacted soil in front of him. 'Don't say I didn't warn you.'

Without the proper building supplies, it soon became apparent that the task of repairing Dong Hung into a habitable camp was next to impossible. Dung could see the end was swiftly approaching and waited for it patiently. He'd no idea if the change would be good or bad, but that there would be a change he was certain. Two months had passed since the storm without any significant co-operation from the commandant. When Hien and the others had approached him he'd promised them supplies, but they never came and by now everyone suspected that they never would. The water remained contaminated with mud and debris from the mountains and even though the adults took great care to strain it through muslin cloth and then boil it, the children were showing rapid signs of deterioration in their health. Winter was also upon them and while the women and children were allowed to use the kitchen as a sleeping place, the men were left to sleep in the open air. It was a miserable time and even the most submissive of people were talking about taking militant action.

Dung wasn't sure what sparked it. It may have been the heavy rainfall of the previous night, when all the men woke to find themselves soaking wet, or it may have been because of the children crying from stomach problems, but as the morning progressed word spread there was to be a demonstration in the compound. Several of the single men, Hien and Cuong included, were preparing to march to the gate and demand to be allowed to leave the camp and continue on their journey to Hong Kong. Dung joined them and watched in wonder as the number of demonstrators grew to around two hundred. It seemed as though every man, woman and child from the camp had joined with them as they marched toward the gate demanding their freedom.

'Freedom! Freedom!' The chanting was both exhilarating and deafening.

When they reached the gates the guards fired over their heads, but seemed reluctant to fire into them. No one took any notice as by now frustrations were running so high that even the threat of being shot would not have stopped them. Cuong was the first to rush the gate, but Dung and the others were so close behind him it was hard to see whose shoulder was at the forefront of the pushing. Dung felt the gates give a little and when they suddenly sprang open, he rushed forward with the surge of bodies.

Everyone was cheering as they spilled out into the road. They were free, and sang forcefully as they marched determinedly down the lane. For the first time in almost four years they were outside the camp fences. It was a moment of victory. Dung could feel his heart pounding in unison with everyone else's. He felt connected and fully alive. The happiness he'd known at the birth of his baby returned and sprang within him like a river in flood. They were ready to sing and march all the way to Hong Kong and if it took a month, two months, six months, no one cared. Their hearts were so full, they didn't need food.

They had walked over a mile and already passed over the bridge when Dung felt his heart skip several beats as he registered the road block of four police trucks ahead of them.

'Run for the fields,' shouted Hien. As three more trucks loaded with police closed in on them from behind, shots were fired creating instant panic and the crowd scattered into the fields. Dung couldn't be sure if the police were shooting at them or above their heads any more. If they had fired level with the crowd, miraculously so far no one seemed to have been hit. As the asylum-seekers fled in all directions trying to skirt the police trucks, the police rushed at them with truncheons.

Dung was running towards the sugar-cane field when he felt a blow to his shoulders as a truncheon came down hard on him. Another strike to the back of his legs sent him toppling forward to his knees. Before he could pull himself up, he was aware of Huong beside him. She seemed close to hysteria. 'They've arrested Hien and several of the others.' Dung pulled himself up just in time to see Hien being forced into a police truck along with Cuong, and three other single men, Duyen, Lap and Tien. He went to run after them but found his way blocked by a policeman with a gun pointing straight at him. His alarm magnified as he watched the police truck with Hien, Cuong and the others, leave in the opposite direction to the camp. Huong looked uneasily towards the guard then glanced sideways at Dung. 'They singled them out. There was nothing random about the arrests.'

'Then why Tien? The way he hangs around with the guards and plays poker with them, I wouldn't put him on their files as a trouble maker.'

Huong shrugged. 'Maybe they made a mistake.'

'They don't make mistakes.'

Within fifteen minutes of the truck leaving, the remaining asylum-seekers had been rounded up and forced into a tight line along the centre of the road. There was nothing Dung could do except move along with them back to Dong Hung.

Several months passed and with no news or sign of Hien and the others returning the rumours surrounding their fates were rife. While some thought they had been taken to the prison at Kham Chau, others thought they had been pushed back across the Sino–Vietnamese border like Mr Kien and Long. The more cynical of the young men suggested it was more likely they had been executed immediately after their arrests. Dung knew Hien wasn't dead and suspected he'd been pushed back across the border. During the long days of waiting for news he tried to convince Huong that even if he'd been handed over to the Vietnamese authorities Hien would find a way to escape again. Hien was a survivor, and besides assured Dung, had Hien been dead he would have joined with Ha and Diep in their night-time whisperings to him.

There was also talk of the commandant being in disgrace and of the Dong Hung asylum-seekers being transferred to Fang Cheng. This new camp was said to have been purposely built for Vietnamese asylum-seekers, and with good accommodation and a table-tennis and television room, it was just the antidote everyone needed to boost moral. Although Dung knew he would never go to the camp himself he was pleased to think that even though they had failed in their bid for freedom, there was at least some hope of better conditions for his friends.

The idea of digging up the bones of his wife and child and returning them for burial in Vietnam had been festering in Dung for a long time. This latest rumour, that his brother may have been pushed across the border into Vietnam, just convinced him that that was where he should be and as he planned his mission he felt his spirits soar. His quest, although dangerous, brought him back into the world of the living. He had an advantage over everyone else since the guards mostly ignored him. They called him the living dead and even the dogs were so used to his night-time prowling that they just wagged their tails when they saw him. Escaping from Dong Hung would be almost like walking through an open gateway.

When the moon was at its fullest, Dung prepared to leave Dong Hung as quietly and as easily as he had arrived. A more sane person would have waited for a moonless night, but then Dung didn't consider himself to be sane, and he didn't need the darkness to hide his departure. He regretted not saying goodbye to Huong and Tuyet, but he didn't want to let anyone know of his plans. Information could only hurt people. It was better if everyone continued to think of him as the 'Ghost Locust' who, already half spirit, had simply stepped over the line between the living and the dead and vanished from the prison as only a ghost could.

No one paid much heed when at dusk he wandered wraith-like along the perimeter of the camp to the walled section. Throwing his bundle of possessions over the wall he silently pulled himself up onto it. The glass which cut into the flesh on his hands and face as he flung his body over gave him a momentary pleasurable sensation of physical pain which reminded him that for a short time, at least, he had a reason to be alive. There were no alarms, no barking dogs. If the guards had seen him climbing over the wall, they chose to ignore it. Maybe they were as glad to see him leave as he was to go.

Following the track to the mountain, Dung passed a solitary cyclist. The man paid him no heed. It was as though he really didn't exist. Since Ha's death he'd become gaunt, his bones shining through his skin like ivory, leaving his lonely figure to barely cast a shadow in the moonlight. Chuckling to himself, Dung could imagine that he was indeed a ghost and invisible to the human eye. Having broken free of his prison, there was nothing to hold him down and he floated, glided, noiselessly along.

As Dung climbed the mountain, the air became sweeter. Like the roots of the rosa canina plant it intoxicated him. Ha's gentle singing, riding on the wind, drew him upward like a warming, gentle breeze. Below him the stream stretched out like a silver thread winding its way down the mountainside and across the sugar-cane fields. That same stream would one day snake its way into Vietnam where it would meet the Red River and join with it in its journey to the open sea. Separate or together, it was only time that made the difference. And wasn't that the way it would be with himself and Ha? Separated in life, they would be joined together again in death flowing in a harmonious tryst with the natural pulse of the universe. Above him the mountain's lavender peaks stretched upward into the night sky, reaching into the heart of creation itself.

Dung didn't even consider that he might not remember where their grave was. He simply followed Ha's voice until he knew he was beside her. Her warmth cloaking him in a lover's embrace, he allowed his tired body to collapse on the soft mound of earth. Resting his head in the intoxicating soil, he slept as he had never slept before.

In the morning Dung woke refreshed. The early morning sunlight bathing his body was energising and he set about digging up Ha and Diep's bones with a feeling of lightness. Several tough grasses had grown over the graves forming a protective blanket, but once Dung uprooted them the soil lifted away easily. By midday his task was complete. Wrapping the bones in his rucksack, he carried them back to the stream where he washed them clean. The bones gleamed white, and when he wrapped them back up in his rucksack and slung them over his shoulder, their weight was negligible. He could hardly reconcile himself to the fact that so small a package could represent such a large part of his life.

The words of a poem written by Ho Chi Minh when he was leaving his prison in China and returning to Vietnam, rang through Dung's mind:

The clouds embrace the peaks,
the peaks embrace the clouds,
The river below shines like a mirror,
spotless and clean.
On the crest of the western mountains,
My heart stirs as I stride forward,
Looking towards the southern sky
and dreaming of old friends.

Dung wondered if Ho Chi Minh might not have taken the same route back into Vietnam. Two different people with two different minds, but perhaps of the same heart. Their love of the motherland and love of freedom leading them on to a path of shared footsteps.

All the time Dung was embracing and kissing the earth, Lieutenant Huu of the Socialist Republic of Vietnam frontier guards, post 212, was watching him. His men grinned and gave each other puzzled expressions. The Lieutenant could have ordered them to shoot the intruder, but it wasn't necessary. The gaunt man they were watching didn't pose a threat. They could arrest him whenever they chose. They had observed him cross over the border from China into Vietnam, and the reason they hadn't moved in on him earlier was that it was more interesting to observe his behaviour. They suspected he might be a spy from China with an assignation to hand over the contents of his sack to someone. Although who the someone might be was hard to fathom since there was no one other than Vietnamese patrols for fifteen kilometres. The intruder's behaviour toward the earth, however, was remarkable. It hadn't escaped the Lieutenant's thinking that they might not be dealing with a spy but a madman.

As Dung prepared to move on, Lieutenant Huu decided it was time to take action. He wanted to question the trespasser and to see what was in his sack. He didn't want all that evidence to get blown up by the man's careless step onto a landmine. Lifting his hand to signal that the time had come for his men to move in and arrest the suspect, he sat back and

The Ghost Locust

waited. The frontier guards silently surrounded their quarry, then before Dung even had time to sense their presence, they were beside him with guns pointed toward his chest. One of the men moved up beside him, and wrenched his arms behind his back, and bound a rope around his wrists. Since the prisoner showed no signs of resistance they bid him follow them back to post 212.

———————◦◦◦———————

Colonel Khiem was one of the senior officers to be notified of Dung's arrest. Picking his way through the old files, he sifted out pieces of information to remind himself of the details of Tran Van Dung's previous arrest four years ago. Khiem was still with military intelligence, and since Tran Van Dung's case overlapped into the case of Nguyen Cao Cuong's, there was a legitimate excuse for his department to become involved. At the time of the original fiasco he'd red-starred Dung's case as one that should immediately be brought to his attention should anything be heard of his whereabouts. Looking back through his notes it was all as he remembered it. Tran Van Dung was the brother of Tran Van Hien. With Nguyen Cao Cuong they had escaped into China just hours or maybe minutes before he was ready to arrest them. The frustration he'd felt in having them escape still jarred on his memory. But these were all minor details in a case that would not normally have kept his unfailing personal interest. What really interested him was the indisputable fact that Nguyen Cao Cuong was the brother-in-law of Major Thanh.

Khiem smiled. Sixteen years had passed since Nguyen Chau Thanh had reported him to his uncle, General Nguyen Tat Chau, for his excesses in the executions of civilians during the Tet offensive in Hue. Major Thanh, although his inferior in rank, had disgraced him and robbed him of the honours that would rightfully have come his way. The memory still ate away at his insides. To have been brought before a military tribunal and to be questioned by General Chau about his conduct during the Tet advance in Hue, was humiliating beyond belief. Riddled with ulcers and too much alcohol consumption Khiem was not a healthy man. He'd survived the criticisms, since others had been implicated in the massacre, but he'd never been officially decorated as a war hero. Until Hue he'd been on a fast rising career path and with his good connections and an outstanding military record he might even have been invited to become a member of the Central Party Committee.

He had never been able to prove it, but he was certain that Major Thanh had assisted his brother-in-law and the two accomplices in their escape to China. He sifted through the file to find the letter Nguyen Cao Cuong's wife had written to her husband in China. Mrs Minh had given the letter to Major Thanh's wife. For a less favoured person than Thanh the letter alone might have been enough to lead to a conviction, but as it was, the incident had fizzled out and Khiem and his comrades had come out of it looking foolish.

With the kernel of a plot formulating in his head, Khiem picked up the phone. Dung's reappearance in Vietnam was exactly the opportunity he'd been waiting for. He was not the only one to dislike Major Thanh. The man was far too much of an independent thinker to have progressed so far in his career without making enemies, and if anything were to come of his idea Khiem knew he would need help.

Chapter 10: Old scores

19th June 1984 to 3rd April 1985

All faces have a harmless look in sleep.
Eyes closed, they all look honest and pure,
Awake, men differ: good and evil show.
No virtue and no vice exist at birth.
Of good and evil, nurture sows the seed.
PRISON DIARY, HO CHI MINH

THANH EASED BACK in the bamboo chair while he waited for Nam to prepare the spring rolls. He'd ridden one hundred and fifty kilometres on his motorcycle from Hong Gai to Hanoi and was glad to remove his sandals and put his feet up. After the assault of sand and grit thrown up into his face by traffic moving along the unsurfaced roads, the air was refreshing. From the rooftop patio, where Nam rented rooms in the Hai Ba Trung district, Thanh could see down onto Le Ngoc Han street. Although it was late the street was still busy with an assortment of anxious traders trying to squeeze out a living wage from the last of the daylight hours. Women with wrinkle-aged faces crouched under conical hats amongst woven baskets of cauliflower, beans and green onions, while young girls staggered up the road under the weight of netted baskets of live chickens. As Thanh watched the street, two plastic-sandalled cyclo drivers lay back in their chairs, watching. . . . Everyone was watching. The traders were looking for customers while keeping a sharp ear for a signal that the police might be coming. It was illegal for them to park their goods in the street, but so long as they were standing up with their baskets suspended from their wooden shoulder rods and tottering along the street, the police would leave them alone.

Thanh turned his attention from the street and visualised the serene tree-lined setting of Hoan Kiem (Returned Sword Lake). He would eat his breakfast there tomorrow before heading back to Hong Gai. He loved Hanoi, not in the same way he loved Hue, which he considered to be truly Vietnamese, but he liked Hanoi's European flavour. He liked the fancy French green and white lime-washed colonial embassy buildings with their shuttered windows and their elegant entrance-ways. He liked the industrious 'thirty-six-street' area of old Hanoi with its tubular narrow buildings and red tiled roofs, where street after street specialised in the product of its namesake: paint street, coffin street, apothecary street. Thanh was tired of Hong Gai with its backwater thinking and was ready to move on. If there were to be any reforms, then he was sure they would come from Saigon or Hanoi where the vibrancy of city life could not be repressed.

Nam interrupted Thanh's thoughts as he carried over a tray and placed it on the table. He set out some plates of spring rolls and shrimp cake, a dish of fish sauce and a bowl of salad herbs, before sitting in the bamboo chair across from Thanh. 'All right, so while we eat, tell me about this "Ghost Locust". What's his story and why are you involved?'

'I don't know why I'm involved, which is why I came to talk to you. I thought you might make some inquiries for me.' Nam nodded. He picked up a spring roll, wrapped it in herb, and dipped it into the *nuoc mam* sauce. 'Do you recall when my brother-in-law Cuong deserted from the army and the escalation of trouble after it was found that his friend was storing TNT at his home?'

'Yes. And I recall that my father advised you to stay out of it, but you didn't.'

'The "Ghost Locust" is Dung, the younger brother of Hien, Cuong's long-time friend. He was arrested and escaped into China with a young girl before the authorities learned of the explosives being stored at his brother's home.'

'Interesting. And now you're the supervising officer in his case. Tell me about him. Whatever madness brought him back to Vietnam?'

'The girl . . . well, his wife, I believe, died soon after giving birth to their son. The baby died shortly after the mother. When the commandant announced that everyone was to be transferred from Dong Hung to a camp in Fang Cheng, he escaped.'

'I know of Dong Hung Camp.'

'Dung couldn't face being further separated from his wife and baby so he brought their bones back to Vietnam for burial.'

Nam drew in his breath. 'He's either a hero or a madman.'

'I think both. The point is I believe his story. He wasn't guilty of subversive anti-government activities before he left, and he isn't a Chinese spy.'

'He's guilty of theft. If I am to accept your version of why TNT was being stored at Tran Van Hien's home, then he was helping his brother to dig up the anti-tank mines for the purpose of selling it to fishermen.'

'Yes, he's guilty of theft.'

'So how do you know he isn't a Chinese spy? His mother is Chinese, and he was in the Dong Hung Camp.'

'Dong Hung is a prison. It's no more a base for training spies than our own central prison in Hanoi. I've spent two weeks talking to him.'

'Talking to him?'

'Yes, he's not the kind of man you interrogate. He's detached. If I were to accuse him of being a spy, I don't think he would really care. There's nothing defensive in his manner. His only concern was that the bones of his wife and child receive a proper burial. I've already seen to that. . . .'

'What are you saying Thanh?'

'I passed their bones over to the wife's brother.'

'On whose authority?'

'I'm the supervising officer in the case. It seemed indecent to keep them hanging round as evidence.' Nam shrugged his shoulders. 'What I'm telling you, brother, is that this man is innocent of the crimes he's being accused of. I've spoken to him at length about his escape and about Dong Hung. He's given me remarkable information about my brother-in-law. All of it makes sense. It fits with. . . . Well, I should tell you, it fits with the information I received from Cuong and Hien when I met with them in Haiphong before their escape.'

Nam smiled as he shook his head. 'I knew you couldn't resist getting involved. You realise you could have jeopardised our own secret work.'

'But isn't the ordinary man just as entitled to freedom and justice as Uncle Chau's important friends? Wasn't ours a People's war, not a war to liberate only the famous and privileged? What of the ordinary people like Cuong and his friends. Why shouldn't they have an escape route?'

'Cuong was a deserter and the other two were thieves.'

Thanh stood up. He was restless and frustrated. He leaned over the balcony wall and looked down onto the street. 'No. That's too simple. We have to look closely at why they were thieves. Didn't our government create the conditions where there was no other choice? Of what value is a government that has no compassion? Look at how we treated our Southern compatriots after the fall of Saigon. We were too impatient and too suspicious to allow the unification of the South to move slowly.' Turning, he came back to Nam. 'And didn't you ever consider deserting?' Of course Nam had thought of deserting and Thanh knew it.

'Sit down, brother. I'll pour you some tea. One day, when the situation in our country eases, you will make a fine defence lawyer. But right now you are employed as a public security officer. If you try to defend this man, you will be dragged down with him. Look at the cases of the other two Dong Hung escapees: Nguyen Son Kien and Pham Van Long. Maybe they weren't spies either.'

'Maybe they weren't.' Thanh could feel the tears welling. He turned away from Nam so that he wouldn't see the redness of his eyes. 'What was it all for? Independence and liberty — wasn't that our battle cry? But where is the liberty for Kien and Long? Where is their justice? If I put in the report expected of me, Tran Van Dung will go to prison as surely as Kien and Long. If I don't and I tell the truth. . . .'

Nam stood up and walked over to Thanh. 'The chances of Tran Van Dung receiving a fair trial are as remote as a rice crop without intensive labour, regardless of any favourable report from you. I don't know who is responsible for assigning you this case. It is certainly someone who knows enough about you to understand how you think. Your sense of justice is hardly a secret despite my father's warnings to you. Maybe they even have some suspicion of our underground escape trail?' Nam laid his hand on Thanh's shoulder. 'Delay your report, brother. Let me try to find out who is behind this.'

Sitting at his desk in Hong Gai, two weeks after his meeting with Nam, Thanh stared at the names on a slip of paper in front of him: Senior Colonel Ngo Tien Khiem. Something stirred in his memory. He tried letting his thoughts drift until slowly recognition of the name seeped in. Hue, Tet 1968! Thanh felt a queasiness rising in his stomach. Khiem had been one of those responsible for murdering civilians and throwing them into a mass grave. There had been no directive from Hanoi or from the National Liberation Front, but Khiem had taken it upon himself to see to it that no one suspected of even the slightest connection with the Saigon forces, however tenuous that connection might have been, would survive.

Dung viewed the man opposite him with distaste. Since Major Thanh had arranged for Tuan to collect Ha and Diep's bones for burial, his old determination and appetite for life returned. For the first time since Ha's death, he began to consider his own situation. He'd known that the transfer of his case from the Hong Gai Public Security Office to the Military Intelligence unit in Hanoi, was unlikely to be to his advantage. What he hadn't been prepared for was that the authorities were not only interested in implicating Dung in anti-government activities, they were trying to get him to implicate others as well. Dung couldn't be sure that

Hien and Cuong were not already being detained in a prison cell somewhere in Hanoi awaiting their own trials. After days of intensive interrogation, this private meeting with Senior Colonel Khiem struck him as being more dangerous than anything which had gone on before.

'Dung, my compatriots don't believe your story and I'm sorry they treated you badly. You see they don't understand you like I do. The story of the "Ghost Locust" — a madman bringing bones back into the country for burial — that's a lot to ask them to take in.'

'I'm not claiming to be mad. It was others called me the "Ghost Locust". I only mentioned it because it was the name and the interpretation of my state of mind that allowed me to leave Dong Hung Camp so easily.'

'Oh, I believe you, Dung. I think you're really the innocent party in all this. You're still a young man with the possibility of a bright future and it saddens me to see how your friends have used you. I would like to find a way to help you.' Khiem stood up from his desk and poured two cups of tea. He offered some to Dung before sitting on a chair nearby. 'I would not ask you to testify against your brother. He has merely been foolish like yourself. The two that are the real enemies of Vietnam are Nguyen Cao Cuong and his brother-in-law Major Thanh.'

Cuong's brother-in-law! Of course, thought Dung. He'd sensed something familiar about Major Thanh right from the first time he'd met him at the Hong Gai Public Security Office, but he hadn't made the connection. It was Thanh who gave Hien and Cuong the money for their escape. Dung not only owed him a debt for helping him make the arrangements with Tuan for the burial of Ha and Diep, he owed Thanh a debt on behalf of his brother.

'Ah, I detect some recognition in you as to who Major Thanh is, of his two-fold plot to trap you. Did you know that he sent in a very damning report about you?'

Dung folded his arms and waited to hear from Khiem what his deal might be. He wasn't as young as he used to be.

'He accuses you of being the mastermind behind a plot to cause internal disorder. He claims the explosives you stored were to blow up Chinese businesses in the northern provinces. This as we all know would have given China the excuse to cross back over our northern border and interfere in our sovereign affairs.' Khiem stopped speaking and leaned toward Dung, looking intently into his eyes. 'I see from your expression that you didn't know of this plot or that you yourself were implicated in it. For years Major Thanh and his lackey Nguyen Cao Cuong have fooled many people with their pretence of reasonableness. But don't be taken in — Thanh, especially is a dangerous man. Cuong, well he's a fool.' Khiem stood up. 'Still, I think I have said enough for now. We will meet again privately. In the meantime I will try to think of a way to help you. But you understand I will need your co-operation.'

As Dung sat in his cell a sense of dread swept through his whole body. He didn't like Khiem. His instincts warned him to be on guard around him and he tried frantically to analyze what exactly was happening. He was sure that what Khiem said about the report wasn't true, yet why lie? Dung had no experience in dealing with such deception and felt out of his depth with Khiem. If Major Thanh had really sent in such a report, then why? It didn't make any sense. There was no anti-government plot so if Thanh believed there was, why would he even bother to listen to Dung's story?

By the time the second private meeting with Khiem came, two days later, Dung had decided he would trust in his own instincts with regard to Khiem and Thanh. He'd felt a kinship with Thanh which had only grown with the passing of time, yet every muscle in his body warned him to distrust Khiem and to be careful of him.

'You've been a disappointment to me, Dung. I really thought that since I was willing to help you, you would work with me in trying to put a very dangerous criminal behind bars. I see I overestimated your intelligence. Well, it won't actually change anything. Lieutenant Huu, of the border patrol already informed me that when you were first arrested and he questioned you about acting as a spy for China, you didn't deny it. You haven't protected anyone. In fact all you have succeeded in achieving is sacrificing yourself along with your co-conspirators and since we already have two of your group from Dong Hung in prison, it won't require too much effort to see that all of you receive your just punishments.'

Several months had passed since Thanh turned in his report and handed Tran Van Dung's case over to Military Intelligence, so he was anxious to learn the outcome, yet when the letter finally arrived instructing him to appear before a panel of seven advisors in Hanoi, he knew with a dreadful certainty that he was in severe trouble.

Having prepared himself psychologically Thanh was not surprised, when a week later, standing before the panel and listening to the allegations made against him, he recognised Senior Colonel Khiem as the central figure sitting in judgment of him. Seeing Thanh's recognition Khiem immediately took the lead in the questioning. 'Tran Van Dung is an enemy of the state. Why would an officer in your position submit a report that waters down his crime to that of petty theft?'

'I'm not disputing that Mr Dung committed crimes against the Socialist Republic of Vietnam. By assisting his brother in digging up the landmines and selling the TNT to fishermen, he was committing a serious offence. But I am quite convinced there was no intention on his part to participate in any terrorist activity.'

'Are you not aware that the prisoner confessed to acting as a spy for China when interviewed by Lieutenant Huu at the border?'

Thanh had not known of any such confession, but he was aware of the interrogation techniques of many of his colleagues. 'I interviewed Tran Van Dung over several weeks. I am quite convinced that the account he gave me is accurate. There could be a number of reasons why he might make a false confession to Lieutenant Huu. I believe that you are renowned for being able to extract an unusually high number of confessions of that sort yourself.'

Khiem glared at Thanh. 'In spite of all the evidence, and I repeat, evidence against the prisoner, it puzzles me that you should be so intent on defending him. One would think that you and I are on different sides.'

'It's quite simple,' said Thanh. 'My objective is to see that justice is served. It's what I fought the American war for and it's what I'm now paid to do. The people of Vietnam not only deserve justice, they demand it. Tran Van Dung is innocent of the crimes you suggest. There is no direct evidence against him to suggest he is a spy or a terrorist.'

The oldest member of the panel of judges leaned across the long table toward Thanh. 'This young man, why did he risk coming back to Vietnam if he wasn't a spy? He didn't need to come back.'

'When I first met him I asked myself that same question. But after speaking with him over time it became very apparent; his love for his country, his love for his wife and child and the desire to return them to our motherland, were the factors which motivated him. Mr Dung is not a spy, he is a patriot in the full sense of the word. After digging up his wife's and his son's bones he turned south, back toward his homeland. A saner man, or a man who loved his country less would have headed north. Mr Dung didn't care that he risked arrest — he didn't try to hide himself when he crossed back into Vietnam, in fact he did quite the opposite. He fell to his knees and kissed the ground because he was so happy to be home. Now does that sound like the behaviour of a man on a spying mission against his motherland?'

'You make an interesting observation. In fact our own dear Chairman, Ho Chi Minh kissed the ground after his release from prison in China.'

'Exactly comrade. Mr Dung's mission was to bring the bones of his family back here for burial. He had just escaped from prison in China and had no thought of betraying his country.'

'Is it true,' interjected Khiem, 'that Nguyen Cao Cuong is a friend of the brothers Tran Van Hien and Tran Van Dung?'

'I believe so.'

'And is it true that Nguyen Cao Cuong also happens to be your brother-in-law?' asked Colonel Khiem.

Thanh gave a half laugh. 'Yes.'

'And is it also true that at the time of Nguyen Cao Cuong's imminent arrest, you and your wife visited your other brother-in-law, Bui Anh Tang.'

Thanh considered the question before answering. If they had been seen at Tang's shop then to lie would only make matters worse. The fact that they linked his visit with Lan suggested that someone had seen them. 'Yes.'

'What was the purpose of that visit?'

'As you yourself just stated, Bui Anh Tang is my wife's brother. It was not unusual for us to visit him.'

'You made that visit soon after you forced entry into your wife's sister's home. She of course, is the wife of Nguyen Cao Cuong. That is correct, isn't it?'

'My wife was concerned about her sister and naturally her husband's desertion was of worry to all of us.'

'And where did you go after your visit to Bui Anh Tang's shop?'

'We went home.'

'And home is Hong Gai?'

'Yes.'

'Interesting, I always thought that Hong Gai was several miles north of Haiphong. You seem to have travelled a considerable number of kilometres that day,' said Khiem. 'Are you aware Major Thanh, that we have a witness who can testify that both you and your wife were in Haiphong later that day?' Thanh felt himself go cold. 'You are not on trial of course, this is just a private, preliminary hearing. Nevertheless, I have arranged for the witness to be present here today. I think what our witness has to say will be of considerable interest to the rest of the panel.' Khiem then turned to his compatriots. 'Will you excuse me, comrades, while I arrange for the witness to join us.'

Thanh waited anxiously, wondering what witness Khiem had managed to rake up. He remembered the man with the pigs who had given him directions, but after all these years he wondered how anyone could have found him, and even if they had, how could the man be sure about the date? Five minutes later, when the witness was brought into the room, it was not the pig man who entered, but an old woman. Thanh stared at her. He thought she was vaguely familiar but he could not place where or when he might have met her.

'Please tell the panel your name.'

Her shoulders were shaking and her voice barely audible as she spoke her name. 'Duong Kim Dao.'

'Speak up,' ordered Khiem.

'My name is Duong Kim Dao.' She looked desperately toward Thanh. 'They have. . . .'

'Keep to the point old woman. Is it correct that you are the mother of Tran Van Hien and Tran Van Dung, and that you live in Haiphong with you married daughter?'

The old woman was weeping. 'Yes.'

'And do you recognise this man?' Khiem pointed toward Thanh. The woman seemed reluctant to look at Thanh. 'Please look at him.'

The old woman gave him an apologetic look.

'Did the man standing before this panel come to your daughter's home.'

'Yes.'

'Can you tell the panel why he came to your house?'

'It was to help my son and his friend escape from Vietnam.'

'What was the name of your son's friend?'

'Cuong.'

'Nguyen Cao Cuong?'

'Yes.'

'Okay, continue.'

'He came to our house, first his wife to see if it was all right. Later he came in.'

'And what was the purpose of the visit?'

'To give my son and Mr Cuong money.'

'Why did he give them money?'

'To escape.'

'And didn't he also give them information as to who to contact for this escape?'

'He gave them the name of a man in Haiphong.'

The silver-haired panelist addressed the old woman, 'Do you recall the name of the man?' Any hopes Thanh harboured as to where this judge's sympathies lay were shattered by this unexpected turn of questioning.

'I don't remember.'

'Very well, I think the witness can leave us for now.'

After Mrs Dao left the room, the panelist, whose name Thanh didn't know, turned his attention back to Thanh. 'What have you got to say, Major Thanh?' Thanh remained silent. In view of the damning evidence there was nothing he could say. To have called the old woman a liar would not have protected him. It would simply have shamed him.

'Before the panel withdraw to discuss this case, there is one more piece of evidence I would like to submit.' Khiem produced a letter which he slid along the table for the other panelists to view. 'As you will note, this letter is addressed to Nguyen Cao Cuong. It is a letter from Mr Cuong's wife informing him of the death of his mother. This letter was passed by Mr Cuong's wife to Major Thanh's wife during a visit she made to Dong Cuong Yen Bai New Economic Zone.' Khiem turned to address Thanh. 'Why, Major Thanh, would Cuong's wife pass a letter for Cuong to your wife?'

'Because they're sisters. There was no one else for her to pass the letter to.'

'I believe you yourself visited Dong Cuong Yen Bai Economic Zone weeks before the mother-in-law died. Had your visit been later and had Mrs Minh passed the letter to you, would you have accepted it?'

'Almost certainly.'

'Why?'

'Because she needed to pass the letter to someone.'

'My thought is that Mrs Minh passed the letter to your wife because she knew that you were in contact with your brother-in-law in China. In fact it is my belief that not only did you arrange the escape of your co-conspirators, but that you are also in regular contact with their Chinese controllers. Isn't that correct?'

As Thanh saw little point in answering the question, the hearing was adjourned for private discussion. Thanh was taken to one of the empty interrogation rooms and asked to wait, however, it came as no surprise when after an hour, Khiem returned with three of the panelists and asked Thanh to sign his detention order.

Chapter 11: Hoa Lo Central Prison

26th July 1985 to 3rd April 1986

After such long disuse my legs are soft like cotton.
Trying a few steps, I stagger and totter.
But very soon the guard bellows:
Hey you no loitering in prison.
PRISON DIARY, HO CHI MINH

THANH PACED HIS CELL, three feet by five. He knew the measurements exactly. He could have paced it with his eyes closed and never brushed his shoulder against the wall or struck his ankle on the concrete slab which served as his bed. The six foot high ceiling seemed to be sinking down into the room robbing him of precious space. The air was acrid. No one ever came in to clean the drain hole which served as his toilet, even though Thanh had put in several requests. The hole had become blocked and the smell permeated through the cell robbing Thanh of breathable air. The absence of natural sunlight deprived him still further — it robbed him of hope and caused his skin to take on a yellow pallor.

Thanh had been isolated for thirty three days. Each day, he found it took more and more discipline to force himself to complete his yoga exercises. The rice, of the poorest quality, normally served only to pigs and cooked with a gritty salt, left him thirsty. On the occasions when he could be certain the guards were not close enough to his cell to spy on him through the peep hole, he would rinse his rice through with the bowl of water meant for rinsing his hands. Usually one of the guards remained by the door and watched him eat. The gritty salt, the guard said, was there to help him focus his thoughts back on the revolution; to cleanse his soul of the corrupting influences in his life. Thanh would happily have shoved the salted pig rice down the guard's throat to let him see how well it cleansed his soul, but since pig rice was better than no rice, he ate it silently.

As the days passed Thanh wondered about the delay in his interrogation. When he was first brought to Hoa Lo Central Hanoi Prison a month after his meeting with Senior Colonel Khiem and the panel of advisors, he'd expected to meet with Khiem almost immediately. His thought was that he might be able to make a deal to protect Lan. The waiting and the not knowing was driving him crazy. He knew he would not receive any sympathy or special treatment in spite of his long service to his country. As far as the Communist Party was concerned, one was either with them a hundred percent, or against them. There was no in between, and the party was always right. By helping Cuong and Hien, two enemies of Vietnam, Thanh had opposed the party. As a former cadre and war hero, his situation would, in fact, be worse than if he had sat idle during the war, or profiteered from it by running one of the Saigon whore houses.

Thanh stopped in mid track. The gentle tapping on his wall was undeniable. Before stooping to make contact with his neighbour, Thanh tiptoed to the peep hole and glanced through it. The three guards were at the far end of the line of cells, making themselves tea. Thanh decided it was safe to whisper: tapping messages was tedious and time consuming. Even though Thanh felt as though he had all the time in the world to tap, it was more satisfying to whisper and hear another human voice. Deprived of almost everything else, human contact kept his spirit alive. The information which filtered through the prison grapevine was more precious than gold.

Thanh sat down on his slab and put his mouth close to the wall. 'The guards are drinking tea. They're out of earshot,' he whispered. Having completed his message Thanh turned his head and pressed his ear firmly against the wall. Linh's response was slow in coming. Thanh supposed Linh was making his own check on the guard's situation. Talking to other prisoners was an offence against the state, punishable by beating. Linh was right to be cautious.

Through earlier conversations Thanh had learned that his cell neighbour, Truong Tu Linh had been a member of the Maquis and although he fought alongside his Northern comrades for the unification of Vietnam, he had suffered under the communist regime. His first arrest occurred shortly after the liberation of Saigon. The thirty days of being checked out, as they called it, had stretched into two years. This second arrest which occurred two weeks prior to Thanh's arrest stemmed from Linh writing a novel critical of the Hanoi government. An overseas Vietnamese friend who tried to smuggle the novel out of the country had been arrested at Noi Bai Airport. Linh knew nothing of his friend's situation, although he hoped that since the friend carried a French passport, the French Embassy would fight to secure his release. Thanh was impressed by Linh's concern for his friend, while seeming to accept his own fate without complaint.

Thanh's patience was rewarded. Linh's whispers floated through the cell wall into his ear. 'I just heard from Madame Quynh. The prisoner in the next cell to her died during the night.' Thanh pressed his ear closer to the wall. 'Madame Quynh saw them take his body out. She didn't know his name because . . . perhaps being closer up the line to the guard room he'd been afraid to respond to anyone's tapping.' Thanh felt a wave of sadness. That the man should die and no one know his name seemed even more cruel than if they had succeeded in communicating with him and were talking of a friend. 'She heard the guards talking about it this morning,' continued Linh. 'They were quite nervous because he wasn't supposed to die. It was suicide. He bit his tongue off, swallowed it, then choked on it.' Thanh sat back. He didn't know what to say. The horror of the prisoner's death left him numb.

Thanh was in a restless sleep when he was awakened by the guard and ordered to get dressed and quickly follow him. He had been sleeping in his undershorts, so he slipped into his trousers and shirt. While dressing he glanced at the scratch marks he had made on the wall to keep account of his days in isolation. Forty-two days had already passed.

'Hurry up. You're taking too long.'

Thanh fastened his trousers leisurely and followed the guard out of the cell. Although it was still dark, the sense of space in being able to walk down a passageway that was longer than five feet was sheer pleasure. His legs hesitated and stumbled a little as he broke the five foot barrier. But as Thanh's confidence increased, he varied his pace to get the full entertainment of feeling his limbs work. His yoga exercises had held him in good stead.

'What are you doing? Just walk at my pace. If you try to escape I'll shoot you.'

In order to get to the interrogation block, it was necessary to walk across the compound. Once outside Thanh felt a momentary panic. The open space was overwhelming. The volume of air flowing into his chest was too much and looking up he was stunned at the loveliness of the night. A full moon contrasted against the darkening sky gave the panorama a depth he'd never before dreamed of, while trees on the distant hillside, silhouetted in tones of deep purple against the skyline, stood out like proud centurions. Up until that moment, he'd experienced a sense of pride in the way he'd faced his challenge of isolation. The maths games he'd played to keep his mind elastic and the recollecting of long verses of poetry, suddenly struck him as meaningless. Tiny mind games to pretend his world was bigger. In the face of the vast universe stretching out in front of him, Thanh realised the full sadness of his confinement and in wonderment of how splendid and vast the earth could be he slowed to a standstill.

'Hurry up. Now you're moving too slow.'

'I was looking at the moon.'

'Just shut up and move.' The guard shoved Thanh into the narrow corridor that led to the interrogation room.

As Thanh stepped into the room, he made a quick survey of his surroundings. Besides Senior Colonel Khiem, a young officer sat with a pencil and paper set out on the table in front of him. Barely glancing up from the file of papers he'd been reading, Khiem ordered Thanh to sit down. There was only one place for Thanh to sit so he placed himself on the chair in front of Khiem.

After seating himself, Thanh scanned the ceiling to discover the source of light: it was a single lightbulb hung miserably from the ceiling. Gazing past Khiem to the window behind, Thanh wondered if he might glimpse the moon again. It was out of view, but it occurred to him that if he could drag the interview out he might snatch a view of the morning light before being returned to his cell.

Khiem began the interrogation by asking Thanh to give an auto-biographical account of himself and his family. He was particularly interested in the details of Thanh's activities during the war years. It was a standard approach to questioning. Thanh spoke slowly and deliberately allowing Khiem's assistant, Lieutenant Ngay, ample time to write the information down accurately. Much to Thanh's surprise, Khiem remained silent during the three hours it took for Thanh to relate his story. The officer asked questions for clarification, but otherwise did not interrupt the flow of Thanh's autobiography. When Thanh felt he had satisfactorily given as many details as he wished Khiem to hear, he brought his account to a close.

Khiem took the sheets of paper from the officer and browsed through them. After asking a few general questions, Khiem then wasted no more time in coming to the point of his personal contention with Thanh. 'Before going to Hue, Tet 1968, you were stationed in Saigon. What was the nature of your work there?'

'My mission in Saigon was to check up on the safe houses to see everything was in order and to alert our compatriots to the coming offensive.'

'You were a spy, then?'

'No.'

'You are credited with having broken into the American Embassy during the offensive, where you destroyed CIA documents relating to the Phoenix programme — does that not make you a spy?'

'No. My connections were with the Sapper troops. My work required that I assume various identities to protect myself were I to be stopped and questioned, but I was not employed by the Saigon government nor was I in a position to spy on their activities.'

'But you knew of such people?'

'Of course. I have just told you that. I acted as a liaison officer.'

Prior to the Tet offensive, Thanh had alerted his comrades to the coded message to be broadcast on Hanoi radio by Ho Chi Minh, 'This Tet is different from the others. Forward, march!' This was the signal to the National Liberation Front and People's Army to mobilise their forces. They had hoped it would also bring about the general uprising of support from the Southern population.

'And how could you have been certain your contacts were not playing you for a fool — their allegiance being to the Saigon government?'

'I suppose I could never know for certain, but I trusted these people and the information they received was preselected on a need-to-know basis. Had they been traitors, or more likely had they been captured and tortured, the information we gave them sustained us only limited damage.'

'Why did you visit number nine, Nguyen Binh Khiem Street?'

'I didn't go inside.'

'You don't deny being near there?'

'If you mean, did I know it was one of the satellite offices of the Saigon government military intelligence, then of course I knew and my being there was quite deliberate. The building was to be a Sapper target during the Tet offensive. I familiarised myself with the area and distances around it. I then radioed that information back to our troops.'

'Why did you leave Saigon so quickly after Tet? Wouldn't it have been safer to go into hiding than to travel at such a time to Hue?'

'It was much safer to get out of Saigon than to remain. By leaving when everything was still chaotic, it was easy to convince the Republican soldiers of my cover. Had I left a few days later, they might have had clearer instructions and been more organised. They would likely have

taken the time to investigate my story more fully. It was a gamble that
paid off.' Thanh smiled to himself as he recalled how he had barely
escaped the reprisals of the Saigon troops. 'Once the Republican soldiers
regained control of the city, they were determined to root us out. Anyone
being stopped on the street or found hiding was shot on the spot if he
couldn't identify himself and show legitimate reasons for being in Saigon.
I was stopped as I was trying to make my way out of the city. I was
carrying the fake identification of a Catholic school teacher, Huynh Huu
San. My knowledge of the Catholic doctrine convinced my captors, one
of whom was Catholic, that I was whom I claimed to be. My story, that
I had been visiting my old father in Saigon for the lunar new year, was
reasonable enough, as was my stated reason for returning back to Ho
Nai. When I expressed outrage over the sneak Tet assault, and worries
that my school may have been destroyed by the enemy, the Republican
soldiers allowed me to proceed. They advised me to take care as there
were still many Viet Cong around.'
   'Viet Cong?' Khiem spoke the word derisively.
   'Their word, not mine.'
   Thanh deliberately expanded his account of his escape from Saigon.
It was safe ground to waste time over. The darkness was beginning to
fade and so long as the interview was civil, Thanh saw every reason to
prolong it. To see the sunrise one more time in his present situation,
would be to glimpse into heaven.
   Although Khiem's face remained hard, Thanh noticed that Lieutenant
Ngay was grinning. Taking the opportunity to draw Ngay into a collusive
relationship, where he could keep Khiem's interests at a distance, Thanh
described how he had hitched a ride with an ARVN troop moving north
to repel the People's Army. Ngay clearly enjoyed the irony and as he
nodded his head and asked more and more questions for clarification,
Thanh could detect Khiem's agitation increase. Finally his tolerance
snapped. 'Who instructed you to go to Hue?'
   It was the moment Thanh had been expecting and he understood
immediately where Khiem's questions would lead. He had always known
his crime was not that he helped his brother-in-law and Hien escape or
even that he'd put in a favourable report on Tran Van Dung. Thanh's
crime was that he had raised doubts about Khiem's competence as an
officer. After Thanh reported Khiem's activities during the Hue massacre
to Uncle Chau, Khiem had been disgraced and it was only after the death
of Ho Chi Minh the following year, that Khiem had slowly regained
favour and been reinstated into his old position. Nevertheless his career

had been damaged by Thanh's allegations, and although Khiem was known to have powerful friends amongst some of the more hard-line, pro-China members of the Vietnamese government, he was never openly honoured as a war hero.

'I was making my way to Hanoi so passing through Hue was on my route.'

'You liar. Your being in Hue was no accident. You were sent there. Who sent you?'

Thanh had no intention of mentioning his uncle's name. He had worked as an agent for his uncle for many years. Khiem had been right about some of his Saigon contacts: they had been double agents and Thanh had known it. He had used these relationships to feed false information to the Saigon government. Ultimately their betrayal had proved to be more useful to Hanoi than to Saigon. Thanh gazed steadily into Khiem's eyes before giving him his response. 'I was sent as a personal agent for Chairman Ho.'

Khiem almost choked, then he seemed to recover himself. Smashing his fist hard against the table he leaned toward Thanh. Sweat had broken out on his brow, his voice was cold and controlled. 'My God, you'll pay for this. Your lies and arrogance go beyond anything I've ever heard.'

Thanh surveyed Khiem's discomfort with pleasure. Khiem's young assistant had dipped his head and placing his hand over his face was trying to hide his giggles. Thanh leaned back in his chair. His answer had not been outrageous. Since his youth Uncle Chau had forged a close relationship with Ho Chi Minh and on many occasions Thanh had sensed Uncle Ho's hand behind the instructions he was being given by Uncle Chau. Having constantly stressed the need for discipline within the People's Army and the strict code of ethical behaviour for the freedom fighters, it was quite conceivable that Uncle Ho was alarmed by the reports coming out of Hue.

Khiem stood up and opened the door calling for the duty guard. 'Take him back to his cell.' But as the guard advanced toward the interrogation room, Khiem changed his mind. Turning sharply toward Ngay he snapped, 'Wait outside with the guard. I want a private word with the prisoner.'

As Thanh remained seated he wondered what Khiem wanted. He knew he was not going to grant him any favours. It would be pointless to even raise his concerns about Lan. If he were to find a way to protect her, it would have to be some other way. When the moment had come, he'd been unable to humble himself in front of Khiem, as he'd promised himself. He'd sacrificed all hopes of negotiation for this one moment of victory. He knew he was selfish, proud even. All that mattered was that he'd succeeded in turning the interrogation round to Khiem's disadvantage. He'd made him lose face in front of one of his subordinates and, petty though his victory might be, it was worth everything.

Khiem turned toward the window and spoke with his back toward Thanh. Although the morning light was just beginning to show itself, Thanh was so intent on listening to what Khiem had to say, he barely noticed it. 'We were retreating. Those men were the enemy. Had we left them, they would have risen up and killed us. And if not them, then their children, and their children's children.' He turned sharply toward Thanh. 'You're a meddling intellectual, an individualist who has no sense of the wider revolutionary picture. Human rights have no place in a war situation. Only the winners have rights.' His eyes narrowed. 'I've watched you for many years. When the rebel Hong Gai miners slowed production because there were no supplies in the shops, it was you who disturbed our internal security by giving credence to their complaints. Don't you understand what will happen if we show weakness? We hold on to our power by a slim thread.' Khiem spat the words out. 'You dare accuse me of commandism. As a leader of the revolution I don't shy away from my duty. Your crime is that of liberalism. By failing to instill our policies upon the masses you encourage their reactionary views. With enemies everywhere we have to stay vigilant otherwise our country will be doomed. . . .' Khiem was shaking. 'I had to take a stand against the traitors — there was no choice in the matter. You're a coward. If it wasn't for your uncle, you would have been chucked out of the party and imprisoned long ago. Those who have no stomach for revolution should stay away from party leadership otherwise they will bring our country back down to its knees.' Thanh realised that Khiem was no longer talking about him, but was referring to Uncle Chau's leadership position within the Vietnamese government. Leaving the window, Khiem strode toward the door, flung it open and marched purposefully out of the room. 'You deserve to rot in a cell.'

Thanh sat there mystified. Khiem hadn't needed to explain his position. Maybe he didn't feel as secure as Thanh had assumed? It was a strange exchange. While Thanh pondered these thoughts the guard put a hand on his shoulder. Thanh stood up and sighed. It was clear to him that whatever he did he could not expect a fair trial. Still he had no regrets about what he'd said to Khiem. In his world of limited freedoms he had exercised choice.

Thanh had barely time to process the interrogation with Khiem before
he was visited by four guards. Two of the guards entered his cell noisily
with irons draped carelessly over their shoulders. Towering over Thanh,
their hugeness crowded the cell. The safety of his earlier silence and
predictability was shattered.

'Stay sitting on the bed,' ordered one of the guards. Thanh's instinct
was to jump up and resist, but he knew that after the confinement of his
cell he was no longer fit and would be easily overpowered. Reluctantly
he remained passively seated on the concrete slab. To resist, he knew too,
would invite beatings which would leave him worse off.

As the guards pulled unmercifully at his limbs, crossing his arms
diagonally to his ankles, Thanh tried to ease himself into a more
comfortable position.

'That's too tight. How am I to move or go to the toilet?'

'You don't move, and you go to the toilet when we take you.' As the
last guard retreated from the cell and slammed the door, Thanh knew
fear. If he were to be kept in irons for a long time he would lose the use
of his arms and legs entirely. Facing death was one thing; in death there
was freedom. To lose the use of his body would be a living hell.

Time dragged even more slowly. With fifteen minutes a day out of chains,
for food, exercise and hygiene, Thanh was aware that his body and mind
were rapidly deteriorating. His wrists and ankles were swollen around
the manacles and the raw flesh was becoming infected. It was as painful
to be released from the chains as it was to be fastened back into them.

Then slowly . . . as the days and nights blurred together Thanh lost
count of time. With his arms and feet crossed it was impossible to lie
down or find a reasonable sleeping position. Fatigue played with his
sanity. He became obsessed with thoughts about the man who had bitten
off his tongue. He was now certain that the reason the prisoner had not
communicated with his fellow cell-mates was because he'd been in chains.
Linh's tapping also ceased and in his delirious state Thanh wondered if
the man who died after biting off his tongue, was not himself; Linh's
earlier whisperings having been a premonition of his own death.

Thanh tried to push back his feelings of despair. It gnawed at his sense
of justice that it was he who was the prisoner in irons, the presumed
traitor, while Khiem was free. Free to extract whatever personal vengeance he sought. Why couldn't the ancient revolutionaries understand that

it was Khiem who was the traitor? By slaughtering his Vietnamese
brothers, Khiem betrayed the revolution, his evil spilling out of his pores
as freely as the streams flowed down the mountains. Where was the
justice they had fought for?

In his lifetime Ho Chi Minh always spoke so eloquently of 'independence and liberty'. Thanh desperately wanted to believe in Ho's
sincerity. He tormented himself with the question of what had happened.
Where had the revolution gone wrong? If Thanh just knew the answers
to these questions, he believed he could survive his isolation. It was the
absence of answers which left him feverish and disoriented. With the
disintegration of the boundaries of time and distance, Thanh's memory
slipped back and forth:

*It was July 1963. Thanh was weaving his way through the crowds. People
were pouring into the streets from the houses and alleyways, to pay their last
respects to the novelist Nguyen Tuong Tam. Young girls in smart outfits
followed the procession. They were the daughters of Saigon's elite. Thanh, who
like most youths of his age had read Tam's controversial novel,* Breaking the
Ties, *understood the reasons for their being there. The book had once been
required reading in the South, while in the countryside and in the North,
Tam was considered to be too much of an individualist to be given just credit
for his ideas. Tam's ideas challenged the traditional thinking of Vietnamese
culture, especially with regard to women's role in society. However, even in
the liberal South, Tam had recently fallen foul of the Saigon leadership. Nhu's
secret police were in full force, mingling with the crowds as though they were
welcome guests at his funeral.*

*The funeral procession was turning into the graveyard. Thanh, conscious
of his peasant clothes, decided not to follow. He was about to turn away when
he saw a girl mingling among a group of students and handing out folded
sheets of paper. Thanh noticed he wasn't the only one who was watching her.
One of Nhu's secret police was nodding to his colleague to move in on her.
Quickly pushing his way through the crowd Thanh positioned himself in her
pathway. As she tried to slip past him he caught hold of her wrist. She spun
round and glared at him in disbelief. 'I'm not going to hurt you,' he said
urgently. 'I just wanted to warn you, they're watching you.'*

'Who? Exactly who are watching me?'

'Nhu's secret police.'

The girl looked round anxiously. 'How do you know?'

*'I just do.' He released her wrist. 'Follow me. I know how to outmanoeuvre
them.' The girl hesitated, saw the men, now urgently pushing their way*

towards her, and nodded. Taking her hand Thanh jaunted through the crowds until they reached a side alleyway. As he glanced back he noticed with dismay that the two men were rapidly gaining on them. He signalled to the girl to turn into the alley and they took off at full speed. Thanh didn't waste time looking behind, but he registered the clipped running footsteps in their wake. Turning again he guided the girl into a covered gully which ran between the houses. Then another turn. Twisting their way through alleys and gullies Thanh didn't slow up until he was sure they had left Nhu's agents far behind. Sweating and out of breath they stood still, grinning at one another. 'We lost them.'

The girl looked around, then doubled over laughing before flopping down on a nearby step. 'That was fun.'

Thanh positioning himself beside her, creased his brow in disapproval. 'It wouldn't have been if we'd been caught.'

'No . . . sorry. I'm grateful for what you did.' She pouted her lips. 'It's normal for me to laugh when I'm scared. Thank you.'

Thanh shrugged. 'It was nothing.'

'How old are you?'

'Fifteen.'

The girl laughed again. 'Well I'm eighteen. I've arranged to meet some friends at the Caravelle after the funeral, so if I invite you to have tea with us, don't get any ideas I'm at all interested in you.'

Thanh felt his face burn. 'I wouldn't think that.'

'Good, because if I was interested in someone, which I'm not, he'd have to be at least twenty . . . thirty even.' The girl continued to grin at Thanh. 'I don't mean to be rude to you. Look my name's Mai. What's yours?'

'Tuyen.' Thanh didn't especially like lying, but his instinct for caution was ingrained.

As they made their way to the Caravelle Hotel, Thanh wondered why this obviously sophisticated and probably wealthy Saigon girl would even bother to waste time with him, especially as she so clearly wasn't interested in him. Thanh had heard of the Caravelle. It was a fancy hotel where journalists and Saigon's intellectual community met to plot and argue over the current political situation.

The clanking of metal, as the guards collected the empty food trays, brought Thanh back to the present. His door clanged open and the guard entered. 'You haven't touched your food. Why?' Thanh ignored the question. What did it matter if he ate or not? They might rob him of physical freedom but they could not take away his willpower. The guard replaced the chains around Thanh's wrists before snatching up the plate, 'Ah, it's your choice.' As the guard retreated from the cell Thanh retreated into his thoughts.

Under the onslaught of criticism by the foreign press — unacceptable to an American President facing re-election within the next year — Diem's and his brother Nhu's days were numbered. As Thanh saw it, the first incident to push events beyond return, occurred on 11th June 1963. Although Thanh hadn't been in Saigon that day and hadn't seen the images which shot around the world's television sets, the portrayal of the revered Buddhist monk's self immolation, haunted him as it haunted everyone else. Every detail of the immolation had been passed by word of mouth through the cities and villages. It was imprinted in Thanh's mind as though he'd shared those last moments with the venerable Thich Quang Duc himself. Thanh knew of the dusty dry heat of the city which hung heavy in the air when the venerable monk arrived at the busy intersection of Le Van Duyet and Phan Dinh Phung streets. He could imagine breathing the city dust into his own nostrils. Walking sedately from the car to the centre of the streets the revered monk had sat down while his brothers encircled him many rows deep. Two assistants bowed before him, then as though performing a normal religious ritual, they poured gasoline over his shaved head and saffron robes. The people of Saigon watched in shocked silence as the venerable Thich Quang Duc struck the match which ignited the fire. With his legs and hands neatly folded in the lotus position, he sat motionless for a full ten minutes while the flames devoured his body. The heavy odour of gasoline and burning flesh scorched the air crimson. All that remained of his body was his heart. Even the local police were rumoured to have prostrated themselves in the street. Mrs Nhu's dismissive remarks, calling the protest merely 'a barbecue', had seemed to Thanh, like more fuel poured on to an already raging fire.

Yet the plots ran deeper than even Thanh had suspected at the time. As Tri Quang, the rebel monk, sought to discredit Diem, so that in the vacuum of power the Xa Loi Pagoda monks could forge an alliance with Uncle Ho, the people of Saigon held their breath. The American presence was becoming intolerable. Thanh had sensed the tensions all around him, in the city, the market-place and the villages. He'd seen it in the darting, furtive eyes of the people. Even the birds sang with an uneasy strain.

For years there had been various plots against Diem, the first whisperings of which were rumoured to have originated from the bar at the Caravelle. . . .

Thanh felt the irons bite into his wrists. It would be almost better if they never unchained him as taking the irons on and off was always unbearably painful now. Better, in fact, if they just left him alone. The images of Saigon in 1963, of Mai with her petite waist and flowing dark hair, were clear. He wondered why this memory should suddenly slip in and out of his mind so easily. After that meeting, he'd never seen Mai again. He thought he'd forgotten what she looked like. Yet, here she was again, in her Western clothes and still eighteen, speaking to him as though the intervening years had melted away to nothing.

'Tuyen, these are my friends, Hieu and Canh. Hieu is studying at the school of pharmacy while Canh here is a student of literature.' Her face beamed. 'Several of his poems have already been published.' Canh, embarrassed by Mai's remarks, gazed down into his empty glass.

Hieu stood up and shook Thanh's hand. 'Our brother Canh looks thirsty. Since it's my turn to fill up the glasses, what would you like Tuyen?'

Thanh, having registered the finely tailored cut of Hieu's suit, was reminded again of his own humble attire. He looked uncomfortably at the image of himself reflected in Hieu's tinted sunglasses. Stumbling over his words he mumbled, 'Tea would be nice, thank you.'

'Tea! Nothing stronger?' Thanh flushed. He felt out of place and wondered why he'd agree to come. If he could have turned and fled without looking foolish, he would have. He suspected that had Phat, his political commissar, known he was there, he would have objected. Phat regarded Thanh as his young protégé whose mind, although bright and idealistic, was malleable and needed to be carefully nurtured — protected from the evil influences of Saigon society. He would undoubtedly regard the bar at the Caravelle Hotel too dangerous a place for his favoured young freedom fighter.

'I'd like tea as well, thank you Hieu,' said Mai. 'I was at the novelist, Nguyen Tuong Tam's funeral. Tuyen rescued me from the arms of Nhu's, Cong An. I want you to treat him as though he were my young brother.'

Hieu bowed his head in a gesture of submission before beckoning to the waiter and ordering the drinks.

'Don't mind Hieu,' laughed Canh. 'He's not so bad really.'

When the waiter had left, Mai leaned conspiratorially across the table. 'Did you know Nguyen Tuong Tam was to be tried for complicity in the abortive coup against Diem three years ago?' she whispered. 'That's why he committed suicide. He was to report back to the police last Monday. My mother is friends with his wife.'

'This is the crack-down we expected,' said Hieu. 'The cards are beginning to stack up. But when they finally fall, who's to say where they will land.'
Canh stared at them incredulously. 'I was at the funeral as well. When Tam's friend, the writer Nhat Tien, spoke, I wrote down his words. I didn't know Mr Tam committed suicide.' Canh pulled his notebook out of his pocket, then read aloud: '"Your death will always be a bright torch to light the dark path we must tread. A great encouragement for us in the hardships we shall encounter. A brilliant mirror in which we, who take up pens after you, must look at ourselves and reflect."'
'I thought his words were beautiful.' Canh's eyes misted over. 'But now I understand the words have a deeper meaning.'

Thanh had always admired the writer, Nguyen Tuong Tam. Perhaps in response to his memory of Canh's recital, or maybe it was as a result of being reminded of his own dark path, Thanh felt the warm tears trickle down his cheeks. He licked the salt from around his lips and wondered if, by licking his wounds clean he could soothe some of the pain away from his heart. Where was he, Saigon, Hanoi? Death, injustice, misery were everywhere. 1963 or 1975, 1984. What was the difference? What of Ho's promises? They had achieved the unification of Vietnam and independence from foreign domination, but what of freedom, justice and happiness? After a hurriedly implemented economic policy, poverty stalked the streets in the faces of children everywhere. The hollow cheek bones, infected eyes and matted hair was not the picture Ho painted for the children of Vietnam's bright future. The masses of arrests and forced exodus from the cities to barren or inhospitable snake-infested New Economic Zones, the re-education programmes; these mistakes all contributed to the mountain of injustice. Where were the answers. . . ?

They were leaving the Caravelle. For a minute Thanh thought she might have been giving him her address. But, when he uncrumpled the sheet of paper she'd slipped into his hand, he realised it was the paper she'd been handing out to her student friends at the funeral. He stared at the printed words:

> *Let history be my judge, I refuse to accept any other judgment. The arrest and detention of nationalist opposition elements is a serious crime, and it will cause the country to be lost into the hands of the communists. I oppose these acts, and sentence myself to death . . . as a warning to those who would trample upon freedom of every kind.*
> *NGUYEN TUONG TAM — SUNDAY, 7TH JULY 1963*

Sitting, day after day, with his back hunched and his blood supply restricted, Thanh slowly lapsed into a state of semi-consciousness. The obsessive thought of Uncle Ho's sincerity or of how long it might take to bite through his tongue, no longer bothered him. Nothing mattered. He found himself floating between reality and a state of dreaming. Slowly his pain evaporated. Death could not be far away and he accepted it with growing anticipation. He was swimming and found himself gently drawn toward a warm light. He became aware that he was no longer alone. As he travelled beyond the dark path of his destiny he felt his body bathed in a warm, healing lotion. Recognition dawned as Thanh looked into the face of his companion and healer.

Uncle Ho smiled. 'You have to go back, *dong chi.*' Ho's voice was gentle. Thanh could feel the vibrations of love emanating from his spirit. It was healing . . . soothing.

The chains melted away and Thanh tried to raise his hand in a gesture of protest. 'No. I don't want to go back.' Thanh had already chosen to give up on life. Chosen also, to forget his earthly illusion of struggling to achieve justice. 'Independence and liberty' are just noble words. 'I lost faith in you. Lost faith in our cause.'

'It's your destiny to return. Our people still struggle. They need you, and others like you — brave enough to speak out — to bring peace and understanding to our country. My name has been cursed by those who have become misguided and use me as a weapon against the people. Our motherland — the soil, the ashes of those who have crossed this bridge ahead of you — still cry out for justice. Our people's quest for freedom, distorted, has lost direction.' There were tears in Ho's eyes. His face although gentle, was pained. 'Have courage. You face a long journey with no promises of success. But, none of us can avoid our fate, however much we would hope for a simple life.' Uncle Ho's figure slowly dissolved. Thanh felt himself being carried along a narrow corridor. The air changed. It was colder, and there were wafts of fresh breezes.

Thanh woke to find himself stretched out on a concrete block with a blur of faces peering anxiously over him. He was alive and he was with people. It was several minutes before he realised that he was in a communal cell. One of the inmates was sitting behind his head and waving a plastic sandal close to his face to create a draft. The air, rancid with the sweat of too many bodies crowded into a small place, smelt sweet to his nostrils. Without being able to fully register his thoughts he knew, with an absoluteness more satisfying than anything he'd experienced before, that he was glad to be alive. The conversation of his fellow inmates was like honey to his starved senses. It washed over him in mellowed tones pushing away the loneliness of his days in isolation.

Thanh lay on the stone block, drifting in and out of consciousness, for a further two days before he was able to register his gratitude. 'When they brought you to us you were almost dead, brother. I'm amazed you were able to come back.'

Recognising the voice of his former cell neighbour, Truong Thu Linh, Thanh tried to lift himself up, but Linh gently touched his shoulder forcing him to stay where he were. 'You had better lie down for a while longer. The infection's almost gone, but your body's in bad shape. We managed to smuggle antibiotics in through one of the guards. Without his help you would have died.'

Seeing his friend's face for the first time Thanh studied him. The dancing, gentle eyes revealed a mischievousness Thanh hadn't anticipated. Linh's lips curved upwards only at the left side and gave his face a comical, mocking appearance. The shocking white hair resting on his shoulders completed the picture of humour which surrounded Linh's character.

'Before your arrival seven days ago, there were twenty-nine of us. . . .'

'Seven days! Have I been here that long?'

'Yes brother. We've listened to your rambling for seven days. We were at the point of taking bets on your chances of survival. I have to confess I was beginning to doubt my common sense in having backed your tenacity to pull through. There were moments when I seriously thought you wouldn't make it.'

'What if I'd died?'

Linh shrugged. 'I'd have forfeited my turn for sleeping on the block.'

Thanh looked around at his cramped cell-mates sitting on the floor with their legs drawn up tightly under their chins and realising the luxury which was being offered to him by letting him stretch out he tried to shift himself into a sitting position.

Linh shook his head and pushed his legs back onto the block. 'There's time for you to take your turn on the floor but for now just enjoy the privilege fate has afforded you.'

Thanh's recovery took several months. At first he could only lie down and submissively sip the nourishing liquids Linh held to his lips. Later, when the swellings were gone and the raw skin no longer wept he was able to sit up and walk around a little. He spent the days talking quietly with Linh. He learned that Linh had been transferred out of the isolation unit to his present cell on the day of Thanh's interrogation with Khiem. It was Linh who had wiped his brow and nursed him back to health when he was delirious.

Thanh's delight in meeting his former neighbour in the flesh, gave his life new meaning. Their whispered conversations were more vital to him than the bowl of watery rice that sustained his body through the eternal days of confinement. Thanh often wondered about his dream, or his death. In a moment of shared trust he confided in Linh. Was there really some higher purpose to his life? It was a puzzle which often occupied his thoughts. If his life held a higher purpose, then what was it? Prison life seemed to offer so few opportunities. Linh didn't question Thanh's spiritual experience. The answers, he said would only come to him as the opportunities arose. By rights he believed Thanh should have died and so the fact that he survived gave him a special responsibility to seek out his life's destiny.

Although the cell was overcrowded and the air stagnated as everyone took turns to lie next to the door and breathe in the few fresh molecules that slipped under it, Thanh continued to enjoy the companionship of his cell-mates. He heard stories of how inmates had been arrested for such minor infractions as playing 'yellow music' (songs popular during the old Saigon regime), or because they had fallen foul of a superior who accused them unfairly of some wrongful doing. He heard tales of his cell-mate's sexual conquests. With each telling, the conquests grew a hundredfold. Nhan, who was propositioned by a beautiful maiden, worthy of being the daughter of the Dragon King, in a later telling was propositioned by all of the Dragon King's seven daughters. They tore their clothes from their bodies and threw themselves on top of Nhan in a wild sexual frenzy. 'What did they look like with their clothes off. Come on, more detail. Then what?' The banter went on. Everyone understood it was a game, but it filled a need.

There were a few inmates who curried favours from the guards by their willingness to volunteer information, but they received such a hard time from the other prisoners Thanh wondered why they thought it was worth their while. Everyone was aware that the government planted informers among them, so although there was a level of honesty among them, it was always tinted with discretion.

Thanh was on his way to a complete recovery when a new prisoner was introduced into their cell. At first there was a groan as everyone was forced to move around to accommodate an extra body, but when the prisoner introduced himself as Mr Tien and told the other prisoners he had escaped from Vietnam in 1979 and been a prisoner in China, everyone's interest was immediately aroused. Thanh's interest was particularly stirred as he realised the camp Mr Tien was speaking about, was the same one his brother-in-law Cuong had been sent to. When Tien spoke of his experiences in Dong Hung and Fang Cheng, Thanh was bursting to ask him questions about Cuong and the others. It was almost certain he would have known them, but it was equally certain that Mr Tien's being placed in Thanh's cell, was also no accident. Khiem would be just waiting for Thanh to bite on his bait. Were Thanh to show an interest in learning about Cuong and the others, Khiem would interpret that as being evidence of Thanh's involvement in their anti-government group.

Mr Tien was eager to talk and so Thanh was able to glean a reasonable amount of information from questions the other prisoners asked. Linh also seemed to have a second sense of Thanh's need to know about Tien's experiences in the Chinese camps. When Tien ambled off on digressions Linh gently guided his conversation back to his experiences in China.

'So, what were some of the things that happened in Dong Hung?' said Linh.

'Three men were put in the monkey house for stealing the commandant's pig.'

'What were their names?'

'Ah . . . one of them Long, escaped. He was shot or eaten by the dogs, I'm not sure. The other two, Hien and Cuong were arrested with me after the demonstration. We all pushed the gate down then piled out of the camp in protest of the way we were treated. Everyone joined in, women, children, babies, everyone.'

'It was a brave thing for everyone to do,' said Linh.

'I knew of a Hien and Cuong who escaped to China. What was the rest of their name?'

'Tran, something Hien and Nguyen Cao Cuong. Were they your friends?'

'No.'

'Although I was arrested along with them, they released me after six months.'

'Why?' said Thanh. It was the first question he'd asked, but there was something about Tien that made him uneasy.

'I don't know. They took me to Kham Chau Prison, questioned me about the demonstration, then released me into Fang Cheng Camp.'

Thanh was just about to ask a further question when Linh nudged him aside and interrupted him. 'And what about the other two, Hien and Cuong?' said Linh. 'What happened to them?'

'They were taken to Kham Chau, along with two others. But as to what happened to them no one knows. In all likelihood they are still there or maybe they were pushed back across the border.'

Through Linh's further prompting, Thanh also learned that Fang Cheng had been the better of the two camps. 'The buildings were solid in Fang Cheng and our water was satisfactory,' said Tien. 'We even started a school programme for the children. I was teacher number one.'

'That's excellent, Mr Tien. I'm sure you were a good teacher, but I don't understand how you came to be forced back into Vietnam,' said Linh.

'When we were in Dong Hung we were promised we could apply to go to resettlement countries. A few refugees from overseas were allowed to visit and select wives. Some people even got away by forging documents for family reunification, but generally we were stuck. Especially the men. There was one really pretty widow, Huong, her name was. She could have got away to England through marriage, but she kept herself aloof. No one really understood her. We thought she had to have been crazy to turn an opportunity like that down. Goodness knows what's happened to her now. I would have married her myself given half a chance.'

'So how did you get to be in Vietnam?' prompted Linh.

'A delegation from the United Nations came. The commandant really wanted to make an impression on them. Normally our food rations were pretty meagre. Rice soup, the odd vegetable and pork fat. You know, just like our cuisine here. Anyway, the commandant put on a good show for these people. He killed off some of his prize pigs, extra vegetables were brought in from the village, and we were even given some halfway decent clothes. Most of us just had the clothes we left Vietnam in. Anyway he made us really smarten the place up. He even gave us some yellow paint.' Tien had gained the attention of the whole cell. 'Well, when the delegation arrived they thought we were living in luxury. You know what I did?'

'What did you do, Mr Tien?'

'I went up to this important looking man and I put him straight. I told him just how things really were. The next thing I knew, the UN people were gone. I was handcuffed, slung in a truck and taken to the border.'

'Shame we couldn't get the UN people to come and visit us. We could elect you as our leader,' said Mr Pham. Thanh chuckled along with his cell-mates at the backhanded compliment Pham had thrown at Tien. 'It's a thought though,' continued Pham, 'We could invite the UN to keep a watch on our lot. Who fancies roast pig on the menu today?' Roast pig sounded good to everyone since food was the second favourite topic of conversation.

'Come on, let's be reasonable,' said Linh. 'It would spoil all their fun. If our communist superiors couldn't torture us and spike our food with salt, what would be the incentive for working here. Not the money, that's for sure. Vietnam is bankrupt in more ways than one.' Linh's comments brought about even more laughter.

At the height of the laughter the cell door was flung open and the guard stood at the doorway with his gun pointed into the body of the group. 'Quiet down. You're prisoners. You have wronged the state. Why aren't you being submissive? We didn't bring you here to enjoy yourselves.' The guard's words brought a rumble of suppressed laughter. His face turned beetroot and he levelled his gun at several of the offending heads. Stepping backwards, so as not to turn his back on the prisoners, the guard yelled for back-up. A second guard hurried to his assistance and slammed the cell door shut. As the door banged back into position the inmates broke out into riotous laughter.

'We'll probably pay for this,' commented Pham. There were quiet nods, but generally the mood was one of exultation. The guard who had opened up their cell was Sergeant Nhu, a known bully with no sense of humour. As Thanh settled back down to his place on the concrete slab, he felt a sense of pride and cohesiveness with his cell-mates. Pham was right, they probably would pay for it, but every victory they won was a statement of their limited freedom to express themselves.

For the next two days their rations were cut in half. The rice, which in normal circumstances was fairly inedible, was served with grit which made it almost impossible to eat. With the water ration kept under tight control, to have rinsed the rice out was an unaffordable luxury. No one complained, although Thanh was disturbed when Tien and the two other cell-mates he suspected of being informers were taken away for periods of questioning. He was even more shocked, however, when a week later, after no further punishment from the guards, his name was called.

Thanh followed the guard down the corridor and across the courtyard to the interrogation rooms. He was taken into a room where he was told to sit still and wait for one of the prison staff. Thanh waited. An hour passed and no one came. Then the guard came back, and with no explanation of why he'd had to sit there, he was led back to his cell. The following day two guards came in and fetched Linh. From the way they handled him, it was obvious he wasn't being called for release. Thanh waited anxiously all day, hoping that nothing was seriously wrong. It occurred to him they might be playing the same game with Linh as they had with him.

When the switch for the night guards came and Linh still had not returned to the cell, Thanh knew his fears had been realised. Linh wasn't going to come back. He had probably been punished for his anti-communist remarks and would be contained in the isolation block. The atmosphere in the cell was sombre. Thanh found that, whereas before, he had been liked and well respected by his fellow prisoners, they now regarded him with loathing and suspicion. Everyone knew Linh was his friend, and had perhaps even saved his life. In the brotherhood of the prison community, to betray a friend placed Thanh amongst the lowest of the low.

Chapter 12: Full circle

3rd December 1985 to 17th August 1986

The supple rope has been replaced with hard irons.
At every step like bracelets of jade they jingle.
Although a prisoner, held suspect for spying,
mine is the dignified bearing of a Court official.
PRISON DIARY, HO CHI MINH

HIEN KNEW AS WELL as anyone how dangerous the border area could be, especially the half a mile either side of the boundary, but after more than a year of isolation in Kham Chau Prison, plus the years of confinement in Dong Hung, it was a relief to be back with his friends and to be facing this opportunity to measure his wits against the uneven odds they were up against. Although Tien had been arrested with them after the escape from Dong Hung, he had not been with the others when they were taken from their prison cells in Kham Chau and loaded into the police truck. Hien could only speculate that he had either befallen a more serious fate or he had agreed to co-operate with the Chinese. Hien suspected it was the latter. The pressure to give in to interrogation, and to accept the financial reward and promises of freedom offered in return for spying against Vietnam, was something Hien had repeatedly closed his ears to. It didn't matter to Hien that he felt at odds with his own government, the country of his birth was Vietnam and he would not be a traitor to her. Tien, on the other hand, was not a man to inspire trust and Hien was glad not to have him along.

Hien still regretted deeply that Dung was not with him. As he reflected back to the time of their arrests Hien wondered yet again how Dung was doing in Dong Hung. Hien was constantly worried about his brother's welfare — Dung was unpredictable and Hien wondered what crisis he might have brought upon himself during his absence. Huong's warning, that he was powerless against the commandant's authority still shadowed him, and served as a constant reminder of his own weakness. Hien had no claim on Huong and Tuyet yet they were as dear to him as though they were his family. His only consolation was that they and Dung were together and could somehow watch out for one another.

Meeting up with Cuong, Duyen and Lap again, after the long separation, gave him the feeling anything was possible. On the eighty-kilometre journey to the border no one spoke. Under the watchful eye of their guards it would have been foolish, besides now was the time to pray, or if not pray then to draw upon all of their survival energy. As the police truck pulled off the road and came to a halt, Hien felt his stomach rise to his mouth. He sat rigid as the guards removed his chains before forcing him to climb out of the police truck along with his three comrades. With guns levelled at their heads Hien wondered if he was about to be shot, but when the guards ordered them to cross the border into Vietnam, Hien saw a chink of an opportunity. Although their survival hung on a thin thread where a misplaced foot on a landmine could blast them to eternity, he determined to try for it.

Cuong was the first to start running. He threw Hien an urgent glance and then instead of running straight ahead as Hien had expected, he ran in a zigzag fashion toward the shelter of a heavily shrubbed area. The Chinese guards fired their guns. Whether it was at them or it was a ploy to alert the Vietnamese patrols to their presence, Hien didn't know. In any event as they grouped together in the dense foliage, out of breath and shaking, miraculously none of them had any visible bullet holes in them or had trodden on a landmine.

'The Vietnamese patrols are going to be on us soon,' said Cuong. 'There's a stream near here. If we can submerge ourselves in it and drag ourselves along, the stream winds back into China.'

'China!' exclaimed Duyen.

'You can go back to Vietnam if you like, but my idea is to double back into China and make my way to the coast. If we can get to Bac Hai there are Vietnamese boats which stop on their way to Hong Kong.'

'Bac Hai is double the distance of Kham Chau. It's all the way back and more.'

'It's the only route to Hong Kong unless you want to try to make it to Mong Cai or Haiphong. For me the route to freedom lies north.'

The sound of gun shots splintering the air was unnerving. It might have still been the Chinese guards, but in any event Hien decided he couldn't hang around debating the issue of where they were going. 'A Vietnamese patrol is likely to be upon us any minute, but they won't risk following us back to China. I'm with you, Cuong. Let's go.' As Cuong led the way toward the stream Hien noticed that Duyen and Lap were following.

Three hours later they were already fifteen miles up the coast of China and Cuong suggested they take a rest before deciding what to do next. The ploy to double back into China had worked. It had fooled the Chinese because it was clearly not what they expected them to do. It had persuaded the Vietnamese patrol, which for a while had seemed to be fast gaining on them, that they were probably Chinese and it was better not to pursue them into what might easily have been a trap. Hien couldn't help laughing at the ingeniousness of it.

'Well, now that the immediate danger is over, what next?' asked Lap.

Hien contemplated the problem. None of them had any money and besides being in a hostile country, they were still several hundred miles from Hong Kong.

'I have a cousin,' said Duyen. 'I haven't seen him in ten years but I believe he lives in Pai Lung. If we could just get enough money for the transport, food or whatever it takes to get us to Bac Hai, then maybe we could get jobs. It's going to take a while to organise a boat to Hong Kong. Besides the boats that stop there will be full so why should they jump at taking us?'

'Duyen's right. The first thing we need is money or at least find the means to obtain it. Your relative in Pai Lung. . . .' said Hien. 'Do you think we can trust him?'

'My cousin's name is Kenong. That's all I know about him. If anyone has another idea I'm open to it.'

Hien cracked his knuckles as he sat across the white-clothed table and surveyed the tanned, rugged seaman's face of Mr Wong. Yes, Mr Wong looked to be a man he could trust. And why not? The very fact that they were alive was proof their luck must have changed for the better. The evidence was there. They had passed through one of the most dangerous places on earth without stepping on a landmine. They had evaded capture by Vietnamese and Chinese border guards and with all of this good luck going for them they had successfully located Kenong, the distant cousin of Duyen in Pai Lung. It was Kenong who had introduced them to the construction manager who'd provided them with casual labour for the past three months, and after travelling with them from Pai Lung to Bac Hai, it was Kenong who successfully located the group of five asylum-seekers from the Chinese camp of Long Chau. The Long Chau asylum-seekers, escapees themselves, were as anxious to get to

Hong Kong and to share the costs as they were themselves. What better luck could a man hope for?

Hien filled the teapot from the hot water flask. He was feeling confident as he surveyed the now familiar faces of his new companions. From the description they had given of the Long Chau camp, it sounded to be as awful a place as Dong Hung. Only the origin of the inmates was different. Located west of Dong Hung, near the Lang Son railway terminus, most of the camp inmates were from Hanoi or from Ha Bac and Lang Son provinces. They all had their own stories and during the past two days Hien had been as eager to listen to their tales of woe as he was to relate the horrors of his life in Dong Hung. Sitting together with this new visitor, Mr Wong, the group of desperate young men were a force to be reckoned with.

'You can have the boat for seven thousand yuan on condition that myself and my family travel with you,' said Mr Wong.

Kenong raised his brows. 'Six thousand.'

Mr Wong shook his head adamantly. 'I could sell the boat for eight thousand.'

'Yes, but that wouldn't secure a place on it for your family,' insisted Kenong.

'I'm already down a thousand. I just can't do it.'

'If you insist on more money,' interrupted Cuong, 'then we'll have to stay here much longer to earn it. And the longer my friends stay here, of course, the greater the risks to both us and to you.'

'Why the risk to me?'

'Look around you. People see us talking together. If we're arrested don't you think they'll have an interest in talking to you?'

Mr Wong looked uncomfortable. 'I'll settle for six thousand, but you must come up with the money for food and fuel.'

'It's a deal,' said Cuong.

Glancing at his new companions from Long Chau Camp, Loc, Xuan, Pham, Toai and Giao, Hien raised his can of beer. 'To Hong Kong and a free life.'

'May the wind be our friend and carry us safely,' added Kenong.

For twenty-one days the boat made steady progress. They had made several stops along the coast to take on machine oil and additional rice, and with no mishaps their journey to Hong Kong looked to be sealed.

Hien leaned back against the stern and let the fresh breeze wash over his face. He noticed that the waves were beginning to increase in size, but he enjoyed their vibrancy. His only regret was that he hadn't somehow organised an escape from Dong Hung earlier. If he could have been making this journey with Dung, Huong and Tuyet, he would have felt more at ease with himself, but the nagging feeling that he'd abandoned them was never far from his thoughts. Hien wasn't sure exactly when he realised that he'd fallen in love with Huong, maybe it even went as far back as Kim Bang's boat. What mattered was that because of propriety, her being a widow, he'd delayed speaking of his feelings. Now it was too late. She and Tuyet would never know how much they meant to him. Since caution was not one of his normal traits, he couldn't believe that he'd been so stupid as to let such an opportunity slide by him. Hien fantasised endless situations where he spoke to Huong of his love for her. He imagined their dialogue, then improved upon it like a script editor, until he was satisfied that the words were just right.

They were within sight of Macau, and only a matter of hours off reaching Hong Kong, so Loc's words disrupted Hien's thoughts with timely impact. 'I've heard stories that the officials of Hong Kong treat those who have been in China differently from the Vietnamese who come straight from Vietnam.'

Hien pulled himself into an upright position. 'What!'

'How do you mean different?' asked Cuong.

'They don't regard us as refugees. I know of men from Long Chau, who after escaping and arriving safely in Hong Kong, were put in Victoria prison. We received letters from them telling us not to go there.'

Hien was stunned at the news. 'So why tell us now?'

'Because if we go into Hong Kong we have to agree on a plan. We have to say we came directly from Vietnam. We need to know things like the current cost of a kilo of rice. Silly details like that.'

'That's not so simple,' said Mr Wong. 'The boat's registered in China. Maybe they can check on that.'

Before Hien was able to register what was happening, Cuong had jumped up and with his hands clasped around Loc's throat, was shaking him. 'You brainless runt. Why keep this secret from us?' Loc's Long Chau companions looked uneasy, so Hien positioned himself ready to take them on should they move toward Cuong.

Loc was red-faced, whether from Cuong's grasp or his own indignation, it wasn't clear. He was gasping as he spoke. 'Look you have to understand, we were desperate. If you'd known about Hong Kong policy would you have come?'

'Bastard. You bastards deliberately tricked us.' Cuong spat the words in Loc's face.

Hien could feel the tension rising. 'Look we're all desperate. None of us wanted to stay in China, so if we don't go to Hong Kong where else is there?'

Loc's companion Pham edged toward Hien. 'Ask your friend to let go of Loc's throat.' Pham's voice was low and calm, but the underlying threat was evident. 'The five of us agreed that if we mentioned anything about Hong Kong either you or Mr Wong might have dropped out of the deal. Everyday we spent in Bac Hai could have cost us our freedom. We thought that once we were on our way we could work out another plan.'

Cuong released his grasp from Loc's throat. 'You're lucky I don't throw all of you off the boat.'

Loc pulled himself upright. 'I didn't say we couldn't go to Hong Kong. I just said we need to have a plan.'

'Plan!' exploded Cuong. 'You just heard the man, our boat's registered in China. Mr Wong and his family are Chinese. How can we devise a plan at this stage? Instead of tossing you overboard, you want me to throw them?' Cuong shoved Loc toward Mr Wong's youngest daughter. 'Here you throw the kids while I tackle the big people.'

Giao pulled out the map. 'There's always Japan. . . .'

Mr Wong looked aghast. 'This boat can never make it to Japan. It's too far away and there's open sea to navigate.'

'Then the Philippines. Look, if you're worried about the open sea, here's what we can do. We continue to hug the China coast north of Hong Kong, then at the narrowest point we cross to Taiwan. We then hug the Taiwanese coast to its southernmost point. There is open sea through the Bashi Channel to the Luzon Strait, but beyond that there are islands we could stop at.'

Mr Wong shook his head. 'This isn't what I planned. I have my children to consider. There are already signs of a storm coming up, and there simply isn't a narrowest point. You're talking about two hundred, three hundred miles of open sea. What happens when there's no shore to take shelter?'

Hien could hear the anxiety in Mr Wong's voice. The helmsman knew his boat better than any of them and the memory of another ethnic Chinese helmsman, Kim Bang, was still raw in Hien's memory. As he looked at Mr Wong's two little girls, he could see in their faces the fear of Kim Bang's daughter Tuyet. He could see the face of Tyan Yu, and then the face of the child who didn't survive and whose name he could no longer remember. 'I've seen how a boat can break up in a storm. If I'm never on another one, that suits me. Whatever happens to us is of little consequence, but the children, they are our future. Who knows anything about Macau?'

'I hate to tell you this but I suspect Macau's policy is no different from Hong Kong's,' said Pham.

Cuong looked toward Mr Wong. 'What were your reasons for leaving China?'

'Their one child policy, it created. . . . But it doesn't matter now. If my children were to drown. . . .' Mr Wong's wife let out a stifled sob.

'I think we should take our chances with the Macau authorities,' said Hien. 'And if we go to prison, what's new?'

The government of Macau proved to be as rigid in its interpretation of 'port of first asylum' as the Hong Kong government was rumoured to be. Since they had come from China, they were not refugees and were the responsibility of China. Mr Wong and his family had barely set foot in Macau before they were handed over to the Chinese officials at the border. For Hien and the others there had been a slight reprieve as the authorities argued it out among themselves as to whose responsibility they were. In the end the Chinese authorities confirmed their registration at the Dong Hung and Long Chau camps, and reluctantly agreed to take them back.

On the morning of the handover, Hien found himself shackled and herded along with Cuong and the other single men to the waiting police truck. He'd prepared himself for a period of detention while he explained his circumstances to the Macau authorities, but to be handed over to the Chinese authorities, without any opportunity to tell their stories was a fate neither he nor the others had bargained for. As the police prodded them toward the truck, Cuong, who was chained at the head of the group, tugged himself forward and threw himself in front of the truck while the others taking his lead threw themselves alongside him. 'Let us die here. For God's sake, just run us over if you want to be rid of us, but don't send us back to China.' Hien couldn't tell who was yelling what. They were all yelling different things and banging their heads into the ground in a desperate hope that the authorities would acknowledge their plight.

The police converged on them with electric sticks and batons. When reinforcements arrived the police advanced on them in force and they were beaten, dragged, and thrown into the truck where they were further secured to the metal legs of the benches. Their continued pleas and banging of heads against the sides of the police truck elicited little sympathy and at eleven o'clock precisely they were handed over officially to the Chinese authorities on the Macau–China border.

Within eight days, Hien and Cuong found themselves separated from their two compatriots from Dong Hung and the five from Long Chau, and taken to the Sino–Vietnamese border. As they were bound and blindfolded, one of the Chinese guards fired his weapon. Then with gun barrels sticking into their backs they were ordered to walk towards the border. They were back where they came from. As they began to walk forward, the Chinese guards fired off several more rounds and at each volley Hien stiffened expecting to receive a back full of lead. Aware of Cuong's close presence he tried frantically to come up with a plan. If they could just get rid of their restraints and repeat their old trick maybe they had a chance. It was a slim hope and as Hien wrestled to free his bound wrists while taking small hesitant steps which led him further into the heavily mined area, he prayed for divine intervention.

Cuong, with a strength enhanced by desperation, freed his wrists from the rope and yanked off Hien's blindfold before snatching at the rope on Hien's wrists. Hien sprinted after him toward the protection of the undergrowth, but had barely taken two strides, when a fresh round of shots was fired just over their heads. There was no mistaking that this time the shots had been fired from the Vietnamese side. An order was shouted in Vietnamese. 'Stand still, or we'll shoot you.' Hien and Cuong stopped in their tracks. The gunfire had been too close for them to have any illusions that they could make a run for it.

Their hands were rebound and they were marched the ten kilometres to the 313 border encampment. The injustice of their treatment in Macau was still incomprehensible. To have come so far in their quest for freedom, the risks, the pain, the long years of detainment and then to be handed over to first their Chinese captives and now the Vietnamese — a full circle without any opportunity to put forward their case for asylum, was more than Hien could take in. He'd always imagined that outside of Vietnam there was justice, that he'd have been welcomed into the free world with open arms.

Upon arrival at the encampment Hien was pushed so brutally into the hut that he tumbled into Cuong, knocking him off balance. Cuong had barely managed to get himself to his feet when one of the soldiers forced him up against the wall.

'Right, what's your name?'

'Le Duc Thoai.'

The officer kneed Cuong in the groin. As Cuong doubled over, the officer pulled him up by his shirt and spat into his face. 'Liar. One of my men recognised you. You are Nguyen Cao Cuong, the deserter and a traitor to all Vietnamese soldiers.' As the man went to take another strike at Cuong, Hien threw himself toward him. Several soldiers rushed forward and flung Hien back against the wall and as he fell to the ground, he felt the sole of a rubber sandal stamp down onto his nose. Warm blood trickled into his mouth.

'Let's show you how we treat traitors.'

Hien was still recovering when he heard them drag Cuong outside. Three of the soldiers remained in the hut with him. Each took their turn kicking him in the face, ribs, groin, anywhere they could get a strong blow in until they grew bored and left him alone. There was nowhere on his body that didn't feel as though it hadn't been run over by a truck. His breathing came in slow painful gasps, but all he could think was, thank God, they hadn't asked him his name.

Several hours of lying in pain and fear passed before Hien was dragged outside. Stumbling along on his bloodied feet, he was led to a clearing. The sight of Cuong suspended by his legs from a tree made him gasp. In one desperate glance Hien noted the bucket of water near by and Cuong's lifeless body. 'Your friend wasn't very co-operative, but I think you will be ready to tell us everything.' As one of the soldiers cut the rope, letting Cuong's body slump heavily to the ground, another moved forward to kick the body into a nearby ditch.

'Bury him.' As Hien was pushed toward the ditch several guns were levelled at his head. 'Bury him.'

Hien crouched down beside Cuong's body. Reaching into the shallow ditch he gingerly touched Cuong's face. It felt warm. It didn't seem as though Cuong were breathing, but he couldn't be certain that he was dead. A rifle butt whammed into Hien's head. Dizziness took hold of him and he snatched to grab hold of something as he tumbled sideways. The gun barrels moved in closer to his head. 'Throw some dirt and branches over your friend.'

'He might not be dead.' Hien heard the click of a rifle. As he pulled himself up to his knees, and scraped some dead leaves and turf into the ditch, he was all the time wondering why he didn't just let them shoot him.

Chapter 13: Thanh Hoa Prison

17th June 1986 to 3rd April 1988

Nostalgically a flute wails in the ward.
Sad grows the tone, mournful the melody.
Miles away, beyond passes and streams, in infinite melancholy,
A lonely figure mounts a tower gazing far and wide.
PRISON DIARY, HO CHI MINH

L AM SON THANH HOA PRISON — renamed by the prison inmates as: 'Place of poisonous water with no exit or hope for the future' — lived up to its name. Since most prisoners' cases had not yet been brought to trial the ultimate torment was that there were no happier times to be anticipated or days to be counted off. Hopes of going home were pounded ruthlessly into the ground by the endless drudgery of their daily lives. The commandant, Ngo Pham Do, could order a man to perform hard labour well beyond his physical capability with the threat that, if he refused or slacked off on his work, it would go against him at his hearing.

When Thanh arrived at Thanh Hoa Prison, his relief in getting away from the silent rejection of his former cell-mates in Hanoi was short lived. He was immediately assigned work with the quarry detail, where suspended from a rope over a cliff edge, his task was to chip away at the rock face with a chisel and hammer before placing a stick of dynamite into the cavity. His only respite was during the few precious moments of refuge when all the dynamite was in position, and inmates were lowered to the ground to take shelter from the explosion.

During one such break, Thanh found himself crouching next to an inmate who had been nicknamed by the other prisoners as, 'Uncle Tung of the South'. There were several former Saigon officials in the prison and since self-confession was as much a part of the prisoners' lives as was hard labour, rumours as to a man's past crimes were common knowledge. Thanh had never spoken to Tung, but knew that he'd been one of the instigators in the coup d'état against President Diem. Since the names of high-ranking political prisoners were often changed by the authorities, Thanh didn't know if Tung was really his name or not. He was large for a Vietnamese, with a shock of grey hair and Thanh thought the name, Uncle Tung of the South, suited him.

As Thanh prepared himself for the blast Tung leaned toward him and whispered in his ear. 'You're new here, aren't you?'

'New to Thanh Hoa, but not new to the Prison Archipelago.'

'Well my advice is keep your head down and don't eat the manioc,' said Tung.

'Why not eat the manioc? We lived on it during the war years.'

'It's bad luck. Especially for those of us who work the dynamite detail.'

Thanh laughed. 'I'll follow your advice brother.'

A month later when Thanh learned that Tung had been transferred into his political indoctrination session and also his smaller self-criticism group, he was delighted. Thanh found the robot-like Xuong's jargon at the indoctrination sessions repetitive, but to have fallen asleep during a session would have been tantamount to treason. During the hour-long meetings inmates were expected to sit cross-legged and keep their eyes riveted on the instructor, however in the smaller self-criticism group with Comrade Thao, participants were encouraged to work through their past mistakes.

It was at one of these smaller meetings that Thanh first heard Tung speak of his involvement with the former Saigon government. 'It's incorrect,' argued Tung, 'to accuse me of leading the army in the attack on the Xa Loi Pagoda. Neither myself nor the army were involved. The raid was carried out by Nhu's secret police and made to look as though it was us. I'm willing to confess to my misguided sense of nationalism: co-operating with the Americans was not the way to bring about freedom for our country. I knew that at the time, but faced with all the conflicting forces operating in Saigon, we were just trying to find our way through. The eventual unification of the motherland was on all of our minds, but we had to first prove that we were strong enough to negotiate a fair settlement for the South.'

'North, South, it doesn't matter. We are one country and one people.'

'I know that, but at the time it seemed important to protect. . . .'

'Protect what? Your self interest?'

'It wasn't self-interest, although I won't deny I had ambitions, but really I did what I thought best for the people.'

'The people of the South.'

'Yes, brother. I bow my head down to your superior intelligence. My thinking was limited. I thought only of the people in the South.'

When the inmates gathered together the next day for their meal, Thanh took the opportunity to speak to Tung. 'I would be careful brother. Thao is not so simple-minded as Xuong. I'm sure he senses the sarcasm in your voice.'

'What I was saying was true. I have made mistakes — far too many. Believe me, I've had more than ten years of re-education to ponder them, but it's Thao and others like him that make me want to throw up. Their arrogance is insufferable. If their purpose is to clone me into one of them it'll never work. I'll always be at odds with their thinking.'

'Although on different sides we both dedicated our lives to fighting for freedom. I wonder if we might not have done better if we had just stayed in bed,' laughed Thanh.

'I don't think there was a chance of our ever being able to do that, but you know, in 1963 there was a chance for freedom — a chance to end the war before it really began.' Tung shook his head. 'It's what all of us wanted so why did we fail so abysmally?'

'From my side I later became aware that Thich Tri Quang and his group of rebel monks were trying to discredit the Diem administration so that the Americans would withdraw their support.'

'That's exactly right. The Kennedy administration were looking for an honourable way out and we were trying to establish a power base to strengthen our negotiations with Ho. Tri Quang's links with the Viet Minh went back years. So with all of us seeking the same thing, why didn't it happen?'

Thanh shook his head. 'I look at our country's history and wonder why our people constantly face such hard trials. Even the rice crop yields itself unwillingly.'

'Diem was not the puppet I supposed him to be. He was at the point of chucking the Americans out. In May, Nhu met secretly with Ho in Cambodia to negotiate the terms of a settlement. I can't tell you how many times I've wondered what would have happened if we hadn't deposed them. The tragedy was that twelve years, and God only knows how many deaths later, on the day of "liberation", when we handed over power, there was none to give. The South didn't even have a bargaining position.'

'I remember that at the time of their assassination, my political commissar made the comment that the Americans had just shot themselves in the foot.'

Tung sighed. 'The Americans supported the coup, but we carried it out. Keeping hold of power wasn't as easy as grasping it. When Thieu finally emerged as the victor at the end of our struggle for the old South regime, I joined in a plot against him. That's how I ended up in Binh Xuyen.' Thanh knew that the old Binh Xuyen was the secret police quarters of the Saigon regime. 'First I was tortured for being a member of the Communist Party, now I'm incarcerated at Thanh Hoa Prison for being opposed to the communist regime. I tell you, next time round I'm staying clear of politics.'

Thanh laughed. 'When the American leaders introduced Thieu as the new president we couldn't believe what we were hearing. We had been all prepared to send out teams of cadres to explain to the villagers that Thieu was just another American puppet, but by their introducing him, they did it for us. From then on everyone saw him as a US puppet without our saying a word.'

'Stop talking,' yelled a guard from across the courtyard. 'You have only five minutes to get your food and eat. Talking amongst prisoners is not allowed.'

Fifteen months had passed since Thanh first came to Thanh Hoa Prison. Tung was preparing the ropes for their descent down the cliff face when Thanh noticed the grey drawn taught lines across his face. It was as though Tung's advanced years had suddenly caught up with him. 'What's wrong?' inquired Thanh.

Tung looked up from his work with the ropes. With no hint of his normal smile the light in his eyes seemed to have died. 'A letter reached me from my wife. It was written over a year ago.'

Thanh realised that the letter contained bad news. So few letters ever reached the prison, that even after a year's delay, it was an event to be celebrated when one made it through.

'My daughter Trinh, our thirteen-year-old twin granddaughters, My and Mai, were raped and murdered. They'd escaped from Vietnam in a boat and were approaching a fishing town called Songkhla in southern Thailand, when their boat was attacked by Thai pirates.' Tung's voice was flat and he spoke as though he were reading a news broadcast. 'When everyone on the boat was left for dead a young boy slipped over the side and swam to a village further down the coast. Although the local police didn't take action against the pirates the boy was taken in by villagers who managed to get word to the Red Cross.'

Thanh didn't know what to say. He felt like crying himself. The Vietnamese saying, that the sins of the father passed through three generations before being laid to rest, seemed horribly evident. Tung had been unable to protect his daughter and her children because, instead of being honoured as a war hero, he was being punished for his courage and love of country. The prisoner's impotence, in not being able to protect his family, was a dire consequence of prison life.

As the news of Tung's personal tragedy spread through Thanh Hoa, it was as though everyone shared his loss. Each man was reminded of his own family — far away and unprotected. Were they safe? Was his wife faithful? Was his old mother still alive? They were all questions that might never be answered. The lack of information coming into the prison was the added psychological pain which no one escaped.

When the mine exploded, three days after the arrival of Tung's letter, Thanh was taken completely by surprise. His rope swung violently and if it weren't for the fact that he'd tied himself in, he would have plummeted to the ground. With each successive thud against the rock face he felt his breath knocked out of him. As the blood ran from his face and chest, his breathing came in uneven, painful bursts and he felt as though a heavy weight were crushing his chest. It was only after the rope began to swing less furiously and the thunder stopped pounding in his ear, that Thanh realised he was injured. His vest and boxer shorts had been almost completely torn away. Amidst the shouting and confusion Thanh felt himself lowered to the ground, but it was only as he was lifted onto the stretcher that the pain eased and he fell into unconsciousness.

The first Thanh knew of Tung's death was when he awoke in the hospital unit of the prison. The explosion which had killed Tung had also taken the lives of five other men. Thanh was one of the lucky ones having only sustained five broken ribs and superficial bruises to his face and head. The commandant Ngo Pham Do blamed Tung's carelessness for the accident, although the truth, as Thanh saw it, was that unless a man was a hundred percent mentally and physically alert, the risk of something going wrong was unacceptably high. Tung had been distracted and that moment of vulnerability had cost his life and the lives of others suspended on the ropes near him. There had been other accidents, too numerous for them to be really considered as accidents, but always the blame was placed on the inmates, and despite frequent protests from the prisoners, nothing changed.

After superficial medical treatment Thanh was released from the hospital unit and returned to his cell block where he was temporarily taken off the job of placing dynamite and assigned to crop growing duty. It was only then that he fully understood Tung's remark about not eating the manioc. The manioc was grown over the dead bodies of former prison mates. When Thanh wrote a formal complaint to Pham Do and requested that the manioc should be grown elsewhere, Thanh was promptly reassigned work on the rock smashing detail.

The rock smashing detail, although less dangerous than placing the dynamite in the rock, was physically harder work. With his ribs not yet healed, Thanh was unable to meet his quota of work and instead of being able to take regular swings at the rocks, he found himself struggling for breath after only a short time. His slowness lead to beatings from the guards, which further set his health on a downward spiral.

When Thanh complained a second time to the commandant he was hauled off to the isolation unit where he was told he could be as lazy as he liked. Being lazy, he soon discovered, meant not lying down or pacing round his cell, but sitting for hours on end without moving. There were no chains, but a guard was assigned to watch him all the time. When he relaxed he was promptly beaten across the shoulders with a rubber strap. Although psychologically distressing, the act of sitting still gave Thanh's ribs a chance to begin to heal and when he was released, after twenty one days solitary, he was able to move and breathe with greater ease.

From conversations with fellow inmates Thanh understood that the prisoners were rarely allowed visitors, so he was surprised when he was collected from his cell block and told he had a visitor. Thanh suspected it was Khiem calling him for further interrogation so he was overjoyed when he discovered that the visitor was Nam.

When Thanh entered the room Nam jumped up from the table and rushed over. Snatching Thanh's hands he gasped at the sight of his emaciated figure. 'You look terrible. You're so thin.'

Thanh laughed. As bad as he might look to Nam, he thought of himself as little different from the rest of his fellow inmates. 'You should have seen me a month ago,' said Thanh. 'Right now I'm doing okay. I just came back from a short holiday.'

Nam looked puzzled. 'How are you going to survive a long sentence? God knows when your trial will come up. My father's been trying to help you, but it's a sensitive time right now. There's a struggle going on between the reformists and the old hard-liners. Nguyen Van Linh's policy

of *"doi moi* — renovation" is like a breath of fresh air. If he can breathe
life into the economy, then it gives credence to those of us pushing for
faster reforms.' Thanh listened intently as Nam spoke of the recent goings
on in the inner circles of government. 'We tried to pay to get you out of
prison, but it isn't possible. You're too high profile. The best we could get
is this visit.' Nam handed Thanh an opened package. 'They gave me
permission to give you this. It's medicines and some salted fish.'

Thanh took the package eagerly and examined it. It was more than
medicines and salted fish. There was a jacket, a woollen vest and some
socks. There were fresh vegetables, cooked pork and a bag of sticky rice
cakes. The temptation to eat some of the rice cakes there and then was
almost irresistible. As Thanh stared at the food supplies in wonderment
Nam continued speaking.

'I have to tell you, though, brother, Tran Van Dung's trial just
concluded. Your friend Dung was found guilty of collaborating with a
foreign country, and guilty of intent to commit acts of sabotage against
the Socialist Republic of Vietnam. He got sixteen years.' Thanh felt his
heart sink. It was what he expected, but he was still disappointed to hear
it. 'I'm sure Khiem's only been holding off on your case to get the results
of Dung's trial. What's worse,' said Nam, 'Tran Van Hien was also
arrested for entering Vietnam illegally. .'

Thanh was stunned. Dung had told him of his suspicions that Hien
and Cuong might have been pushed across the border by the Chinese,
but it was such a long time ago, Thanh assumed that they must have
made it safely to Hong Kong. 'Hien is in Vietnam?' The shock was still
too great for him to take in, but an overwhelming feeling of hatred toward
Khiem shot through him. 'Sixteen years for Dung is hardly a lenient
sentence.'

'No. Well, that's how it is.' Nam was obviously uneasy about being the
bearer of bad news. 'I should tell you Lan met with Minh two weeks ago.'
Nam's voice broke into Thanh's thoughts. 'Minh and the children were
released from Dong Cuong Yen Bai. Minh couldn't get her old house
back because it is now occupied by the nephew of the district chairman.'

Thanh felt a wave of despair. It was almost certain now that he would
not just be facing charges for helping his brother-in-law escape; Khiem
would not be satisfied until he fabricated enough evidence to charge
Thanh under Article 72: Treason against the motherland. Thanh remembered Minh's situation after Cuong spoke on New China Radio when he
had been branded as the lackey of China. His fears for Lan resurfaced.

'How is Lan?' He spoke her name quietly, afraid his showing any regard for her would put her in danger.

'She's doing okay.' Nam fished into his trouser pocket. 'I have a letter for you.' Thanh took the letter and studied the familiar handwriting. Before opening it he sniffed the envelope and then pressed it close to his heart.

My dearest Thanh,

It breaks my heart to think of you in that awful place and to never know if you are sick or in pain, lonely or hungry. I have always been a selfish person, but knowing you are there because of my family is humbling and makes it even harder to bear. The days and nights pass slowly and I never know if I will see you again.

Five months ago Senior Colonel Khiem came to visit me. It was a strange visit. Although he asked a few questions (none of which seemed to be of any significance), he was not unpleasant. I really have no idea why he came. Maybe he was feeling guilty, I just don't know.

Don't worry about me. My life is fine. I have a job at a small carpet factory. The money is enough. I know that Nam has been trying for a long time to get news of your situation and to help you. He always visits me to see that I am well and he keeps me informed about his father's efforts to try to gain your release. It was such good fortune he could have this visit. Nam thinks that after your trial it may be possible for me to see you.

I go to the temple every day and pray for you. I wonder how I ever came to know such an honourable man. Sometimes I think I don't have the courage to be worthy of you, and then at other times I'm angry with you for not being satisfied with just being ordinary. But those moments pass. I wait for you.

All my love,
Lan.

Nam will bring you some rice cakes and warm clothes I knitted for you. Take care, my love. Stay alive.

Thanh felt a lump rise in his throat. He wiped the tears from his eyes before folding the letter and carefully placing it in his shirt pocket. He would take it away and read it over and over again. Reading Lan's words it was possible to imagine their relationship had been what he'd always hoped it would be. She was so beautiful, he wondered how he could ever have neglected her. Only when he had memorised every word of her letter would he insert it into the lining of his trousers. The letter would be his most treasured possession so he would make sure no one stole it.

However, neither the letter nor Nam's answer that Lan was fine, reassured Thanh. The horror of Tung's loss haunted him. Khiem hadn't visited Lan because he felt guilty. The visit, although pleasant on the surface, had much more sinister connotations. Thanh had known what he needed to do for over a year so this opportunity of meeting with Nam made it easier, inevitable even. . . . 'Nam, I want you to do something for me. If I ever come to trial, Lan is going to be punished for the crimes I'm accused of. You know how it is. How it was for Minh.'

'Of course, I will do what I can to protect her.'

'I want you to marry her.'

Nam looked at Thanh in astonishment. 'She's married to you.'

'I've already put in a request for our divorce. Look, I know that had it not been for our close friendship you would have stolen her away from me years ago.' Nam looked at Thanh steadily, his eyes never leaving Thanh's face. 'You love her don't you, Nam?'

A pained look crossed Nam's face. 'I've always behaved honourably toward you both.'

'I know that, but you do love her.'

Nam looked down at his hands. 'She is the most exquisite creature I've ever set eyes on. How could a man not be aroused by her beauty? But I thought I hid it very well. Yes, I love her.'

Thanh felt his throat knot tighter. Was it just Lan's beauty that drew men to her? He hoped not. He hoped that she'd meant more to Nam. 'My life is doomed here. You must never tell Lan about our conversation. I will simply make the arrangements for the divorce. Her pride will be hurt, but she loves you, too, Nam. During the years when I was going crazy in myself, I know you could have taken her from me whenever you wanted. It's to your credit that you honoured our friendship, but now I'm begging you. It's the only way we can protect her. Will you promise me?' Nam hesitated in responding. Thanh leaned toward him, 'Otherwise I'll have to kill myself. If I'm dead there's no reason for Khiem to punish her to get at me.'

Nam was shaking. Even at the height of the war, Thanh had never seen him so affected. Nam, the composed, handsome, warrior, Thanh had spent his life looking up to. Nam, who from boyhood boasted that the revolution was everything, was losing his facade of discipline.

Nam slung his head back and sighed. Thanh could see that he was trying to repel his tears. 'I've dreamed of expressing my love to Lan, but this isn't how I wanted it. I would rather I fought you for her. Your words devastate me.'

'There's no other way.' Thanh's voice held a note of desperation. 'Promise me.'

Nam stood up and prepared to leave. For a moment, Thanh thought he'd leave without making any reply. Nam turned. Looking Thanh full in the face he grasped both his hands. 'I promise you.'

After Nam's visit Thanh continued with his job on the rock-smashing detail. Although it appeared that the guards were less inclined to react when he failed to complete his work load, Thanh worked as well as he could and it was only as his strength returned that he increased his work pace. He was not a slacker and did not want to put an extra load on his prison mates. Besides, the physical work took his mind off Lan and his growing sense of loneliness.

Several months passed before Thanh learned that his application for divorce proceedings had been finalised. At first he felt a tremendous sense of relief, but as the enormity of what he'd lost crept insidiously into his thinking, he fretted over how Lan would receive the news. Would she feel betrayed, or would she feel relieved to be rid of him since she was now free to enter into a more meaningful relationship with Nam? Always at odds with himself and seeking answers that were illusive, whichever way Thanh interpreted her reaction, it always left a bitter taste in his mouth.

Since Thanh now had no responsibility to anyone, for the first time in almost three years of incarceration, he became obsessed with the idea of escape. How or when he would make his move he wasn't sure. It struck him as ironic that he should suddenly think of himself as free — not free of prisons walls, but free all the same. His parents, sister and brothers were dead; his country, Uncle Chau and Nam could no longer expect anything from him because of his confinement. And Lan . . . it grated him to recognise it, but he was free of his responsibility toward Lan too. So there it was, for the first time in his life, at the age of thirty-eight, he was obliged to no one. But where he expected to feel relief, he felt only emptiness.

Thanh had barely drifted into sleep when he was woken by a guard entering the communal cell. He didn't need to be told the guard was seeking him — instinct warned him his turn had come. Any thoughts he'd harboured about escape would have to go on hold. While his case was under investigation he'd have no quiet moments to make any plans. Hien's trial had finished over two months ago, so Khiem would be anxious to turn his attention back to Thanh.

It was a surprise therefore, when after being marched down to the interrogation room, Thanh learned that Khiem was not in charge. He was informed that because of the severity of the charges against him his case had been turned over to Tran Nhu Toai. Toai, a short, wiry man with cropped brittle grey hair, wore a permanent smile across his face, and as the interrogation progressed through the night, Thanh became increasingly irritated by his sarcasm.

'You were the personal agent of President Ho. I regard it as a great privilege to be working with you.' Thanh chose to ignore the provocation. 'But tell me, were you as loyal to our great leader as you were to Nguyen Binh Long?'

Thanh knew that Toai would have read the transcripts of his interrogation with Khiem thoroughly. He would be aware Thanh had told Khiem that he trusted all his Saigon contacts. The fact was, however, that Thanh hadn't trusted all of his contacts; he knew several of the people he contacted, although purporting to be loyal to the revolution, were also being paid by Saigon. Nguyen Binh Long's loyalties had always been divided and he was arrested after the liberation of Saigon for his activities against the revolution. Thanh had seen him recently in Thanh Hoa Prison and although they exchanged pleasantries, Thanh deliberately avoided any further contact with him. It wasn't that Thanh held a grudge against Mr Long, indeed he recognised Long had played out his time during the war years doing what he believed to be right. If it meant playing both sides off against each other to get money to feed his family, that was a matter for Long's conscience alone. For Thanh to have renewed their acquaintance, however, would have been foolish. Mr Long understood this as well as Thanh.

In answering the question, Thanh decided against treating Toai with the same disrespect with which he regarded Khiem. Toai was as renowned for his brutality as was Khiem, but already Thanh could see he was more intelligent and a much more shrewd interrogator. 'Nguyen Binh Long was arrested for his activities against the revolution. Clearly the government in Hanoi had suspected him for a long time. I'm sure that when I was given information to pass on to him, his disloyalty was taken into account.'

'And what about your disloyalty? Was that taken into account?'

'We both know the leaders of our revolution don't make mistakes. If I had been disloyal, they would have known it.'

'So what made you support the traitors, Nguyen Cao Cuong and Tran Van Hien?'

'Nguyen Cao Cuong's only crime was that he deserted from the army. It was against the law for me to assist him in his escape, but since he's my brother-in-law I felt it was my duty to help him.'

'What about your duty to the motherland?'

'I made my choice and I'm ready to accept the consequences.'

'Tran Van Hien and his brother, Tran Van Dung, have both been convicted of treason. Had Nguyen Cao Cuong not died while crossing the border back into Vietnam, he would also have been convicted of treason.'

Thanh drew in his breath. This was the first news he'd had of Cuong since Dung told him about the demonstration in Dong Hung and Cuong and Hien's arrest. Nam had mentioned Hien's trial, but Thanh had supposed Cuong escaped. Hearing of his death was like a bomb shell. It brought the futility of all their efforts to achieve freedom into sharp focus.

'And,' said Toai with a broad grin across his face, 'as you say, the leaders of our revolution are never wrong. Your friends are traitors. That much has been established. They stored dynamite on their premises for the purpose of conducting terrorist activities for China.' Thanh remained silent. 'Our purpose in meeting is to establish exactly what your role was within this terrorist group.'

'There was no terrorist group for me to be involved with. My crime is simple. I gave my brother-in-law money and advice so he could leave Vietnam.'

'He left Vietnam to escape being arrested. You also tried to subvert the course of justice a second time, by distorting the evidence against Tran Van Dung. He'd already admitted to being a spy before you attempted to change his mind. You tried to turn him into a folk hero. The noble Ghost Locust honouring his dead relatives by bringing their bones back into Vietnam and this thing about his kissing the ground. How dare you draw a comparison between the traitor and our great leader.'

'I didn't make the comparison. I was making the point that a traitor doesn't kiss the soil of his motherland. It was an observation of fact.'

'Don't patronise me. We know you to be more subtle and clever than your friends. We see you for what you are Mr Thanh — a very dangerous man.'

During the course of the interrogation Thanh was transferred from his communal cell to an isolation block. Night after night of endless questioning left him worn out. He grew increasingly resentful of Toai's probing and accusations. He was still assigned to the rock smashing detail, although the guards hovered near him to make sure he remained isolated from the other prisoners.

After eight days of this unyielding regime Thanh's body screamed out for sleep. He was confused and found it impossible to relay detailed events in any logical order. He contradicted himself during the sessions, not because he was lying, but because places and dates became muddled in his mind. The beatings he took when he fell asleep during the sessions only increased his weariness. Several kicks in the ribs brought back his old problems: his breathing was tight and the shrapnel wound he had taken in his shoulder years ago, was inflamed.

During those few hours after he was led back to his cell, before the early morning indoctrination sessions began, the guards banged metal cans outside his door. The light Thanh once craved was now continuous with his cell lit up as though it were permanently under magnesium flares. Gradually Thanh lost count of the nights he was subjected to interrogation. As he was pushed back to his cell for maybe the thirteenth night in a row, and heard the thunderous echo of the door as it clanged back into its brackets, he felt an uncontrollable urge to strike back.

Thanh imagined he could feel his brain drying out from lack of sleep. If he couldn't extinguish the lights and find a peaceful place to lay his head, his sanity would desert him. Dragging himself onto his feet, Thanh drew upon the last reserves of his energy. With the strength only a crazed person could muster, he leapt at the ceiling. Smashing his fist hard against the brittle surface of the lightbulb, he let out a demented laugh as the glass shattered into a thousand particles and darkness prevailed. Instantly the door banged open. The guards rushed in, pushed Thanh over with an elbow swipe to his head, then dragged him bodily across the glass and back along the corridor to the interrogation room.

'We're not making very good progress, Mr Thanh,' said Toai. 'I'm disappointed. You understand that we must, of course, punish you for the damage you caused to government property . . . otherwise how will you learn to avoid future mistakes?'

Dung stood in line two rows behind Hien. He'd been in Thanh Hoa for two months, Hien a little less time. Both knew that the prisoner to be publicly beaten was Cuong's brother-in-law, Major Thanh. It seemed incomprehensible that since their meeting in Hong Gai three years ago, Thanh's life should have taken such a downward spiral. Although Dung did not know the details of Thanh's case, he could not help feeling that his own bad luck had rubbed off on Thanh. When Thanh was dragged out by the guards and forced down onto the ground, Dung hardly recognised him. He remembered Thanh as being tall, athletic, with gentle, angular good looks and soft penetrating brown eyes. The emaciated, broken body stretched out over the concrete block with glazed eyes hidden behind the huge swellings on his face, was not recognizable as the man Dung remembered.

As the beating began Dung wanted to turn away. The impulse to close his eyes was compelling, but he knew the guards were scanning the faces of the inmates. They would have delighted in hauling a victim out and making an example of his anti-revolutionary spirit. Each crack of the cane was a message to all of them — the pain was their pain and they all felt it keenly.

'Nine ... ten ... eleven.' The voice droned on, never faltering. With each strike Dung's anger flared. He thought of all the injustices he'd ever suffered — his father's going away to war and never returning, the confiscation of the family home, the allegations of his betrayal to the motherland, his brother's beatings. He thought of Cuong's broken body rotting in a ditch. 'Twelve ... thirteen.' As his hatred became more focused the seed of an idea began to take shape. 'Fourteen ... fifteen.'

It was over. Two rows in front, Hien's shoulders looked as though they had shrunk. The atmosphere among the prisoners was tense. It was as though everyone had stopped breathing in deference to Thanh's courage. He hadn't screamed out once, and as his wrecked body was dragged away there was a low, but distinguishable rumble among the prisoners. The assault on one prisoner was an assault on everyone.

Four weeks had passed since Thanh's beating and the memory of it was never far from Dung's thoughts. If he achieved nothing else with his life, he was determined to get Thanh out of Thanh Hoa Prison. Fortunately

Hien was of the same thinking and upon hearing of Dung's plan he was eager to help bring it to fruition. Getting himself assigned to quarry detail had been easy since the other inmates generally preferred the laborious task of smashing rocks to risking their lives placing dynamite on the cliff edge. However, stealing the dynamite took time and if Dung took too much in any one go, his assigned explosions would be noticeably less intense than those of his neighbours. It was a matter of balancing risk against time. While Thanh remained in the hospital unit, there was a chance their plan would be successful, but once he was moved back to the isolation unit it would be impossible to get him out. The isolation unit was the most heavily guarded area of the prison. By comparison, the hospital was hardly guarded of all. Prisoners rarely knew the luxury of a full recovery because once their life was out of danger they were moved out of the hospital.

It was tempting to grab an extra stick of dynamite to speed his plan along, but Dung knew the dynamite was all accounted for, so Dung collected his sticks of dynamite as instructed before making his way to the cliff edge. It was only when he was strapped into his harness and was lowering himself down the cliff face that he dared cut into the dynamite stick and allow the slim stream of powder to pour into the pouch he had hidden underneath his shorts.

Dung was making his way over to Hien with the freshly stolen powder when a fellow prisoner walked over to him. Instinctively Dung rested his hand over his boxer shorts.

'I hear our brother Thanh is beginning to make some recovery. It will not be long before he's transferred back to the isolation unit.'

Dung felt his body go tense. It was almost as though the prisoner had read his thoughts. 'Brother Thanh's a good man,' said Dung.

'I know.' The inmate then sidled closer to Dung and taking his hand as though in greeting pressed a small packet into it. 'Good day, brother.' With his fist tightly clenched over the package Dung stood rooted to the ground and stared after him as he ambled over to his place of refuge for the coming explosion.

'Get moving,' yelled the guard. The countdown for the explosion was already underway so Dung sprinted over to where Hien was taking cover.

'That was Truong Tu Linh, the writer. What did he want?' asked Hien.

'I'm not sure. Look, he gave me this.' Dung opened up the crumpled note paper. Inside was a grey-brown powder. 'Gun powder?'

'Looks like it.' Hien wet his finger and put some of the powder to his tongue. 'He knows what we're doing.'

'How?'
'God knows.'

Hien waited until the work details were lining up to be transported back to the prison before approaching Linh. 'What's the meaning of giving this to my younger brother?' Having emptied the gun powder into his own private supply, Hien handed Linh back the crumpled paper.

'There are no secrets in Thanh Hoa. Your trials were well publicised. Thanh and I are old friends. If it's your intention to include him in your escape, then I'm ready to help.'

Hien eyed him suspiciously. Why would Linh be so concerned about Thanh, and how was it even possible that he should know that he and Dung were planning the escape for Thanh?

'Thanh has many friends. None of us like what's happening to him. I arrived here two days before his public beating. It was not a sight I will forget.'

Hien continued to gaze at Linh intently. Linh obviously knew Dung was pilfering gun powder and if it had been his intention to report them he could have done so already. In spite of Linh's confinement, his book criticising the government had eventually made it to France and been published. He was quite a celebrity in the prison and it was rumoured that Amnesty International and Hong Kong PEN, the writer's group, had taken up his case with the Vietnamese government. It seemed unlikely that a man of such high principles would be an informer. Hien shrugged. 'All right. What if I am willing to trust you? How can you help us?'

'Before I tell you my plan, you must promise me that when you escape, you'll take Thanh with you.'

Hien felt affronted. 'That has always been our intention.'

Linh nodded. 'Good. Then it's as I thought. When you get him away from here tell him that you spoke to me. Tell him that I knew how he was set up at Hoa Lo Central Prison, and that the friendship between us is unstained. You must be sure to tell him that.'

'If you are indeed Thanh's friend, then please, brother, join with us in our escape.'

'No. It will be more useful to have me stay here to orchestrate a diversion.'

'We can't let you do that. There has to be a way for us all to get out.'

'My plan is better.' Linh's eyes sparkled. 'Don't worry I have my own idea of leaving here.'

When the first explosion came, throwing the kitchen roof skyward, no one seemed to know what had happened, Thanh least of all. He'd been lying on his stomach in a half sleep. Hearing the commotion he tried to pull himself up onto his elbows, but pain forced him down again. 'Maybe a boiler's blown in the kitchen,' suggested one of the patients.

Thanh could hear shouts and he was certain that the loud cracking noise above the series of explosions was gun shot. As he strained to listen two hospital orderlies rushed over to him with a bamboo sling. 'Get on.' There was no way Thanh could have scrambled onto the sling. He'd barely time to acknowledge his inability when strong hands rolled him from his mat onto the sling. The agony of the movement sent shock waves through his body but he was too weak to retaliate and his protest amounted to no more than a groan. Without any regard for his well-being the orderlies snatched up the sling and raced with him down a corridor.

A guard ran out of a side door and tried to stop them. 'What's going on?'

'The fire's spreading to the hospital unit. We have to evacuate everyone.' The guard leapt out of the way and ran back toward the hospital ward. By now Thanh had no confidence in the two orderlies and was anxious to rid himself of their assistance. Taking advantage of the interruption he tried to ease his way out of the sling, but he was pushed back.

'Let me walk,' moaned Thanh.

'No time. Besides you're not capable of walking.'

Everything was happening at great speed, but it wasn't until they hauled him into a waiting ambulance that Thanh's suspicions surfaced. The door slammed shut and the ambulance accelerated forward at breakneck speed.

Thanh turned on the two orderlies. 'What is this?'

Dung smiled. 'We're breaking you out of prison. Don't you remember us, brother?'

Thanh could hardly believe what he was hearing. The pain slamming through his body and head befuddled his thinking into a dazed fog. It was years since he'd last seen Hien, but seeing the brothers leaning over him with self-congratulatory grins on their faces, brought some recognition. 'The explosives? This is a prison break?'

'Yes.'

Thanh wanted to laugh, thank them, scold them — he wasn't sure what. 'How did you get here?'

'Same as you. We're prisoners.'

'Here, change into these clothes,' said Hien urgently. 'We can celebrate our victory later.'

The exercise of putting on the officer's uniform in the fast moving vehicle, even with Dung's help, was as painful as the hurried journey along the corridor.

'Sorry, brother, but here's something else you won't like.'

Before Thanh could anticipate Hien's next move, a sickly warm liquid splashed down over him. Wiping his hand over his face so that he could open his eyes Thanh looked aghast at his reddened fingers. 'Oh, my god.'

'It's pig's blood. You're all right. We need a disguise to get past the gate so I'm going to wrap these bandages on you. Don't say anything, just moan.' Thanh closed his eyes. At that moment moaning was what he felt he could do best.

The sirens were blaring as they slowed for the gate and came to a halt. Thanh held his breath, but as the door of the ambulance was thrown open and two guards peered in, he let out a low and painful moan. Hien pointed toward Thanh. 'It's the prison commandant. There's been an explosion — you must have heard it. He's injured and if we don't get him to hospital in Hanoi, he'll die.'

The guards looked at one another and seemed uncertain what to do. 'You have papers?' One of them asked.

'Papers! That's absurd. Can't you see this is an emergency? What's your name? You want to be responsible for the death of Commandant Do?'

The guard looked at his partner, but getting no support stepped back. 'You'd better go.'

Somewhere along route they must have stopped because Dung produced a bottle of rice wine and after easing Thanh into a raised position he poured the liquid into his mouth. 'Drink this brother. You've been moaning up a storm for the past six hours while drifting in and out of consciousness. At one point we worried we'd killed you. Our treatment was pretty brutal, eh? I'm sorry brother.' Thanh drank a good half of the bottle before dozing back to sleep.

When he awoke the second time they were easing him out of the ambulance. 'I'm sorry to disturb you,' said Dung, 'but it's time to ditch the ambulance. You can rest up here for a while before we start the trek into the mountains.'

Bleary-eyed, and a little giddy from too much alcohol, Thanh tried unsuccessfully to raise his head. 'The mountains!'

'It's not as bad as it sounds,' assured Dung. 'Hien and I know these trails and the pathways are not too rough. We'll make a proper stretcher with poles, and this time you can lie on your stomach.'

The wine had made Thanh's pain more tolerable and the irrepressible urge to laugh kept sweeping over him. 'Where are we?'

While Dung sat with Thanh on the bank, Hien and another prisoner, Dinh Hung Luong, guided the ambulance over to the edge of the gorge before pushing it over. 'We're in Lao Cai,' said Dung. The sound of crashing branches and undergrowth as the ambulance smashed its way down the slope before burying itself in the undergrowth below, brought a broad grin to Dung's face. Looking back at Thanh he said, 'After leaving Thanh Hoa we kept away from Hanoi and drove toward Son La. It was risky keeping the ambulance for so long, but since you were in no condition to travel we had little choice.'

Hien came over to join them. 'We'll clean up the mess we just made with the ambulance so no one will find it, then we'll set off into the hills before nightfall. Dung, you help us while Thanh gets some more rest.

Thanh still couldn't believe he was free. It had happened so fast. One day he was lying in a prison hospital with absolutely no hopes for the future; the next he was stretched out on a bank trying to wipe the dried pig's blood from his eyelashes. All the while he was conscious of the sun shining down onto his face, and the sound of birds singing. It was almost too much to take in. Then, suddenly exhausted and overwhelmed by his feelings, he let his arms sink back in the sweet smelling meadow grass and cried and laughed both at the same time. After all the sorrow and pain of the last three years, to know freedom, even were it to only last a day, was heaven.

Chapter 14: Back to the mercy of the seas

29th May to 12th October 1988

Pure Brightness! Yet a drizzle falls monotonously
And the prisoners' hearts suffer grievous agony.
Which way to freedom, we plead, pray?
To the yamen the guard points, far away.
PRISON DIARY, HO CHI MINH

SINCE RELATIONS BETWEEN VIETNAM AND CHINA had moved from ice cold to lukewarm, the border area was less heavily patrolled and life in the tribal villages had taken on a sense of normality. There were days in the Hmong mountain village when Thanh thought he'd never recover well enough to make the overland journey to Zhanjiang, but as the weeks passed, so did much of his pain. His breathing eased and he was now able to extend his walking from the immediate vicinity of the village to a little way beyond it. Each morning would see him getting up from his mat, with the first crow of the cockerel. Hobbling along on his stick, he would go beyond the bamboo hedge which bordered the village, then follow the three kilometres of red earthen mountain track to the stream where he would bathe his sore muscles in the icy cold water. Refreshed by his bath, he would try to push on a little further each day before giving in to fatigue and retracing his steps to the thatch village in time for a late breakfast.

While his mornings were taken up with this ritual, his afternoons were spent in a more leisurely fashion. Thanh would either sit with Hien, Dung and Luong mulling over maps and documents as they finalised plans for their escape, or when there was nothing left of importance to discuss, Thanh would go off alone and stretch out on a hammock under the umbrella shade of two coconut trees. Listening to the whispering as the branches brushed intimately against one another, Thanh realised how tempting it would be just to stay where he was.

The tranquillity of the Hmong village, the simplicity and gentleness of the women as they nursed him back to health, the laughter of the fresh faced children, provided the respite his body and soul craved. Not only had Thanh felt his own strength return, but he'd watched Dung blossom from a troubled gaunt old man to a vibrant handsome youth. Thanh suspected that the attention of the young village girls with their smiles, silver looped earrings and indigo robes, had contributed to this transformation. The magic of the village was intoxicating for all of them. Even Luong, whom Thanh hadn't been sure of, proved to be a capable hunter and fisherman. Luong knew almost as many stories as Dung, and between the two of them they would keep the children enthralled for hours. However, there were dangers and Thanh had to struggle to keep himself from falling under the village spell. He could never be sure that the authorities wouldn't, one day, find the ambulance and trace their tracks up to their mountain haven.

Their plan was to cross the border at Dong Dang with the early morning flow of market traders and then make their way to Zhanjiang on local buses. Hien had managed to secure false papers from a contact Thanh knew of in Mong Cai. For a while they had considered crossing at Mong Cai, but their Hmong friends assured them that if any suspicion arose as to the authenticity of their papers, the officials at Dong Dang were much more likely to accept a bribe than those at Mong Cai. All they were waiting for was the money to come through from Nam. There was no question that he wouldn't send it; it was just a matter of arranging the contacts to get it to Lang Son market where one of the Hmong traders would bring it up to the mountain village.

Thanh was dozing in his hammock when Hien approached him. 'Luong just came back from Lang Son with the Hmong traders. He has the money from your friend. There's a letter here with it.' Thanh sat up and taking the package from Hien he pulled out the letter:

Dear brother,

I hope your health is now fully restored. It was such a surprise when I heard of your escape from Thanh Hoa. Your friends have served you well and my only regret was that I could not have done as much for you. Still it pleases me to be able to assist you in obtaining some money. I have carried out your wishes as you asked. I sold your bike for a little more than the price you asked. I am also enclosing some money of my own. One day, when you become a rich man in the free world, you can pay me back, but until that day the money is yours. I still wonder over your plan. My idea would be for you to avoid going into China but to come back to Haiphong where I could arrange passage for you to Hong Kong. I know of the rumours filtering back into Vietnam regarding Hong Kong's detention centre policy and their plan to introduce stringent screening is not good, but surely your cases would warrant refugee status. Your friend's idea to try to get to the Philippines by way of Taiwan sounds very dangerous. The sea in this area is notoriously rough and I fear for your safety. If it is a matter of your not wanting to let your friends down, then forget it because I am willing to help them as well. It is the least I can do since it was they who helped you when I could not. Your brother and friend always.

Thanh set the letter aside. Nam had not signed it and there was no mention of Lan. He wasn't surprised, but it nevertheless saddened him not to hear any mention of her circumstances. The money was exactly what they needed. However, he would not accept Nam's offer to assist them in obtaining a passage from Haiphong to Hong Kong. He had not heard of the intention to introduce a screening policy, but Hien's reasons for not wanting to go to Hong Kong or Macau were legitimate and their plan to meet up with other asylum-seekers in Zhanjiang and to purchase a boat to get them to the Philippines was the best they had.

As they approached the border area with their cart of empty apple baskets, Hien slipped the border guard a twenty thousand dong note. 'Please hurry us through. If we can get to our supplier before the other traders we can select the best of the crop. On our way back, there'll be a five-kilo bag of apples for you.' The border guard nodded and waved them through the Vietnamese side of the border. Five minutes later as they passed into China with equal ease, Thanh grinned at his three companions.

The bus journey, zigzagging its way across country, although tiring because of the long hours of sitting on wooden seats, was largely uneventful. When the pain in Thanh's ribs gave him trouble, he refocused his thoughts to the scenery outside. After the years of confinement, the view of open fields and the hustle and bustle of small Chinese villages absorbed his attention totally. It was only as they approached Zhanjiang and met with a road block they had any reason to be concerned.

Thanh was sitting beside Dung when one of the policemen stepped onto the bus. As he made his way up the aisle, he examined each person's papers. To some he made a comment while to others he just handed the papers straight back. When he came to Dung, he scrutinised his papers for several moments. 'Why are you going to Zhanjiang? It says here that you are a market trader doing business in Qinzhou. So why come this far west?'

'My mother lives in Zhanjiang. She's dying, so I'm making this trip. . . .'

As Dung gave his explanation, a small girl sitting on the seat opposite suddenly emptied the contents of her stomach into the aisle. The vomit splattered over the policeman's trousers. Seeing his look of horror, the child's mother jumped up and frantically tried to wipe his trousers with a cloth she'd snatched from her bag. The cloth was covered in oil and the more she wiped the dirtier the trousers became. 'That's enough, woman.' Thanh suppressed his laughter as the policeman pushed the woman aside and rapidly vacated the bus.

The centre of Zhanjiang was a bustling town of shops and motorised bicycle carts. Thanh enjoyed its surface chaos as vendors, cyclists, and pedestrians criss-crossed each other's paths while hurriedly going about their business. He delighted in the variety of smells emanating from the street stalls. Cart loads of hot red peppers from the countryside were sold by the catty while fish were strung to dry in the sun. It reminded Thanh of the seaside towns in Vietnam where the activities of both the country-side and the sea flowed together.

After finding a place to sleep at a cheap hostel, Thanh rested while the others diligently set about the task of locating a boat. What they had expected to achieve in days took weeks, so when Thanh felt well enough he joined in the search. Trudging round the tea houses and dock areas day after day, making inquiries to locate the kind of boat they needed for the open sea voyage to the Philippines, he began to despair of ever finding an affordable vessel capable of making the voyage.

However, their luck changed when Luong located three Vietnamese asylum-seekers, Vu, Thai and Tam and brought them back to meet the others. They had already located a boat and were looking for other asylum-seekers to share in the cost. As they sat round drinking beer and talking of their past experiences, Hien grew excited to learn they had been in the Fang Cheng Camp.

'There was never enough food,' said Vu. 'Many times we'd catch rats and roast them over a fire. That was a real luxury.' He laughed. 'It wasn't long before we'd cleared the place of them.'

'I left Dong Hung before the transfer to Fang Cheng,' said Hien, 'but a friend of mine would have gone. She was with the group that arrived in 1983, or maybe '84 — so much has happened that I'm no longer sure.'

'I remember the Dong Hung people coming,' cut in Tam. 'When they arrived they looked even worse than us.'

'My friend was called Huong. She had a young daughter with her,' went on Hien. 'Do any of you remember seeing them?'

'The pretty widow,' laughed Tam. 'I quite fancied her myself, but she was too aloof. Besides at that time the Chinese were allowing overseas Vietnamese with British passports to come in and select wives.'

'Did she marry one of them?' asked Hien.

Tam laughed. 'I suppose. Wouldn't you if the offer were there. I tell you this thing with the women was really hard. It forced us into a bachelor life. That's when we decided it was time to escape. One moonless night we climbed over the fence and here we are.'

With a fresh coat of red paint and a new tarpaulin cover the boat looked to be in excellent condition. After staying close to the coast of China for ten days, they were five days into the sea journey to Taiwan before engine problems appeared. Hien worked with Tam trying to get the engine started. It would start, then stop. Meanwhile the currents were carrying them off course. Instead of moving closer to Taiwan, they were drifting away from it. When an island came into view no one questioned Tam's decision to stop and seek help. But as they moved closer toward it and saw the concrete bunkers hidden in amongst the hills with the machine guns trained on to them, everyone became alarmed.

'Bloody hell. Look at those,' said Dung.

Thanh had already seen them. 'And they're aiming straight toward us.'

Before they had time to retreat a shower of bullets rained into the boat. Thanh and the others flung themselves to the floor. The shooting stopped and three speedboats, loaded with uniformed men, circled the boat before moving up alongside them. An officer shouted across to them, 'Is anyone dead or injured?'

Slowly they pulled themselves up from the boat deck. By some miracle no one had been hit. The bullets had all lodged in the boat. 'Not for your bloody want of trying,' yelled Hien.

'I'm surprised. I would have expected some injuries. This is Republic of China government property. You leave this area within fifteen minutes or we will have no alternative but to shoot you.'

'You've just shot our boat full of holes. You seriously expect us to leave like this?' said Thanh.

The officer looked embarrassed. 'I can't let you land here. This is government property. It's your own fault. You shouldn't have come here.'

'We're lost and have engine trouble,' said Thanh. 'We're refugees, heading for the Philippines and were hoping for some assistance.'

'You're nowhere near the Philippines.' The officer ran his fingers round the top of his collar. When he spoke he sounded apologetic. 'Stuff rags in the holes. I'll order one of our boats to tow you south away from the island. We can only escort you a little way. It's the best I can do.' He started to turn away, then stopped and added, 'Don't come back. This is restricted military defence property. Our orders are to shoot at any boat that approaches.' There was little choice but to stuff the holes with rags and accept the offer of an escort away from the island.

The days passed slowly. Having eaten all the rice and tins of fish, their daily diet consisted of dried biscuits and tinned fruit. The strain of not seeing land and the constant struggle of keeping the boat afloat was beginning to show on everyone's nerves. Thanh was dozing while the others took turns to bail out the boat, when Luong suddenly cried out, 'It's Russian. We're near Vietnam. They'll take us prisoner.'

Thanh looked toward where he was pointing and saw a Russian tanker making a steady course southward. 'We're nowhere near Vietnam,' said Thanh. He'd just woken from a sleep and although he spoke confidently, doubt was creeping into his mind.

Seeing their expressions of concern, Tam laughed. 'We are, absolutely and positively nowhere near Vietnam. You have such little faith in me. With any luck we should sight the mainland of Taiwan in a day or two.'

The Russian ship passed without incident and Thanh breathed a sigh of relief. He realised that although the currents were carrying them south, which was ultimately where they wanted to go in order to reach the Philippines, they would not be able to negotiate the difficult crossing through the Bashi Channel to the Luzon Strait without spending several days in Taiwan to replenish their food stocks and repair the boat. Permanently blocking the bullet holes required time and money. Time they had, but finding the money for repairs would mean working illegally. It seemed to be the same everywhere. The cost of freedom came high.

Later in the day it began to drizzle and the clouds held the threat of a storm. 'It's hard enough to keep afloat as it is. If there's a storm and heavy rain. . . .' Tam didn't need to say more. From the concern on everyone's face it was clear they had all been thinking the same thing.

Darkness came early and as the evening wore on the rain became heavier forcing the boat to sink lower into the water. Hien and Luong helped Tam stretch out the boat's tarpaulin cover and attach it to the sides in the hopes of keeping some of the water out. The waves, however, continued to roll in with monotonous repetition, seeping under the tarpaulin, they formed into secondary waves that sploshed backward and forward as the boat was forced skyward before dipping back dangerously. Thanh felt his muscles tighten. His wartime experiences had taught him to cope with many things, but he was not a sailor and as the boat lurched, he felt his stomach rise until there was nothing he could do but give in to the urge to vomit. He'd barely recovered when a huge wave cascaded into the boat splashing them in the face and tearing off the tarpaulin. The boat rocked unsteadily and sank still lower. Hien snatched hold of the cover while Tam and Dung tied it back in place. The wind tore in again, fiercer this time. The cover flew upward and as Thanh leapt to grab it, he slipped and smashed his head against the side of the boat. Blood spilled down his face. Dazed, he pulled himself to the side of the boat and vomited.

'Look!' yelled Thai. 'Help us. Help!' Thanh forced himself to peer through the gloom. At first he couldn't see anything and as the seconds passed he thought Thai was must be imagining things. But when the lights of a Taiwanese fishing trawler suddenly flared over them Thanh couldn't believe their luck. Ten minutes more and the boat would be completely underwater.

In response to Thai's shouts the trawler manoeuvred toward them. It was too dangerous for it to come close so the fishermen threw a rope across. Hien attached the rope to the boat. 'We're going to pull ourselves through the water. Dung, you go first, then Thanh.' With Hien's urging Thanh slipped over the side of the boat into the sea and grabbed for the rope. He was dizzy from the blow to his head and was barely able to keep a grasp on it when Dung's arm clasped round him. 'Come on, old friend. We didn't get you out of prison to let you drown. It's not the end yet.' As Dung's words of encouragement floated in and out of his hearing Thanh tried to pull himself along the rope. The waves splashed blood and salt into his eyes and with each immersion he swallowed mouthfuls of water. The current was tugging at his body and he had barely enough stamina to carry on when he felt someone catch hold of him and haul him into the fishing trawler. With a blanket wrapped around his shoulders Thanh was led into a dry cabin where he stripped out of his wet clothes and lay down to rest.

Thanh slept fitfully through the remainder of the storm and it was only as daylight was beginning to show itself that he felt strong enough to get up and join the others. When he located them, they were sitting amongst the fishing nets on the deck with the captain, deeply engrossed in conversation. 'What is it you need us to do?' asked Hien.

'We gave you protection from the sea, now we need you to protect us from our government. It is against the law for us to pick up refugees. We will set you down safely on shore, but we ask that you do not tell anyone that it was us who rescued you.'

'We owe you our lives. None of us here will inform against you.'

'Thank you. I am sorry it has to be this way.'

'Thanh!' Hien jumped up. 'How are you feeling?'

Thanh wandered over to the nets and sat down. 'Last night I was preparing to leave this world. Today I'm filled with the wonder of it.' Thanh breathed in, 'I feel great.'

After the fishing trawler deposited them on the beach and left, they wearily trudged the seven kilometres into the village. Despite Thanh's sense of well-being he was weak and when Dung offered to let him lean on his shoulder he accepted. As brothers, Hien and Dung were alike in some ways, but Thanh found their differences more striking. Hien was strong and self-assured while Dung had a shy playfulness about him and was more contemplative, perhaps spiritual, if that was the word. Dung was the poet while Hien was the warrior. If he had died last night, thought Thanh, he would not regret his life. Miserable though it had been at times, he'd seen the best in people and the worst. He regretted Cuong's death, but the bond of friendship he'd developed with Hien and Dung gave his life perspective. It was as it had been during the war years. Friendship was more intense because life and death depended upon it. His relationship with Lan, although sexually passionate, never included the same level of comradeship.

When they eventually arrived in the village, it occurred to Thanh how God-forsaken and dejected they must look; a frightening sight to the civilised world. Thanh was wondering how they might present themselves in a less shocking light when Hien, who clearly didn't share the same concerns, strode up to the first cottage they came to and knocked on the door. An old lady answered and seeing their bedraggled state hurriedly invited them in showing not the slightest sign of fear. She spoke an odd version of Mandarin, but Thanh could understand what she was saying. 'Oh my poor drowned boys come home from the sea. What a state of

affairs.' Within minutes of entering her home steaming bowls of noodles
appeared on the kitchen table. 'If you eat this all up there's always more.'
    With the neighbours' curiosity came bundles of dry clothes and
blankets. Thanh was grateful. It meant that by the time the policeman
came to interview them and take details of their circumstances, they were
looking quite human. 'I can't tell you what will happen until after I return
from the city, but since Mrs Yim says you can stay here then I have no
objection.'
    'All seven of us?' asked Dung.
    The policeman smiled. 'Mrs Yim has had seven sons of her own,
grown up to be sailors. Any of them ever get the wrong side of her and
they'd be beating on my door asking me to lock them up for the night.'

They stayed in the village for three days before a government truck came
to transport them to Tainan. It was evident from the first that the
hospitality they received from the ordinary people was quite different
from the treatment they received from government officials. In every
country it appeared to be the same. The police in Taiwan were more
interested in determining that none of their own ships had been involved
in rescuing than they were in recognising them as refugees. Thanh's
experience of them reminded him of Hien's encounter with officials in
Macau and he found it hard to answer their questions with civility.
Although everyone told the same story, the officials remained suspicious.
They argued that since there was no wreckage along the coast someone
must have helped them. However, after five days of intermittent questioning with no variations to the original story coming forth, the officials
gave up and informed them that the following morning they were to be
transported to an open refugee camp in Kaohsiung.
    When the covered police truck arrived early the next morning, they
obediently climbed into it. They drove for several hours before the truck
pulled off the road and they were ordered to climb out. As Thanh took
in the small harbour he immediately suspected they had been duped.
There was no sign of a camp anywhere, just a few fishing trawlers floating
on the water.
    Hien was the first to react. 'What's going on? This place isn't Kaoh-
siung.'
    'No. They can't take you in Kaohsiung.'

'Have pity. One of our compatriots is sick and needs medical attention. We don't want to stay in your country, but we need time to prepare for our journey,' pleaded Dung.

'You're not taking us to Kaohsiung because there probably isn't a camp there,' yelled Hien. 'You lied.'

'Move.' The official pushed his rifle against Hien's head as the rest of his colleagues herded them along the jetty. 'We are giving you a boat and some supplies. You can go where you like, except Taiwan. South of you are the Philippines, to the west is China. If I were you I'd go back to where I came from.'

Hien glared at him. 'I'm not you, and you wouldn't.'

Aware of Hien's increasing agitation Thanh feared that he might get himself shot by provoking a fight with the man who held a gun to his head. Linking his arm in Hien's, he led him swiftly forward. 'We'll make it to the Philippines, start our own business and become millionaires. That'll show them. Then come back here and flaunt our money in their top hotels.'

Hien forced a smile. 'Yes, let's do that.'

When Thanh saw the boat, his heart sank. It was not even as good as the one they had set out from China in. They climbed aboard reluctantly. It was as though they were in a never-ending nightmare yet to have protested further would have only invited trouble. With a sad heart Thanh and his compatriots sat silent for close to six hours while the authorities towed them out into the open sea before cutting the rope. 'You're not welcome in Taiwan.'

'For pity's sake give us a compass at least,' shouted Tam.

'Go with the current.' The police boat swept passed them and tossed in a container of water and several packets of dried biscuits before rapidly pulling away.

Thai checked the boat over with Tam. 'We have very little fuel and it's doubtful we have enough food or water to get us as far as the Philippines. I don't know what else there is to do but chart out a route from the sun and the stars,' said Thai. 'If you want my opinion we're going to die out here.'

'We don't,' said Vu.

The engine ran slowly, and in spite of their desire to go south it seemed as though the boat was drifting west. 'If we keep this course up we'll end up in Da Nang,' moaned Thai.

'I wouldn't worry about that,' said Tam. 'There's about a thousand or more kilometres between us and Da Nang. If the boat does drift there, all that will be left of us is our bones. The seagulls will have picked us clean.'

'Oh lovely,' said Hien. 'What else is there nice to talk about?'

'Well, now that we are on one of the major sea lanes, it's likely a foreign ship will pick us up,' said Vu. 'Let's just hope it isn't Vietnamese.'

'Or Russian,' laughed Hien.

'I know of an asylum-seeker,' said Thai, 'who was picked up by a Greek ship. The captain told him that they would take him with them to Greece, but when the ship made a stop in Hong Kong, the shipping company or maybe the Greek government said he had to stay in Hong Kong, so they put him in a detention centre and he's still there now.'

'Well my choice of country,' said Dung, 'is Italy.'

'Why Italy?' asked Vu.

'I imagine that Italy must look something like Vietnam. It has the same kind of shape, the same mountains and a similar climate.'

'And the same what else? Are you homesick brother?' asked Hien.

'Okay, the first to spot an Italian ship gets to sleep with the first willing female we come across,' said Vu. 'The others have to wait their turn.'

It drizzled for the next two days. Thanh suggested they collect the rain-water so they spread out the boat's canvas cover and made it into a shallow pit to let the rain run in. Since the sky was overcast, they could not navigate by the sun and stars; all they could do was ration out the biscuits and wait for the next clear night or sunny day. There wasn't long to wait, and for a while their good spirits returned as it seemed that in spite of the odds against them, they might successfully chart their course toward the Philippines. Then the fuel ran out and as the sun continued to blaze down on them hour after hour, day after day, each man's hope drained away and he slowly retreated into his own thoughts. With no place to seek shelter other than to crawl under the scorched tarpaulin which was suffocating, the sun burned uninterrupted through their skulls. Hunger gnawed into their stomachs, but with the rationing of water, the biscuits were too dry to digest so they were left untouched.

When a ship passed on the horizon the sailors either didn't hear their desperate calls for help or they didn't care. Their earlier camaraderie evaporated under the relentless glare of the sun; there was nothing left to do but let their minds drift with the flow of the current. It seemed to

Thanh they had used up all of their will and determination, so it was now down to fate to take them where she would.

The water ran out on the seventh day. On the following morning there was a slight drizzle — just enough for them to tilt their heads back and wet their mouths — but it didn't last long and as each person took a turn at licking the moisture that had collected on the cover, Thanh could see the situation was desperate. 'From now on we save all our urine. We can use the old water container and hang it over the side of the boat to keep it cool.'

No one questioned his instructions. The thought of drinking cool urine held none of the repulsion it would have done in normal circumstances. But as the days continued to stretch out with no sign of further rain they soon found that they drank the urine faster than they could produce it, and after two-and-a-half weeks at sea since leaving Taiwan, it was clear to everyone that the end must be near.

Someone would claim to see an island; then it would disappear. Thanh was having serious problems with his head. He felt as though all his old injuries were opening up. He drifted in and out of sleep without really being able to determine the difference. He was vaguely aware of shouting. Someone was drinking sea water. He would have drunk it himself if he'd had the energy to sit up, but it was easier to just lie there and ignore the fuss.

He could hear groaning. At first the groans were human, but slowly they took on a wild and eerie quality. Thanh lay terrified, shivering with every surge of the water. His head pounded and his throat was so dry that he felt as though it might close over and suffocate him. He thought he might be feverish but he wasn't sweating, his skin was dried out. He wished the groaning would stop but time had no reference any more. It shifted back and forth as the birds' screamed overhead. One minute he was drifting on a boat, the next he was following the Truong Son Trail. It was November 1967, and several weeks had passed since his leaving Hanoi, although how many exactly he didn't know. After spending a year working with Soviet technicians he'd been glad to be back amongst his own comrades. A major offensive was being planned and he was heading back south to the action. The bout of jungle fever which had forced him to fall behind the rest of his group now consumed his whole being like a blanket of fog. It weighed down upon him crushing his shoulders into his chest. His breathing came in short jerky bursts and, although each step was agonising, he forced his limbs to press forward. He knew that if he stopped again he would never stand up and would become one of the skeletal corpses which littered the trail like macabre signposts.

As Thanh approached the way station he could just make out the rows of hammocks slung carelessly between the trees. Through his blurred vision the hammocks took on the shape of huge draping cocoons. The low eerie moans emanating from the ghostly slings drew him forward, but as he peered into the hammocks, one after another — inspecting each and every one of them, two and even some of them three times — all he could find were the rotting remains of something that had once been human. . . .

'Thanh!' As the damp cloth gave moisture to his dry lips Thanh heard Dung's voice. He opened his eyes. 'You're ill,' said Dung. 'But you're going to be all right. We managed to get the attention of a Taiwanese fishing boat. They have given us water, maps and fuel.'

Dung lifted him up a little and raised a flask of water to his lips. 'Here, drink some of this.' Thanh drank, but his head and back hurt so much he was not sure he wanted to come back alive. The water, however, revived him and after some minutes he ate some of the melon Dung offered.

'I was back on the Truong Son Trail. I had wandered into a way station where I could hear the moans of my dead comrades. They screamed out to me but when I uncovered them they were dead. . . .'

'You were dreaming.'

'No it happened. It was real.'

Hien pulled himself alongside Thanh. 'You heard the moans of Vu and Thai. They drank sea water. Their bodies swelled up and they went crazy. It was a blessing when they died two days ago and we threw their bodies overboard.' Thanh closed his eyes as he took in the horror of what he was being told. 'We've given up on any idea of getting to the Philippines. The currents are against us at this time of year. The Taiwanese boat gave us a tow to help us get back on course to the China mainland. We are only a day out from Hong Kong.'

'Hong Kong!' Thanh glanced toward Hien. 'Is that where you want to go, brother?'

Hien gave a hollow laugh. 'Where else is there to go?'

Chapter 15: Pearl of the Orient

*Whitehead Detention Centre for Vietnamese Boat People, Hong Kong
6th September to 12th December 1990*

*Without the cold and bleakness of winter
The warmth and splendour of spring could never be.
Misfortunes have steeled and tempered me
And even more strengthened my resolve.*
PRISON DIARY, HO CHI MINH

T HE AIR CONDITIONER HEAVED its last dying splutter as it, too, gave into
the relentless oppression of the sun. Yesterday the problem had been
the water supply. When Thanh returned to his bunk, having sweated his
way through the torrent of questions thrown at him by the immigration
officers, he'd been desperate to wash himself clean of the day's events, but
he was afforded no such luxury. Today he felt the malady bite its way
deeper into his stomach. He could cope with the heat. Heat, or cold, it
didn't matter, he had faced much worse during years of fighting in the
jungle. It was the tousle of lies and the sour after-taste of betrayal he
seemed unable to escape from.

Maintaining his rigid posture Thanh watched the immigration officer
shuffle his papers around his desk. As if to emphasise his boredom, the
officer sighed and shifted uncomfortably in his chair. For the hundredth
time that day he pulled the moist handkerchief from his trousers pocket
and wiped away the pearls of sweat spilling onto his brow. He leaned
forward. The unspoken words behind his glare left little room for doubt
about what he was thinking. It was as if he, Thanh, were responsible for
the misery the immigration officer was experiencing.

When he did speak, his words were brittle. The accusation barely
disguised, he asked Thanh again, 'So why were you outraged by the man's
arrest. You said yourself you barely knew him.'

'What happened to him wasn't right.'

The immigration officer sneered. He'd heard Thanh make the same
simple statement before, but it clearly didn't satisfy him. 'You've got to
do better than that to get refugee status. To be outraged by an injustice
in a country where injustices occur all the time. Why not just keep your

mouth shut?' He leaned back in his chair. 'I'm supposed to believe you were crazy enough to risk your freedom for some nutter called the Ghost Locust, put on trial for treason because he took bones back to Vietnam. Come on. . . . Let's just be honest about it. You are all economic migrants.' The immigration officer laughed. 'And even if this story of the Ghost Locust were true, why should you care? Why should anyone care? If a man chooses to be so stupid let him face the consequences.'

Thanh cared what happened to Dung, just as he cared about what happened to his country. These feelings were inextricably bound together. But the assumption that justice only belonged to the people of Western countries irked him more than anything else. Freedom from the brutal injustices of colonialism was what his people had sacrificed their lives for. It was Ho Chi Minh's promise. Tired of the endless probing and sarcasm of the immigration officer, he let his gaze wander through the bars of the cubicle window. For Thanh, Hong Kong was a contradiction. From the sea its landscape glittered, rising pearl-like out of the water. A promised land with gold and silver sparkles gambolling off the buildings, which beckoned desperate voyagers with offers of sanctuary and freedom. From his prison, Hong Kong was a different place: a colony of false hopes with only the pretence of democracy, amounting to nothing more than a tinsel-town facade.

'You know, the lies you people tell make me sick.'

The sun, catching on the rolls of barbed wire led Thanh's gaze beyond the baseness of his immediate surroundings, beyond the outer fencing, to the velvet slopes of the mountains. All his life Thanh had tried to live with honesty and integrity. The lies he told were a matter of survival. As a young freedom fighter he'd hidden his loyalty to the National Liberation Front from Nhu's secret police. Later he'd lied to protect his uncle and their secret intelligence work from the hard-liners within the Communist Party. Thanh had seen very little of Hong Kong since his arrival in May 1988, but he knew with sorrow that for such as himself, it was not so very different a place from his own desperate Vietnam.

'And what about this colonel you say held a vendetta against you? So far your answers on that score have been very unrevealing. It seems to me that everyone who left Vietnam has some one who was trying to get even with them.'

Thanh glanced momentarily toward the immigration officer before turning his attention back to the window. Unable to trust that the immigration officer could comprehend his disillusion, Thanh chose not to share his thoughts. Pride and a sense of injury caged his feelings. The shame of Hue still hung over him. If they knew more of his past service with military intelligence, they would want him to reveal information about his country he was unwilling to give. Maybe the information would get back to Vietnam and it would endanger Uncle Chau and Nam. He was not a traitor or a deserter; his love for his country was always paramount in his thoughts. He'd spent too many years in prison in Vietnam to be intimidated by immigration officers. It no longer made any difference that his claim for refugee status hinged on his ability to satisfy the officer's ego and to give a plausible account of his story. Silent and alone in his thoughts, the realization that he was throwing away this slim chance of freedom seemed less important than clarifying in his own mind that what he had done was right and that, despite all the evidence against him, he had remained loyal to his beliefs and to his country. If he were to give an explanation for his actions, or offer an apology, it would be to Uncle Chau.

Thanh knew that by not revealing his once trusted position within the Communist Party, and his special duties for his uncle, it was unlikely that he would be able to convince the immigration officer of his legitimate claim for refugee status. One inconsistency detected meant everything he said was now a lie. Thanh stood up and walked over to the window. He could see no way out of the trap his destiny led him into. The immigration officer shot up from his seat. 'What are you doing? You have to sit down. I'm conducting this interview.' Thanh didn't care to hear. He left his place by the window and walked out of the immigration officer's room, gently closing the door behind him.

Thanh hesitated outside the editorial office as he read the familiar sign over the door: TAP CHI, DOC LAP TU DO — MAGAZINE, INDEPENDENCE AND LIBERTY. When the asylum-seekers had first gained permission from the Hong Kong government and the United Nations High Commission for Refugees (UNHCR) to start up the magazine five months ago, Thanh had watched Hien painstakingly hand-paint the sign. In spite of the poor quality paint and threadbare paint brush Hien had still managed to produce a professional finish by carefully measuring out the size of each letter and painting over it several times. Thanh considered it to be a good sign and one worthy of the quality of work produced for the magazine.

Even within the short time the magazine had been in operation, it had grown from a few pages of poetry to a professional standard publication.

Besides inmates' work, news and articles which came into the camp from outside always managed to find their way to the editorial office in Temporary Camp One (TCI). With few jobs available for asylum-seekers and even fewer jobs which posed any creative challenge, Thanh knew he was privileged to be working on the magazine. As chief editor, he held a pass which allowed him to leave his bunk in Section Eight every morning and be escorted by one of the guards to the school area in TCI until the late afternoon.

Upon entering the office a chorus of voices rang out from the other editors. 'Hey, welcome back, brother.'

'How was it with immigration?' inquired Binh. 'You were only gone for two days. We expected it to be longer.'

Thanh shrugged. 'I walked out on them.' There was a gasp followed by a hushed silence as his friends took in the significance of Thanh's words.

'You walked out on immigration?'

'Yes.'

Binh shook his head. 'Screening's an aberration for all of us, but if you don't co-operate they won't recognise you as a refugee. The power's in their hands, and you gave up your chance!'

'That was suicidal, brother,' said Hien quietly. 'They'll send you back to Vietnam. After all we've been through, why would you do that?'

Thanh didn't know — something the immigration officer had said. He supposed something inside him had just snapped. 'Let's forget it. It's behind me now and we have the September magazine to get out.' Thanh knew that neither he nor the other editors were going to forget it. News of what he'd done would spread through the camp like fleas on a diseased rat. It was far too outrageous a thing to be kept quiet. But Thanh knew the others well enough to expect them to give him some space for a while. They would save their questions until later.

'We haven't been idle while you were gone.' Hien walked over to the desk tray and presented Thanh with the sheets of paper which constituted the almost-completed magazine. 'You want to look through it?'

'Thanks.' Thanh took the manuscript from Hien and seated himself at the child's school desk in the corner of the room. His legs were too long to slide under it, so he sat sideways. As he leafed through the sheets he noticed that besides the poetry and short stories, much of the issue was devoted to the translation of current news articles. He smiled. It had taken months of negotiations with the Correctional Services Department (CSD) and the UNHCR to convince them of how important it was for asylum-seekers to receive information from the outside. If they were to make realistic decisions about their lives, they needed to know of the changes that were taking place in Vietnam and in Hong Kong government policy toward the asylum-seekers. 'It looks like you've translated some interesting news items.'

'Your battle with Clarence Kwok paid off. Since Monday the guards have been bringing us both English language newspapers and a couple of the Chinese papers as well.'

'Great,' said Thanh, nodding his head in approval. After scanning the news section Thanh read through some pages of poetry. Some of it was very touching. He was especially moved by a poem written by a young teenage boy, Trung; 'It was raining the day I left Vietnam'. The verse was beautifully ambiguous as to whether the boy was referring to the tears of his mother, his own tears, or the tears of his motherland, they were delicately intertwined. It was the way most of his people felt about their homeland. The soil where they grew up was as much a part of their being as their ancestors who lay buried within it. To live in exile was to be rootless.

Thanh read the poem through twice more. Still smarting from his brush with immigration, he decided the poem was worth publishing in English as well as in Vietnamese. Enough Hong Kong officials read the magazine and he wanted them to know that although they had left their homes, it didn't mean they didn't love their motherland and weren't desperately homesick. Trung was an unaccompanied minor who stowed away on a boat going to Hong Kong after his widowed mother's boyfriend beat him up. His ambition was to go overseas, study at university and after getting a job as a journalist arrange for his mother to come and join him. Thanh had no doubts that he would achieve it. Trung's work was of such consistent high literary merit he'd won several cash awards for the Youth Prize in Poetry and short story competitions held by the magazine.

Thanh would ask Dung to work with Trung on the translation of the poem. Since their arrival in Hong Kong in 1988, Thanh had taken it upon himself to teach English to a small group of friends. Dung and Trung were two of his best students. Although Dung's education had been interrupted by the war, he was quick to learn and was a natural poet. Whether he wrote in Vietnamese or English he now knew how to use both languages with sensitivity and subtlety.

Setting the poem aside, Thanh turned his attention to an article written by Ngo Duc Binh. Binh, the most radical of the editors,

consistently wrote inflammatory articles attacking Hong Kong government policy, the UNHCR or the Vietnamese communists. Thanh hadn't
chosen to be chief editor; the position had been thrust upon him after a
vote taken amongst the other editors. He didn't like to be the one who
was always drawing attention to Binh's articles, but he felt he couldn't let
this article pass. Sometimes Binh's criticisms were valid, but his writing
was so scathing, it detracted from the important points the asylum-
seekers needed to make. This particular article was entitled: 'Master
Deceiver — Ho Chi Minh'. The contents described how Ho Chi Minh
deliberately fooled the people into believing he cared for them, when his
real motive had been to trick them into fighting for a communist
Vietnam with him as its ultimate dictator.

Standing up from the desk Thanh wandered over to the long table
and pulled it away from the wall. 'We need to have a meeting.' Binh's
face darkened as he looked up from his writing. Thanh wondered if Binh
didn't deliberately write the articles just to provoke a reaction from him.
Binh had wanted to be chief editor, and since he'd been a journalist in
Vietnam he thought he was the most qualified for the position.

Hien pulled some chairs around so they could gather for their
conference. 'I know what you're going to say,' he said. 'So let's discuss it.'

As the editors sat down, Thanh began speaking. 'Our compatriots
have been deprived of literature, history books and a free press for many
years. Many of them will take what we write as being absolute truth. That
places an extra responsibility on us that normally wouldn't apply.' Thanh
looked directly at Binh. 'This article about Ho Chi Minh is rubbish and
you know it.' He hadn't meant to be quite so direct, but the article
irritated him. Binh irritated him, and above all he was still irritated with
the immigration officers who'd interviewed him. They all seemed bent
on taking a simplistic attitude. There was no middle road and no interest
in searching out the subtleties of a complex truth. One was either
supposed to be hard-line communist or hard-line anti-communist.

Binh stood up, towering threateningly above Thanh. 'You fucking
communist. What right have you to censor my writing anyway?'

Thanh sighed. He was weary of political extremism. Maybe he was
even weary of life. 'Sit down, Binh. Let's discuss this.'

'Fucking right we will. I'm going back to my section.' Binh strode out
of the editorial office slamming the door behind him.

Hien leaned toward Thanh. 'He's dangerous, you know, Thanh. He
has a lot of overseas contacts who share his views, friends who have
enough money to pay someone in the camp to do you an injury.'

Thanh shook his head. 'Binh's blood runs hot, but I don't see him seeking out personal revenge. The pressure to take an extremist view is his ticket out.'

'What about this article? Is there any way we can edit it to make it appear more reasonable?'

'Have you read it?'

'I've glanced through it. But it's true, most people here believe they were betrayed by Uncle Ho.'

'I understand the bitterness. I think we were betrayed, but not by Ho. He juggled relationships with the Soviets and the Chinese brilliantly so that we didn't align ourselves too closely with either of them. We have always been masters of our own destiny. But there was a punishment to pay for taking an independent route.'

'How do you know Ho's loyalties weren't first to Moscow and Peking, asked Hien.

'His first loyalty was always to the people of Vietnam. We're a fiercely independent people. Gaining our independence was such a long and bitter struggle that it just wasn't in our nature to humble ourselves before the three super-powers. We were always ready to negotiate, but to give up our right to self-determination ... never. We had no choice other than to defend ourselves against Pol Pot, but the protracted war in Kampuchea, engineered by China and the United States, bled us dry.'

'Look, one solution,' interrupted Vinh. 'Print Binh's article as it stands, but write your own article and have it printed alongside. Let the people decide for themselves. Binh's article is so inflammatory, it wouldn't take much intelligence to realise which has the ring of truth. You could analyze his points one by one.'

'I don't think Thanh should do that,' said Hien. 'This isn't just a simple lesson in history we're talking about. People are passionate on the subject of Ho.'

'Whatever we decide to do, I need to resolve things with Binh,' said Thanh. 'We have enough opposition against us as it is. If we fight among ourselves, and don't keep our integrity as editors, we'll be digging a grave for the magazine.'

As the sun shone through the cracks of the corrugated siding, Thanh roused himself into wakefulness. Forcing open his eyes, he scrambled up onto his knees and poured himself a beaker of water from the plastic bottle he kept in his bunk. Climbing down the ladder and making his way over to the wash houses the issue of Binh's article was now far from his thoughts. The continued threat by the Hong Kong government to forcibly repatriate asylum-seekers occupied not only his thoughts, but, it seemed, the thoughts of everyone in Whitehead.

After a thorough wash in cold water, Thanh returned to his bunk and dressed quickly. Neither he nor any of the other asylum-seekers would be leaving their own sections that day. They had all agreed earlier not to report to work but to participate in a series of planned demonstrations which were to take place throughout the morning. Thanh tied a white band around his head and made his way over to the chairman of the peace and order committee's bunk. The head bands had been smuggled into the detention centre, along with banners and art materials, from overseas groups in preparation for the demonstrations. Thanh grinned to himself. It seemed that as fast as the Correctional Services Department tried to block the smuggling, their friends from outside found new ways to get the items in.

When Thanh entered the Nissen hut, he saw that the others were already gathered and sitting cross-legged in Ky's bunk. With serious faces they fixed their attention on Human Rights Hung. Thanh scrambled into the bunk beside them just in time to catch the concluding words of Hung's speech. 'It is unanimously agreed, then, there will be no violence.' Thanh respected Hung and nodded his agreement along with most of the others.

'Yeah,' said Ky. 'But if they make a grab at me to force me on a flight to Vietnam, I'll fight with everything I have. And believe me, I'm not the only one who thinks that way.'

As Thanh arranged his legs into a comfortable position, Hung poured him some tea. Anxious to dissipate Ky's call for violence, Thanh leaned forward. 'There are going to be news helicopters flying overhead. We can never fight all of CSD, the police and maybe even the army, if the government chose to pull them in. They can draw on all the manpower and resources they want. What do we have?' He paused and looked round at the faces gazing at him. 'We have our bodies and our minds. We have an opportunity here to demonstrate our peaceful intentions. Once we resort to violence, we'll lose outside support.'

'Thanh is right,' said Hung. 'When a sympathetic world sees our men, women and children collectively forming the SOS, they will understand our desperation. It is only with the free world's support that we'll ever achieve security and freedom.'

Ky shook his head. 'I just don't see it. Even if we can't win, it's better to go down fighting than not to try.'

Thanh swallowed hard as Ky's words triggered a memory from his youth. He understood Ky's fervent passion not to submit to the power of the Hong Kong government since it was perhaps this same stubborn passion which had persuaded him to walk out on the immigration officer. He'd never liked Ky, but for the first time, he could see that in many ways they were of the same stubborn mold. Fixing his gaze on Ky he nodded. 'I agree with you. We do fight to the bitter end, but this isn't a situation that can be won by violence. We have to be creative in how we fight.'

Ky scowled across at Thanh. 'Oh, the "pen", yes. You call yourselves intellectuals, but your lives are no more useful than mine. We're castrated oxen; not even free to roam the pasture at will. This wire tiger cage we live in strangles away our manhood. What I say is, if they treat us like animals then that's what we'll become.'

'Ky, all of us feel castrated, but we have to get our thoughts out of our pants and into our heads.' As Hung spoke he pulled himself up onto his haunches. 'Come on, brothers, it's almost time. Let's join our compatriots in the compound.'

Thanh knew of nothing he could add to ease Ky's anger. Three months ago Ky's wife and two daughters had volunteered to return to Vietnam. Although Ky had tried to prevent them, a social service agency worker had arranged for them to be transferred out of Whitehead to the closed section of the Kai Tak Camp while they awaited their repatriation. It was this final defeat to his manhood which had pushed Ky beyond normal reasoning.

As Thanh walked across the compound with Hung, he saw the banners had already been set in place. Men, women and children were filing out of their huts in small groups and seating themselves in the compound. From the ease with which each person placed himself on the ground it was evident that everyone knew exactly where to sit, and by ten o'clock the inmates from each section had formed a perfectly shaped sos of human bodies.

Wearing white headbands they bowed their heads for fifteen minutes of silence. It was a moment of sombre reflection where only the roar of aeroplane engines and the thump of helicopter blades rebounded upon the stillness. Headbands fluttered from the downdraft of the news helicopter but no one on the ground moved or uttered a word. The Correctional Services men, on full alert, remained watchful from their posts. At precisely fifteen minutes past ten, the body of asylum-seekers broke their silence and began a steady chanting. The sound was low at first, but like a distant herd of stampeding buffalo, the sound gradually gained momentum. 'Down with the forced repatriation policy of the Hong Kong government. Down with. . . .'

Thanh noticed that as the chanting became more emotional and specific in its content, the Correctional Services officers looked increasingly nervous. They had clearly been given instructions not to intervene unless necessary since it was in everyone's interest that the demonstration should remain peaceful, yet as the helicopters came in closer to get good pictures for their news coverage, it seemed they not only stirred up the dust from the concrete compound, but they charged up the emotions of those underneath.

Thanh sensed the change, although when four youths rushed out of Nissen Hut B with their hands gripping burning blankets wrapped tightly round their shoulders, he was taken totally by surprise. The youths ran screaming towards the line of Correctional Services officers shouting, 'Our today is your tomorrow. Down with the government of Vietnam. Down with the Hong Kong government. Down with Chinese and Soviet domination.' The flames, whisked up by the helicopter propellers, caught hold of their hair. Three of the young boys let go of their blankets as they beat the flames from their heads. The fourth, however, charged on towards a young Correctional Services officer and collapsed in a heap of flames at his feet. The officer, stunned by the spectacle, stood immobilised as the news helicopters buzzed in closer.

Overcoming his initial shock, Thanh leapt to his feet and ran toward the boy. He snatched the blanket from the youth's shoulders and flung it aside. Dropping to his knees he frantically tried to extinguish the flames from the boy's head. Several other asylum-seekers and Correctional Services officers sprang into action. Thanh flinched as a torrent of cold water beat against his ear drum then cascaded over the boy's head. With the flames extinguished, Thanh lifted the limp child into his arms. The raw open wounds — the smell of burnt flesh. . . . The war years flooded back. For a moment the young boy was Anh, the scout from Thanh's former unit. Thanh was shaking; tears welled in his eyes. Then slowly, as the crowds pressed in, the image passed and Thanh realised that the boy was not Anh, it was his young student, Tran Man Trung.

Thanh was still in a daze when three ambulances arrived. The medical crew came to Trung's assistance first. They soaked his head in wet bandages, administered an injection, and gently lifted the small limp body onto the stretcher. As the second crew turned their attention to the three other youths and ushered them over to the two remaining ambulances, Thanh prepared to walk back to his hut. The pain in his hands escaped him, but he was feeling dizzy from shock and thought only of lying down.

'This man needs attention.' The voice came from the young Correctional Services officer who had been a witness to the whole event. Addressing Thanh directly this time he said, 'I'm sorry. I should have reacted. It happened too quickly. . . . Look, your hands are badly burned. You have to go to hospital.'

One of the medics put his arm on Thanh's shoulder, and led him over to the waiting ambulance. 'Come this way, we can soon clean you up.' Thanh didn't resist. He was too preoccupied with his thoughts. The image of Anh's body numbed out all other senses.

It wasn't until after he was registered and ensconced in his hospital bed that Thanh was able to reflect on what had happened. He worried over why Trung would have done such a thing. Even though Trung didn't have any parents in the camp and hung around with the other orphan kids, he stood out amongst them. Not only were his writing skills superior, but people liked him and the younger children regarded him as something of a leader.

As Thanh watched the pictures of the demonstration flash across the television screen on the evening news, he felt dissociated from the actual event. It was as though he was watching a replay of someone else's life. The aerial view of the bodies in their sos formation was more emotive than he'd imagined, yet he wondered how it would seem to the people of Hong Kong. The pictures of the boys rushing in with their flaming blankets and then a close-up of Thanh smothering out the flames on the boy's head with his bare hands seemed unreal. He felt as though he'd just watched a television drama, where once the camera was switched off, the actors would walk off the set uninjured. But this was no staged drama. While the group of unaccompanied minors from Section Eight watched in awe at the actions of their young hero, Trung's life hung in the balance. The news commentator reported him to be in critical condition in intensive care while the three other youths and a man, who'd come to one of the boy's assistance, were described as comfortable.

A heavy sadness hung over Thanh. As he stretched down between his sheets he realised he was physically very comfortable. This was the first bed with sheets he'd slept in since Khiem summoned him to the board of inquiry. The bed's softness stimulated his memories of Lan, and he wondered how she was doing. After his visit from Nam at Thanh Hoa Prison, he'd received no further news until he arrived in Hong Kong. When he'd settled down to prison life in Hong Kong, he'd written to Nam. Nam wrote back to inform Thanh that he'd honoured their agreement and married Lan. Nam hadn't enclosed photos of the wedding, but he'd sent a photograph of Lan with their young son Toan. Toan as a one-year-old, he said, was as precious as his name suggested.

Thanh tried to push his longing aside. Lan was no longer his. There was no handsome dark haired son for him to be proud of. It was time to forget her. He'd made a decision and needed to live by it. There were many pretty girls in the camp and he fleetingly wondered if he should turn his attention more seriously towards one of them. There had been liaisons, but nothing serious. He had no future. If this fact had ever been in doubt before, his walking out on the immigration officer had secured the final bolt.

Yet as Thanh looked around at the almost non-existent hospital security it occurred to him how easy it would be to escape. He could get a temporary job in Hong Kong to earn some money while he considered his next move. The thought played with his imagination and he forced himself to recall the layout of the building.

'Speak English?'

Diverted from his musings Thanh glanced up at the English doctor peering down at him. 'Some.'

'You fellows must be pretty desperate out there to set fire to yourselves.'

'I didn't set fire to myself.'

'Just shift over a minute please. Nicely does it.' As Thanh was speaking the doctor thrust a needle into his backside. 'So, you're the chappie pulled the blanket off the kid. Good for you. It's not everyday I meet a hero.'

'How is he? Are you his doctor?'

'We can't say yet. It depends on how he gets through the night. At this stage it's. . . .' The doctor paused as though he'd decided against saying anything more about Trung's condition. 'Well, at least you'll have a good night's sleep. I've just given you a sedative with a shot of morphine. The doctor patted down the blanket. 'Night, old chap. Enjoy your night's luxury.'

Thanh's rest at the hospital was short lived. The following morning he was taken in a Correctional Services Department prison van back to

Whitehead where he made his recovery under the care of the camp
agency doctors of Médecins Sans Frontières. The first he knew of any
trouble with the magazine was a month later when he was called to the
UNHCR field officer, Anders Boern's, room. Clarence Kwok, the welfare
officer, sat with another Correctional Services officer in the corner. 'This
won't do, Thanh. We're going to have to consider closing the magazine
down,' said Boern. 'We set up censorship just so inflammatory garbage
like this wouldn't get through. If you guys slip articles past CSD, then we
have to say "no" to the magazine.' Boern passed a copy of the October
issue across to Thanh. It had been folded open and a huge red circle was
drawn round one of the articles.

Thanh studied the circled article. It was a piece written by Binh
describing the ruthlessness of the Hong Kong government's policy of
forced repatriation. The article first criticised the UNHCR for kowtowing
to the government, then went on to incite asylum-seekers to set fire to
themselves. He even added suggestions of ways they might get hold of
gasoline to show their attempts were serious. Thanh passed the magazine
back to Boern.

'This is the first time I've seen this article,' said Thanh. 'As you see, it's
written on a separate sheet with no number to put it in sequence with
the rest of the magazine. I'm not sure how Binh slipped it in. I'll speak
to him.'

'That's not good enough,' said Clarence. 'We have a system of trust
here. You've abused it. It's a privilege for asylum-seekers to have their own
magazine.'

'Other than this article we've done a good job on the magazine. We've
even helped you communicate information. If you close us down, I
guarantee there'll be trouble. Our people are desperate for news and with
the forced repatriation flights leaving with such regularity, tension is
high. Something like this could spark off a riot.'

'Are you threatening us?'

'No, of course not. I just know how things are. The other editors and
I can deal with Binh. I promise you he won't write any more articles that
are not approved of by us or that bypass your censorship.'

'Hey, he's off the magazine. If I had my way, he would be sent to Upper
Chi Ma Wan or be on the first repatriation flight out of here. We're not
negotiating Binh's continuing as an editor, we're talking about the
survival of your magazine.'

'No one in the camp likes the idea of forced repatriation, so what Binh
is saying voices most people's concern. If you send him to Upper Chi Ma

Wan or even dump him from the magazine, you'll turn him into a martyr. It's much better I speak with him. He can retract what he's said and in the future adopt a more moderate tone.'

Boern raised his brows at Clarence. 'What Thanh says is right. The tension amongst asylum-seekers is at an all-time high. I think for now, at least, we should consider keeping things low key. The first thing we do is get Binh to retract his statement.'

Clarence stood up. 'Okay, you can leave us now, Thanh. This isn't the end of the matter though. The fate of your magazine still has to be determined. Get your man to retract what he said and we'll get the retraction circulated round the detention centres by midday.'

As Thanh strolled in front of the guard back to TCI, he speculated on Binh's likely reaction when he reported his conversation with Clarence and Boern. In many ways this would be the ideal opportunity to force Binh off the magazine, so Thanh was surprised at his own reluctance to do so. It wasn't that he feared a reaction from the other asylum-seekers as he had indicated to Clarence. Although Binh's radicalism could be extreme, often his articles stretched the content of the magazine to a healthy balance.

When Thanh walked into the editorial office, he was immediately accosted by the other editors. Binh's reluctance to join them was noticeable. 'What was the meeting about? Are we in trouble again?' asked Vinh.

Thanh placed the October magazine on the table and flipped through the pages to the article on immolation. Hien read it out loud then said, 'We didn't write this. How did it get in the magazine? Whose name. . . ?' He looked up aghast. 'Binh, you wrote this?'

Binh looked away from his work. 'Yes, I wrote it. So what?'

'I don't give two shits about you criticising the Hong Kong government, but inviting kids to set fire to themselves. Why?' asked Hien.

'Look, you saw the news. It was those kids running out with burning blankets over their heads which got the attention of the media.'

Thanh shook his head. 'That's not what we're about. None of us like forced repatriation, but the way those kids went about protesting it, was wrong. Trung isn't going to die, but he'll suffer with those burns for the rest of his life. Besides the pain of endless operations to restructure his face, he'll have to deal with how he looks. That has to be a challenge for any young boy, but especially for one with no parents to turn to.'

'I wasn't responsible for what happened to Trung.'

'No, but you're suggesting others do the same. That's sick, Binh.'

'Sometimes desperate circumstances require desperate measures.' Binh clenched his fists together.

'Then set fire to yourself,' said Dung.

'All right. I admit I'm wrong. I don't want kids getting hurt. Especially kids like Trung. Next time anyone sets fire to himself, it'll be me.'

'That's not the answer,' said Thanh. 'We're on the same side, brother. I just want you to retract what you've written.'

'Retract it. Like hell I will.'

'Then you're off the magazine.'

'That's what you want isn't it?'

'No. But if you want to stay with the magazine then you will write something to retract what you said.'

'It will make me look like an idiot. It'll make us all look like idiots.'

'That's not my problem. If you don't write something you will be off the magazine and I'll write it.'

'Why don't you chuck me off the magazine anyway?' said Binh.

Thanh laughed. 'And make you a martyr. Not likely?'

'Oh, fuck it. I'll write the article. But you're hardly the one to criticise me for not kowtowing to those shits. I wasn't the one to walk out on immigration.'

Chapter 16: A switch of identity

7th September to 4th October 1990

In the autumn night, with neither quilt nor mattress,
I curl myself up for warmth but cannot close my eyes.
Moonlight on the banana-palms adds to the chill.
I look through the bars: the Little Bear has lain down in the skies.
PRISON DIARY, HO CHI MINH

AS THE THREE BIG BROTHERS THREADED their way through the corrugated domed Nissen hut, Hien climbed down from his third-level bunk to meet them. He knew what they wanted and preferred to be on solid ground when he met them. Whatever nervousness he felt inside, he wasn't going to let it show.

'Brother Hien,' said Tong. 'We know you got paid today.' Tong spoke with the throaty rasp he'd cultivated to send a chill through his victims. As though unmoved by Tong's tone or words, Hien looked up absently and gazed steadily into his pockmarked face.

'So?'

'That's not friendly. We ask all our compatriots paid by the agencies, to contribute a share of their wages. It's only reasonable that we should also get paid for our services.'

'What services?'

'We keep law and order in the section. Without us you wouldn't sleep easily in your bunk at night.'

'Without you I'd sleep much easier in my bunk, thank you. I'm not interested in contributing to your protection racket. Go string yourselves up with chicken wire, and leave those of us who want to live peacefully alone.'

Tong stepped up close and exhaled heavily into Hien's face. The stench of stale garlic and fish oil was overwhelming. Hien's immediate impulse was to step back and it was only through the most determined effort that he managed to hold his ground. 'Well, we'll see how easily you sleep tonight, you buffalo shit,' he spat.

Hien wiped his face. 'Ugh. . . .' Rage, revulsion, fear. . . . 'How about dog fart,' he taunted in between gasps of slightly hysterical laughter.

'That has a much classier ring to it than buffalo shit. In fact a friend once likened. . . .'

As applause and laughter rang out from behind several of the curtained bunks, Tong's face flared crimson. He turned abruptly and with his cronies following closely at his heels, fled from the hut.

'Tong's not going to take your insult easily. You better watch your back brother.' Hien looked through the half-open curtain of his neighbour's lower bunk.

'Do you pay them money?'

'No, but then I don't earn any.'

Hien climbed back up to his bunk. He had no intention of paying and what's more, he realised he was in a position to warn other asylum-seekers that if they stood together, they didn't need to give in to Tong's threats either. The concept of having a peace and order committee was a good one and in some of the sections it worked. In his section it didn't. Tong, and the men who trailed round after him, were natural criminals. In any society, they would be criminals, thought Hien. Sitting cross-legged with a sheet of writing paper on his lap he scribbled out an outline for his article.

'If we print this article,' said Thanh, 'it could put you in danger. Tong's not going to ignore it.'

'I can look after myself,' said Hien. 'I did my bit in the army too. The Tongs of this world don't threaten me. He's about as useless as a capon strutting round the camp with his gaggle of hens.'

'Maybe so, but with us being in different sections, who's there to help when he goes looking to pluck a fowl?'

'What would you do, Thanh? Pay him the money? I don't think so. You're even more stubborn than me.' Thanh shrugged. 'Look, brother, I didn't go seeking this fight, but I can't walk away from it either.'

'You're a good friend, Hien, and a good editor. We'll print the article if that's what you want, but I don't feel easy about it.' Thanh's voice trailed off as Niki bounced into the editorial office and dumped a pile of newspapers and articles onto the table.

She was becoming a frequent visitor to the magazine, and Thanh wasn't sure what he felt about her. He suspected she was probably at least ten years younger than him. If it were not for her dazzling blue-green eyes, she could easily pass as full-blooded Vietnamese, though in fact she was of mixed Vietnamese and European descent. She was of slight build and although Niki didn't have the Asian, classical good looks of Lan, she was certainly striking in a way that Thanh found difficult to ignore. It irritated him that she always encouraged the editors to speak about themselves, but was uncommunicative when they asked questions about her past. Niki viewed the world with a gritty naïveté Thanh couldn't always fathom. She officially worked for Rights for Refugees (RFR), but the support Niki gave the magazine was indispensable.

'What have you brought us today?' asked Binh. He flipped through the magazines.

'I was speaking to someone in UNHCR,' said Niki. 'It seems there's to be a forced repatriation flight every month. A hundred passengers each time. The government is really serious about it. There is pressure from China that the problem of asylum-seekers coming into Hong Kong has to be sorted out before the handover since they don't wish to deal with it.'

'It's six years before China takes over. Why are they panicking?' said Binh.

'Five-and-a-half years. They say with fifty thousand asylum-seekers here already and more arrivals every day, at a hundred a month, it'll take years to clear the camps. Besides the government wants to send a message to Vietnam, that coming to Hong Kong is a waste of time.'

'Just whose side are you on?'

Niki's face blushed crimson. 'I didn't make this policy. I assumed you wanted news — good or bad. Ignoring this is like sticking your head in the sand.'

Thanh listened to the conversation between Binh and Niki for a while before interrupting. 'Binh's annoyed because his girlfriend just ditched him for someone else.'

Binh picked up one of the magazines Niki had brought in, and threw it across the table toward Thanh. 'It isn't true. I ended the relationship. She was driving me crazy with her insistence we get married.'

Thanh nodded his head mockingly then turned his attention back to Niki. Speaking in Vietnamese he asked her about her weekend.

'I spent most of my time reading *Life and Death in Shanghai*. It's a fascinating book. I'll let you have it when I'm finished. But Thanh, why do you always speak to me in Vietnamese. It isn't as though you're not fluent in English.'

'You're Vietnamese. Why shouldn't I address you in our language?'

'I'm half-Vietnamese and since I mostly grew up in America, it's hard work for me to speak Vietnamese. You know that.'

'Exactly. It's my job to re-educate you.'

Niki scowled at him. 'Ha, ha, ha. So why were you two looking so serious a moment ago?' Thanh passed her Hien's article. Niki read it slowly before handing it back. 'You shouldn't print this. The *dai go* aren't going to take it lying down.'

'So everyone says,' said Hien. 'What do you suggest I do? Pay them the money?'

'Well, I suppose you could do nothing.'

'No, sister. It doesn't work like that.'

As Thanh sifted through the magazines with Niki, Vinh bounded into the editorial office. 'I've got news for you, Thanh. I met your brother-in-law yesterday. He's just been transferred from High Island to Section Nine.'

Thanh stared at Vinh in astonishment. The reference to his past marriage, especially in front of Niki, irritated him. 'I'm not married.' Cuong was dead and surely Tang would not have escaped from Vietnam? 'I don't have a brother-in-law.'

'Tran Van Cuong. He say's he is related to you.'

Hien was about to transfer an armful of papers from the desk. Hearing Vinh's words he dropped them on the floor. He was shaking. 'Cuong's dead. I buried him.'

'Well, maybe he's the resurrected Christ. Hey, I saw him. What can I say? He was so excited when he heard you were here. He said I must put a word in with you to get him on the magazine. He's desperate to meet you.'

Thanh couldn't take it in and spoke almost mechanically as though it was just another applicant they were considering. 'It'll take a few weeks to get him a pass. . . .' Then as the impact of the what he'd heard registered his excitement surfaced. 'Why are we looking so serious? What's wrong with us? Cuong's alive.'

'I'm stunned,' said Hien. 'If you'd seen him when they beat him up and dumped his body in the ditch . . . I'm afraid to believe it.'

'Death is a doorway we pass through,' said Dung. 'Maybe he has some reason for passing back through it.'

'If it is Cuong,' said Thanh, 'then it means he was never dead.'

'How can you be so sure?'

Thanh wasn't sure. If Dung had really challenged him about his own experience in Hoa Lo Central Prison he could not have said if he'd passed through that door or not. Alone at night in his bunk, he still pondered over whether his meeting with Uncle Ho been real, or if it had just been the dream of a prisoner delirious with pain.

'Who's Cuong?' asked Niki.

Thanh tore himself from his thoughts and turned to face her. 'He's an old friend of ours from Vietnam. We thought he was dead, but if the man Vinh has spoken to is Cuong, you'll meet him soon enough.'

━━━━━━━━➤●◄━━━━━━━

When Cuong was escorted into TCI, three weeks later, Hien sprinted down the stairs to greet him. Thanh stood back as the two friends hugged each other silently. After the disaster of his screening interview, Cuong's arrival lifted his spirits. Since Cuong had survived his brutal attack it seemed anything was possible and the celebration they had planned promised to be perfect.

Hien was shaking his head. 'I buried you. Can you ever forgive me?'

'Well, you did a lousy job,' said Cuong laughingly. 'Next time I'll get a professional.' Noticing Thanh, Cuong sprang up the stairs. 'I'm both sorry and happy to see you here. You can't imagine what my feelings were when I heard you were in Whitehead. It seems we've a lot to catch up on.'

Thanh slapped his shoulder. 'I'm glad you're alive, Cuong! It gives us all back some hope.'

'I heard about your screening, brother. So what happens now?'

'We forget about it. We'll talk later. First we celebrate.'

Thanh led Cuong into the editorial office where a spread of fine Vietnamese delicacies was laid out on the table. Cuong gasped. 'How in the world. . .?'

In the centre of the table Thanh's crab noodle soup had been served up in a baby's toilet training bowl. Thanh had given Niki his month's wages to buy the crab in the Sai Kung fish market. She hadn't been able to stay for the celebration, but earlier that morning she'd called in to his section with a bag of crab meat hidden in the bottom of her back-pack. In addition to the crab she'd brought noodles, fresh fruit and vegetables. Thanh was impressed at how much she'd been able to purchase with his HK$100 note. If he'd suspected that things were so cheap in the market he might have suggested she purchase a saucepan. It was only on reflection that it occurred to him that she might have added some of her own money to make his purchases go further.

Next to the soup was a plate of spring rolls with a side dish of fish sauce. Quang had spent the morning soaking mushrooms, chopping up shrimp, pork, and green bean to make a filling before rolling it altogether into the rice paper. On the table was a fresh green salad with mint, coriander and crushed peanuts from Dung. There was shrimp cake from Hien. Chopped onion and cucumber in a vinegar sauce, from Binh. Vinh had prepared a bowl of chicken wings. Everyone on the editorial staff had been eager to make their contribution. The bucket of stuck-together rice and stewed cabbage was courtesy of the Hong Kong government.

'I haven't seen food like this since, I don't know when,' said Cuong. 'Perhaps it was at the time of. . . .' He glanced at Thanh. 'Yes, it was your wedding to Lan. Do you remember?' Thanh winced inside, but quickly catching himself he managed a smile. 'Well, I have a surprise for you,' continued Cuong, 'Just wait a moment — I hid it downstairs.'

Cuong disappeared briefly then returned with a guitar. 'It's not in very good shape, but I won it in a poker game. I thought Hien might like to repair it then keep us all entertained with his playing. What do you say, Hien?'

Hien was already looking at the guitar with great interest. 'There's some quality to this instrument. Where did you get it?'

'I told you. I won it. It's not much use to me, so I'd like you to have it.'

Hien looked embarrassed. 'I can't take this from you. I could teach you to play and it would give you hours of enjoyment.'

Cuong shook his head fiercely. 'Forget that. I've better things to do. I'd rather listen to you play than risk making an idiot of myself. Keep it, I insist.'

As Binh rushed up the steps and ran into the editorial office, Hien lovingly inspected the guitar. 'Look, if some of you guys can distract the guards,' said Binh, 'Xuan, in Section Eight, has some rice wine which he's willing to siphon through the fence to us. I've already located a jug.'

Thanh beckoned to Quang to follow, before heading downstairs and wandering over to the guard box where the small group of guards regularly gathered round. In an unusually authoritative voice for an asylum-seeker, Thanh addressed the senior guard, 'Clarence Kwok promised us we would receive the morning newspapers first thing, but we're not getting them until early afternoon. Sometimes later than that. If we are to get a daily newssheet out, that doesn't give us time to translate and get it typed up.' As he spoke Thanh deliberately positioned himself so that as the guards turned to look at him they had their backs to the compound.

The senior guard looked perturbed. 'It's nothing to do with me. If you have an argument about it, then you need to take it up with Clarence Kwok.'

'That's easy to say. Are you willing to unlock the gate and escort me to his office in the administrative block near Section Ten?' Quang wandered over to the gate as though he expected the guards to open it.

'If you want to see Clarence Kwok, then put in a written request.'

Thanh discreetly let his eyes wander to where Binh was still siphoning the wine. 'So, if I write something out now, when will you deliver it to him?'

'Now look here. I've said the written request will get to him, but I'm not your messenger boy.'

Quang burst out laughing. 'Thanh, the service in this establishment is not up to scratch. I think we should consider taking up residence elsewhere.'

Thanh caught his tone. 'I hear the Mandarin Hotel is pretty good, or maybe we should consider the Peninsula.'

By this time the guards were intrigued by the conversation and were waiting to see how the senior officer would respond. It was at that moment Binh hurried past, and casting a sideways look, winked at Thanh. Thanh immediately turned to Quang. 'I prefer the Peninsula. I hear they serve a nice afternoon cream tea with salmon and cucumber sandwiches.'

Quang leaned toward him. 'Cream tea ... is that anything like Vietnamese tea?'

The guard studied their faces as though they had gone out of their minds. Thanh nodded politely toward the guard then, hardly able to disguise the grin on his face, took Quang's arm and turned him toward the editorial office. 'Let me tell you exactly what a cream tea is. I read about it in an Agatha Christie book.'

Having eaten his fill, Hien leaned back in his chair. 'Tell me, Cuong, why aren't you dead?'

Cuong laughed. 'Well, perhaps it's like the time we went on Kim Bang's boat instead of Mr Luyen's. We thought it was bad luck, but then we saved the lives of Huong and her daughter. Later we met Dung in Dong Hung. That's good joss, yes?' He paused. 'Maybe there is a reason I'm alive when I should be dead. If, as Thanh says, my survival is a statement of hope when everything else is pretty desperate, that's a good reason to be alive.'

'I believe you. But how did you survive?'

Cuong lit a cigarette. 'I remember the beating and the drowning. Obviously I passed out. Much later I woke up in a mountain hut amongst a family of Nhung peasant farmers. They neither cared nor knew that my mother could have been related to them. When two of the young men from their village found me in the ditch, badly buried by my friend here, they saw I was in trouble and carried me back. They were days away from their mountain retreat, but that didn't discourage them.'

'I'm glad I did such a shoddy job. If I'd been thorough, you might still be rotting there.' Hien lifted his glass. 'More wine, everyone.'

Cuong gulped back his tumbler of rice wine. 'With that thought, I think I might just have another.' Hien filled the cut down plastic coke bottle which served as Cuong's glass. 'My recovery was slow, but when I felt better I crossed into China and made my way north. I stayed six months in Wanqingsha, a sugar plantation along the Pearl River estuary. It was there I met up with other Vietnamese seeking freedom, and we earned the money to build our boat. It wasn't our intention to go to Hong Kong, but after three failed attempts on the high seas and the deaths of some of our group, we arrived in Hong Kong, defeated. We spent seventeen days on a pontoon in Victoria Harbour before being transferred to Hong Kong Island. There was no more fight in me, so I accepted my lot and went to Victoria Prison. It was a miserable time where we spent hours just sitting on benches not able to talk or do anything. When the meals were served, we had to squat down in a line. It was humiliating. I'm not sure how I kept my sanity.' Cuong took another gulp of wine. 'It took three years for them to change my status from Chinese illegal immigrant to Ex-China-Vietnamese illegal immigrant. That's when I was transferred to Hei Ling Chau Detention Centre. From Hei Ling Chau I went to High Island and then here. I had no idea about any of you until I met Vinh. He was telling me about the magazine when suddenly the names started to fall together. You can't believe how excited I was to learn you were here.'

'Your journey sounds about as pleasant as ours,' said Hien with bitter sarcasm. 'Immigration don't really want to understand what we've been through. Screening's a game where they look for loopholes to prove we have no case.' Hien filled his glass and drank it down quickly. 'After all, we're economic migrants looking for a better life.' Hien's eyes looked bleary and Thanh suspected he was becoming a little drunk. Noticing Thanh's concerned look, Hien laughed and patted him on the shoulder.

'Except Thanh here, who refuses to fall into any of their categories. He walks out and doesn't even pretend to play the game.'

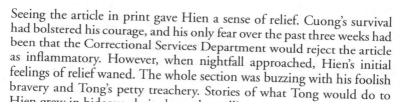

Seeing the article in print gave Hien a sense of relief. Cuong's survival had bolstered his courage, and his only fear over the past three weeks had been that the Correctional Services Department would reject the article as inflammatory. However, when nightfall approached, Hien's initial feelings of relief waned. The whole section was buzzing with his foolish bravery and Tong's petty treachery. Stories of what Tong would do to Hien grew in hideous clarity by each retelling.

Before settling down to sleep, Hien pulled out an old leather suitcase given to him by one of the agency workers and unpacked his umbrella. After stripping off the material cover and the spokes he pulled out his nail file and painstakingly rubbed away until he'd produced a sharp point. Sitting back, he admired his work. Transformed, the umbrella would serve as quite a substantial weapon. It wasn't Hien's intention to go after Tong, but if they came for him during the night, he would be ready.

The night passed without incident and so next morning, bleary-eyed, Hien made his way to the editorial office. Dung was the first to greet him. 'Looks like you had even less sleep than me. I was awake most of the night worrying about you. This situation's no good. What if I climb the fence tonight and keep you company, or better still, you climb into my section?'

'And for how many nights would I have to do that? I have to show Tong that his threats don't bother me. If I slept in Section Eight they would say I was running away, and if you came into my section all they have to do is have a little word with one of the CSD officers, and you'd find yourself in Upper Chi Ma Wan. I have no choice but to see this out.' Hien patted Dung on the back. 'It'll be all right, little brother. I shall stay awake at nights and do my sleeping in here where you can watch over me.'

The second and third nights passed without incident, but even though Hien took naps in the editorial office, fatigue was catching up with him. By the fourth night he was beginning to think his fears were unfounded and comforted himself with the thought that since he'd survived so much already, Tong's petty vendetta was, by comparison, a mere drop in the ocean. As Hien settled himself into a comfortable dozing position he pulled his umbrella next to him. He wouldn't sleep exactly, but just to rest his eyes would be enough to get him through the night.

Hien snapped his eyes open and pulled himself upright. He hadn't intended to fall asleep, but he must have, because suddenly he was wide awake and in the blackness he could feel his assailants. Dark shadows loomed around and above him, their breathing warm against his face and down the back of his neck. He tried snatching for his umbrella, but as he reached out one of them smashed his guitar down onto his wrist. Hien heard the guitar strings snap, the wood splinter, felt the spasm in his wrist sharp and savage. Consumed by his anger and pain he punched blindly into the darkness, but he was outnumbered and they had caught him by surprise. He was being dragged, his arms and legs clutched forcefully by firm hands, then tumbling . . . falling too fast. He snatched at the air — to grab anything at all that would help break his fall. His hand smashed against the middle-level bunk. Next instant the concrete floor rose up and slammed hard into his body. The impact, sending tremors through his chest, stole his breath. A flood of lights, stars dancing in front of his eyes, voices, then the blackness caved into his head and there was nothing. What had seemed like long drawn out minutes had lasted seconds.

Niki made her way over to the Ex-China Vietnamese Illegal Immigrant (ECVII) Unit partitioned off from Section Five. Formerly the asylum-seekers who entered Hong Kong from the camps in China had been detained at Hei Ling Chau; however, in a recent shuffle the ECVIIs were moved to the Whitehead Detention Centre. For more than two years Niki had been working with a group who arrived from a camp in southern China called Fang Cheng. Although the majority of this group escaped from Vietnam in the late seventies and early eighties, they were not entitled to be considered for refugee status. Having spent several years living in China it was deemed that since Hong Kong was not their first point of asylum the responsibility to determine their status lay with the government of the People's Republic of China.

'Niki! Thank God you're here. I worried that you wouldn't have access to us any more.'

The voice was familiar to Niki. It was her friend Huong, who having spent six years in the Chinese camps of Dong Hung and Fang Cheng, escaped three years ago with her daughter Tuyet to Hong Kong. 'Huong, how are you? I had to make a special application to get in here, but it's okay. How do you like Whitehead? It's different from Hei Ling Chau.'

Huong looked close to tears. 'Can I talk to you privately?'

'Of course.' Niki followed Huong to her second-level bunk. With barely room to sit up straight, Niki sat cross-legged with her head stooped forward and waited to hear what Huong had to say. Huong had always impressed her as being strong so she wondered what awful thing must have happened to upset her so much.

'I think you know someone who was very dear to me a long time ago.' Huong spoke hesitantly. 'He wasn't exactly a boyfriend. He protected me. In fact he saved my life once.'

'What's his name?'

'We were good friends in an earlier camp.'

Niki leaned toward Huong. 'His name, Huong?'

'Tran Van Hien.'

'You know Hien?' said Niki with surprise. 'He works on the magazine with me. In fact I visited him in hospital just three days ago. He's doing okay. He had an injury to the head, some broken bones. We thought his back was broken, but the doctor says it's just badly bruised.' With Thanh's unrequested language lessons, Niki found that her Vietnamese was coming back to her. She didn't know the word for concussion but she was able to express her thoughts well enough. 'He'll be in hospital a little longer. But truly, he's all right. I promise you.'

Huong reached forward and hugged Niki. 'Thank you. Hien doesn't even know I'm in Hong Kong. I didn't know he was here until this incident with Tong, and then suddenly he was a hero and everyone was talking about him. We left Vietnam on the same boat and were together in China. Our boat was ripped apart by the sand banks which was when he saved my life. I was afraid to love him because I'd been married before. My husband was the helmsman and drowned on the trip. It was an arranged marriage and although he wasn't a bad man, he treated me like I was his daughter.' Huong was talking fast, obviously compelled to explain herself. 'Loving Hien was very natural.'

At that moment Huong's daughter crawled into the bunk. 'Mama, have you been crying?' asked Tuyet.

'No, of course not.' Huong looked embarrassed and quickly wiped her eyes. 'Remember Uncle Hien from the China camp. He's in hospital, but Niki tells me he's going to be all right.' The child looked bewildered. 'No, I don't suppose you do, it was a long time ago and you were very young.'

'Niki, are you going to stay and eat with us?' said Tuyet.

'Not today, but I will sometime soon.'

'I can't tolerate this place,' said Huong. 'We have to wait here until China identifies us. Hong Kong want to send us back there. I don't want that, so I'm thinking of applying to see if I can go to Vietnam. I did nothing wrong there; it was my husband they didn't like.'

'Our agency has been pressuring the UNHCR and the Hong Kong government to look into your situation again. I can't promise anything. If you want to return to Vietnam you should, but don't do it because you're afraid of being sent to China — just wait a while and see what happens.'

'I want to see Hien so much. Please tell him about me. I must know what his feelings are toward me. For years I've wondered what happened to him. I was certain he wasn't dead. I just felt, if he was, I'd have known. . . .' A look of alarm crossed Huong's face. 'He doesn't have a girlfriend, or a wife does he?'

'No. I'm absolutely certain he doesn't. I'm going to see him in a couple of days. I've been taking messages to the hospital from his friends. If he did have a girlfriend, I'd know. I promise I'll tell him about you. Then I'll come back and visit you.'

'Oh sister, you don't know what your coming here today has done for me. Look, I have something for Hien.' Huong rummaged through a box of personal papers. She took out a crumpled sheet of waxed toilet paper. Niki smiled. 'It's the only paper I had. It's a poem. Will you take it to him?'

Niki took the paper, and folding it carefully put it in her pocket. Then clasping Huong's hands into her own she said, 'There are some other people here I must talk to before I leave, but I'll see you next Tuesday.'

As Niki made her way to the main gate, the meeting with Huong weighed heavily on her mind. She felt guilty. While her life was comfortable and privileged, her own people lived in miserable conditions. It heightened her sense of loneliness. She could barely remember her mother's face any more, but she remembered the years of being small and wandering the streets with the other orphan kids. When she'd been taken to America, she'd felt lost. Her new parents were kind and slowly she'd grown to love them, but there was always the feeling of not belonging — the feeling that she needed to find her mother and discover who her father was. At night in the safety and comfort of her own room in Hong Kong, it haunted her that her mother might have escaped from Vietnam and might be living in one of the detention centres. They might even have spoken and not recognised each other. So many lives were torn apart.

Niki thought of a woman she knew, whose husband left on one boat with their son while she left with her two daughters on another. Having split up as a way of doubling the odds, so that at least part of the family would survive, the woman now faced the despair of not knowing if her husband and son were alive.

By the time Niki reached the main gate an idea was already taking shape in her head. When she flashed her card at the guard and noted his casual glance, the idea cemented itself. It was simple. So simple she wondered why she hadn't thought of it while she was talking to Huong. She wouldn't go and visit Hien as she planned. Instead she would come straight to Whitehead. She would have to wear sunglasses because of the odd colour of her eyes, but since the days were still clear and sunny, no one would think it strange. Huong would be able to visit Hien in hospital while she could ease some of her own discomfort by sharing something of her privileged life. The chances of anything going wrong were negligible.

The school line was beginning to form in the compound when Niki and Chinh arrived breathless at Huong's bunk. Huong stared at them amazed. 'I didn't expect to see you until Tuesday.'

'Never mind that. I'm glad I made it in time before Tuyet left for school.' Niki stooped her head to address Tuyet. 'Listen, Tuyet, I'm going to arrange for Mummy to visit an old friend in hospital. When you come back from school, I'll be here. It's just for today. Is that all right?'

'I don't mind if Mama goes out. I have my walk through the camp to school everyday. Mama never goes anywhere.'

Huong was still confused, but hearing her daughter speak brought a lump to her throat. 'You are a funny goose. Give me a kiss before you join the school line up.'

Tuyet gave her a kiss. 'You enjoy yourself, Mama.' Huong followed her daughter to the door of the Nissen hut and watched as she dashed off across the compound. The female Correctional Services officer was calling out the names of each child before having them take hold of the rope line. Once she completed all the names, the guard opened the section gate allowing her to lead the children through. As Tuyet passed through the gate, she turned and waved.

When Tuyet was out of sight, Huong left her place at the door and hurried back toward Niki. 'Huong, meet Chinh. We often work together so you can trust him.'

'I've already met Chinh, but trust him for what? How is it possible for me to leave Whitehead?'

Niki grabbed her hand and climbed onto the bunk with her. 'What we are about to do is illegal, so it's up to you to decide if you want to do it. If we get caught you could be sent to Upper Chi Ma Wan Camp.' All the time Niki was speaking she kept her voice low. Then she fished into her wallet and pulled out two cards. 'Listen, this is my Hong Kong ID card, and this is my camp identification card. I know my eyes are a different colour, but otherwise we look enough alike. We've always said we could be sisters and our long black hair is what people notice first. Do you speak any Cantonese?'

'Yes, I was in China for over six years. I speak it okay.'

'That's great. That was the only thing worrying me. My plan is, you borrow my cards and pretend to be me. Chinh will help. When you leave the section, he'll walk over to the CSD desk with your card and his. This will be the hardest section to get through because the guards might recognise you. Do you know any of them?'

'No, not especially. We haven't been here long, and besides I stay out of their way.'

'Good. I'll give you some Hong Kong dollars and instructions on how to get to and from the hospital. Taxis are not expensive here and I'd rather you take one than risk getting lost on a bus. Are you ready to try?' Huong stared at Niki. It was the most incredible and wonderful plan she'd ever heard. She was shaking inside in anticipation of seeing Hien. There was no way she could ever express her thanks to Niki. 'I know this is dangerous and if you think it's a crazy idea, that's okay. I won't think any the less of you. I've thrown the idea at you suddenly. The thing is I don't know how much longer Hien will be in hospital. Maybe there's time for you to think about it and you could go next week.'

'No, really Niki, I'm desperate to go. You're the most wonderful sister in the world. I'll always be grateful for this.'

'So you want to go today?'

'Yes. Today.'

'Okay, this is the plan. First we exchange clothes.' Niki turned toward Chinh. 'Disappear, Chinh.' Laughing, Chinh left the Nissen hut and disappeared outside to speak to some of the other asylum-seekers. 'You need to be wearing newish clothes so I deliberately put on my best things this morning. Even on the outside, the police rarely stop people for an ID check if they're nicely dressed. As you pass each gate you have to show your camp card. At the main gate there's no hassle, just flash your card and walk briskly through the gate. Don't look back. Chinh will stay with you to the main road and help you get a taxi, but after that he has to come back here. There's a young boy who suffered some serious burns. He's coming back to his section so Chinh needs to be there to meet him. I've written the name of the hospital and ward number in Cantonese. Pay the taxi driver what he asks, then add a HK$5 tip. Can you do that?'

'Yes, I think so.'

'I've also written down instructions for when you get to the hospital. You can stop and buy Hien some fruit or flowers if you like. There's enough money. Get a taxi back, remember. When you arrive at the main gate show your camp card, but stay in the taxi until you get to the section gates. Chinh will be looking out for you in TC1. He'll escort you back into the ECVII section.'

'How can I repay you?'

'Just be sure to come back.'

As Huong walked through the hospital lobby and approached the moving staircase, she could feel her stomach turn somersaults. Outside had been terrifying enough with the masses of cars and heavy vehicles, but inside.... She glanced back. The hospital door attendant was watching her and beckoned towards the stairs. Huong slowed her pace allowing a small Chinese woman in white overalls to stride past. She was three steps behind as the woman stepped onto the stairs so drawing in her breath Huong took a huge leap and landed on the same step as the woman. To stop herself falling backwards she snatched hold of the woman's arm. The white coated woman looked startled and then laughed. 'Oh, these modern inventions. We get lots of folk from the country and they don't like them any more than you. Here, take my arm and when we reach the top we take a big jump that lands us on solid ground. Are you from the mainland?'

'I'm from the countryside,' mumbled Huong. Huong wondered about Niki's wisdom in dressing her in so smartly. She might look like a sophisticated Hong Kong Chinese, but her behaviour gave her away. Still, being from the countryside was permissible; being an illegal immigrant wasn't.

After helping her off the escalator, the woman looked at her with concern. 'Where are you trying to go, dear?'

Huong felt close to tears. The woman couldn't fail to recognise something was wrong and might turn her in. Niki's plan had been wonderful and crazy, but after being locked up for ten years, Huong felt like a small child who didn't know how to behave on the outside, and her primitive life in Vietnam was nothing like the way things were in Hong Kong. If she were to get caught because of her own stupid behaviour, it wasn't only her that would be in trouble, but Niki as well. It also hadn't occurred to her before, but Hien might not want to see her. Why should he? It had been at least eight years since they last saw one another. The whole thing was madness.

'You've come to visit a friend, perhaps?'

'Um . . . I'm here to visit Tran Van Hien, he's um, he's in Ward Eight.'

'The young Vietnamese man, of course.' The woman's face beamed. 'He's in a special room off Ward Eight. I'll take you there myself since I'm going that way.' As they wound their way along the corridors, Huong tried to slow her breathing. She was sure the woman must be able to hear her heart racing. 'Don't worry, dear. No one really likes hospitals. It reminds us of our own mortality, but a hospital is actually a good place; our aim is to help people, not to contribute to their troubles.' The woman stopped and pointed down a hallway. 'It's just along that hall. You enjoy your visit.' The woman started to walk away then stopped. 'There may be a guard on duty so have your ID card ready in case he asks to see it. You don't need to be afraid of him.'

There was no visible sign of any guard, so Huong hurried through the ward to the end room. As soon as she entered the room and recognised Hien, her fears dissolved. Taking the sunglasses from her face she ran over to his bedside. 'Hien, do you remember me?'

Hien was staring at her as though he'd seen a ghost. 'Huong! Am I dead? Have they drugged me? How can you be here?'

Huong pulled a chair over and sat down beside him. 'I came here because I had to bring you some mangoes. How are you?'

'Some mangoes. . .! Huong, how can you be here? I can't believe it. You've haunted my dreams for years. How can you just walk into my life again like this?'

'I'm at Whitehead too, Section Five. I didn't know you were in Hong Kong until this incident with the big brothers. Then everyone was talking about you. I made inquiries, and people said you were the same Hien from Dong Hung.'

'Did you escape from Whitehead?'

'No. I know Niki. It was her idea. We swapped places for a day so I could see you.'

'Niki! How long have you known Niki?'

'Oh, a long time. Don't you think we look alike?'

Hien stared at her. 'Yes, I suppose you do.' He pulled himself up to a sitting position. 'It's fate brought us back together. You might say I'm rushing things, but I'm not. Life rarely gives us second chances. Marry me, Huong? Marry me today?' Huong stared at him in amazement. Her mouth dropped open and she didn't know what to say. 'I've spent the last eight years regretting that I never told you I loved you. I want to marry you more than anything else in the world.'

'You're crazy.' The tears were freely running down Huong's cheeks. 'How can we marry today? I'm not even the person I'm supposed to be.'

'Of course I'm crazy. I love you. Marrying you will be the only sane thing I've ever done. Your mourning time is over, so I can speak freely.' Hien pulled himself forward and grabbed Huong's hands. 'Tell me yes, please, please tell me yes.' As Huong hesitated Hien suddenly looked anxious. 'You didn't marry anyone else did you? I heard you might have gone to England.'

Huong's mouth was quivering. 'No, of course not.' She sat stunned for a minute. Her life in Vietnam suddenly seemed far away. The normal codes of behaviour which bound society didn't make sense in her situation. There was no time or shared place for the rules of courtship to happen. They had let the years slip by before because it wasn't proper to show their feelings, but here was Hien again and he was offering her marriage. If she said no she might never see him after today. Their paths would take different directions. She would have severed that thin thread of hope which had kept her going. Huong looked directly at Hien. Allowing the happiness inside her to spread across her face she said, 'Yes. It would be a great honour for me to become your wife.'

Thanh knew something was wrong when Chinh rushed up the stairs to the editorial office minutes before everyone was packing up to leave. 'Look, it's like this. Niki loaned her ID card to Huong. She's in the ECVII unit off Section Five. All the outside agency workers have to leave now and Huong's not back. I expected to meet her here hours ago. Niki will have to spend the weekend here.' Chinh was almost breathless as he spoke. 'Maybe she can handle that, but the longer she's in Whitehead the greater the chance that one of the guards will recognise her. In the daytime they'll assume she's working, but at night. . . .'

Thanh couldn't take everything in. 'Who was supposed to be here hours ago, and why does Niki have to stay in Whitehead?'

'Niki loaned Huong her camp card and Hong Kong ID so Huong could visit Hien in hospital.'

Dung ambled over to Thanh. 'Did you say Huong?'

'Yes, they transferred the ECVIIs over from Hei Ling Chau. These are Vietnamese who were held in Fang Cheng in southern China. Several of them escaped in family groups and came here.'

'I know of Fang Cheng. I never went there because I escaped, but those who stayed behind did. If this Huong's from Fang Cheng then I know her. She was on the same boat as Hien and Cuong. After Hien saved her life they became close friends. Hien would never have left her in Dong Hung had it not been for his arrest after the demonstration.'

'Yes, that's who she is. She didn't know Hien was here until Tong dropped him from his bunk. When she asked Niki to get a message to him Niki devised the plan for them to swap.'

'Swap!' Thanh was beginning to grasp the meaning of what had happened. He'd expected to meet with Niki that afternoon after she'd been to the hospital. He'd been surprised at her not coming because she had wanted to meet Trung. 'So where's Niki now?'

'She's in the ECVII unit part of Section Five. Huong hasn't come back, so Niki will have to stay here.'

Chinh had barely finished speaking when one of the Correctional Services officers came running up stairs. 'What's the delay?' he demanded. 'We're closing TCI. I've got men at the gate waiting to escort you to your sections.'

'We were just coming,' said Chinh.

As they trudged downstairs after the officer, Thanh hung back and tugged at Chinh's arm. 'Don't worry. I'll make sure she's safe.'

Thanh waited until nightfall before making his way over to see Niki. He was glad of the opportunity to do something for her for a change. Being a detainee at Whitehead was demoralising and in relationships with people from the outside he'd always felt at a disadvantage. From his first meeting with Niki he'd been fascinated by her. She was attractive to look at, but more than that he liked the way she ignored the detention centre rules. Although lists were posted on most of the section gates, he suspected that she had never bothered to read any of them. She lived by her own rules. However, unlike the asylum-seekers who knew how painful it was to lose one's liberty, she had always been free to pass unhindered through the detention centre gates. He worried that her courage might stem from naïveté. If bringing in food, cigarettes, alcohol, cameras and an assortment of other restricted items carried a six-month prison sentence, plus heavy fine, he wondered what the punishment for trading identity cards and allowing a detainee to escape would be.

Once over the fence Thanh sprinted across the open compound to the sheltered darkness of the Nissen huts. Most of the asylum-seekers were preparing for sleep, although as he crept between the huts he could hear the discordant blare of several radios competing with one another. When Thanh entered the single women's hut and peered into bunk number seven, Niki visibly jumped. 'Bloody hell, Thanh. How on earth did you get here? For a minute I thought you were Clarence Kwok.'

'Do I look like Clarence Kwok?'

'No. But I was just worrying about his catching me here when you stuck your head through the curtain.'

Thanh leaned into the bunk. 'I didn't mean to startle you, but I thought I should hop over and see you were all right.'

'Hop over?'

'I just hopped over the fence.'

Niki grinned. 'You didn't just hop over the fence. There's thirty feet of wire fencing with barbed wire on top. How did you really get here?'

'Over the fence.' Thanh produced some iron hooks. 'It's easy with these. I hook them on and off the fence as I climb up. Even you could do it.'

Niki laughed. 'Forget that. I'm not climbing over any fence.'

'Well, you might have to. If Huong doesn't come back, you can hardly walk up to one of the CSD officers and say, "Let me out. Sorry it was a mistake and I'm not supposed to be here."'

'Huong will come back.'

'Maybe she will, but it doesn't hurt to have a plan in case she doesn't.' Despite Niki's feigned bravado, he could see she was looking worried.

'What do you think happened to her?' asked Niki.

'If she found Hien, she'll be safe. Escaping from the hospital would be as easy as walking through an open door. Maybe he decided it would be fun to show Huong the sights of Hong Kong.'

'Except Huong promised she'd come back. It's not that I mind. If I thought that was true, I'd be delighted. It's just I don't think she would deliberately stay away longer than we agreed.'

'I've never met Huong, so I can't say. Hien has good reason to escape. He just failed screening. He received his first chicken wing last month.'

Niki drew in her breath. 'He failed, even after all he's been through?'

'That's not so unusual, is it?'

'It's grossly unfair though. You really think he would escape?'

'Why not? I would and probably will at some point.'

'But not if it meant leaving me stuck in Whitehead?'

Thanh grinned. 'Well, I don't know. That would require some thought.'

Niki pointed to the sleeping figure of Tuyet curled up in a corner of the bunk. 'A man might do that, but not a woman. This is Huong's daughter.'

'Let's hope you're right.'

'I know I'm right, but something could have gone wrong, though? Huong could be in trouble somewhere?'

'Look, I didn't come here to alarm you, but I want you to know that if something has gone wrong I can get you out of here. Just don't go giving yourself up to CSD.'

'Over the fences?' Niki heaved a sigh and shook her head. 'It might seem like nothing to you. There's barbed wire on top, and then to actually get outside of Whitehead there are several fences with connecting poles to walk across. I just couldn't do that. And what about the surveillance towers and the patrol guards? Would they just turn a blind eye when all of this is going on?'

'You could do it Niki. I promise you with my guidance I could get you out of here. Do you want me to stay awhile, or would you rather I leave so you can go to sleep?'

'No, don't leave. Come and sit down instead of standing out there.' Thanh was hoping to stay and talk, but he hadn't expected it. In the magazine office there were always the other editors around and he never felt comfortable in asking Niki about herself. Without waiting for a second invitation, he clambered onto the bunk, crossed his legs and made himself comfortable.

'Do you think Huong's in danger?' asked Niki.

'I think she's having a wonderful time with Hien.'

Niki still looked anxious. 'I hope so.'

'I'm sure she is. It's their happiness which compromises you.'

'I don't mind. She'll come back.' Niki ran her fingers through her hair. 'In fact, in an odd way I'm not as unhappy as I would have expected to be. My being here evens things up. . . .' Thanh was puzzled. 'Anyway,' she laughed, 'it means I can question you about yourself.'

'Oh, yes?'

Niki suddenly looked uncomfortable. 'I didn't mean . . . ask questions like immigration. It's just your walking out on them and the conflicts between you and Binh. Many times I wanted to ask you about your side of things. I've heard Binh's opinion often.'

'There's nothing complicated about it. Binh and I have different ideas. Mostly I respect him, but sometimes his ideas put the magazine in jeopardy. Then I have to take a stand.'

'Is that it? It seems deeper to me.'

Thanh shrugged. 'Well, perhaps it is. I love my country . . . our country. Even though I left Vietnam, I haven't abandoned her. We live in this prison hoping to impress upon our Western benefactors that we're refugees. We are refugees, but the reasons for our fleeing are complex.' He paused, uncertain whether to go on. 'Maybe this isn't interesting to you?'

Niki's face became serious. 'Please go on. I am interested. There's so much I don't know about my own country, my own people even. It's like I'm an outsider wherever I am.'

Looking across at the sleeping child cuddled in the corner of the bunk and then at Niki's intense scrutiny of him, Thanh drew in his breath. If he was serious about getting closer to her, this was his opportunity, but he'd kept his feelings locked up for so long he wasn't sure how to begin. Talking about an abstract ideology seemed the safest way to bridge the gap between them. 'To many Westerners communism is bad and capitalism is good. It's that black and white. Clearly communism has failed in many ways — it's also become contaminated by corruption, power, fear, greed. You name it. But, then what system doesn't continually have to struggle with these issues? Besides, this was never Ho's dream for Vietnam. His main objective was independence.' Thanh shifted his position. He hadn't spoken like this in a long time, particularly to a woman. He'd never discussed his ideas with Lan and wondered why he felt at ease with Niki, but she seemed genuinely interested, so he continued.

'Ho was looking for justice, equality, freedom. He wanted education for our children, jobs for the people, and happiness. There is nothing wrong with these aspirations, but it's the labels we put on systems that cause us damage.' Niki remained silent, but slowly nodded her head. 'Perhaps,' Thanh hesitated as he pulled his thoughts together, 'ultimately all of us are seeking the same thing. A system which works best for the most, yet still allows room for the individual's needs to be met.' He breathed in deeply. 'Community versus the individual. We need to find a balance, but the problem is if we tend to favour one above the other then the labels jump in.' Thanh leaned toward Niki. 'Binh takes a hard-line anti-communist position because this is what he feels our benefactors expect of us. It's all part of a game. But if you play the game long enough, there is no backing out. It's the trap we set for ourselves and we become what we play.'

Niki nodded. 'I think I understand.'

'Do you understand the concept of *dau tranh?*'

'Struggle — I don't know, something like that?'

'More than struggle. It's political, it's armed, it has to do with everything we do, however small or insignificant, that takes us further towards our goal.' Thanh was elated. His disillusionment temporarily shelved, he felt a resurgence of his youthful passion. 'The peasant planting rice in the paddy fields, then sharing his harvest with the freedom fighters. That's *dau tranh*. I think all Vietnamese shared a dream of independence and liberty. Even those who sided with Diem.' Thanh stopped speaking. He trusted Niki, but he suddenly felt it was foolish to be saying so much.

Niki waited for him to continue speaking, but since he was still hesitant she continued with their exchange. 'You know my father was a French journalist,' she said. 'If he supported American intervention in the beginning, he quickly changed his mind after living in Saigon. Also my mother used to be a member of the Maquis.' Thanh looked at her, uncertain as to why she was telling him this. 'As a child she was part of the resistance movement against the French. Then when the Americans came she went down in the tunnels with the freedom fighters. If you're going to help me escape from Whitehead, you should first be sure I'm worthy of your help.'

Thanh laughed. 'It doesn't matter to me what your parents' ideologies were. I would help you anyway. Actually, I was told by one of the camp workers that you were an orphan.' Niki's cheeks suddenly became inflamed and she drew back as though Thanh had struck her with a knife. 'I'm sorry,' said Thanh. 'I didn't mean to upset you.'

Niki clasped her hands tightly as tears sprang to her eyes. 'The dust of life. That's what they used to yell at us in the streets. I was one of the children who should never have been born.'

Thanh could have kicked himself. He couldn't believe how insensitive he'd been in challenging her. He didn't want their conversation to end like this. 'Niki, I'm really sorry. What I said . . . I'm an idiot. "The Dust of Life", that's a cruel name only worthy of the people who use it. You are who you are. That is,' he paused daring himself to go on. 'You are one of the most special people I have ever met in my life.'

Opening her eyes wide, Niki scrutinised his face as though she were unsure whether she could really trust him. 'Really?' she said hesitantly. 'Do you mean that?'

'Of course I mean it.'

Niki relaxed and something of her usual smile returned. 'But, you're right. I don't know who my parents were. My father could have been American as easily as he could have been French. Maybe he was a soldier and my mother was a prostitute. I was ten when I made up the story of my parents. It helped me cope. All I really know is that my mother left me with an aunt when I was young. But the aunt was old and she couldn't take care of me; when she died no one knew that she was supposed to be taking care of me. There were lots of kids like me so we banded together to take care of each other.' Niki looked down at her hands. 'Do you despise me for lying to you?'

Thanh wanted to clasp his hands over hers but resisted the temptation for fear of insulting her. 'Why would I despise you, sister? There was a time when I lied just as easily as I breathed. If I hadn't, I could never have survived the war. Whoever your parents were, they must have been worthy, honourable people. And all of us were forced to do things we regret. War destroys more than just lives. But, look at your situation now. I don't know anyone else who would have put themselves in your position.'

'Then it really doesn't matter what my parents may or may not have done, or whose side I was supposed to be on?'

'Our people faced a struggle which tore brothers and sisters apart. My own parents passively supported different sides in the early stages of the war. My mother used to say that President Diem was as much a patriot as was Uncle Ho. All that was needed to unite the country, she said, was for them to sit and drink tea together. After Diem was assassinated there was no real government in the South and any hope of a settlement faded with the massive build-up of American troops. Years later when a bomb fell on my parents' home, it didn't matter who they had supported. The bomb didn't fall on just half of the house.' The memory of his parent's death was still raw, and for a moment Thanh lapsed back into his own thoughts.

Niki seemed sensitive to his mood. Reaching among Huong's kitchen box she took out a metal bolt and some wire. 'If you can rig up the electricity to this bolt I can heat some water and make us coffee.' Thoroughly educated in the tricks of survival in the detention centre,

Thanh took the bolt and wired it at both ends with some electrical flex. He then took the other end of the flex and wired it into the strip lighting to tap into the detention centre electricity. After placing the bolt in a plastic bowl of water he waited for the water to boil.

'I'm sorry I lied. I just wanted you to know I supported your different opinion on things. I should have trusted you and spoken truthfully. It's just that this thing about my parentage has caused me years of pain.'

'You don't have to apologise, Niki. I've spent my whole life being secretive. It starts out as a way of survival. Later it becomes a habit, that's hard, if not impossible, to change.'

When the water boiled Thanh removed the bolt before pouring the hot liquid into the cups. 'If there had been free elections, Ho Chi Minh would have won. It was Uncle Ho's leadership which led us to independence. Binh and others here at Whitehead believe we were betrayed by Ho Chi Minh because the better life promised by *dau tranh* never came.'

'Maybe we were betrayed, Thanh. Why did so many people leave Vietnam? Why are they still leaving? You left.'

'There was betrayal of sorts, but it's not so simple.' Thanh clasped his hands around his coffee cup. 'My uncle was a personal friend of Uncle Ho. He's a Party Central Committee Member.' He paused and looked straight into Niki's eyes. 'I've never told anyone here that.' Thanh drank from his coffee. He suspected Hien, Dung and Cuong must know, but it was never a subject any of them discussed. 'For years I struggled over why Uncle Ho had allowed the excesses of the land reform to take place. It was this that made not only my mother, but many people, question his integrity. It was only later, when my own feelings about our country were in tatters, that I dared speak to my uncle about it.' Setting his cup aside, Thanh stretched his shoulders back to make himself more comfortable. There was something about the coziness of the bunk, the soft night lighting, that encouraged him to keep talking.

'Uncle Ho was such a respected figure in our history that nothing has ever been written about the times of his falling out of favour. It is something that isn't spoken of in Vietnam, but between 1954 and 1957 our leadership was very much in a pro-China mode. Uncle Ho was considered weak. He'd trusted the French and their promises had failed to materialise — there were no promised Geneva elections to reunite our country — and even the Soviet Union seemed disinclined to really support the nationalist movement. It was Truong Chinh, the General Secretary of the Lao Dong, and his pro-Chinese faction that followed

Peking into the tragic excesses of the Land Reform. His policies almost severed the bonds between the people and their leaders and it was only Ho's stepping back into power that stopped the North from falling apart altogether.'

Thanh sat back. 'Although Vietnam has always struggled to remain independent of Chinese and Soviet influence, there have been times when circumstances have pulled us dangerously closer to one camp or the other. Our losses at Tet in 1968 were excruciatingly high. I don't think the American people realised the extent to which our troops were depleted. The National Liberation Front never fully recovered. Although the US troops began their withdrawal because of anti-war pressure from the American people, their bombing over Tay Ninh and Cambodia intensified. I was there. The Americans were trying to destroy our headquarters and to obliterate the network of pathways along the Truong Son mountains — the Ho Chi Minh trail, as they called it. After Ho died in 1969, our dependency on the Soviets increased. The Soviet intelligence ships, disguised as fishing trawlers in the South China Sea, picked up the B-52s as they came in from Guam or Okinawa. Without their radioed messages, the headquarters of the NLF and the Chinese advisors would have been destroyed.' Thanh suddenly laughed. 'The bombs crashed so close to us that it was not unusual for us to wet our pants.'

Niki nodded her head. 'I would have done more than wet my pants if I'd been there.'

'Well, perhaps that happened, too.' Thanh picked up his cup and sipped his coffee. 'At the same time China, who was now seeking a new alliance with the US, began to block the passage of Soviet arms through their border. It was a time of considerable strife. Had Ho Chi Minh been alive, my uncle believes we could have remained independent of the Soviet Union, but without Ho's brilliant skills as negotiator, we slid into a closer alliance with the Soviets and there was nothing we could do to halt it.' Thanh sat back. His mind was racing. If he could have trusted the immigration officers in the same way he trusted Niki then perhaps he could have explained himself to them and gained his recognition of refugee status.

'How did the Soviet influence change things?'

'It was subtle at first. I was in the South for some of that time. I was spending my time between NLF brothers in Saigon, but then retreating into the jungle to our headquarters every now and then. Through the sixties we had trusted one another. Ho had always treated the Front ministers with respect — they were to be the new South Vietnamese government. They were mostly not communist and as the American war neared its conclusion, the distrust and fear between our differing ideologies deepened. Cadres were introduced into the South who had no sense or respect for our Southern brothers. They were so full of their own self-importance and superficial ideology, they rammed it down everyone's throats. It was nauseating. I spoke to my uncle about the changes taking place, but the tide was too strong for us to withstand it.'

'What about your reasons for leaving Vietnam? It seems you might have done some good there.'

Thanh offered Niki more hot water before pouring some into his cup. 'Did you know the asylum-seekers from Dong Hung called Dung the "Ghost Locust"?'

Niki looked shocked. 'I didn't know Dung was the Ghost Locust. But then it was only a few days ago I learned of the connection between Huong and Hien. I've heard tell of a story of the man who smuggled his wife and baby's bones out of China and into Vietnam. They say he wandered around the camp and became so gaunt and crazy that even the guards thought of him as a ghost. Was that Dung?'

'Yes. The ghost locust is a particular species of dragonfly that carries bad luck. When Dung caught one and offered it to the children, an old woman screamed. She believed he was bringing ill fortune upon himself and upon them. It wasn't long after that Dung's wife and baby died, so the name stuck. I believe after that, Dung even thought of himself as the carrier of bad luck. I compare his ill fortune with my own good luck. It's like my life was charmed. Success came easily to me. When others died I remained alive. Unlike Dung who became a victim of the ghost locust, I can say I have actively sought the chaos and torment which has afflicted my life. I could have avoided trouble.' Thanh laughed. 'I could have been one of the bright stars, but it's as though the ghost locust is in my soul. This stubbornness to refuse to submit to a stronger force, even though I know it will bring ill-fortune, is what keeps driving me into trouble.'

'A bit like our own motherland,' suggested Niki. 'I love her as much as you do and after what you've said I can see why you walked out on immigration. Not that I'm condoning it mind, because I think what you did was rash and dangerous, but I do understand.'

Thanh shifted uncomfortably. 'Anyway, it's late. You have to sleep.' He gently pressed Niki's hand. 'You'll be all right. I shall come and visit you tomorrow, after dark.'

Chapter 17: Over the fence

5th to 7th October 1991

In jail we also celebrate mid-autumn,
But moon and wind carry the sting of sadness,
Barred from enjoying the autumn moon in freedom,
My heart wanders after her across the boundless heavens.
PRISON DIARY, HO CHI MINH

THANH WOKE EARLY the next morning feeling oddly at ease with himself. Speaking to Niki last night had lifted a heavy weight off his chest and the prospect of spending another evening with her filled him with eager anticipation. He was tempted to go and talk to her through the fence, but realising that it would have created an unnecessary risk he decided against it. Above anything else, he wanted to protect her.

Burying himself in his writing to keep his mind off wanting to visit Niki, Thanh scribbled out an outline for a short story. The story, about a young performer who joins the revolutionary theatre and becomes steadily disillusioned as he discovers that he is less and less free to express his own ideas, had been drifting around Thanh's mind for some time, and he wondered why he hadn't thought to use it as a cover for his own screening with immigration. He was quite capable of creating his own life history and convincing someone else of its authenticity, but he had hoped he would be able to communicate his true feelings to the Hong Kong immigration officials. It wasn't their trying to trip him up at every turn which disturbed him, he'd expected that, but what he hadn't expected and what he couldn't tolerate, was their arrogance in assuming that because the asylum-seekers were from a poor, war-torn country, they were less deserving of justice than anyone else. Walking out had been a matter of pride, his only avenue of maintaining his integrity and restoring his dignity in the face of such an insult.

Thanh was putting the final editorial touches to his work when Mr Phu came running into the Nissen hut and yelled up at Thanh's bunk. 'Thanh, come down. There's trouble for your friend.'

Thanh didn't wait to hear more but clambered down quickly from his third-level bunk. 'What is it?'

'Clarence Kwok was just in the ECVII section. He bumped into Niki and spoke to her. He made some comment about her being in Whitehead on a Saturday so all he has to do is check the register at the guard's house and he'll know something's wrong.'

'Yes, and he will. Clarence is not a man for ignoring details. Where is she?'

'She's still in the section, but hiding in the single men's hut. It seemed better than having her draw attention to her friend's absence in the women's section.'

'I have to get in there even if it means climbing the fence in broad daylight.'

As Niki sat with Mr Tien in his bunk several of the young men came running into the Nissen hut. 'Clarence hasn't let the matter rest. After leaving the section he went to the guard house and spoke with the entry guards. He then came back into our section and wandered over to Hut A asking us if we'd seen you. Of course everyone acted as though he was crazy. He then left the sections altogether, but we just got a report relayed from Section Eight that he's coming back this way with fourteen CSD officers. When they search these places, they uncover every toothbrush and nail. There is nowhere left unturned.'

Niki took in the news soberly. As she examined the physical reactions of her body, the thought struck her that people were right in how they described fear. Her whole body was trembling and her knees felt decidedly like jelly. She closed her eyes in an effort to end the nightmare she was confronted with, and the grim realization that her crime was likely to result in a prison sentence. It was just as she was anticipating her imminent arrest that she felt a warm arm rest gently over her shoulders, then a soft reassuring voice in her ear. 'It's the fence Niki, I can get you over it.' Niki opened her eyes to see Thanh crouching down beside her.

'Some things I can handle, but I never told you I'm terrified of heights.'

'You can do it, Niki. It's only one fence to get us into Section Five. It's not like the outer fences and with any luck you can stay there. Our brothers are going to create a diversion near the gate while Tien and I go over the fence with you. I will guide your hands and Tien will be below you to guide your feet.'

'I can't go. What about Tuyet?'

'Tuyet will be fine. My wife will keep an eye on her,' assured Tien.

Niki breathed in deeply. This was real. She couldn't offer any more arguments to put off the inevitable. 'Niki, listen to me. We have to go now. Our brothers are ready to start a fight.' Taking her hand Thanh guided her along the back of the buildings towards the fence. Niki felt dazed as though someone had hit her on the head. 'Okay, we're going over,' said Thanh.

Niki was too preoccupied with her own fear to pay attention to the shouts going on at the other side of the section. Thanh held her hand as Tien guided her foot onto the first hook. Then he was guiding her second foot and somehow she was moving upward. Thanh continued to hold her hand as he coaxed her to lift her body higher and higher up the fence. 'You're climbing, Niki. See how easy it is.' Niki felt the strength of Thanh's will draw her towards him. She was actually climbing the fence, each step moving her steadily upward, when all too quickly they were at the top and she was having to climb over the barbed wire. Someone, maybe Thanh, placed a blanket over the wire, but as Niki tried to manoeuvre herself over it she glanced down. Seeing the ground far below, her eyes lost their focus and for a minute she thought she might pass out. 'Look at me, Niki.' Thanh was speaking again, his voice firm and encouraging. Struggling to keep her eyes fixed on his face she allowed Thanh and Tien to guide her over the wire. They were on the other side, then they were descending. Tien had scrambled ahead and was guiding her feet while Thanh remained beside her, cupping his hand over hers, forcing her hand to snatch onto the fence.

'We're on solid ground. You did it,' said Thanh. As Niki looked down at her feet she was barely aware Tien had left them and was scooting back up the fence. Removing the blanket from the wire he quickly descended back into the ECVII section.

'I'll see you early Monday morning, Niki,' shouted Tien through the fence before disappearing toward the raucous brawl at the section gate.

'We need to disappear, too,' said Thanh. Several asylum-seekers from Section Five gathered round Niki to make a small crowd as they escorted her across the compound to the alleyways between the Nissen huts. 'You're going to stay with Miss Mai. I even found a quilt for you to sleep on.' Niki was shaking from her ordeal and paid little attention to the promise of a quilt, but when she climbed up into Mai's third-level bunk and saw the quilt spread out for her, she felt ashamed.

'I can't take this quilt. If you all have to sleep on a hard board, so shall I.'

'Niki, we've spent our whole life sleeping on wooden boards. It means nothing to us,' said Thanh. 'You're body isn't used to it. It has to hurt you to sleep that way.'

'Please, I prefer to sleep on the wood. Don't press me.'

'Just as you please, but Niki, you don't need to feel ashamed. I'm really proud of you.' Thanh put his hand under her chin and lifted her head so she could gaze straight into his face. It was the most intimate human gesture she had ever experienced. 'You confronted your fears today. That takes tremendous courage.' Niki didn't know why, but Thanh's gentle touch, his words of praise, brought tears to her eyes. 'I'm leaving you in Mai's care. She will make sure no one disturbs you. If there's further trouble, I'll hear of it and I'll be back.'

Thanh arrived early the next morning just as Niki was finishing her breakfast of noodles. Seeing him approach she set down her bowl and bounced over to greet him.

'Did you sleep well?' asked Thanh.

'It was strange. I slept better than I've slept in years.' Niki didn't dare admit she'd spent the night dreaming of Thanh.

'Well, I had thought about taking you out on a boat ride to one of the islands, but since my freedom is a little restricted right now I was hoping you would settle for a walk around Section Five. Actually there's someone I would like you to meet. He's from my section, but we had him climb over the fences before daybreak so he could talk to you. He's waiting in Luong's bunk. Luong, by the way, was one of the people from my boat. I'm not sure if you know him, but my experiences with him go back several years. Dung is here as well.'

'I can't believe what I'm hearing. You all climb over the fences as though it's nothing.'

'It's easy. You did it.'

'I didn't think it was easy and besides the fence I went over was one of the smallest. It's not like the fence between Sections Seven and Six. That's a really serious fence.'

Thanh laughed. 'You think when the buffalo boy leads his ox on a piece of string to the field the ox could not run away if he chose. If all the asylum-seekers decided to leave here tomorrow there is no way the Hong Kong government could prevent us. They spend thousands and thousands of dollars on fencing thinking they can keep us contained, but in the end a fence is a fence, and it all depends on how desperate we are to get over it.'

They were entering Hut C when Dung jumped up from a bunk and ran over to meet Niki. He gave her such a tight hug that when he let her go she almost lost her balance. 'There's talk in all the sections about what you did for Hien and Huong.'

Niki looked aghast. 'What about CSD informers. Will they tell Clarence I'm here?'

Dung laughed. 'Don't worry. No one will tell. We're proud of you, sister, and Hien stood up to the big brothers. The story will become legendary.' Dung grabbed her hand. 'Come and meet Trung. Oh, and please forget about practicing your Vietnamese; you must speak English. I will quietly translate what you say to Luong so he doesn't feel left out.'

'Of course.'

As Niki climbed into one of the lower-level bunks she gave a start. Seated in front of her was a young boy. While his face was hidden by a plastic mask, the tufts of hair springing out from the top of his scarred head gave him the appearance of something more animal than human.

'Trung is an unaccompanied minor. He was the child who put a burning blanket over his head at the time of the demonstration against forced repatriation,' said Thanh.

Reaching for Trung's hands Niki clasped them between her own. 'I've wanted to meet you for a long time. I've read many of your poems and stories and thought they were wonderful, although. .,' shaking her head in disbelief, 'I imagined you to be much older.'

'Trung is old,' said Thanh 'He just happens to live in a child's body, which is why we were anxious for you to meet him. UNHCR traced his mother in Haiphong. It's their intention to send him back.'

Niki looked at him seriously. 'Don't you want to go back and live with your mother?'

Trung moved the mask from his face to reveal his scared distorted features. 'My mother mustn't see me like this. I need time to make a better recovery. It isn't that I don't love her. In fact I love her terribly, but for me to go back to Vietnam would mean going back out on the streets begging.' Trung laughed, 'Maybe my ugly face would make me into a successful beggar, eh? But what kind of ambition is that?'

As Trung spoke it became more and more evident that the effort of speech was still difficult for him. Taking out a handkerchief Trung wiped the dribble from his mouth. 'I have an aunt and uncle in Canada who want me to join them. If I go there I can get a good education. I can make something of myself. When I'm bigger I can earn enough money to arrange for my mother to join me so I can take care of her in her old age.'

Niki didn't know why, but she was feeling really angry with Trung's mother for having let her child take such risks. She remembered the news broadcast of his having set fire to himself. No one does that who hasn't suffered. 'That's a huge responsibility for a child to take on.' When she spoke her voice was accusatory but she couldn't keep the tone out. 'Why couldn't your mother take care of you? Why did she let you leave? You might have drowned trying to get here. Thousands of other kids did. And the pain from the fire. . . .'

As Trung and the others sat looking at her, Luong took out some oranges and began squeezing them into a jug of water, then stirred in some sugar. 'I heard you were a street child yourself. You must know something of what it feels like to be out there alone.'

'I do. Which is why I wonder about Trung's mother.'

'The UNHCR case workers don't respect my mother either.' Maybe to hide his tears, or perhaps to shield his embarrassment, Trung slipped the mask back on his face. Whatever his reason Niki saw it as a gesture of withdrawal and she felt her heart sink. 'Many years ago my mother worked as a teacher while my father worked as a journalist for the provincial newspaper. We were doing okay, but during the early eighties my mother had some difficulties with the school administrators. She challenged them over the fact that children from better families, by that I mean peasant, revolutionary backgrounds, were being given higher marks than the children from not such good families, even though these children were often doing better work. Anyway, because she was out-spoken, she lost her job. My father was so angry he wrote an article about it. The article was never published, but he was told to apologise for writing it.' Momentarily taking a rest from speaking, Trung dabbed at his face under the mask. 'Anyway, things went from bad to worse. My father was shamed and he became sick. Maybe he was sick anyway, but he died within two years of the troubles beginning. Now my mother has no job, no husband and she has a young child to raise.'

As Niki waited for Trung to continue with his story, Luong poured out five plastic beakers of orange juice and passed them round. The level of concentration in the crowded bunk was intense, and it seemed that everyone was grateful for the distraction. Niki regretted having har-boured such horrible thoughts against Trung's mother. She regretted even more having spoken out so harshly.

It was difficult for Trung to drink the juice with the mask on, so he removed it again. Trying not to stare at Trung's face, Niki wondered how long it would take to heal. He would always be scarred, but maybe with good surgery the doctors could reshape his face so his features wouldn't appear so distorted. The hospitals in Vietnam could never attempt such extensive surgery, but in Canada they just might.

Trung set down his plastic cup. 'Many times my mother and I had no food to eat. She would try hawking on the street, but that was illegal and it seemed she was always in conflict with the authorities. By then I wasn't allowed to go to school so I ran around with the other kids. We begged, we searched for fallen vegetables in the markets, sometimes we even encouraged the fruits or vegetables to fall just so we could pick them up. We were like a pack of feral dogs and learned all sorts of tricks.' Trung spoke slowly and was careful to pronounce each word.

'One day four of us decided to go to Hanoi on the train. We thought that people were rich in the capital and that it would be possible to make good money begging. Getting there was easy. We just jumped onto the back of the train and hung on, but when we caught the train back we jumped on the wrong one. It was a fast train. We travelled at such a speed and since we had no real handle to hang onto, my friend Phu fell off.'

'Was he killed?'

'I don't know. We asked about him but no one ever said. We were detained by the police and then taken to the place for street children. My two friends had no parents so they are probably still there. I was lucky because some old friends of my father helped my mother to track me down. When the police returned me to her she was angry. Not so much with me, but with herself. It was then that we moved in with an uncle. I think my mother felt she couldn't care for me on her own or that I needed a father to keep me out of trouble. Anyway the uncle beat me. It was then I thought if I could find a way to support myself and mother, she could leave him. In Canada I could become a journalist, or maybe a famous writer. In Vietnam I could never do that. My family history is against me and besides, what could I ever write about there? Everything I want to say is forbidden.'

'How old are you Trung?' asked Niki.

'I'm fourteen. I've been here two years.'

'Your uncle and aunt in Canada — how closely are they related to you?'

'My uncle is my father's elder brother.'

Niki shuffled her way across the bunk and put her arms around Trung. 'I'll bet your mother is really proud of you. I'm sorry about what I said earlier, it must have broken her heart to let you go.'

'She wants me to go to Canada. We are alike in many ways. She should have been quiet about the children at school, but she wasn't. She knows how much I want to write. If I went back to Vietnam it would be too easy for me to get in trouble again. Maybe there would even be some trouble because of what I wrote for the magazine.'

'Listen. I have a friend, she's a solicitor. I think she would be really interested to hear about your situation. She's a wonderful person, gentle, kind, although when it comes to fighting for people's rights, especially the rights of children, she's really fierce. Many of the immigration officers are afraid of her.'

'I know who you mean,' said Luong. 'Mrs Pambakker.'

'Her name is Pam Baker.'

'Do you really know her?' asked Luong. 'Is she your friend?'

'Well, I hope she is because I would hate to have her as an opponent. She might look frail, but underneath she's as strong and determined as an ox. If she takes on Trung's case, she won't let go until she's won.'

Niki kept out of sight while the bins of rice and vegetables were brought into the section by the Correctional Services staff. However, after they had eaten, Thanh invited her to walk with him. It was a clear cloudless day, and as they were weaving their way between the huts, Thanh asked Niki how she liked Trung.

'I was impressed. He's so mature, but then I always thought his writing didn't fit that of a fourteen-year-old.'

'Do you think Mrs Pam Baker can help him?'

'I don't know, but I know she will give it everything she has. Trung is so bright. Why did he set fire to himself, was that really just to demonstrate against the forced repatriation policy?'

Thanh guided Niki over to the back wall of one of the Nissen huts. 'Let's sit here. We have a good view of the mountains so while we sit and gaze at them I'll tell you more about Trung.'

Niki leaned back against the wall. Thanh was right. If one ignored the concrete compound with its thirty-foot wire fencing, and looked above and beyond Whitehead to the mauve mountain-tops outlined by a silver thread against an azure sky, the view was breathtaking.

'I was in TCI when it happened. One of the agency workers had brought in materials for the children to make kites. The kids were excited since the kites were probably the first toys any of them had ever owned in their lives. And I have to hand it to him, Trung is a creative genius. He made the most beautiful kite of all. It was a phoenix with yellow and red wings.' Thanh shuffled his position. 'The next part I didn't witness since I was involved in my own work, but I soon heard the commotion. Trung's kite had flown over the fence and become stuck in some bushes outside the main camp sections. As you might imagine, Trung was devastated by the loss, so he climbed over the fences to retrieve it.'

Looking over at the outer fencing Niki gasped. 'Oh, he didn't climb the outer fencing as well did he?'

Thanh grinned. 'I thought you'd appreciate that. He did just great climbing out, snatched his kite free and was about to climb back when some of the girls asked him to bring back a flower for them. When you live for years without being able to touch wet grass under your bare feet or smell the scent of a flower. . . . Anyway Trung understood, so instead of racing back and maybe avoiding detection, he stopped to pick flowers.'

'He stopped to pick flowers. Oh, that sounds so much like him.'

'Those few moments cost him a beating. One of the guards saw him from the tower and gave the alarm. When the officer came round to arrest him, Trung tried to explain why he climbed out of the detention centre. The officer didn't understand his Cantonese so Trung spoke in English. That seemed to enrage him further and he shouted at Trung that he was not allowed to speak English to him. He then took swipes at Trung about the head, before forcing him to climb back over the fences. Trung was so upset that he tore his arms and legs quite badly on the barbed wire.'

Niki breathed in deeply. It was as though she were climbing the fence with Trung. His fear interspersing with hers. 'My God, he must have been terrified. I was, and mine was the little fence with no one yelling at me. Why did you have him climb the fence this morning to meet me? I could have met him in TCI another day.'

'It was important he climb the fence again. It was also important that he spoke English with you. It has to do with believing in his self-worth and believing that the world is not all bad. It's hard to always say what goes on in a person's mind, but I think the incident with the guard really shattered Trung's belief in humanity. His not being allowed to speak English to explain himself, affected him more than the actual beating. And then the forced repatriation policy just convinced him that it was impossible for him to achieve any of his ambitions.'

In response to Mai's whisperings, Niki dressed quickly and clambered down from her bunk. It was still dark, although a hint of morning light was beginning to show itself. Seeing Thanh at the doorway, she rushed over to him. Crazy as it was she was sad to see the weekend end.

'Are you ready?'

'After the story you told me about Trung, how could I dare be afraid? I can do it.'

Tien was waiting for them at the fence line. 'Okay, we do exactly as we did before,' said Tien. Thanh had hardly set the pins in place before Niki was pulling herself up the fence. At the top she hesitated, but seeing that Thanh was right beside her and ready to guide her over the barbed wire, she regained her confidence. Within seconds they were standing on firm ground on the other side.

Thanh scrambled back over the fence. Before departing he whispered through the fence. 'See you in TCI later this morning, okay?' Niki nodded. 'If Huong doesn't come back, then next time we go for the outer fences as well. I was thinking it might be time for me to consider escaping anyway.'

'I'll see you in TCI,' said Niki emphatically. 'Huong is coming back.' Thanh shrugged his shoulders and grinned. As he retreated into the early morning mist Niki watched him go, then turning toward Tien she ran with him across the compound toward Huong's bunk.

As Niki snuggled down, Tuyet opened her eyes. 'Did you have a nice time in Section Five?'

'Yes, I did, actually. How about you? Were you all right?'

'I did fine. I'll bet Mummy had a wonderful time too.'

'Oh, I hope so,' said Niki.

When the message reached Niki that Huong and Chinh were registering into the ECVII section, she raised herself quickly and sat with Huong's neighbour, Mrs Phuong, on the lower bunk. There was little point in hiding at this stage. If Clarence decided to accost Huong at the gate, then they were doomed. There would be no more clever tricks to get them out of trouble. It would be more dignified to face Clarence than try to escape and then wait for the police to come looking for her.

As Huong dashed into the Nissen hut, Niki jumped up to greet her. 'Thank God, you're okay. I was worried. . . .'

'I'm really sorry, Niki. Look, I think we better change clothes quickly. Chinh says something's wrong. He's waiting outside the hut.' Niki didn't wait for a second warning. She slipped out of Huong's clothes and scrambled into her own as quickly as she could. She'd barely time to put on her sun glasses and join Chinh outside when Clarence came striding across the compound towards them.

As he approached, he stared straight at Niki. From his expression it looked as though it was more than he could do to stop himself from grabbing hold of her and shaking her. 'What are you up to?'

'Good morning, Clarence. I'm not sure what you mean,' replied Niki.

'You were here Saturday. How did you get in and out? There's no registration of you being here, either in this section or at the main gate.'

'Saturday! I went on a really great junk ride with some friends. We went to Lamma Island, walked round, ate some sea food and came back early evening.'

'That's not possible.'

Niki shrugged and gave him a look as though he were losing his mind.

'You think you can trick me, but you can't. I'm watching you. Put a foot wrong and I'll know.' At that last remark Clarence turned, but as he strode back across the compound toward the gate, hushed ripples of laughter trailed after him.

Niki watched him leave. 'Wow, that was close.'

'Closer than you think,' said Chinh. 'We were at the gate when I heard them radio through to Clarence. I sensed the guards were going to make us wait there until Clarence arrived so I snatched Huong's hand and we took off through the gate before they had time to make their protest.'

Niki shook her head. She couldn't believe how lucky she was. 'Before we go to the magazine office, I must hear from Huong about her weekend.'

Niki was not the only one anxious to hear Huong's story. It seemed that all the ECVIIs in her section wanted to hear what she had to say. Huong placed herself near the doorway so there was room for everyone to gather round. 'I did exactly as you said, Niki. I caught the taxi to the hospital. I bought some mangoes at a fruit stand. The traffic on the roads was a bit scary, but then when I got inside the hospital it was even more bewildering. A woman took me to the ward where Hien was staying.' Huong's eyes lit up when she mentioned Hien's name, then shyly extending her hand she proudly displayed the gold band on her finger. 'It's not real gold, but it's the most precious ring in the world to me.' At the crowds' insistence Huong displayed her ring for the others to see.

'Oh, sister, tell us your story,' said a petite, spotty faced girl.

'It was wonderful finding Hien again. He thought he was dreaming when he saw me. He asked me to marry him there and then. How could I refuse, Niki? I love him. Loving him is the most incredible experience in the world, but I didn't intend not coming back. The guards locked the gate on me.'

Niki took hold of Huong's hand and squeezed it. 'I'm so happy for you, Huong. It was fine here. In fact it was quite an adventure so go on with your story.'

'Hien told me to go back outside to the hospital garden and wait for him there. We weren't sure about there being guards around, so he had to be careful. As I waited in the garden, he didn't come for ages and I was worried something had gone wrong. But he did fine. He stole a white overall and just walked out the main door as though he were a doctor. We dumped the overalls in the garden, then, using the rest of your money, Niki, we took a taxi to Tuen Mun. Hien knew a Vietnamese Catholic priest. He didn't care we weren't Catholic. He instructed us in the Catholic doctrine and had us say some things, then he married us.'

A chorus of cheers went up among the group. Tuyet kissed her mother. 'I'm happy for you mama and now I have a real dad.'

Huong put her arms round Tuyet then turned to Niki. 'Sister, I'm really sorry about my not coming back as I promised. We tried. The priest gave us money and instructions on how to get to Sha Tin. That part was easy. But time was passing quickly and we couldn't get a taxi to White-head. It was rush hour and none of the taxis would stop for us. It took ages before we found out which bus to catch and then we got off several stops too late. When we arrived at Whitehead, Hien kept out of sight as I approached the gate. The guard said all the camp workers were leaving and that it was too late for me to enter. He looked at me so oddly I panicked and ran away. Hien and I were wondering what to do when we saw Chinh. We were so happy to see him, and he to see us so he took us back to his place.'

'I thought it best we leave it until this morning before trying to get in. I hope that was all right,' said Chinh.

Niki laughed. 'You were probably right not to try to get in, but it did make for an interesting weekend. So now that Hien's escaped, what's he going to do?'

'We discussed this. If he stays escaped then that would mean per-manent separation from Huong and Tuyet. The only way for them to be together and to start a new life is to go through the system. For one thing although they are married, the Hong Kong authorities will never recog-nise it because as far as they are concerned Huong never left Whitehead. We can hardly tell them what we did. Your helping Huong get out of the camp is a criminal offence.'

'It's complicated.'

'Don't worry we have a simple solution. Hien is going to hand himself in a little later this morning, if he hasn't already done so. I'll make inquiries among my UNHCR contacts and try to find out what's going to happen to him. I suspect he'll have to spend six months at Upper Chi Ma Wan.'

Huong grimaced. 'He was all right about it. We are really sorry, Niki. I cried when they wouldn't let me in.'

Niki reached over and hugged her. 'I'm really happy for you, Huong. Hien is a lovely person and he'll be a good husband to you. All we have to do now is figure out how to make your marriage official so that you can be reunited as man and wife.'

'We've already discussed that,' said Chinh. 'The government generally doesn't like the ECVIIs to marry into other sections because their status is different, but if we show that Hien and Huong were living together in China, I'm sure we can create enough pressure to get permission for them to marry at a registry office. It might take some time, but in the end I think we have a good chance.'

'I can marry Hien again. That's wonderful.' Huong turned to Niki. 'Niki, Hong Kong is so beautiful. Chinh took us to so many places and we ate in a Vietnamese restaurant. Then we ate Western food in an expensive hotel.' She took Niki's hands. 'I have to thank you and Chinh for the best honeymoon ever. Will you ever forgive me?'

'When you didn't come back, I was scared you'd been in an accident. I realised that I was irresponsible to send you off on your own. If anyone needs to forgive anyone, you should forgive me. I could have been less impulsive and arranged it so Chinh was free to take care of you.' Niki stopped speaking and, lifting Huong's hands, she pressed them hard against her lips. 'But I'm glad I didn't. It was an honour to be able to give you a honeymoon in Hong Kong. Thank you for coming back safely.'

After saying goodbye to Huong and Chinh, Hien waited two hours before limping up to the guard house at the main gate. He didn't care what happened to him. He was so buoyed up after his marriage and the weekend with Huong there was nothing they could do to him to dampen his spirits. He felt playful. 'Excuse me, I'm an asylum-seeker from this detention centre and I'm just returning myself from the hospital.'

The two guards inside the guard house gave him a quizzical look. 'Oh yes, so why are you out here and not inside?'

'As I told you, I am returning myself from the hospital.'

'The economic migrants don't just return themselves from the hospital. What's your game?'

'Would you rather I left then and went back to the hospital to wait for an escort?'

One of the guards looked at his colleague then stood up. 'Well, maybe you shouldn't leave. What papers do you have?' Hien was carrying his camp card which identified him as working on the magazine, so he handed it over to the guard. 'What's this?'

'It's what it looks like. I told you I'm an asylum-seeker here. This card has been signed by your welfare officer, Clarence Kwok. It gives me permission to be escorted from Section Seven to TCI every morning so I can do my work for the magazine.'

'You know Clarence Kwok?'

'Yes, I told you I live here. But if you don't want to let me in, I'll go and find somewhere else to live. I never really liked it here anyway.' Hien acted as though he were going to wander back up the road.

The two guards ran out of their shelter. 'No, no, I don't think you should go away. Look, I'll radio someone for you and find out what's going on.' The guard who'd so far remained silent walked back into the shelter and put in a radio call to his superior. 'We have a man here, claims he's an economic migrant. . . .'

Hien advanced toward the shelter and thrust his head through the window. 'I don't claim to be an economic migrant. I told you I'm an asylum-seeker. If we don't establish that point right now, I'm leaving.'

The guard standing next to him took hold of his arm. 'Calm down, we'll sort things out in a minute.'

The guard speaking into the radio continued. 'We have an asylum-seeker here. He has a card signed by Clarence Kwok.' There was a pause as the person on the other end spoke back. 'The name on the card says Tran Van Hien.' Several seconds passed. 'Yes sir.'

The next moment a Correctional Services van spun through the gate from inside the detention centre and pulled up beside Hien. Several officers jumped out and ran toward Hien. Hien tried to pull back as they grabbed hold of him. 'Look, you don't need to grab me like this. I already told your men I'm returning myself to Whitehead. I'm not fully recovered from my injuries, so please be careful with me.'

The officers paid no attention to his request for gentler treatment and shoved him into the back of the van. They drove round the outer road before coming through the second gate leading to Sections One to Eight.

At Section Seven they pulled through the gates and quickly unloaded him. Before being forced into the administrative block, Hien managed a wave toward a group of kids who were hanging round the inner gate of the compound.

Inside the Section Administrator's Block, Hien was shoved into a room and forced to sit down. Two Correctional Services officers eyed him warily. 'Why did you leave the Queen Elizabeth without being discharged properly? You have no right to do that.'

Hien looked at his interrogator and smiled. He was home. What a place to call home he thought. 'I was homesick. It was lonely in the hospital so I decided to come home.'

His interrogator looked at his associate. 'Was this man receiving psychiatric treatment at the QE?'

'No sir, he was the one pushed from his third tier bunk. Maybe he damaged his head.'

'I did damage my head,' said Hien. 'In fact I had a bandage round my head when I left the hospital and somehow I lost it.'

'You left the hospital on Friday. It's now Monday, so where have you been all this time?'

Hien wiped his brow. 'You know, I'm not sure. I think I lost myself. I was trying to get home, but I couldn't find the way.' He smiled. 'But here I am. I'm home.'

The younger of the officers whispered in his colleague's ear. 'The man's cracked in the head.'

'You were gone three days and nights. Where did you sleep?'

'Oh, I slept in the street, on a beach. Yes, two times in the street.'

'You look clean.'

'Of course. I wash myself in the sea.'

'The hospital is many miles from here. Did you walk back?'

'I walk. I take the bus. I smell the flowers.'

'Do you have money then?'

'No.'

'Then you're lying. You need money to catch a bus.'

'No. No money. The man on the bus he listens to my story and he helps me find the way home.'

The Correctional Services officer shrugged. 'Put him in lock up. We'll get a medical report, then decide what to do.'

Chapter 18: Hidden cameras

20th May to 13th November 1992

The morning sun into the prison penetrates:
The smoke clears away, the mist dissipates.
The breath of life suddenly fills the skies,
And the prisoners' faces are all now smiles.
PRISON DIARY, HO CHI MINH

A CLOUD OF SMOKE hung over the editors as they perched on their stools in the magazine office, drawing heavily on their cigarettes. It was an all too familiar scene, and had it not been for Thanh's increasing fondness for Niki he was not sure he could have retained his sanity. Yet since the weekend that Niki had been stuck in Whitehead, there had never been a time when she and Thanh could be alone together, so that any hopes for a developing a closeness always seemed frustrated. Standing in the doorway, looking at the drawn faces around him, Thanh felt his muscles tighten across his jaw. Although his friends looked older it was as though time hadn't advanced at all. Its slow progression grated on all of their nerves terribly, leaving them frustrated and listless. Thanh likened it to being frozen in a time capsule while their life blood dripped away unnoticed through the cracks in the plywood floor.

At least once a month the editors would gather together to discuss the news items and try to foresee what impact it might have on their lives, or analyze its affect on Communist Party policy in Vietnam. When the Gulf War escalated to dangerous proportions threatening world peace, it had seemed as far away and as unreal as a staged movie flickering across the television screen on the nightly news. The collapse of the Soviet Union in December 1991, and the resulting domino effect had also seemed unreal, but it had occupied their discussions for almost a year. But the saddest event to impact on their lives had been the fire at the Sek Kong Detention Centre during the eve of Tet, the Lunar New Year in February 1992. It was quite conceivable that the already volatile situation in Whitehead could erupt in a similarly disastrous fashion.

Thanh looked at his compatriots and sighed. He spent too much time thinking — it was like a disease, a curse with him. There was work to do, and despite the permanence of his underlying sadness, he could already see that today's meeting promised to be a little different. For once they were not just discussing the news; they were talking about making news — about having a voice.

Thanh had stopped smoking several years before he was first imprisoned and didn't want to be drawn back into the habit, so he pulled a chair over to the doorway and positioned himself so as not to breath in the stale air. Neither Niki nor Chinh smoked, so it was not long before they squeezed into the narrow doorway beside him.

'Why are you smoking, Hien?' asked Niki. 'Huong told me you promised her you'd give it up.'

Hien looked at her alarmed. 'You won't tell her will you? I will give it up, but after six months in Upper Chi Ma Wan, a man needs to do something to calm himself down.'

'Of course I won't tell her. But it's not too much longer to wait, and after your marriage you'll be living in the same section. Then she'll know you for what you really are.'

Binh laughed and prodded Hien in the back. 'Hitching yourself up to a woman. Now that's far more dangerous than making a secret film.'

Thanh looked across at Chinh. 'What do you know about this film-maker?'

'His name is Martin Broderick. He's from England. The company he works for is independent of the main television networks, although I understand it is they who have commissioned the documentary. I don't know much more than that.'

'How much influence do we have as to the final version of the film?' asked Thanh.

'It won't be like in Vietnam. This is not a propaganda film. If we decide to help him, it will be up to us to decide on the material we shoot, but once the film is back in England, then of course, he can edit it as he wishes. I do know, though, that he's sympathetic to your situation. You face two risks. One obvious risk is that CSD will find out what we're doing.'

'Well, Upper Chi Ma Wan isn't pleasant, but it's survivable,' said Hien. 'But what about you and Niki? What would happen to you?'

'Who knows. No worse than you,' said Chinh.

'We're used to prison,' said Dung. 'I think the risks you and Niki take are greater. Since we no longer have our liberty, we've really very little to lose.'

'That brings me to my second point of concern. I think we're all agreed that the risks we face in Hong Kong are manageable. What con. . . .'

Thanh interrupted Chinh as he was about to make his second point. 'Are we Niki?' he asked, looking toward her. Niki looked hurt. 'Are we agreed that the risks in Hong Kong are manageable?'

'Yes,' protested Niki. 'Anyway the Hong Kong government would never put us in prison. Imagine how it would look. Human rights workers imprisoned for helping asylum-seekers reveal the truth of their miserable lives. It would make a great headline. Let's face it, it would help our cause more than theirs.' Thanh nodded. It was perhaps unfair of him to focus on Niki. He knew she had courage, but he didn't want to expose her to any more unnecessary risks. He recognised in her a stubborn pride which, like his own, if not tempered could lead her into trouble.

'The Hong Kong government's not the problem. What concerns me,' continued Chinh, 'is that someone might be a little too critical of the Vietnamese government. You have to realise that when the documentary is aired in England, the Vietnamese Embassy in London will monitor and record it from the TV. We need to make it clear to everyone who participates that the Hong Kong government is never going to grant refugee status in such a contrived situation.'

'What you're saying,' said Binh, 'is that with the forced repatriation flights going ahead at full speed, if an asylum-seeker says something critical of the Vietnamese government, he's on his own when he gets repatriated.'

'That's exactly what I'm saying,' said Chinh. 'I shall ask Martin to edit out anything of that nature, but, of course I can't tell him what to do. I just think everyone should know that, and be careful. Protect yourselves as interviewers and protect others. Don't film anyone saying anything that is anti-communist or against the Vietnamese government. There can be no acting out mock trials of cadres. If you think something is controversial you can always switch the camera off, or you can rewind it and record over it.'

'Does anyone have any objections to our co-operating with this film-maker?' asked Thanh.

'Really, we would be foolish to turn the offer down,' said Cuong. 'It's what we moan about all the time — our lack of real contact with the outside world.'

Chinh looked round. 'Is everyone of the same opinion as Cuong? Are we to help make this film?'

There was a unanimous 'Yes' amongst the remaining editors.

'I'd like to make a film about the unfairness of screening,' said Hien. 'Meeting with immigration is like having bees up your trouser leg. You have to sit still and take the stings without saying a word; otherwise you come out worse.'

'Hien, you had your chance for freedom. You should never have come back,' said Quang.

Hien smiled. 'I know, but that's what love does for you. It dulls your brain and sends all your reasoning powers into your pants.'

'How about inviting Martin Broderick to your wedding ceremony, Hien,' said Chinh. 'The guards standing near you at the registry office and Huong climbing into a prison truck in all her finery. It will make a poignant picture.'

'You're right,' said Niki. 'And if you talked about saving Huong's life and of your being in Dong Hung prison together, then the separation, it would make an incredible story. Most of the people who came in from the camps in China are trapped. It would be a good way to get publicity for their plight. What do you think, Hien?'

'Why not? And I'll just tell them about your switching places with Huong so we could meet up.'

'No, I think that should be left out,' said Niki.

'Too bad, that was the most fun part of the story.'

Niki leaned toward Thanh. 'Thanh, I've been talking to a man in Section Ten. He just failed screening even though he was a famous writer in Vietnam and went to prison for criticising the government. I thought he would be a good person to interview.'

Thanh was just pulling himself out of his chair to pour some water when Niki's remarks stopped him in mid track. He couldn't dare hope it was Linh. The man was from Section Ten so that would make him a Southerner, and imprisoned for criticising the government. . . . 'What's his name?'

'He calls himself Diep.' Thanh could barely contain his disappointment. It was too much to have hoped for. There were many writers imprisoned for criticising the government. 'That's not his proper name though. I've written it down.' Niki pulled out a crumpled piece of paper from her pocket. 'Truong Tu Linh. Have you heard of him?'

Thanh leapt up. 'Linh! My God, he escaped. He made it.' He pulled Niki up onto her feet. 'How long have you been speaking to him, Niki?'

'A few weeks I suppose. Do you know him?'

'Know him?' said Thanh. 'He's an old friend from my past. Niki I don't know how I could survive without you. I just love you. . . .' At his remark her face coloured and she quickly glanced down at her feet. He wasn't sure how to read her reaction, so letting his words trail off he gently removed his grip on her arms and quickly carried on talking to the others.

'You could invite him to join the magazine,' suggested Chinh. 'That way if you wanted to visit him you wouldn't have to climb over the fences.'

'Yeah,' laughed Quang. 'Climbing from Section Eight over to the new area of Section Ten might pose a few problems, even for Thanh.'

Since there was no objection from the Correctional Services Department and the United Nations High Commissioner for Refugees, Clarence Kwok reported that Linh would be able to join the magazine. While Quang and Binh sat at the two computers translating the day's news, Thanh paced the floor of the editorial office waiting for him to arrive. The results of Thanh's screening with the review board had come through with a negative determination on his refugee status. It was what he expected, but seeing it in writing still had a chilling effect. It was his second chicken wing. Although UNHCR had the power to reverse the decision of the Hong Kong government, they were frugal in its application. Linh's coming and the prospect of being able to voice their grievances through Martin Broderick's film were two more reasons why he should delay his escape. His plan was to travel across China to Tibet, then cross into India through Nepal. It might take him a year, or even longer. Thanh had no idea how difficult the journey would be or how the Indian government would view his request for asylum, but it was better than just wasting his time in Whitehead with only the prospect of being forcibly repatriated to Vietnam at the end of it.

The other reason for Thanh's delay had been Niki. There was no future for them together — he knew that. Niki's future lay in the free world; his didn't. Until he was in a position of freedom and self sufficiency, he couldn't even seriously consider entering into a relationship. Still Niki's presence in the detention centre provided a pleasant distraction which he was unwilling, as yet, to give up.

At ten o'clock Linh breezed into the editorial office. 'I heard you're looking for an editor to represent Section Ten,' said Linh. 'Do you think I might qualify?'

Hearing his voice, Thanh sat at his desk motionless taking in Linh's gaunt, shrunken frame silhouetted in the doorway: Linh's pain-ravaged face stood out. 'You look thin, brother, but I suppose we can work on that. Yes, you'll do.' Then, unable to contain his feelings of delight, Thanh bounced across the office and wrapped his arms round Linh. The moment passed silently and Thanh pulled back. There was nothing he could say to express his gratitude to his friend. Words would only have demeaned his feelings. 'We have a magazine to put out and a film to make. Are you ready for that?'

Linh smiled. 'Yes, if we die protesting the injustices of this world, at least we go down fighting, eh? How are you, brother? You look better than the last time I saw you.' Thanh looked puzzled. 'I was there when you received the public whipping. I'd just been transferred from Hanoi so it was quite a shock.'

'Hien and Dung told me how you assisted them in the escape. You didn't think I betrayed you?'

Linh smiled. 'An old man like me, I'm wise to their tricks. I understood how and why they had set you up. Was it bad with the others?'

Thanh shrugged. 'It's all in the past.'

'Maybe, but you were tried in absentia brother. They gave you a fifteen year prison sentence.'

Thanh felt himself go cold. 'It's what I should have expected. Fifteen years, eh?'

'Yes, brother. Not something you want to go back to.'

As Linh was speaking, Dung walked into the editorial office with Niki and Chinh. Slinging his black backpack from his shoulder, Chinh spread it out over the table and fished out a small video camera. 'The camera can stay here a month. Take it where you like and film whatever you think is relevant to our cause. Niki and I can take film in and out as needed. Once a tape is full, we get it out.'

'Since you're so keen to get yourself in trouble again, brother Linh, perhaps we could start with a practice run filming you,' said Hien. 'I, for one, would like to hear how you escaped from Vietnam. Maybe the viewers at home would also like to hear.'

Quang left his place at the computer and came over to examine the camera. 'It's smaller than I expected. Can it really take quality pictures?' Chinh nodded. Quang turned it over a few times then lifting it to his eye he focused on Linh. Niki was standing next to him and put Quang's fingers on the switch to show him how it operated.

'Mr Diep, tell me how you escaped from a prison in Vietnam.'

'Firstly, I should say my name is not Diep, but Truong Tu Linh. I was imprisoned in Thanh Hoa because the Vietnamese government took exception to some of the books I wrote. Twelve months after the dramatic

escape of my three close friends, Amnesty International and the writers'
organization PEN managed to get a release for me of sorts. After leaving
Thanh Hoa, I was kept under house arrest. No going out, no visitors. It
was a luxury to be away from Thanh Hoa, but I found the isolation of
my life miserable.' Linh leaned closer to the camera. 'I was detained at
the local public security office on each public holiday. There was always
the threat that if I transgressed any of the rules, or if the government
changed its mind, I would be back in prison.' He shook his head. 'After
six months I decided, enough was enough. My wife was constantly
watched, but my young son was fairly free to speak to whom he liked,
so through him I managed to communicate to friends my intention to
escape to Hong Kong. Some of my books had been published overseas
and I was owed money from the book sales. My friends used that to buy
passage for myself and family on a boat. The night guards used to
frequent a café next door to my home so it wasn't difficult to arrange for
them to have a good night's sleep while we slipped out of the house.'

'Well, welcome to Hong Kong, brother,' said Quang. 'I hope you find
your new quarters more to your liking.'

'It's true, I'm not lacking for anyone to speak to. The loneliness of my
former life has ended. There are about three thousand inmates in my
section. We live in boxes all piled on top of one another, like chickens in
a coop. Whenever I make love to my wife everyone in Nissen Hut B, is
aware of it.'

'You do have a little curtain to pull around your bunk?' asked Dung.

'I do, of sorts. You are right, brother. My complaints are unjustified. I
just wish you could convince my wife of our privacy.'

'Oh it's like that, is it,' said Cuong. 'I have to say that in some respects
I've found this place quite to my liking.'

'We won't use this exactly as it is, because the general TV viewer won't
understand some of the things you refer to, but let's run the tape back
and see how it worked,' said Niki. The editors gathered round and took
turns to view what was on the camera. Thanh took his turn and peered
through the view-finder. For such a tiny camera the pictures were
amazingly clear. Technology in the West had advanced way beyond
anything he'd dreamed of. When he finished examining the film, he
passed it back to Niki.

'We should experiment with the zoom,' continued Niki. 'I was speaking to Annie, the cinematographer, and she suggested we try not to move
while holding the camera. It's better to get a shot, switch off and then
move to another speaker and switch on again. The same with the zoom.

It's okay to go from a wide shot to close-up, but to zoom in and out makes it difficult for a viewer to watch.'

'A bit like being seasick,' suggested Thanh.

'Exactly,' said Niki.

While Niki was explaining how the camera operated, Thanh drew Linh aside. 'After our escape from Thanh Hoa, what happened to you? Your account just now sounded too simple.'

'Well, perhaps a little simplified.'

'So what happened, brother? I've thought about you so many times.'

'The guards eventually managed to quash the riot and put out the fires which started after the explosion. There was an investigation into what caused the explosion. In the end they named Hien, Dung and Luong as the main culprits although there were suggestions you had master-minded the whole thing from your hospital bed. Commandant Ngo Pham Do was criticised for allowing a dangerous man to join a work party where he had access to dynamite. The whole thing became quite nasty. If I were you, brother, I would slit my throat before ever going back to Vietnam.'

'What about the inmates involved in the rioting? What were the repercussions for them?'

'About twelve of us . . . those considered to be leaders were hauled off to the isolation block. There were questions, some beatings. You know how it is.'

'How bad was it for you?'

'I think, maybe it was good, brother. I took some beatings. A broken jaw, ribs.' Thanh cringed as he thought of Linh and others being beaten on his account. 'There was some internal bleeding which persuaded them to transfer me to the hospital. But the reports of my condition led to my being transferred from Thanh Hoa, to my home. Not a bad outcome, eh?'

'Except one small detail.'

'What's that?' asked Linh.

'Neither of us has been recognised as refugees.'

'My case is already high profile because of Amnesty and PEN, so even if I fail screening there is always UNHCR to lean on. It's not me I worry about, brother, but you. What will you do?'

'I have a plan to escape, but not yet.'

'I heard tell of two men who escaped from the High Island Detention Centre. They stowed away on a container boat going to Brazil. They were on the boat for several weeks. When they got there, the Brazilian government exptradited them back to Hong Kong and Hong Kong repatriated them to Vietnam.'

Thanh breathed in. 'That was bad luck. Still the idea of stowing away on a boat isn't bad, unless of course the boat is going to Brazil. But there must be other countries which are not so hard-nosed. Maybe I should do a little research.'

Niki stood between Martin Broderick and his camerawoman, Annie, as she filmed Hien leap from out of the police truck, then lift first Huong and then Tuyet, to the ground. It was a relief for Niki to see Tuyet with them, because up until the last few days it had not been certain she would be allowed to attend the wedding. Neither Dung nor any of Hien's and Huong's friends from the detention centre was allowed to attend, but then they had not expected it. The real celebration would take place at Whitehead and since Huong and Hien were already married, the civil wedding ceremony was as much a show for the camera as it was to satisfy the authorities' legal requirements.

Huong looked across at Niki. Her face was glowing, and in contrast to the bleak backdrop of the police truck, looked radiant in her lavender silk *ao dai*. Since Niki was much the same build as Huong, it had been easy for the dress-maker to achieve a perfect fit. Tuyet's outfit had caused more problems, but after several trips to and from the detention centre, Niki had eventually achieved the correct fitting. Standing at her side, Hien looked the perfect groom in the fawn light weight suit Martin had given him as a 'thank you' for allowing them to film. All that was lacking were the flowers. As Huong and Hien walked arm in arm toward the registry office, with Tuyet trailing close behind, Niki strode over to them and placed a bouquet of deep purple roses with white lace baby's breath into Huong's hands, then attached a rose into the lapel of Hien's jacket. 'There, you two look perfect now.' She stooped and placed a bouquet of pink roses in Tuyet's hands. 'This is a special day for you too, Tuyet. You look gorgeous.'

Tuyet could barely contain her excitement. 'I've never dressed like this in my life, it's like being a princess, but what I'm really thrilled about is being outside in Hong Kong. I saw all sorts of wonderful, tall elegant buildings, gleaming cars and everything through the barred window. I even saw some ships on the water. Oh, so beautiful.'

'Well, I promise you, one day you will view the world without bars to block your vision. And let's hope that what we are doing today marks the beginning of your freedom.' Niki glanced back at Martin and Annie. 'Annie's looking at you, Tuyet . . . smile.'

Huong flung her arms round Niki. 'Thank you, sister, for being here. I know that connecting yourselves with the film-makers carries risks. I'll always remember what you and Chinh have done for us.'

Taking Tuyet's hand, Niki followed the bride and groom into the registry office. The guards seemed embarrassed and although one of the officers escorted Hien and Huong over to the registrar's desk while they wrote down the details of their marriage, the other officer hung around the doorway. Niki and Tuyet took a seat beside Chinh and Martin while Annie carried her camera discreetly to the corner of the room where she could gain shots of them during the ceremony without drawing attention to herself.

As the ceremony came to a close, Chinh slipped out ahead of the others to Martin's hire-car to fetch their gift. When Hien walked from the registration office with Huong at his side, Niki had already joined Chinh and they were waiting at the door. Placing a guitar in Hien's arms Chinh grinned.

Hien looked startled. 'What's this!'

'Niki and I brought it to replace the one the *dai go* smashed. It's a selfish gift really because all of us are eager to hear you play again.'

Positioning the guitar across his chest Hien strummed out a few chords. 'It's magnificent . . . and it's even in tune.' Looking up at Niki and Chinh, 'How can I thank you?'

'Just play for us sometime,' said Niki. 'It'll be your life-long servitude to keep us entertained.'

Hien brushed the tears from his eyes. 'It will be my pleasure.'

As Hien strummed out the chords to Procol Harem's *A Whiter Shade of Pale*, Martin pulled a bottle of champagne from out of his leather shoulder bag and uncorked it. The wine fizzed into the air before splashing over them. 'I haven't any glasses but if you don't mind drinking from the bottle we can all share this.' Offering the bottle to Huong, Martin declined his head deferentially, 'The bride first.'

Before Hien could respond one of the Correctional Services officers had stepped forward. 'I'm sorry this isn't allowed. "No alcohol is allowed inside the detention centres."'

Martin laughed. 'Haven't you noticed. We are not in a detention centre. Though I tell you I'd like to get in.'

'You can drink,' the officer stepped in front of Martin splitting Hien and Huong, 'but these two are not allowed.'

'Oh, have a heart man. This is their wedding day.'

The officer shifted uncomfortably and looked to be on the point of giving in when he suddenly noticed Annie filming him. 'What are you doing? This is a private wedding. No video cameras are allowed.'

Annie glared at him. 'So what are you going to do about it?' The officer's face turned scarlet and even though Annie blatantly continued to film despite his warning, he did nothing.

It was only after Hien and Huong had climbed back into the police van with Tuyet that Annie switched the camera off. 'That was quite something,' she said. 'Actually it's the kind of wedding I like — short and sweet. It's what I'll do when I'm ready to get hitched, but what do we do now since we can't celebrate with them?'

'They're happy enough,' said Chinh. 'I know a good pizza place in Sai Kung. Let's go and eat there. We can drink the champagne in their honour.'

'It seems so mean they can't join us.'

'That's the difference between those who are free and those who are not,' said Chinh.

Niki shrugged. 'The ceremony was only important to them in that Tuyet could be with them. What's really important is that now their marriage is official with the Hong Kong government, they'll be allowed to live in the same section.' Taking Annie's arm Niki led her toward the waiting taxi. 'I went to another wedding where the bride climbed into the truck with CSD officers, and the groom got into a taxi alone to go to the airport. In making this film, there will be lots of injustices you'll hear about, but I promise you Hien and Huong will consider it an honour if we eat pizza together and raise our glasses to their happy and free future. And besides that,' she laughed, 'we're going to have a party tomorrow in Huong's section. All of the magazine editors will be there, so actually it's a good opportunity for us to do some quiet filming. Hien and Huong will tell their story. Dung too, Hien's brother. His story is incredibly sad. Then there will be others who can talk about the Fang Cheng Camp in China.'

'I wish I could be there,' said Martin. 'My biggest frustration in making this film is dealing with all the restrictions placed upon us. We're not allowed to do this, and we're not allowed to do that. It's like trying to make a film of a top security prison.'

'Tell us about it,' said Chinh. 'The gate locks from both sides, but I promise you Hien and Huong's celebration tomorrow will be more exciting than our celebration in Sai Kung, so let's forget about being guilty and enjoy ourselves.'

Thanh was crouched in one of the third-level bunks as he peeled back a part of the aluminum roofing so that he could angle the camera into a good position. If any of the guards were to see him he could be prosecuted for destruction of government property, besides the offence of filming in the detention centre. It wouldn't be the first time he'd been punished for such an offence and Thanh was ready to take the risk. Below him outside the ECVII section, Hien and Huong were celebrating their wedding. It was only Dung who seemed not to be enjoying himself and Thanh suspected that the camp wedding must have brought back memories of his own loss. He was glad when Niki walked over to Dung and locking her arm in his dragged him over to the table to join in with the others.

The lighting outside was good. Later on they would be forced to film inside as they set about the more risky task of recording the stories of the Dong Hung and Fang Cheng people. Chinh would discreetly bring them in small groups, to tell of their personal experiences while the others kept the party going on outside.

As Thanh heard the soft pad of footsteps approaching he leaned across the bunk and peered down. Looking up at him was Linh. 'Brother, what if we swap over now? You should be celebrating with your friends.'

'I only wanted to scan the sections and get a little footage of the celebration. We have a lot of interviews to get through so we have to be sparing with the batteries. I'm coming down now to eat something before we start filming inside.'

When they walked outside into the sunlight to join the others at the table Cuong was in the middle of telling a story. 'This girl and I were in the single women's dormitory. She wasn't exactly Miss Proper, but she was good fun and knew how to stop a man from feeling lonely. Anyway that's when we got word Clarence Kwok was looking for me. There wasn't time for me to get out of the Nissen hut so as Clarence was walking through the door my young friend leaps down from the bunk, rips off her bra. . . .'

'So her bra was actually on her before Clarence walked in?' said Thanh.

'Whatever. Braless she heads straight for the door and almost bumps into Clarence. Seeing him she then does this wonderful act of hysteria. He turns crimson and tries to flee the Nissen hut, but unknown to him some kids have dragged a bowl of soapy water in front of the doorway. Clarence tries to avoid it, steps in it then goes hopping out of the hut like a bouncing ball.'

'Oh, come on. Is that exactly true?' laughed Dung as he wiped the tears from his eyes.

'Well given a few changes here and there, it's almost true.'

'So the real story,' said Thanh, 'was the CSD officer wasn't Clarence, and the girl was a boy, and there was no bowl of. . . .' Cuong jumped up and pulling the legs from under Thanh's chair sent him sprawling onto the ground in a fit of laughter.

Thanh joined in with the celebrations for half an hour before deciding it was time to slip away and begin the filming. It seemed that everyone in the section felt they had something of importance to say and the filming proved to be more time-consuming and arduous than any of them had anticipated. The time went by rapidly and as the camera gobbled up rolls of film at a phenomenal rate they were close to having to pack it in when Cuong remembered there was some spare film in his bunk in Section Four. 'How about it if Dung and I shout across the corridor to Section Four and see whose attention we can raise.'

'Just make sure it isn't one of the guards,' laughed Quang.

Cuong had been gone barely five minutes when Dung returned alone. 'We need a long thread of wire so we can set up a pulley to get the film across.'

'What about string?' suggested Binh. 'We could knot it round a stone and toss one end across.'

'I have a tennis ball,' said Tuyet. 'I don't mind if you put two holes in it and we also have the washing line us kids use to skip with. We throw balls into Section Four all the time.'

'Brilliant,' said Thanh, 'Let's have a try.'

The plan worked smoothly. However, time had been wasted. The editors had permission to be in the section until 3 PM, but it was now 3:15. Since none of the guards had come to tell them they must leave the section, they carried on filming.

Keeping the close-up on Mrs Phuong's face as she was speaking, Thanh listened to her words with sadness. 'After our failed escape from Fang Cheng, I was separated from my husband and son and taken back to Dong Hung. The Commandant and other staff beat me so bad it resulted in my miscarriage. I was in a state of shock because of the loss of my baby and because I couldn't get news of my husband and son so I cried and pleaded with the camp master to tell me what had happened to them. At first he told me nothing, but much later he told me they had pushed them back across the border into Vietnam.' As Mrs Phuong stopped to regain some of her composure Thanh took the opportunity to widen the camera angle to take in the distressed faces of the wider group, however, when Mrs Phuong prepared to speak again, Thanh switched the camera off, flicked it back into close-up and switched on. 'I was so desperate I decided to kill myself. I set fire to my body, but some people in the camp. . . .'

Binh rushed into the Nissen hut. 'Quick! Clarence is on his way over.'

Thanh flicked off the camera and had barely time to stow it under a blanket when Clarence Kwok marched into the Nissen hut accompanied by two other Correctional Services officers. 'What are you doing in here? The agreement was for an outside celebration until three. It's now almost four. I tell you I don't trust any of you people.' He gave Niki a particularly meaningful glare before advancing on Thanh and herding him out of the Nissen hut. There was nothing Thanh could do except to leave the camera where it was. However, as the guards prepared to escort Thanh and the other editors back to TCI, Niki and Chinh quickly made the excuse to stay behind to clear up the table.

Back in the editorial office, Thanh pulled out the film cassettes from his ankle socks and hid them underneath the air conditioner unit, but when Niki and Chinh checked into the section at the Correctional Services hut an hour later, Thanh was aghast to see that they were both subjected to a search. Watching from his vantage point at the bottom of the stairs, he was even more surprised to see that the officers found nothing.

When Niki and Chinh ran up the stairs laughing Thanh rushed anxiously to meet them. 'Where's the camera?'

Niki pointed to the far corner of the section. 'It looks like it just bounced in.' Thanh watched, wide eyed, as a football bounced across the compound having just flown over the fence from Section Eight.

'Oh my God! That's the camera?'

'It bounced its way from the ECVII section to Five, to Six, to Seven, to Eight, and into here. Pretty ingenious eh?'

'Ingenious! It's probably smashed to pieces,' said Thanh sharply, not even bothering to hide his dismay.

'It's okay,' laughed Chinh. 'When we got word CSD were suspicious of our activities we padded it with a piece of old blanket. Maybe someone in one of the sections informed about the filming, I don't know. Anyway we unstrung this old leather football and put the camera inside.'

'Well, we hope it's okay,' said Niki. 'Otherwise Martin Broderick might charge us for it. I'll bet a camera like that cost a few thousand Hong Kong dollars.'

Chinh shrugged. 'He can put it down as a tax write-off.'

'Oh, yes and let the British government pay. Poetic justice. I like that,' said Niki.

Still anxious about the camera Thanh sprinted across the compound and snatched up the football before it could suffer any more bounces. The idea of breaking something that cost so much money made him uncomfortable and Niki and Chinh's laughing about it made it worse. It was only after he'd brought it back into the editorial office, unlaced it from the football and inspected every inch of the camera to make sure it was undamaged that he nodded his head for the others to see.

Niki was grinning. 'We told you it was okay. You didn't really trust us did you?'

Thanh felt humbled. 'You handled it great. I'm sorry.'

'Before we left we managed to finish filming Mrs Phuong telling her story,' said Chinh. 'That was too important to cut short. Otherwise I think we're finished with the Dong Hung and Fang Cheng people.'

A few days after Hien's and Huong's marriage celebration, early monsoon rains began, and it rained and stormed for several days. Day after day the wind belted the rain across the mountain ranges and down toward the sea making conditions in the Whitehead camp Nissen huts miserable. Since the editorial office was on the second level it did not become flooded, so Thanh and the others decided to keep on working, although when Niki turned up at the magazine office Thanh was surprised. 'I didn't expect to see you. How are the roads?'

'Passable. There was a bad mud slide at Sai Kung, but I came via Sha Tin. How come you're the only ones within ten miles of here who have electricity?'

'Binh is our electronics wizard. Ask him,' said Thanh. Binh looked up from the computer and smiled at the compliment.

'How did you do it, Binh?'

'Easy.' Binh shrugged his shoulders. 'I just climbed up onto the roof and tapped us into an emergency supply.'

'Haven't CSD said anything? They're downstairs in semi-darkness and your up here lit up like a Christmas tree.'

'They haven't come upstairs yet. Presumably they don't know,' said Dung.

Niki laughed. 'I don't believe it. You guys are incredible. The music you're blasting out is enough to wake up the dead for miles around.' She dragged her backpack off her shoulders and pulled out some new packages of film from a secret lining sown into her bag. 'Martin asked how you were doing. I think he's anxious to see what else you have.'

Thanh climbed up onto the desk and slipped some film cassettes from the gap under the broken air conditioner. Jumping to the floor he handed the film to Niki. 'Give him these. I think he'll like what we've done.'

'Did Dung tell his story?'

'Yes, we've done everything of importance we can think of right down to the way the children line up for school and the serving of our meals from the plastic dustbins. I'm not sure how much more it is worth us doing. The camera's been in every section. We even managed to tape a musical performance by some of the professional artists in the detention centre.'

'That sounds great.' Niki looked round the room. 'Is Cuong here today?'

'No. They had a weapons search in Section Four, so no one from his section is allowed out.'

'Oh, I need to talk to him. I was at Green Island Reception Centre earlier this week and met his wife.'

'What!' Dung came up beside Niki. 'She's in Hong Kong?'

'Yes. At first I didn't realise who she was. She has three children with her. She was telling me her story and how she came here to find her husband, when it slowly dawned on me who her husband might be. She had an envelope with the return address as Victoria Prison written in English. When she left Vietnam, she had no idea what the English word prison meant, but soon after she arrived here immigration officials told her that from the address on the envelope her husband was in Victoria Prison and so he must be a criminal. They persuaded her to put her name down to return to Vietnam.'

'Oh no. She mustn't do that,' said Dung, suddenly alarmed.

Thanh was of the same thinking as Dung. 'I agree. We have to tell her to stay here.'

'I would have done, but Cuong has a serious girlfriend. I thought it best to say nothing about knowing him and then find out from him what he wants me to do. If he doesn't intend breaking up with his girlfriend, then maybe it's better she thinks he's a criminal. She might be less hurt.'

'With a weapons search they won't even let camp workers in.'

'What if I go into Section Five and do what we did with the film cassettes? I could throw a tennis ball across with a message and then wait for the reply. It's probably better we don't shout in case his girlfriend is around and Cuong doesn't want her or anyone else in the section to know he has a wife and kids.'

'They've probably rounded everyone up so they can complete their search,' said Thanh. 'Still it's worth a try. How long before Minh gets transferred back to Vietnam?'

'I'm not sure. I did suggest she take her name off the list and give me time to see what I could find out, but from what she said, there's a lot of pressure on her to go. They said that since her husband's a criminal, the resettlement countries won't take him and he'll eventually be sent back to Vietnam anyway. They said she should go home now and prepare a life for him so when he gets back it will be easier.'

'Well, if Cuong does abandon her, I'll take responsibility for her,' said Dung. 'It would be too cruel for her to go back now. God, what a nightmare this has all been. Niki, do whatever you can to stop her going back. I'd even marry her if that would help. I wouldn't expect anything in return.'

Niki looked surprised. 'You would do that?'

'Since my wife's and son's death, my life has finished. I really don't care what happens to me. If I can use my life to serve someone else, I will.' He looked squarely at Niki. 'It would be an honour. I used to think Minh was foolish, but after everything she went through in the NEZ and then having brought the kids here, I think she has a lot of courage.'

Niki grasped Dung's hand. 'I wish I could have met Ha and Diep. I know we would have been friends.'

Niki was gone for twenty minutes before she came back into TCI. Although the heavy rains had stopped, it was still drizzling and her hair and face were dripping wet. When she saw Thanh and Dung she shook her head. 'It's as you said. They have everyone contained in the television hut. I can't communicate with anyone.'

'Niki, go back and visit Minh as soon as possible. Tell her Cuong is here and that he's waiting for her. I'm certain this thing with his girlfriend isn't serious. In fact there have been several of them,' said Thanh. 'He's lonely that's all. If we let Minh and his kids leave for Vietnam, he'd be heartbroken.'

Minh's initial distress in learning that her husband might be a criminal deepened within her. She couldn't imagine why Cuong should have changed so much. Nothing in Hong Kong was as she'd expected it to be. From the time the police boat had intercepted the fishing trawler she'd made the voyage to the colony in, and the police, with their rubber gloved hands, had searched everyone for weapons, she'd been in a state of shock. Later when they cut off her long hair and threw delousing medicine all over her, she'd known with clarity that this was not the Hong Kong of her dreams. Straining her eyes she stared through the wire cage to where the government boat was just docking, and prayed that the mixed Asian-Western girl would keep faith with her and come back with news of Cuong. All week she'd avoided speaking to her neighbours in the bunks next to her, for fear of what they might say. The immigration officials were still pestering her about keeping her name on the list of returnees, even though she'd told them she needed time to think. If they were right and Cuong was a criminal with no hope of resettlement, then she would go back ahead of him. She would begin her illegal hawking again and earn the money to make a home for them. It was just something Niki said, or perhaps not what she said so much as what she had hinted, that had persuaded her there might be some hope.

When Minh saw Niki step off the boat, her heart lifted. If she could just have news of Cuong, everything would change. The long years in the new economic zone, the struggle for survival after her release, her long voyage, the insults from immigration — none of it mattered if she could just be reunited with her husband. Running from the fence to the gate she pressed herself against it to be sure that Niki would not walk past without seeing her, and perhaps forget her promise to Minh, go and visit someone else in another section.

It was twenty minutes before Niki, escorted by the guard was allowed to enter her section.

'This is your second visit in a very short time,' said the officer, 'so we cannot let you stay as long as last time. The boat returns in an hour and you have to be on it. I'll collect you in fifty minutes.' Niki thanked the guard before he left.

Minh couldn't contain herself any longer. Grabbing at Niki's hand she pulled her away from the gate. 'Do you have any news?'

Niki smiled. 'Let's talk privately. Can I come and sit with you in your bunk?'

Minh didn't need her to say any more. She ran with her, and once inside looked at Niki expectantly. 'Tell me.'

'For a start this thing about your husband being a criminal is rubbish. He was in Victoria Prison for about three years which must have been when he wrote the letter to you. He was there because he'd come into Hong Kong from China. The Chinese illegal immigrants are treated differently.'

'Yes, he was in China. I knew of that.'

'Well that's the only reason he was in prison. Later he was transferred to the detention-centre gulag for the Vietnamese boat people. Right now he's in Whitehead Detention Centre. You probably know that all asylum-seekers are detained while in Hong Kong pending their meeting with immigration officials to determine their refugee status.'

Minh could hardly take in what she was hearing. 'So Cuong is here and there's nothing wrong.' Minh thought she detected a slight frown cross Niki's face but dismissed the impression almost as soon as she'd registered it. Cuong was in Hong Kong, and he wasn't a criminal.

'I've heard that the Security Branch Refugee Co-ordinator for the Hong Kong government can be a reasonable man if approached directly. I'll go and see him personally and ask if he can reunite you and the children with Cuong as quickly as possible.'

'Is that possible? Can you do that?'

'I'm sure I can.'

At the prospect of being back with Cuong, Minh's emotions welled up and she found herself laughing as well as crying. 'Oh, I'm so happy. You can't imagine how awful my life has been since he left. First I was put in a terrible camp because he'd spoken on the New China radio. They tried to get me to hate him, but I stayed loyal to him always. It was years before they released me. Then my home and everything we used to own was gone. I couldn't find any of my family because they had moved as well. In the beginning I'd been allowed some visitors because of course they were looking for ways to implicate my sister's husband in Cuong's activities. I heard much later they put him in prison and charged him with being a spy. He was publicly beaten for breaking a lightbulb. Then he escaped with Cuong's friends.'

'Your sister's husband?' Niki was staring at Minh. 'What was his name?'

'Thanh. Do you know him?'

'Maybe. I know Cuong and I know some of his friends. Hien, Dung . . . Thanh is married then?'

'Yes, to my sister Lan. She doesn't look like me — she's very beautiful. I knew Hien and Dung. They are all long-time friends. But you said you know Cuong. Do you know him well? Oh, tell me about him.'

Niki looked close to tears herself as she described Cuong's life in the camp and the magazine they all worked on. 'He's healthy. He's funny. When I met you the first time, I wasn't sure you were Cuong's wife so I was afraid to raise your hopes. He will be so happy to see you and the children; I'm sure of it.'

'He doesn't know we're here?'

'Dung will have told him by now. I couldn't myself because when I was at Whitehead there was a weapons search. .'

'A weapon's search?'

'It's routine. It's nothing. If I could have told him about you, I would have. Dung or Hien will tell him.'

'When I came out of Dong Cuong Yen Bai, I was so lost. We had heard Cuong was dead.' Minh heaved a sigh and sank her face into her hands as she recalled how painful those years had been. 'For a while my children and I just roamed the streets looking for our relatives, but they had all gone.' She looked earnestly at Niki. 'An old hawker was sorry for us and gave us some sticky rice cakes because the children looked so pitiful.'

Minh felt the tears spring back to her eyes. 'You know, my own mother used to be a hawker. It was like her soul continued on in the old lady and she wanted to help us . . . her newly found daughter and her grand-children.'

Niki nodded. 'Yes, I believe that's possible.'

Minh smiled as she remembered how kind Mrs Hanh had been to them. 'The old lady, Mrs Hanh, shared her business and her home with us. She said she was too old to carry her heavy basket any more and needed us. Of course it was a lie. She was as strong as an ox.'

'It sounds as though she saved your lives.'

Minh's face glowed. 'Oh yes. I'm sure she did. Without her we could have starved.' Minh pulled out an old photograph and pressed it into Niki's hands. 'Just look at her eyes. You can see she was someone of special dignity.' Niki studied the photograph.

'After she died,' continued Minh. 'I kept her business going. Then one day I met someone from my old village who told me how to locate my elder brother Tang. He told me about the trials of Thanh, Hien and Dung. That's also when Tang gave me the letter from Victoria Prison. He'd had the letter for years.' Minh crossed her arms over her chest and momentarily closed her eyes. 'Then I knew Cuong was alive. Oh, it was such a moment. I cried so much I became almost mad in my head.'

For a moment Minh was overcome by her emotions and couldn't continue. She gratefully accepted the tissue Niki passed over to her and wiped her eyes. 'By then,' she said. 'I had some money saved because of Mrs Hanh's business, so I sought out the snake heads and I came here. It wasn't easy, but we all made it alive.'

'Every time I hear a story like yours it breaks my heart. I'm Amerasian and since I was adopted by an American family and taken out of Vietnam, my life has become so easy. I never worry about food or shelter. Even now if I needed money I know my parents would send it to me.'

Minh reached for Niki's hands. 'My dearest friend, without you I would have lost my husband a second . . . third time, and gone back to Vietnam.'

Niki put her arms around Minh. 'I'll go to the refugee co-ordinator today and tell him your story. You'll be together again soon. I promise.'

Dung couldn't explain his feelings. When Cuong had come into the magazine office and told them of his incredible reunion with his family, Dung found he'd had to leave. He made up some pretext of having to return to his own section, not because he wasn't truly happy for Cuong, their reunion was the most amazing story ever, but, Hien's marriage to Huong and now Cuong's reunion with Minh opened up his own wounds, reminding him of his terrible loneliness. The review board had turned down his application for refugee status, and he'd received the notice of his second chicken wing just a week ago so it was now almost certain he would be returned to Vietnam.

Vietnam, or one of the free countries, it didn't matter any more. The horrors of Dong Hung were years away, yet freedom without his wife and son would have been mental torture. It was almost more comforting to think of being imprisoned again in Vietnam because at least, there everyone was miserable. A common thread pulled the prisoners together — and his loneliness would bond with theirs. And what if Ha and Diep had lived? At least in death, they had been spared the desperation of endless imprisonment.

Dung didn't dare to talk about volunteering to return to Vietnam, to Hien or the others, but the idea stuck in his thoughts. It was actually a relief that he didn't need to volunteer because soon the choice would be taken from him, and he'd be sent back anyway. It was easier that way since he wouldn't have to explain himself.

It was several months since they had smuggled the last of the film tapes to Martin Broderick. In all of that time Thanh had hardly seen Niki. She'd come into the office with bundles of papers and magazines, but she didn't stop to talk and always seemed to be in a hurry to go somewhere else. When he'd tried to get her to talk, she'd pulled away. He'd sensed her distance, but wasn't able to penetrate it. The first Thanh knew of the film having been aired was when Anders Boern and Clarence Kwok marched into the editorial office. 'Switch off those computers. You lock this office up and give me the keys. The magazine is being shut down pending an investigation into a film of the detention centre shown last night on British TV,' said Clarence. 'Chinh, I've collected your camp card from the section gate and am confiscating it. You are to leave here now. I'll instruct a guard to escort you to the main gate.' The blood drained from Chinh's face as Clarence addressed him. 'Is your colleague, Niki Clemenceau, in today?'

'I don't know. I haven't seen her.'

'Well, if you do, you can tell her she needn't bother coming in. She'll be turned away at the gate just the same as you. And maybe later when there's an inquiry into the British film, you will both be summoned for questioning.'

Chapter 19: Return to Vietnam

22nd March to 3rd April 1993

During the long and sleepless nights in prison,
I've written more than a hundred poems on thraldom.
Often at the end of a quatrain I put down my brush,
And through the bars look up at the sky at freedom.
PRISON DIARY, HO CHI MINH

THANH MOVED FORWARD as he sat on the bench opposite Niki in the visitors' room. The only advantage of the poor acoustics, and the high volume of voices as friends and family tried to communicate to one another across the long trestle table, was that it made it more difficult for the guards to listen in on their conversation. Niki looked pale as she took in the significance of what Thanh had just told her. 'I watched the spectacle on television: the last mandatory repatriation flight — asylum-seekers kicking and fighting as they were dragged onto the aeroplane by Correctional Services officers — never suspecting that Binh was amongst them. What's going to happen to him?'

'Binh wrote some pretty provocative articles for our camp magazine, but what he managed to send to overseas magazines was far more radical. I can't see the Vietnamese government ignoring it.'

'It isn't just the articles he has to worry about. A friend recorded Martin Broderick's film and mailed it to me. The documentary concludes with Binh burning the Vietnamese flag and shouting, "Down with the Vietnamese government."'

Thanh sat back exasperated. 'Binh's an idiot. Doesn't he understand he harms all the asylum-seekers by such stupid provocation? If he thought the gesture would get him refugee status, his plan backfired. The Hong Kong government would consider his action contrived. So far as they're concerned a person cannot become a refugee because of their political action after leaving their home country.'

'Will he go to prison?'

Thanh shrugged. 'Maybe not immediately, but long term, I don't know. They say things are changing there, but could they really have changed that much? His behaviour is going to make them very nervous.'

'Thanh listen, since they closed the magazine and we were banned, Chinh and I have been working with other people. No one has any confidence in UNHCR's programme to monitor returnees, so we're planning to operate our own. It won't be large but if we can at least have a presence in Vietnam, it will be a start.'

Thanh opened his eyes wide. He didn't like what Niki was saying. 'What do you mean have a presence in Vietnam? Are you going there?'

'It's quite simple really. We will open three restaurants: one in Hanoi, another in Hue, and a third in Saigon. They will be the kind of places where travellers can come to eat or drink tea and be introduced to others travellers. We will arrange the cars and the interpreters so the money we make will keep the programme financially solvent. The thing is the drivers and interpreters will also have an opportunity to travel round the country and meet with people. We can check up on returnees. Or if any returnees experience trouble they can come to us.'

'And just who exactly will be checking up on these people? They would end up in serious trouble.'

'Don't be so critical. I didn't say it would be returnees. Right now everything is in the exploratory stage. We'll make sure everyone who works with us has a foreign passport.'

'But you can't set up a business in Vietnam unless you have local involvement.'

The bell to end the visiting time hammered across the hall. Thanh was feeling panicky about what Niki had just proposed. Standing up he leaned over the table. 'Niki, the idea's absurd. You don't understand how it is in Vietnam. If returnees know they can contact you for help, then the government will know about you as well. It just won't be allowed.'

'So what if they do eventually know about us? It's better we try to get a gauge on what's going on than sit here and do nothing.'

One of the guards put his hand on Thanh's shoulder as though to shove him along with the other asylum-seekers. 'Visiting has ended. Move along. We have to clear the hall before the next group come in.'

Thanh stood his ground. 'When is all this going to happen?'

'I have already applied for my visa. Chinh and I are leaving for Hanoi next week.'

'Whom have you spoken to about this?'

'I've spoken with some of the camp workers and human-rights people here in Hong Kong. I also spoke with some asylum-seekers who were going back and were worried about their situation.

'Niki, no.'

The guard was becoming impatient with Thanh and gave him a hard push. 'I said move along.'

As Thanh took a stride forward he turned back to Niki. 'We have to talk more. You're a Vietnamese national so it makes no difference that you have an American passport.' Niki seemed as though she heard, but she was also being pushed along in the other direction by the Correctional Services officer ushering the visitors out.

Weaving her way through the busy streets of Kowloon, Niki made her way towards the travel agents. Going up in the rickety lift Niki drummed her fingers impatiently on the wall. There was just time to pick up her visa, grab some lunch and then dash over to Whitehead to see Dung. He'd seemed quite depressed since the magazine closed down and she was worried about him. Despite the deprivation of freedom, Hien and Huong were ecstatic in their new family arrangement and even Cuong had emerged as a new man. He didn't smoke and although he missed being able to work on the magazine, he was so busy getting to know his children and reacquainting himself with Minh that he felt relatively comfortable with his life. Whatever tomorrow brought it could not be worse than what they had been through already. The publicity from Broderick's film had created a huge interest in the Dong Hung and Fang Cheng asylum-seekers' plight so there was some hope of pressure for their status to be changed from overseas advocates.

Inside the travel agency, Niki checked her papers. The tickets were fine, but the dates on the visa were incorrect. 'What's this? I asked for a month's visa.'

The travel agent leaned forward. 'That is a month's visa.'

'The dates are wrong. I'm travelling for a month, but look at this date. It's three days short of when I arrive. It means I'll arrive in Vietnam without a valid visa. They could refuse to let me enter.'

The travel agent scrutinised the visa. 'It's not us that made the mistake. We submitted your application form with the proper dates to the Vietnamese authorities so they're the ones who messed up.'

'What can you do about it? I'm leaving Hong Kong tonight and I have lots of things I have to do to get ready.'

'If you can give me a couple of hours, I'll take the visa along to the Vietnamese authorities myself and get it changed.'

'One hour. That's all I can give you.'

'Okay, an hour.'

Niki made her way to the post office to mail some letters before heading for her favourite street restaurant. She hadn't really wanted to waste an hour over lunch but since there was little choice, she decided to go somewhere she really liked. It was annoying that her visa was messed up and the practice of only issuing it a day before travel seemed like a deliberate ploy on the part of the Vietnamese authorities to make travellers uneasy.

Niki sat the hour out before heading back to the tourist agency. This time when she picked up her visa, the dates had been shifted a week back. It meant that her visa was valid for three days before she was due to fly into Hanoi but would have expired three days before she was due to fly out. Exasperated, Niki made no pretence at being polite. 'What's going on? Is this deliberate, or can people really be that stupid?'

The travel agent shrugged his shoulders. 'It's nothing to do with me. I did the best I could.'

'Where's their office? I'll go there myself.'

'The Vietnamese government doesn't have an official office here. There's no embassy or consulate to go to.'

'You went somewhere.'

'I'm sorry you can't go.'

If it hadn't been for the fact that time was running out, and if Niki didn't leave Kowloon soon she would never make it over to Sha Tin in time for visiting-hours at Whitehead, she would have pursued the argument with the travel agent. As it was, she'd promised Dung she would see him before she left, and she did not want to let him down.

Thanh lay stretched out on his bunk with his torch suspended over his book. He was reading Henri Charriere's *Papillon*. The light was imperfect, so he shuffled himself and the book around to get a better cast of light. The problem was that the batteries in the torch were weak and since he was now confined to his section all the time, he had no immediate way of replacing them. He found the book both depressing and inspiring. Papillon's escapes were as ingenious as they were harrowing.

'Thanh.'

Thanh pulled himself up and leaned over the edge of his bunk to see Dung standing on the ground looking up at him. 'Dung, what are you doing here? Come on up.'

Dung scrambled up to Thanh's bunk. 'I waited till dark before climbing the fence. I wanted to speak to you.' Thanh pulled out a flask from his box of possessions and set about making some tea. 'Today was visiting time for our section and I saw Niki.' At the mention of Niki's name, Thanh put the flask down and gave his full attention to Dung. Although Niki had faithfully visited him since the magazine office had been closed and they had shared what news they had on the progress of the government's inquiry into the film, he still felt unable to get close to her. If he'd thought her reckless before, he felt she was now even more determined to push the system to dangerous levels.

'She wanted me to tell you that everything would be all right. None of the returnees will be involved in their scheme. There is enough support within the overseas community to make everything work.'

Thanh took out two plastic containers he'd cut from the end of lemonade bottles and poured the tea into them. 'It's not enough for them to have challenged the government here. Now they think they can change things for us in Vietnam.'

'Well, I'm really not sure what their plans are with this monitoring programme. She seemed reluctant to talk about it. Maybe because she thinks you're critical of her.'

'I'm not critical of Niki. It's her hare-brained ideas I'm critical of.'

'Maybe it's hard for her to make that distinction. She told me she'd seen Cuong, Minh and the kids last week. She said they seem really happy together. Cuong must have said something to Minh about there being odd girlfriends over the years, but since that's over, Minh told Niki she understood and had forgiven him. Cuong also said there have even been some signals that maybe UNHCR will review their case for refugee status. It seems the film raised a lot of emotions and has caused criticism of the whole screening process. Hien's case is also up for a special review.'

Thanh looked earnestly at Dung. 'That's good news, Dung. It's bound to have repercussions on the status of your own case.'

Dung lowered his eyes. 'I know. That's what everyone here wants — to be recognised as a refugee, but for me it's different. I don't think I could face going off into the free world any more; I've spent too long in prison. Without Ha. . . .' Dung couldn't say any more, but Thanh understood.

'It will be hard at first, but in time . . . and surely you could apply to go to the same resettlement country as Hien and Huong.'

Dung shook his head. 'I know what I want to do. It's why I went back to Vietnam from China all those years ago. Burying the bones of my wife and son wasn't enough. I wanted to stay there and be close to them.'

'Here drink some more tea.' Thanh filled Dung's cup. 'You came here because you had a dream. Try to find it again, Dung. Vietnam would just mean prison for you.'

'When Niki and Chinh are in Vietnam, they're going to visit Tang. I think both Cuong and Minh feel responsible for his losing his bicycle shop. Cuong wants Niki to give Tang all the money he saved from his wages on the magazine. Of course its not a lot of money here and wouldn't be in the free world, but in Vietnam it would be enough to help Tang get started in something else.'

Hearing of Tang reminded Thanh of what his own life had been in Vietnam all those years ago. He knew that Nam and Lan were living in Hanoi with their young son. It all now seemed so far away, yet if he were forced back, it would all begin again. It was like a book he'd read, the *Myth of Sisyphus;* he was doomed to push a boulder up a hill only to see it roll down again, over and over. 'Would you really want to go back again to Vietnam, go back to prison?'

'I've thought about it a lot. You know when Binh was forced back, I really envied him.'

Thanh shook his head. 'Maybe in some twisted way, it's what Binh wanted, too. He certainly didn't do himself any favours by the things he did. Unless he really was naïve enough to think his overseas friends could get him out. I can't fathom what his thinking was.'

'Niki said she was going to try to find him and see that he's okay.'

'How can she find him? She doesn't know where he lives.'

'She told me he lives in Hoanh Ma. She has his parents' address.'

'Hoanh Ma! That's almost on the Chinese border. They can't go there and they shouldn't be checking up on Binh anyway. It isn't as if the Vietnamese authorities won't know who Niki and Chinh are. They will have questioned returnees and will know they worked with us on the magazine. They'll already have been labelled as potential trouble-makers and the authorities will have read everything Niki has ever written for the magazine. If Binh's in trouble, it's his own fault. How did Niki get his address anyway?' Thanh breathed in heavily, and letting his head sink forward, he closed his eyes. It was a nightmare. Living in confinement year after year made him feel as though he was being drained of his masculinity. He'd lost Lan through his own neglect, but with Niki he'd really tried hard to be open. For a while it had been good and he felt there was an understanding between them. Working on the magazine and then filming in secret around the detention centre had given him a sense of purpose. But since the closure of the magazine, all that had gone.

He felt impotent. And then the change in Niki. She'd still been sensitive to his situation, but the trust had gone. Thanh wiped his hand across his brow. This crazy recklessness and her trip to Vietnam were risks she didn't need to be taking. He'd obviously hurt her. They had never spoken of their relationship, but she must have known how he felt about her, and surely she'd understood that he couldn't speak of it because he wasn't a free man.

'I don't know. Maybe an agency worker from UNHCR passed it on to them. Through their group they have lots of contacts.'

'What? Yes, the address.' Thanh put his cup down. His mind was racing. 'We need to break into one of the agency offices and use their phone.'

Dung laughed. 'Thanh you're talking like a criminal.'

Thanh wasn't amused. Frustrated and angry, because it was Niki taking the risks to help his compatriots while he sat helpless, his normal good humour deserted him. 'When those who dictate the law lose their humanity and integrity what choices are left to us? If there were public telephone booths in the detention centre I would use them.'

Thanh clambered down from the bunk ahead of Dung. Even though the fence lights were still blazing, there was enough darkness between the rows of Nissen huts to allow them to make their way over to the UNHCR field officer's hut without anyone noticing them. Taking out a piece of wire, Thanh twisted it into several folds before sliding it into the padlock key hole. After a few jolts, the padlock snapped open. Glancing round to make sure there was no one in sight, Thanh opened the door and slipped through, leaving Dung as sentry.

Inside the room Thanh quickly determined that the field officer's desk was empty, and that the telephone had been disconnected. He cursed under his breath. 'Damn, if he's taken it with him I'm wasting my time here.' With his wire key Thanh clicked open a couple of file draws before locating the hidden telephone. He plugged the phone in and dialled. After three rings an unfamiliar female's voice answered.

'Can I speak to Niki, please?'

'I'm sorry she's not here.'

'I need to speak to her before she leaves for Vietnam. When will she be home?'

'Niki has already left for Vietnam.'

'What! She said she wasn't going to Hanoi until early next week.'

'Yes, that's right. But there are no direct flights to Vietnam from Hong Kong. She and Chinh left this evening on a flight to Bangkok. Niki said she was going to visit an old school friend in Bangkok while Chinh was going to take a train to Chiang Mai, for a few days hiking in the mountains. I don't know how to contact either of them. Do you want to leave your name and number? I'll have her. . . .' Thanh slammed down the phone. His brow was sweating. He knew the next few weeks of just hanging round with nothing to do were going to drive him crazy.

As the plane swooped down into Noi Bai, Niki marvelled at the blanket of darkness surrounding the airport. Isolated lights shone from villages and the motorised traffic, but for the airport of a major city the area seemed magically unspoiled. It was the first time Niki had returned to Vietnam since leaving Saigon in 1978 with the adoption agency social worker. The excitement of coming back tingled in every part of her body and she couldn't wait to explore Hanoi. She'd read so much about it and she knew that besides Hue, it was one of Thanh's favourite places.

The plane touched down just a short distance from the airport buildings and as the passengers walked across the tarmac, Niki breathed in the moist early evening air. Odours of scalded tarmac, river bed spinach, soil, baggage, and smells Niki couldn't identify, filled her nostrils. Then there were the screechy, hollow sounds of motorbike horns honking in the distance. Old memories stirred as Niki absorbed the sights and sounds. Her senses of how to survive on the streets engaged into full gear — the country, both strange and familiar at the same time, was home.

Inside the congested customs hall and passport area, passengers milled around in anticipation of finding a short cut through the crowd. The majority of people from the plane were Vietnamese although Niki recognised a few nervous looking white-faced foreigners amongst the crowd. Most of the foreigners looked like government officials or tired, overworked businessmen with open necked white shirts and crumpled trousers and it was only when she heard them speaking that she realised they were Russian expatriate workers.

After waiting her turn in the line for passport control, Niki stepped in front of the cubicle and handed over her passport and papers. The customs official stared at the photograph in the passport and then scrutinised Niki's face before tapping some information into a machine. 'Where are you staying in Vietnam?'

'Hanoi.'

'Where in Hanoi?'

'We've yet to arrange a hotel.'

The official sorted through some papers then stood up. 'Wait here a minute.' He left his cubicle and disappeared for a few minutes. When he returned he handed Niki her papers and waved her through without another word.

Soon after clearing passport control and customs, Niki was approached by a young man. 'I can give you a ride into Hanoi. Ten US dollars. That's the best deal you will get here.' Niki had heard the fare could be anywhere upward of fifteen.

'Yes, okay.' When Chinh joined her they checked their backpacks through customs, then trailed after the man as he led them to his car.

Outside the crowd of bystanders converged on them. 'You want a ride to Hanoi, twenty dollar.' Niki raised her eyebrows and grinned at Chinh. 'Fifteen dollar.' As the drivers persisted, the young man, who was escorting them to his car, turned round and shouted something at the group. Hearing his words they backed away and quickly dispersed among the crowds.

'What did he say to them?' whispered Niki.

'I'm not sure. I'm not so familiar with the Northern accent and he spoke rapidly. Whatever it was, they didn't like it.'

The ride into Hanoi took close to an hour. There were no street lamps so the only lighting came from the vehicles, which for some reason Niki couldn't fathom, used the main beam only when another vehicle was approaching. Cars favoured side lights while motorbikes seemed to just keep the lights dimmed. Although the distance wasn't far, the road into the city was full of potholes and the oxcarts, bicycles and Honda bikes competed for the best bits of road. The favoured place for traffic from both directions seemed to be the middle where the potholes weren't so deep. While Niki and Chinh sat rigid on the back seat their driver seemed unperturbed, and maintaining his fairly rapid speed, honked his horn vigorously while forcing his way through the mass of slow-moving vehicles. The oxen were the slowest and several times Niki closed her eyes when it seemed as though they were about to hit one of them head on, but miraculously the animals always moved out of the way, and they reached the city without any incident.

'What hotel are you staying at? I take you there.'

'We are looking to find somewhere cheap and clean. A small guest house,' said Chinh. 'Do you know of somewhere?'

'I can take you to a good, cheap, clean place. No problem.' The driver swung the car away from the tree-lined streets, which accommodated the embassy buildings, and turned down several busy side streets before pulling up outside a narrow-fronted building with a wire grating pulled three quarters of the way across its front. 'Stay in the car while I talk to them and see if they have vacancies.' Jumping out of the car, the driver squeezed round the metal grating and entered the guest house. Niki would like to have followed, but since the driver asked them to wait and it seemed as though he was trying very hard to be helpful, she decided not to challenge him. He came out ten minutes later with a man and a woman. 'It's okay. You can stay here. This is a nice place and they give you a good rate.' The woman, in her early fifties, showed them into the guest house. The beds looked pleasant and since the couple were only asking ten dollars a room, Niki and Chinh agreed to stay. After thanking the driver, Chinh offered him some extra money for his help, but with his hands up in front of him as though Chinh were offering him a bribe, he retreated backward toward the door. 'No, I don't take, thank you.'

Chinh looked after him. 'Do you think he was for real?'

'I suppose. This is Hanoi, not Saigon.'

While Niki spent two days taking in the tourist spots of Hanoi, the parks and pagodas, the puppet theatre and the Ho Chi Minh mausoleum, Chinh made inquiries as to how to get to Cam Pha. On the evening of their third night in Hanoi, they sat in a restaurant looking over the maps Chinh had purchased from the street children. 'Without a car, there's no easy way to get there. The cheapest way that I can see is to take a bus to Haiphong, the ferry to Hong Gai and then a bus to Cam Pha. There's a train, but I found out that if we wander over to the far corner of the lake we can wave down a mini bus. The buses are semi-illegal and they pack them full like sardine cans, but it's the way most locals get from here to Haiphong. If you're game I think we should go for it.'

Niki nodded. 'Sounds okay to me.' She looked over the map again. 'We need to inform the people at the guest house we'll be leaving.'

After finishing their meal they wandered back to the hotel. The woman of the house, whom Niki had come to know as Mrs Dieu, was watching television in the front reception and since Niki had already established a friendly relationship with her it was agreed that she should be the one to inform her of their departure the next morning. Chinh wanted to rinse out some of his clothes, so he carried on up the stairs while Niki sat down beside Mrs Dieu.

'We have enjoyed staying here, Mrs Dieu. Your guest house is very comfortable and lovely.' Mrs Dieu turned away from the television set and with her brows knitted together looked toward Niki. 'I want to inform you that tomorrow morning we will be leaving.'

'Leaving!' Mrs Dieu looked alarmed. 'Where are you going?'

Niki was taken aback by her manner. 'Oh, we wanted to see Halong Bay. I've heard it's very beautiful.'

'I'll speak to my brother and we'll make the arrangements for you to go there. You spend two, three days, looking round then we arrange for you to come back. Maybe you don't leave tomorrow, but the next day.'

Niki shook her head. 'It's not necessary for you to make any arrangements. We have our own plan on how to get there.'

'What plan? How do you think you're getting there? It may not be safe.' Mrs Dieu paused in her speech. 'Besides it's not allowed for you to go just like that.'

Niki wasn't sure what to say. She could hardly mention to Mrs Dieu about the illegal bus. 'Some friends made arrangements for us through a travel agency. I think it's the government travel agency.'

'I've not been informed of this.'

'I'm informing you. Please, Madame Dieu, we think your guest house is excellent. We would like to come back here before we leave Vietnam. In fact I would recommend your place to all of my friends.'

'That's not the point. You're a foreigner, and I am responsible for you.'

'What!' Niki was regretting she was alone in dealing with Mrs Dieu while Chinh was probably whistling to himself upstairs as he happily rinsed out his underwear.

Mrs Dieu reached toward Niki and lifted her hands. 'Your body, your face, your hands are all so youthful. The young men must admire you. You have a special young man?' Mrs Dieu was smiling, but slowly her expression changed. She became distant and her eyes misted over. 'Look at me. See how ugly I have become.' Niki cringed as she saw the gnarled, twisted fingers with the dead, broken nails embedded in the stubs. 'They did this to me. They stole my husband and my womanhood.'

'The communists?'

Mrs Dieu's eyes flashed. 'No. I was a communist cadre.' She held her head up. 'I was leader of the women's brigade. It was the Americans did this to me. They did this and many other things I shall never ever talk about.'

Niki felt her heart racing. It wasn't that Mrs Dieu were accusing her of having harmed her, but she felt responsible anyway. 'My father was a journalist.' Niki caught herself in the lie. 'I'm sorry Mrs Dieu, I shouldn't have said that. The truth is I don't know who my father was. I don't even know who my mother is.'

Mrs Dieu looked steadily at Niki. 'The war's over child and what has happened is behind us. I didn't mean to judge you. You and I we have both suffered in our different ways, but you must understand it takes time for a country to recover. I'm trusted here and we want you to have a good stay in Vietnam.' Mrs Dieu wrapped her hands under her black *ao ba ba* blouse and looked back toward the television screen. 'We will discuss the matter of your leaving in the morning.' Niki sat stunned for a moment, then excused herself and fled upstairs.

In the morning nothing was said about their leaving. They settled up their account and after thanking Mrs Dieu and her husband for their excellent hospitality, they prepared to leave. It was only as they were walking through the reception lounge that Mrs Dieu hurried over to Niki and thrust a bulky cloth into her hands. 'Daughter, I purchased these sticky rice cakes for you from the early morning vendor. You and your young man might get hungry on your travels.'

Niki smiled. 'He's not my young man, he's my friend. But, thank you anyway Madame Dieu. Your kindness to me has been gracious and. . . .' Niki hesitated. 'I feel humbled by your experience of life. Thank you for our talks.'

The news of Hien's and Huong's new status as refugees spread through the wire fences from section to section at an incredible speed. Dung was one of the first to send his message of congratulations back through the sections. He knew it was just the beginning. The families of Dong Hung and Fang Cheng Camps were being looked at first, but later it would be the single men. From gossip picked up from the more open UNHCR agency workers, there was a hint that Cuong and his family might be recognised next. Dung felt sick inside. If he were to volunteer to go back to Vietnam, it could jeopardise the other Fang Cheng cases. The authorities would hold him up as an example that since he'd obviously felt safe enough to return to Vietnam, the others need not fear returning, yet if he waited too long and was recognised as a refugee, he would be thrust out into the free world.

What had once been a dream was now a nightmare. Maybe he should just stab a knife into his stomach — that way he would be with Ha and

Diep without bringing harm to anyone else. When life held some hope of happiness he'd feared death, yet now when the pain inside him was totally consuming and he could no longer visualise his future, death played on his thoughts as a welcoming liberator.

Dung dragged himself up from his bunk and wandered round the compound. Some small children were playing near an open drain and he watched as they dropped little sticks into it to see if they floated. Dung was horrified, however, when several of the children picked up the sticks from out of the sewer water and put them in their mouths. Jumping up he scolded them before shooing them away from the drain. It saddened him to think that the children's' mothers, who had once been attentive were now too institutionalised and depressed to notice what their children were up to.

As he walked away Dung contemplated his fears. He knew that his feelings of lethargy were due partly to the deprivation of his environment, but it didn't change matters. When he was working on the magazine, the camaraderie of his friends, and Niki and Chinh's visits from the outside, had given him a purpose. He'd learned to speak English, he'd written poems and found the energy to dream about the future, but now the thought of life terrified him. It was as though the madness he'd experienced in Dong Hung was creeping back into his brain.

If he were to stab himself it would end his torment, but it would cause pain to Hien. He needed a way to just disappear — to just stop existing without there being any consequences. Thanh was always plotting his escape. He didn't talk about it, but Dung knew. He was sure that one day they would look round and Thanh would have vanished. His friends would miss Thanh, but secretly they would envy his escape and his going might even bolster their own courage in taking charge of life. But freedom had come to Dung too late.

Halong Bay, with its limestone crags rising almost vertically from the sea, was as dramatic as it was beautiful. Niki breathed its beauty into her soul. She could feel herself beginning to relax and fall under the spell of her ancestral home. The way of life in the countryside of Vietnam was still both familiar and strange. Taking the hollowed-out metal ferry boat to Cat Ba Island then the burned umber sailing junk to Bai Chay, was like sailing through a Chinese silk painting. The monkeys screeching and swinging from the trees of a nearby island added merriment to the journey. One day she would join her 'father' in his import-export business and later, when she was successful she would extend the business to Vietnam. It had always been her dream to return to her childhood home and bring wealth back to her motherland. Chinh was all for finding ways to make his country prosperous too, so perhaps between the two of them they could come up with a plan where they could work together. If she was able to bring wealth and jobs into the country Thanh could hardly accuse her of being hare-brained. Niki lazed back in the boat and cracking the shell of a second freshly cooked crab, she decided that life at that moment was perfect. She'd slipped into the role of tourist as easily as if that had been her only purpose in coming to Vietnam, and Chinh with his uncomplicated, easy-going ways was as pleasant a travelling companion as she could wish for.

As the kilometres increased, Niki was able to distance herself from the episode with Mrs Dieu. It wasn't that Mrs Dieu had threatened her. She admired Mrs Dieu and aside from the bitterness toward her past, she saw in her a strength and protectiveness which reminded her of how she'd imagined her own mother to be. What Mrs Dieu challenged was Niki's naïve view of herself, her view of the world. Thanh did the same thing. It was as though between them they had forced her to glimpse into a deep pool where truth turned itself upside down.

It was only after they reached Cam Pha and began the search for Tang's house that Niki resurfaced from her holiday mentality and took on a more guarded role. From the beginning Cam Pha struck her as a hostile place. It was dirty. The pollution was suffocating and there was coal dust over everything which stifled out the life of the trees and covered the houses and roads in a layer of black dirt. There was a small park, but with a few scrawny plants even that seemed sadly neglected. The old cinema sat in the centre of the town like a huge empty tomb, the life having fled from it years ago. With rats running unconcerned through the main street, the evidence of poverty was everywhere and she wondered what it would take to bring the town back to how it might once have been.

While Chinh made inquiries of the local people, Niki sat silently behind her dark sunglasses. She soon realised, however, that it wasn't her mixed blood which gave them away — it was everything about both of them. Their smell was cosmetic, their teeth and fleshed out bones exposed their nourished upbringing. Their hands looked smooth and pampered. Besides their accent, their clothes and manner exuded a wealth and confidence alien to the people they met. Yet, despite these differences and the furtive glances as the villagers looked them over, the people welcomed them with a curiosity and hospitality which rapidly overshadowed every other impression. Niki gazed at the smiling faces crowded round them in the street café as a man sitting perched on the stool opposite leaned forward. 'I can show you Mr Tang's house if you want to follow me.'

Tang was out when they arrived at the house, so Tang's wife invited them to drink tea while one of the children went to fetch him. Several neighbours crowded into the small living room to get a look at them and since Tang's wife didn't ask the neighbours to leave, Niki carried on a conversation of small talk with them. However, when Tang arrived at the house half an hour later, he seemed nervous. His eyes scanned the room furtively. 'Why are you looking for me?'

Niki stood up from the table and walked over to him. 'I wonder if we could talk privately.' Tang looked Niki over, then caught her hand and walked to the kitchen.

'You're not from Vietnam?'

'We're from Hong Kong.' Out of sight of the neighbours, Niki pulled out the letter from her cloth moneybelt. 'I have a letter from your sister, Minh.'

Tang's eyes lit up. 'You know Minh, and she's safe?'

'Yes.'

Tang hurriedly opened the letter and thrust the crisp hundred-us-dollar notes into his pocket before reading it. 'Minh says you are friends, that you helped her find Cuong.' Niki nodded. 'Where are you staying?'

'Nowhere yet. We were talking earlier to someone who suggested we find accommodation at the Russian expatriate Coal Mining Centre.'

'Yes, maybe you could stay there. We have no hotel in Cam Pha. I'm sorry, I would like to invite you to stay at my home, but I can't. However, if you would stay and eat with my family, we would consider it a great honour.'

Niki wasn't sure about accepting the invitation. The family were obviously poor and their visit could cause trouble with the authorities. 'I think really it would be better if we ate at the centre.'

Tang looked hurt. 'No. Please you must eat with us. We have so many questions to ask you about my sister and brother-in-law. It would bring us so much pleasure if you would stay. Our food is simple but we give it with all our hearts.'

Niki didn't see how they could refuse. 'Of course we'll stay. Thank you.'

When the meal was finally spread out on the table, the quality and variety of dishes were excellent. There were shrimp cakes, pieces of chicken still on the bone, pork spring rolls, tiny shellfish mixed into a salad dish, sticks of lemon grass and a huge assortment of herbs and salad vegetables as well as rice and fish soup. Niki felt embarrassed as she realised that they must have sent the children out to make special purchases on their behalf. If Tang had really wanted to ask them questions, he suddenly seemed shy. A couple of the neighbours had stayed and after everyone talked casually for about an hour-and-a-half, Chinh suggested that since it was getting dark they should leave to sort out their accommodation for the night.

The guest house wasn't far and after checking in, Tang came upstairs with them to drink some tea. While Chinh sat on one of the beds and offered Tang the only chair available in the room, Niki used the hot water in the flask to make some tea.

'Is Cuong in some trouble in Hong Kong?'

'No. Why do you say that?' asked Chinh.

'I've been visited several times by Public Security recently. That's who I thought you were when you called for me. When I saw you I was confused. They know Cuong is alive and that Minh went looking for him. They told me Cuong was part of an anti-communist group in Hong Kong.'

'No. He isn't,' said Niki handing him his tea. 'I work with Cuong. Or at least I did.'

'Then what's he been doing, or saying, for them to come and visit me? You must tell him he can never come back here. Besides what he did in the past, some of the returnees have said other things which make his situation even worse.' Niki noticed Tang's hand was shaking as he took his tea cup and gulped the hot liquid down. 'Hien is my friend too. I've heard he's also done some bad things. What's going on over there? Are they together?'

'They're not in the same section,' said Niki, 'but both are at the Whitehead Detention Centre.'

'I heard that Thanh is the leader of their anti-communist group.'

Niki caught her breath. She could feel the anger rising inside her. Unable to stay seated, she strode over to the window before turning to face Tang. 'We had a camp magazine at Whitehead. Thanh was chief editor. There was nothing anti-communist about it; in fact Thanh took risks to defend Ho Chi Minh — so if they're trying to create trouble for him, go and tell that to your Public Security Bureau friends.'

Tang went white. He was trembling quite visibly. 'They are not my friends.'

'Niki.' Chinh bounded over to Niki and caught her by her arms. 'This isn't Tang's fault. You need to apologise to him, now.'

The anger in Niki drained from her. She realised she'd behaved horribly toward Tang and felt ashamed. As Chinh released her arms, she walked back over to Tang. 'Tang, I'm sorry. I should understand how it is here and I know they're not your friends. What I said was stupid, unforgivable. I don't know why I reacted so badly. I promise you, we came to you in friendship.' She hesitated and looked earnestly into his face. 'Can you believe that?'

The muscles in Tang's face relaxed. He nodded and blinked his eyes. 'I know. We all do and say things we're ashamed of here. The fear creeps up from behind and takes you by surprise. You have to be very strong not to get caught up.' They sat silent for a moment taking in the full weight of Tang's words.

Tang finished his tea. 'I should leave soon or they might ask questions. How long are you staying in Cam Pha?'

'We really only stopped here to meet you and give you the letter from Minh. Tomorrow we will try to take a bus to Hoanh Ma,' said Chinh.

'Hoanh Ma is close to the Chinese border. It's a dangerous place. There are bandits up there. Besides that, are you even allowed to go there?'

Chinh shrugged. 'I'm not actually sure if we are allowed to go anywhere. It's hard to get a grip on what we can and can't do, but since we are already this far north, we should try to go.'

'Hoanh Ma is remote. It will be difficult for you to take buses. If you like, I can probably help you rent a jeep to get you there and back.'

'Tang, that's risky. We can't involve you,' said Niki.

'I have contacts. I can rent a jeep for you at a good price.' He paused and picking up the photographs Minh had enclosed in the letter, he ran his finger's slowly across the faces. 'These people in the photographs, they're my relatives and friends. Please allow me to do this for you. It would be an honour.'

Niki finished packing away her few possessions before wandering down to reception to meet Chinh and Tang. Tang had telephoned and they had arranged to meet Tang with the driver and have breakfast together before setting off on their journey. Chinh walked over to her. 'I thought I'd go ahead and settle our bill here. There's no sign of Tang or the driver and the receptionist says our visas are being held by Public Security.'

'Public Security!'

'She says it's routine for them to be sent there, but I can't see that it would be routine not to return them. I don't know what's going on.' Niki glanced over toward the receptionist. She was a young girl, and seeing Niki staring at her, she quickly looked down at some paper-work on her desk. 'Tang's already almost half an hour late. I think we might as well go ahead and start breakfast. We can eat slowly and have the receptionist ask Tang and the driver to join us when they arrive.' Chinh shrugged. 'There's nothing we can do about our papers, but I asked the girl to hurry up and get them back because we intend to leave.'

Niki followed Chinh into the dining room. With its rows of tables covered with stained white tablecloths, it reminded Niki of a school dining hall. A group of Russian Expatriate workers were talking together in one corner and although they glanced up as Niki and Chinh entered the room, they quickly lost interest in them and turned their attention back to one another. There was no menu since breakfast at the centre always consisted of two fried eggs, French bread and coffee. The coffee was already sweetened with sugar as well as condensed milk. Niki would normally have preferred to drink coffee without sugar, but after drinking it this way for several days she was beginning to enjoy it.

They ate slowly, hoping that Tang and the driver would join them before they finished eating. After more than an hour of nibbling away at their food, they were getting impatient. Chinh looked at his watch. 'It's gone nine-thirty. This is ridiculous.' The Russians had all finished eating breakfast long ago and left the dining hall. 'Our plans for an early start were a waste of time.'

It seemed pointless to drag breakfast out any further and the cleaners were hovering around them waiting to strip their table of its cloth and empty the hall. Niki suspected that the dining hall might double as a meeting room, so they left and made their way back to the receptionist. A nervous expression spread across her face as she saw them approaching. 'Your friend called. He says the driver has to stop and get some petrol. They will be here soon so will you wait back upstairs.'

'What about our visas?' The girl avoided looking at him and mumbled something they couldn't comprehend. 'I'm sorry. What did you say?' said Chinh more irritably this time.

'Your papers will be here soon. Please wait in your room and I will bring them up.'

'We've already checked out. We're not going back up there so you can charge us another day's stay.'

The receptionist looked scared. 'I wasn't going to do that. Please go back up. I'll bring up a flask of hot water. The room's not locked and there will be no charge.'

'What if we go for a walk round the flower garden?' said Niki grabbing at Chinh's arm. 'I feel like I need some fresh air.'

They had barely wandered round the garden when Niki spotted the receptionist approaching them. Niki had been examining a flower bed with an arrangement of small plants patterned to form HO CHI MINH VA LENIN, but as the girl approached she drew her attention away from the flowers. As she stood waiting to hear what the receptionist had to say, an uneasy feeling crept over her. Chinh left the tamarind tree he'd been inspecting and wandered over beside Niki.

'Maybe Tang and the driver have come,' said Chinh. Niki suspected he was wrong, but since the receptionist was already in listening distance she thought it better not to voice her concerns.

The girl came level with them before speaking. 'The Public Security officers invite you to work with them. Please come back this way.'

Niki felt the blood drain from her face. Glancing across at Chinh she saw that he was as pale as she must have been. Seeing her look of alarm he shrugged. 'We'd better follow her. It'll be all right.'

When they entered the room and saw Tang sitting between two men, Niki wanted to go over to him and apologise. He was clearly aware of their presence but didn't dare look and kept his head drooped forward. Niki also noted with dismay that he was wearing the same clothes she had seen him in last night and it looked as though he hadn't slept at all. Besides Tang and the receptionist, there were three uniformed men. The two men sitting either side of Tang were in street clothes, but she did not get the impression they were his friends.

'Please, sit down. My name is Captain Bui. There are some formalities we need to discuss with you.' The words were spoken by a large man in uniform with several red stripes and stars on his jacket. In a glance Niki was able to take in the narrow room with its window set into the wall at the far end. A coffee table stood between two benches so Niki edged her way between the table and the bench, making sure there was enough space for Chinh to sit next to her. With Chinh in place to her left, one of the younger officers manoeuvred so that he was sitting to her right.

Niki glanced over toward Tang. His eyes were red and swollen and he looked sick. She wanted to reach out to him, protect him from whatever threat it was they were facing, but there was nothing she could say without making it worse. She wondered if one of the men in civilian clothes sitting next to him was the driver, but then as she tilted her head forward and peered at them through her hair, she decided they were both too confident to be other than officials. One of them was sitting leisurely in his chair dragging on a cigarette while the other man was pouring himself some tea.

The man who called himself Captain Bui leaned toward them. 'May I see your passports, please?'

Captain Bui examined the documents, scrutinising their faces to compare them with the photographs before handing the passports across the table to the officer sitting next to Niki. The younger officer then examined the passports before laying them on the table in front of him. They were just within reach of Niki so she stretched over and prepared to retrieve them. She was just about to pick them up when the officer sitting next to her promptly placed his hand on top of hers and with his other hand slipped the documents out from underneath. Without saying a word he let go of her hand and passed the documents back to the senior officer. Niki stared at him in disbelief.

'You need special permission to travel to the border area. You also need permission to be in Cam Pha,' said Captain Bui. 'Your visas are not in order. This visa, belonging to Clemenceau, Niki Trinh, has been altered. Explain to me.'

'I don't know,' said Niki. 'I'm not sure what you mean.'

'The dates are not correct. There are alterations here. And this other visa, look, there's no official number on it.'

Chinh glanced at the visa and laughed. 'That's nothing to do with me. If the number's missing it has to do with your people. It was your people who issued my visa, just the same as they issued Niki's. What game are we playing?'

Captain Bui glared at him, then handed him a document. 'I need you both to read this and sign it.'

Niki and Chinh leaned over the paper and started to read it. The document was a detaining order and charge sheet. Besides the charges regarding having faulty visas, they were also charged with travelling to Cam Pha and to Mong Cai. 'We haven't travelled to Mong Cai, and Halong Bay is a tourist area,' protested Niki.

'Sign the paper,' said Captain Bui.

'No,' said Chinh. 'If you're going to detain us, then you have to be the one to sign it and give us a copy to keep. We don't agree to being detained.'

Captain Bui looked irritated. 'We will arrange for you to hire a car and accompany us to the Public Security Building in Hong Gai.'

'What!' said Chinh. 'If you want us to go with you, then you have to pay for the transport. Besides, if you detain us then other tourists won't want to come to Vietnam. I thought Vietnam wanted tourism. There's an openness in Saigon and Hanoi that maybe you don't know about yet.'

Captain Bui's face reddened. He stood up from his seat and stepped over to the window. Silhouetted against the window, his frame appeared to be larger than it actually was. When he spoke, his voice was low. 'We don't have transport suitable for you. We have Honda bikes. It will be much better if you co-operate with us.' Neither Niki nor Chinh made any response and as the time dragged on a morbid silence descended over the room. Niki was desperate to go to the toilet but didn't dare ask to be excused. She just crossed her legs and hoped the stalemate would end.

Half an hour passed before Captain Bui drew himself away from the window and came back to the table. When he spoke his face was full of disdain and Niki held her breath as she prepared herself for what he had to say. 'Very well, you can make your own way over to the Public Security Building in Hong Gai. There is a bus and my assistant will write you out instructions on how to get there. You have an appointment for 2:30 PM. The guest house receptionist will keep your room open so you have somewhere to stay until your appointment.'

Niki watched dismayed as Captain Bui strode over to the table and placed their visas and passports back into his brief-case before officially dismissing them.

Chapter 20: To go forward is to go back

12th to 29th April 1993

The first watch . . . the second . . . the third watch fades.
I toss about, restless: sleep will not come, it seems.
The fourth watch . . . the fifth. . . . No sooner have I closed my eyes
The five-pointed star is there to haunt my dreams.
PRISON DIARY, HO CHI MINH

T HANH PACED THE PERIMETER of the compound several times before he felt capable of sitting down and reading through the letter from Nam again. He wanted to absorb every detail so taking the letter from his pocket, he leaned his back against the wire fencing and let his body slip down until he was in a squatting position. Folding out the sheets of beautifully hand-written script he carefully began to read:

Dear Thanh,
  My best wishes to you. I am sending this letter to you via my acquaintances in the Vietnamese Shipping Company in Hong Kong. I hesitated to involve you, but after long deliberation, I decided I had no choice. Our friendship has spanned many decades and you know you are as dear to me as though you were my brother. I trust your judgment as well as I trust my own. After reading the letter you may have some idea how you wish me to proceed. You may say the matter is unimportant to you, in which case I regret having disturbed you, but on the other hand there may be something we can do for one another.
  Thanh, the purpose of this letter is to inform you that something happened here regarding several of your friends/acquaintances — I don't know which. Not knowing these people, it is hard for me to see where guilt and innocence lie. The first incident involves a young man, Vo Van Binh. As you have probably already surmised the government here knows about your work on the camp magazine, Doc Lap Tu Do. *They also know that Vo Van Binh was one of your colleagues on the magazine. This man is not a good man and I wonder about your association with him. When he first returned to Vietnam, we questioned him fairly minimally, but we did not trust him so we kept a*

close watch on him. When he crossed the border into Laos we were curious about his intentions. We held back from taking any direct action and with the co-operation of our Laotian compatriots we extended our watch. In Laos he met with some former soldiers of the old South puppet government. We did not arrest them until they re-entered Vietnam with a substantial cache of weaponry. As you know this is a politically sensitive time for us. After intensive questioning, Mr Binh and the others admitted that the money for their project 'Black Fairy' had been raised in the United States from political groups who oppose our sovereignty. Their plan was to target foreign businesses with their explosive devices to make it appear to the international business community that our country is unstable. This, as you can imagine would have the effect of persuading foreigners not to invest here. It would also put in jeopardy the three-stage road map toward the lifting of the US trade embargo.

The case of Mr Binh is clear. However the second matter is in many ways more complicated. It involves two Vietnamese nationals with foreign passports. When Clemenceau Trinh Niki and Phan Boi Chinh entered Vietnam, we knew about their work with the asylum-seekers in Hong Kong. We also knew of their intentions to try to set up an unofficial monitoring system for returnees. They were of some interest to us, but basically we regarded them as manageable. Unfortunately one of our senior officers in the provinces took it upon himself to arrest them over some minor visa matter. Had the matter ended there, there would not have been a serious problem, but your two friends/acquaintances decided to ignore the instructions of Captain Bui to report to the Public Security Building in Hong Gai, and left the guest house in Cam Pha by way of a balcony window. Although Captain Bui held their passports and had arranged for them to be watched, they were not apprehended again for two days. This is where the matter becomes serious. They were arrested in Hoanh Ma. Not only is this a restricted area, but they were arrested inside the home of Vo Van Binh.

Thanh, bringing Vietnamese nationals with American passports to trial is not an easy matter for us, especially since the girl is not fully Vietnamese. The Western world is ready to criticise us at every turn, but if these two are involved in this conspiracy against our sovereignty, then we have no choice but to see they are punished. I should add that while my father and I are still speculating on the subject of their guilt, many of our colleagues are of the firm opinion that, just like Mr Binh, they are a serious threat to us.

I am sad that at this time of sensitivity when we are anticipating the lifting of the trade embargo by the US government, we should be forced to confront this dilemma. There are people in the government who are trying hard to establish greater reforms and push Vietnam toward the kind of bright future Uncle Ho imagined. All I can say is if Ms Niki and Mr Chinh are not terrorists and are only guilty of monitoring the rehabilitation of their compatriots, then it would be better for them and for us if they were not in our country. You know them, Thanh. Advise me.

Take care, brother. I shall await your response through our contacts in the Vietnamese Shipping Company.

Nam
My father sends his warmest regards.

Thanh folded the letter up. Nam wasn't saying it directly, but Thanh sensed what he was asking him to do. He'd wait until darkness before climbing over the fence to talk to Dung. It was Dung's section's visiting time in two days so if Dung agreed to his plan, Thanh would then break into the UNHCR field officer's room and telephone Nam's friends in the shipping company to set things in motion.

As Dung climbed down from the police truck and was herded into the visitors' room, along with the other asylum-seekers whose camp numbers had been called out as having a visitor, he wondered what these two officials of the Vietnamese government would be like. Thanh obviously trusted them otherwise he wouldn't be involving them in his planned escape from Whitehead and his re-entry into Vietnam. It struck him as a bizarre turn of events that an ex-general in the army and Party Central Committee member of the Socialist Republic of Vietnam should be the silent puppeteer behind Thanh's idea to rescue Niki and Chinh. Thanh hadn't said as much, but Hien had told Dung years ago who Thanh's uncle and benefactor was.

Dung also knew that it wasn't Thanh's intention to take him along. Thanh was quite convinced that it was now only a matter of time before Dung would be recognised as a refugee along with his brother and Cuong. He was equally convinced that Dung's idea to manoeuvre events so that he ended up back in a Vietnamese prison was due to the temporary insanity which gripped Dung's soul, and that given time and nurturing in an open society, Dung would one day be free of it and later wonder at the strangeness of it. But, that was where Thanh was wrong. Dung was quite determined to go back to Vietnam regardless of the consequence. His insanity wasn't temporary, it was the same madness which had shadowed him since Ha's death and the thought which plagued his mind, as he anticipated his meeting with the Vietnamese officials, was how could he convince Thanh to allow him to accompany him.

As the outsiders piled into the visitor's room and took their place at the benches along the trestle tables, Dung focused his attention on two fairly well-dressed men. Unlike the other visitors they were not smiling or laughing. After they seated themselves at the furthest point in the hut from the Correctional Services officers' desk and a little distance from the other visitors, Dung was convinced that these were the men he had come to meet. When the Correctional Services officer nodded to the asylum-seekers that it was their turn to enter the inner rectangle of the tables, Dung walked directly over to the two men and sat himself in front of them.

'My name is Tran Van Dung. I believe you are here to see me?'

'Good-day, Mr Dung. You will excuse me if I just introduce myself and my colleague here as Mr Hai and Mr Ba. When you leave here, you must collect the tray at the desk of food packages we have brought for your friend. These packages must all be given to him, you understand.'

Dung felt irritated at the suggestion that he might hold anything back from Thanh. 'Of course I understand. I am not a thief.'

'Not a thief of your friend's property,' laughed Mr Hai. 'We know that, Mr Dung. Otherwise you would not be entrusted with this task. When will you speak to your friend?'

'I can see him after dark this evening. I will give him all of the packages then.'

'That is very good. There is time for him to prepare.' Mr Hai cast a look around. Although two Correctional Services officers independently sauntered up and down the isle between the visitors and the caged windows, neither was in listening distance. The other visitors were totally engrossed in their own conversations with the friends and relatives they had come to see.

'A container ship will be leaving for Haiphong in five days. She is moored outside Victoria Harbour, but we can arrange for a motor launch to be cruising a little way off the shore of Whitehead early Thursday morning — between 4 AM and 5 AM. It will appear that the men on board are fishing. If the boat is intercepted by a police launch we may leave the

area, but will make three more passes until 6 AM. Your friend is to swim
out to the boat at the first opportunity. If no contact has been made on
Thursday morning, we shall repeat the same process on Friday. If again
nothing, then you can tell your friend we shall meet him in here on his
section's next visiting day. If, however, there is any sign of suspicion from
the authorities, we must withdraw our involvement. Our presence in
Hong Kong is, as you might say, tentative.'

'Or, not authorised,' suggested Mr Ba.

'How is he going to get out of here?'

Mr Hai laughed. 'He's capable of figuring that out, but basically he
must be prepared to leave Wednesday night, so that he is ready to make
the connection with us Thursday morning.'

As Dung sat watching him, Thanh cut open one of the packets of dried
noodles. Breaking the contents apart into an aluminum saucepan, he
pulled out a pair of wire cutters. 'Oh, that's why I wasn't to steal your
noodles. That's an excellent hiding place.'

Thanh looked across at Dung and smiled. 'Are you hungry?'

'You're going to eat the noodles?'

'Of course.'

'So they're real. What other surprises have you got hidden in there?'

Thanh sifted through the other packages. 'Well let's see, there's prawn,
chicken. . . . We have a packet of green bean. . . .'

'Okay.' Dung laughed and gave up his questioning. If Thanh wanted
to tell him what else was hidden, he would. While Thanh poured some
boiling water from his flask over the noodles and set a lid on the saucepan
for them to soak in the liquid, Dung examined the shape of each of the
packages and from its feel tried to imagine what might be inside. He still
hadn't thought of the way to convince Thanh that he could be of help
in his plan to rescue Niki and Chinh, but if he didn't broach the subject
soon the opportunity would be gone. 'Thanh, I was thinking. . . .'

Thanh looked up at him. 'Before you say anything, there is something
I want to ask you.'

'What is it?'

'With Cuong and Hien being recognised as refugees, it is likely that
your own case will be looked at in a favourable light. I think you are
foolish to dismiss this opportunity for freedom, but if you are still of a

mind to return to Vietnam, then I am willing to take you along as my assistant.'

Dung stared at him. He didn't know what to say and as his throat knotted up he could feel the tears gathering under his lashes. Afraid that Thanh might see his struggle to contain his feelings, he quickly glanced down at his hands. 'Vietnam is my home. It's where my wife and son are buried. If they hadn't died, there would have been my son's future to consider. Perhaps. . . .' Dung wiped his hand across his face before looking up. 'I want more than anything to put all this behind me and return home.'

'The past isn't going to disappear. There are consequences. . . .'

'I know that. I could hide myself among the mountain people. This obsession of going back, it's not something that I can explain to anyone. If I were to die away from Vietnam. . . . That was Ha's greatest fear and I understood her.' Dung laughed nervously. 'To come so far and be this close. . . . I know everyone here will say that it was the madness in my head drove me over the edge . . . and who's to say that isn't the truth?'

'Madness, I wonder. Maybe this madness is more. . . .' Thanh sighed. 'Well, why don't you tear open those other packages for me so that we can see what materials we are working with.'

Thanh grabbed a couple of hours sleep before rousing himself from his bunk. It was 3 AM and even the late evening poker players had settled down for the night. He slipped into a pair of dark shorts before rubbing the black mixture he'd found hidden in the prawn noodles over his body and face. He then strapped the plastic belt holding his carefully arranged possessions around his waist. Being careful not to disturb anyone, Thanh unscrewed the wire net caging from his window and slipped out of the Nissen hut. In normal circumstances he'd use the door and take the risk of being caught, but this time he was being more cautious.

Luckily, the moon was obscured by a heavy cloud cover. Conducting his movements as though he were on a Sapper operation, he moved silently between the Nissen huts before clambering over each of the section fences. When he saw Dung pressed into the shadows of Nissen Hut G, Thanh crept up to him and touched him lightly on the shoulder.

Dung looked startled. 'I was watching for you. How did you just appear like that?'

'Call it "training to run with the ghosts". It's something I thought you were already good at.' Thanh eyed Dung's appearance. 'You blend in with the background pretty well. Without a trained eye I might not have spotted you myself.'

Before climbing the fence into TCI, Thanh took a moment to watch the spotlights dancing from the look-out points on the outer perimeter to register their pattern. At the moment he determined to be the best, he signalled to Dung to go. They were up the fence and over the top in seconds. As they jumped down into TCI they grinned at one another before sprinting across the open compound to the shelter of the school buildings.

The outer fence was separated from TCI by an inner core fence and a five-foot-wide sewage drain. There were several watch towers along the perimeter of the camp, and Thanh knew that the night guards would be alert to any odd movement. The lights were also much brighter here and Thanh was grateful to have the wire cutters.

Thanh stretched himself out flat along the inner fence and began to cut a two foot curved tear into the wire, but with each cut he stopped short of totally cutting the wire through. By twisting the wire apart with his hands he was able to eliminate the risk of alerting the guards to their presence by the sudden noise of snapping wire. Since the wire was thick it took several minutes to break his way through, however, when he was satisfied that the cut was large enough, he signalled for Dung to prepare to squeeze through. As the brightness dimmed Dung sprang forward, dragged himself through the hole and dropped silently into the drain. Thanh waited a moment for the lights to dim again then scrambled after him. Before sliding down into the sewer he carefully pulled the wire back into shape so that at a glance it was not obvious it had ever been tampered with.

Lying on their stomachs, they dragged themselves through the slimy liquid. The stench was nauseating, and Thanh tensed his neck to keep his face as far away from it as possible, but as the bright light of a watch tower beam skimmed over them, there was nothing for it but to hold his nose and submerge his face into the slime. At the corner of the perimeter, Thanh waited for the search light to pass over before pulling himself up into a crouching position and hacking into the wire. The wire was double layered and Thanh cursed his compatriots at the Vietnamese Shipping Company for purchasing cheap Russian wire cutters. In a place like Hong Kong they could have gone for the latest in Japanese or American technology. It took him almost thirty minutes before the hole was large enough for them to squeeze through.

Dung went first. After pulling himself through, he ran across the camp road to the protection of the trees, and waited. Seconds after the lights skimmed over him, Thanh jumped up and pushed his way through the hole. He pulled the fence back into place and sprinted over toward Dung. As he reached the shelter of the trees seconds before the light flooded over the road, he felt a tingle of exhilaration run through his body. He was free. Free of the cramped spacing, free of having no privacy and eating the same bland food day after day, but most of all he was free of having nothing to do, of having no purpose to his life. He was back in control of his own destiny.

After creeping through dense undergrowth for several hundred yards, Thanh found his way toward the sheltered beach where the rendezvous was to take place. It was still early so Thanh stripped off his shorts and rinsed them in the sea before taking a swim. Dung scrubbed himself clean, dressed into his street clothes and stretched out on the sand for a sleep. It was too risky to light a fire so Thanh dried himself with leaves before dressing and settling down to wait for the motor launch. Four o'clock passed and then five with no sign of the boat. Thanh tried not to show his irritation but inside he worried that something might have gone wrong. 'Let's just go over the instructions they gave you.'

Dung pulled himself up. 'The boat was to meet us Thursday morning 4 AM till five, then keep passing by until six. If there was no contact they would repeat the process Friday. I don't know why they're not here.'

Thanh waited until six fifteen before deciding it was too dangerous to hang around any longer. 'We need to retreat into the mountains for the day then come back here tomorrow morning. The guards will soon be switching over and the agency workers will be coming in. This place will become as busy as Mong Cai market and if they discover the damage to the fence, the alarm will go off.'

By ten o'clock Thanh and Dung were several miles into the mountains. They had made a temporary camp by a stream and had already cooked and eaten a breakfast of roasted fish, before the screeching blare of a siren reached their ears. Thanh cursed as he realised the implications of it. 'We have to forget our rendezvous with the motor launch. They'll never get a boat within miles of this place now. Let's clean up camp and then head for the main road.' As Thanh kicked soil over the cinders to put out the fire and smother the thin trail of smoke which was drifting visibly upward with the current of wind, Dung cleared away the remains of their meal.

Besides a flashlight and various tools, Thanh had retrieved a fake Hong Kong identity card, some money, and a map from inside the food packages. It worried him that Dung didn't have an identity card, but as they made their way down the mountain and saw the police blockades being set up between Sha Tin and Sai Kung, Thanh resigned himself to the fact that his plan to catch a bus into Sha Tin would have to be ditched. The police were checking all traffic along the road and without a valid identity card Dung would be identified as an illegal immigrant and arrested immediately.

Thanh knew from his earlier intelligence training that it was foolish to introduce another element into a plan at the last minute, but he'd sensed Dung's desperation, so putting his good judgment aside he'd included him in the escape. Now there was nothing for it but to hike across country and avoid the roads. It would take them longer, and if the police widened their search to include the countryside, the risk of being caught would increase.

As they strode through small villages dogs ran out to bark at them, and several villagers gave them suspicious glances before retiring into their homes. Thanh could feel the tension rising. The siren, the massive accumulation of police in the area, all it would take was one phone call to have the police closing in on them in minutes. They had to find a way to move quicker. Once in Sha Tin, they could mingle with the crowds and Thanh could risk taking a taxi or bus, maybe even the underground railway, but this side of Sha Tin the area was too isolated. The Whitehead Detention Centre was situated on a strip of coastline between Sha Tin and Sai Kung with only one road linking the two places. It was an area of small villages and mountain scrubland where strangers could be identified easily.

When Thanh saw the bike lying against a brick wall, he decided Fate was watching over them. He sprang across the track toward it. Stripping the bike of its baskets, he took a wad of Hong Kong dollar notes from his pocket and wrapped them into one of the bundles in the baskets: within seconds he was pedalling full pelt along the rough dirt village pathways with Dung clinging on behind. The speed, the bumpy track as the bike hurtled forward, and the fresh breeze battering across his face, lifted Thanh's spirits. He felt like a teenager, and the urge to giggle was irrepressible. Dung must have sensed his mood because he too was laughing as he wrapped his arms desperately around Thanh's waist.

They reached Sha Tin within half an hour, and abandoning the bike, made their way over to the railway station. They were about to approach the turnstile when Thanh spotted a policeman checking the IDs of people entering. He instinctively caught hold of Dung's sleeve and pulled him over to a street vendor who was selling glasses of sugar-cane juice. After purchasing a couple of glasses Thanh sipped his drink slowly while thinking out what their next move should be. A policeman eyed them suspiciously, but since they appeared to be in no hurry and were simply two men enjoying a glass of sugar-cane juice he soon lost interest in them. When a taxi approached Thanh handed back his glass and ran to the curb with his arms in the air. As the taxi screeched to a halt a few yards in front of them Thanh leapt in and slid across the seat to make room for Dung.

Speaking in his good Hong Kong Cantonese accent, which he'd learned to mimic from the guards, Thanh instructed the driver to take them to Mong Kok. He then leaned back and relaxed. However, they had barely covered a few miles and were heading toward the Lion Rock tunnel when Dung pointed out the second road block. Thanh had already seen it and his mind was racing as he weighed up what action they should take. As the taxi joined the slow-moving traffic and edged its way toward the police blockade, he could see that the police were checking the cards of every person going through. Cursing under his breath Thanh tossed the driver more than ten times the fare on the meter and nudged Dung toward the curbside door. Dung understood and sprang out of the taxi with Thanh following close behind. As they headed toward the mountain undergrowth, Thanh half expected to hear a blast from the taxi driver's horn, but the driver cruised off as though nothing strange had happened.

Although the taxi driver had decided to keep his mouth shut, Thanh couldn't be certain that some law-abiding citizen, sitting in one of the other cars, hadn't seen them and would feel duty bound to tell the police. As they stopped for a minute to get their breath back, Dung grabbed hold of Thanh's arm. 'Look, if you split from me now you could make it on your own. You have an ID card. It's my fault you're in this trouble.'

Thanh laughed. He could feel the adrenalin running through his veins again; it was like past times when he had to live on his wits to survive. 'When you think of our non-existent life in Whitehead, this is heaven. Don't you feel alive, brother? We'll outwit them yet, don't worry. Compared to our earlier foes, they are like babies.' Dung grinned and broke into a steady run beside him.

Thanh wasn't as confident as he sounded, but it was important to ease Dung's fears a little. He knew that the Hong Kong police trained thoroughly and that their Sapper training was probably as disciplined and effective as his own. Once the alarm was given, they would call in tracker dogs and helicopters. Their only chance of escape was to get past the open terrain of the tunnel area as quickly as possible and mingle in with the crowds in the busy city area on the far side of the mountain. Thanh suspected that the authorities had not yet established who exactly they were looking for. He knew his people and he knew that once the Correctional Services tried to take an identity check of all the inmates in the detention centre, his compatriots would do everything in their power to frustrate the effort. It didn't matter that the asylum-seekers would not know who was missing; it was just an extension of the code of the prison brotherhood. They would protect anyone they thought was being threatened by the authorities.

They had barely gained any distance from the road when the rapid thud of helicopter blades and the sound of barking dogs reached their ears. Thanh spotted a grating cut into the hillside. It was just what they needed. To have climbed up over the mountain would have taken forever, and the dogs would soon be at their heels. He pulled out his pliers and cut through the grating of the drain, ducked inside with Dung, then pulled the fences back in place. It would at least hold the dogs until the police came. The drain had been cut through the mountain to carry excess storm water away from the tunnel road and was filled with wet slime. They were both sweating and breathless as they ran stooped over through the shallow water. If they could just get through the tunnel and back into the busy Kowloon area on the other side, the tracker dogs would be delayed and it would be easier for them to blend in with the crowds. Fortunately both Thanh and Dung had kept themselves fit during their time at Whitehead, so they both ran swiftly. Thanh had been almost fanatical about exercising every morning and had jogged round the perimeter of the section compound most evenings just for the sensation of feeling he could run. This desperate need to keep exerting himself stemmed from his time at Loa Cai Central Prison in Hanoi when he had been barely able to take three strides before bumping into a wall.

Reaching the far side, Thanh cut his way through the wire grating and they were off running again. Ignoring the hard rocks smashing against their sandalled feet, they ran and slithered their way down a sloping mud track which led from the tunnel area into a shanty town. When Thanh surveyed the packed, bustling market and streets of Kowloon beyond the tin houses he threw his head back and laughed. 'Let them find us now.'

Mr Hai was not overly thrilled when Dung accompanied Thanh into his private office at the Vietnamese Shipping office. 'You could have been caught. Then it would have blown all our plans into disorder. You had one ID card. If I had known about your idea of bringing this man along,' he gave Dung an unfriendly glare, 'maybe we could have authorised another fake ID. What you did was irresponsible, brother.'

Thanh sat himself down and eased back in the chair. 'The point is we weren't caught and besides, if the motor launch had been waiting for us as arranged, we would not have needed fake IDs.'

'We did try with the boat, but it was intercepted by a police launch. They thought our men were smugglers and took them in for questioning. Apparently no one in their right mind fishes round the Tolo Harbour area — it's just too contaminated.'

Thanh burst into laughter. 'What a detail to overlook. Anyway it doesn't matter. We're here and we are in time to meet with the container ship before she sets out for Haiphong.'

Chapter 21: Returning home

Haiphong
4th to 9th May 1993

The wind hones its sword on the mountain rocks.
The boughs of trees are pierced with the spears of the cold.
The bell of a far-off pagoda hastens the traveller's steps.
Slowly the flute-playing buffalo-boys ride home to the villages.
PRISON DIARY, HO CHI MINH

As the tugboats guided the *Hy Vong* within a few kilometres of Haiphong's busy port, Thanh leaned against the rail and breathed in the salty, rank seaweed air. He was home. It had been five years since he had left Vietnam and more than a decade since he'd been a young Public Security officer searching the streets of Haiphong for his brother-in-law, Cuong. So much had changed in his life that he hardly dared think he knew himself any more. Peering down into the water he realised that his feelings were as unclear to him as the sea below. All that mattered was he had to find Niki and Chinh. After that he could contemplate his own future.

As Dung wandered up beside him, Thanh barely registered his presence. 'There's a motor launch approaching,' said Dung. 'The Captain suggests we keep out of the way. How about we go below for a game of poker? I'd like the chance to win back my Pocket English Dictionary.'

Reluctantly, Thanh drew himself out of his thoughts. Turning away from the rail, he followed Dung down the gangway steps to the crew's sleeping quarters. 'What's left for me to win if you lose again?'

'This shirt's a good one. It was given to me by Mr Lieu. He was doing some translating for a British barrister and besides paying him cash for his work, he gave him two shirts.' Dung pulled the back of the shirt collar open so Thanh could read the label. 'See, it was made by a tailor in the Peninsula Hotel.'

Thanh nodded. He could see from the cloth alone that it was definitely a shirt of some quality, but he didn't want Dung to know how much he admired it. 'To my knowledge that shirt has been carried through at least two sewer drains. I'm not sure if I want it.'

'One was a sewer drain. The other was a storm drain, and besides it was wrapped up in my pack and I've washed it since then.'

'Okay, it's a deal. The shirt and/or the pocket dictionary goes to the winner.'

They were barely into the game when a young deck-hand interrupted them. 'The Captain requests you come to his cabin.' Dung furrowed his brows and looked anxiously toward Thanh. Thanh shrugged. If there was going to be trouble they might as well face it quickly. Without speaking, they followed the deck-hand up to the Captain's cabin. They had already prearranged what to do should there be any attempt made to arrest them. If there was a chance to help each other they would take it, but basically, if it came to jumping overboard and swimming ashore, each man was on his own.

Thanh had barely entered the cabin when Nam approached him from across the room. Grinning from ear to ear he clasped his arms round Thanh. 'Brother, it's so good to see you.' It was a long time before Thanh felt able to pull away. For so many years their lives had been knitted together, and their very survival had depended upon one another. 'You look so much better than the last time I saw you. Hong Kong must have treated you well.'

'Yes, very well, brother.' Thanh knew that Nam probably knew as much about the detention centres in Hong Kong as anyone could who had never entered into them. The years hadn't distanced their communication, and they were still able to play their game of double-talk.

'Sit down and drink some tea while we catch up on our lives. We can concern ourselves with other matters later.' Nam held his hand out to Dung. 'Join us, brother. I heard of your coming some days ago. Welcome back to our motherland.'

'How are Lan and Toan?'

'They are both well. You will forgive me that I have not told Lan of your coming to Vietnam. In time I will tell her about our meeting, but for now it is better to remain silent.' Thanh nodded. 'You should marry and have children of your own, brother. The bright future we fought for is for them.'

Thanh felt his throat tighten. 'Good advice, brother. When the time is right there is nothing I would like to do better.'

'I came across someone from your past,' said Nam, 'a man who even now would try to do you harm.'

'Senior Colonel Khiem.'

'You know that I am now working for the Interior Ministry, but there was some overlap in my work with Military Intelligence. I encountered Khiem at a meeting. Predictably he's opposed to the changes that are taking place in our country and claims that *doi moi* — renovation, brings little money but huge problems. Unfortunately he's not alone in his thinking. Many feel that since most of us are former soldiers who fought against the foreigners, we should not forget our dead patriots, or ignore the many plots against us by our former adversaries.'

'Khiem is of the old thinking. Our future lies with opening up our borders to the rest of Asia and the West. One day many of those who fled our country will return and they will bring the gifts of their new learning. We must welcome them back.'

'Yes, that's my thinking, too, but maybe some of their new ways will challenge our old traditions. I don't mean just communism, but the simple values of our people which have gone unchanged over thousands of years. We have to be selective in how we embrace this new thinking.'

They drank and spoke for over an hour before Nam drew the conversation back to their shared concerns. 'Tell me about your friends, Thanh. Ms Niki and Mr Chinh, who are they?'

Thanh sat back in his seat. The Captain's room was comfortably furnished with upholstered seating. Even in his earlier days, when he considered his life to be relatively comfortable, he had never sat in an upholstered chair. 'I understand your concerns about Binh. He was always an extremist, but the situation with Niki and Chinh is quite simple. As you suspected, their issue is human rights, not politics. Just before they left for Vietnam, I told Niki about Binh's forced repatriation. She was concerned about his having burned the Vietnamese flag on a television documentary. I would have advised her to stay away from Binh, but there was barely time for us to talk.'

'This plan to set up a scheme to monitor the resettlement of the returnees — how serious was that?'

'In many ways Niki thinks like a Westerner: she has an idea and she pursues it. When I pointed out to her that if the returnees knew about this clandestine monitoring business scheme, then so would the Vietnamese government. Her thinking was, you would support it.'

Nam laughed. 'Well, maybe she's right. We could pretend not to know, and who knows, it might even suit us. But, actually as far as central government policy is concerned, we are not singling out the returnees for punishment. We have legitimately gathered information because we have to know what these people think and if they are a threat. Look at the case of Binh. We have behaved quite reasonably toward him.'

'What concerns returnees is not the central government policy,' said Thanh, 'but the power that local officials have to target people they don't like. And, to be fair, there have been times when our government has appeared to move forward with reforms and then leap back. Look what happened during the "hundred flowers" era. We were encouraged to criticise the government and then those who did were punished for it.'

'That was years ago.'

Thanh shrugged. 'People have long memories and the distrust and fears are real.'

'Yes, I understand. There are changes that need to be made and in time they will be. So, Thanh tell me more about Ms Niki. What is she to you?'

Thanh was conscious of not only Nam's scrutiny but also Dung's. 'I came back to Vietnam to rescue her. Does that not tell you something of my feeling toward her?'

Nam nodded. 'And I have your solemn word that neither Ms Niki nor Mr Chinh pose a threat to our new revolutionary government? That they are not in any way connected with the CIA?'

Thanh laughed. 'Of course they aren't. Look, the American government probably wishes to pretend that the place they know as Nam no longer exists. They want to forget about it. There are so many other concerns in the world — troubles escalating in the Middle East, North Korea, terrorism, the list is endless — we are nothing to them. Oh, with a population of over seventy million and rapidly moving upward, I suppose the business community see us as a virgin marketplace.'

Nam's face looked serious. 'They invaded us once. Who's to say they wouldn't try again. Look how suspiciously they regard Cuba.'

'Unfortunately for Cuba they live on America's doorstep. Anyway, as far as Niki and Chinh are concerned, you have my solemn promise that they are no threat to us. Remember, I fought in our revolution too. I may have left our homeland, but I still believe Vietnam should be one country under her own rule.'

'Then it's enough. We have much planning to do if we are to protect both your friends and our country from making a mistake which could harm all of us.' Nam stood up and walked over to Thanh. 'I can't express how I feel about your taking the risk to come here.'

Keeping his head low Thanh discreetly looked at his watch. It was 1:34 and if the two Public Security officers in charge of watching Niki and Chinh had eaten their meal and not let it go cold, then the drug should have taken effect by now. As a signal to the young receptionist to go and fetch the empty trays, Thanh glanced up from his newspaper and made eye contact with her. If she were to return with the trays, it meant they were awake. If they were asleep, she should leave quickly and not disturb anything.

Since Niki and Chinh were considered foreigners despite the fact that they were also Vietnamese nationals, they were being detained in one of the government hotels near the centre of Hanoi. If they had been detained in a prison, Thanh's task would have been many times more difficult. As it was, it was relatively easy to arrange for the normal receptionist not to report to work that day because of an urgent telegram informing her that she had to take the train to Vinh to visit her sick father before he passed on, and then substitute a woman they could trust. When the receptionist returned without any trays and set about some busy work at the desk, Thanh took it as the signal that he and Dung could enter the rooms where Niki and Chinh were being detained.

As Thanh entered the communal hallway of the room and noted the Public Security officers stretched out across the benches, Dung stood watch outside. Thanh could hardly contain his excitement when he turned the door handle and walked into the room. Chinh was lying across one of the beds while Niki was standing, staring out of the window. Hearing footsteps she turned suddenly: the fear in her eyes turned to amazement, and she froze in her tracks.

'Come on you idle lazybones. We have to get out of here,' laughed Thanh.

Niki was across the room in seconds. 'Thanh!' He caught her in his arms and for the first time in their long acquaintance he pulled her close to him and held her tightly.

She held on to him for several seconds before suddenly pulling away. Fear returned to her eyes, 'It's dangerous for you. . . .'

Thanh put his fingers up to his lips. 'We have to go.'

Dung had already slipped into the first room and was pulling off one of the officer's uniforms. While Niki and Chinh recovered from their surprise, Thanh stripped down to his underwear, snatched up the second uniform, and changed into it quickly. Dung then proceeded to bind the wrists and ankles of the two sleeping officers.

As they left the room, Thanh took the lead while Niki and Chinh, with their heads drooped forward, walked behind him. Dung took up the rear as they walked calmly, although purposefully, along the open passageway to the stairs leading down to the ground floor. It was only when they passed a laundry maid that anyone showed them any attention. As Dung was level with her she said, 'Can I do that room now?'

Thanh halted and spun round on her. 'You do not enter that room. It must not be touched until my men have had time to inspect it.' The girl sniffed and said something under her breath before turning her attention back to her laundry trolley.

Thanh led them away from the main entrance to where Nam was waiting with the jeep, but as he ushered Niki into the back seat, she sprang backwards almost knocking him flying. 'He's one of them.' Thanh snatched hold of her arm before pushing her roughly into the jeep. Chinh jumped in beside Dung, but seeing Nam sitting in the driver's seat, he looked almost as nervous as Niki.

Tears ran down her cheeks and she dug her fingers into Thanh's arm as they hurtled at full speed away from the hotel. 'Thanh, the driver, he's one of them. What are you doing here? You've been tricked.'

Thanh put his arms around Niki to try to stop her trembling. 'Listen to me, Niki. Nam is my cousin. We have known each other since we were young boys. I'd trust him with my life. I have, many times.'

Slowly his words seemed to get through and Niki stopped shaking. 'He was one of my interrogators. How can this be?'

'He needed to know you were not a spy. It had to be that way. It was Nam who asked me to come here and to see that you get safely back to Hong Kong.'

Niki looked uncertain. 'Are you sure this isn't a trap and that he hasn't used me to get to you?'

'Nam is like a brother to me. I love him.' Thanh stopped speaking, and ignoring the fact that he was wedged into the back seat between Niki and Chinh so that his most private thoughts would no longer be private, he lifted Niki's chin and looked into her eyes. 'And I love you, Niki. That's why I risked coming back.'

Her eyes misted over. 'I love you too, but. . . .'

'My future is undetermined. I know I have no right to love you.'

'You have a wife,' protested Niki.

'Wife! No Lan and I divorced years ago. In fact Nam is now married to Lan.'

Niki looked suddenly confused. 'I thought. . . .'

Thanh gripped her hand. 'I'm sorry. I should have explained to you about Lan. But it was a long time ago and I wanted to leave it in the past.'

It wasn't until they were safely on board the *Hy Vong* that Thanh was able to steer Niki and Nam away from the others so that he could give Niki a fuller explanation of why he had been able to come back to Vietnam. 'We owe Nam a lot Niki. I hope when you two have become better acquainted you will understand Nam's behaviour as well as I do.'

Niki stared at Nam. 'You asked me questions about the detention centre and about Thanh, why?'

Nam smiled. 'At first I was interested to learn more about you. I didn't know if you were a spy or not.'

Niki looked shocked. 'Why would you think that?'

Catching the surprise and indignation in her tone Nam laughed. 'For one, we are suspicious people by nature. It's the result of our turbulent history and the vulnerability of being a young revolutionary government, but, I can tell you, it was your association with Binh that aroused our concerns. We had records of your background, so I knew you worked with Thanh. The profile you presented was perplexing. Of course I was interested, and then when I asked questions about Thanh and you became defensive, it aroused my curiosity further.'

Niki softened her expression. 'You frightened me terribly. I still don't understand, but since Thanh says I can trust you, and you just helped us to escape, I owe it to you to accept the reasons for your questioning.

'Believe me, I had good reasons for wanting to understand the depth of your relationship with Thanh, and they do not all relate to the security of our country.'

'Did you know how I felt about Thanh then?'

'Not immediately. Of course, later on I understood.'

Thanh drew Niki over to him. 'I suspect Nam understood that better than I did. It's why he brought me here. You see our love and your freedom is also Nam's freedom. He is no longer bound by the duty of a husband to love his wife. He is free to love her without any obligation to me.'

Niki's face clouded. 'I was hurt because Minh said you were married to her sister.'

'I was married to Minh's sister, Lan. We have been divorced for many years now. She's now married to Nam and they have a young son.'

Nam stepped forward and bowed his head. 'Thanh is right, of course. Lan was the latter reason for my interest in you. There were both personal and political reasons for my wanting Thanh to return.'

'I'm beginning to understand.'

'Please come with us and meet my father. I know that he's eager to become acquainted with you.'

When they entered the Captain's cabin, Uncle Chau was lounging in one of the upholstered chairs, chatting to Dung and Chinh. Upon seeing them, he stood up and walked over with his arms outstretched. Although his hair was more silvered than Thanh remembered, his eyes glittered with the same youthful intensity as they had always done. 'Uncle.' Thanh savoured the strength and warmth of his uncle's embrace for several seconds before pulling back and sliding Niki in front of him. 'Please, Uncle, meet Niki.'

Uncle Chau clasped his hands over Niki's and squeezed them. 'Welcome home, daughter. I apologise for our earlier inhospitality, but maybe as you and I become better acquainted, you will understand that the shadows of our past still haunt us.' He waved toward the chairs. 'Please sit down. Captain Toai is preparing a special feast for us, but first we will drink tea. There are many things for us to discuss.'

As Captain Toai excused himself from their company, Thanh guided Niki toward the Western-style upholstered sofa and sat down next to her. After his sleepless nights of the past few weeks, he felt comforted in having her close by. He knew it couldn't last, but he wasn't going to hold back on his feelings any longer. She nestled close to him as though she was also anticipating the pain of their pending separation.

Uncle Chau bent over the low table and poured tea into five small cups. Offering a cup first to Niki he then handed tea to the others. After taking a sip he placed his cup on the table and leaned back, steadily fixing his gaze upon Thanh. 'Although our being here together brings me a certain happiness, I must confess that it also brings me some concern. When I suggested Nam write to you it was not my intention that you should come here. At that time I was simply seeking your advice. Thanh, you of all people know this is a dangerous place for you.'

Thanh could feel the suppressed irritation in his uncle's voice. He sat resigned, ready to hear him out. 'Of course,' continued Uncle Chau, 'I understand the situation — it suited Nam to have you make this foolish chivalrous gesture and I should have foreseen what could happen. Nam's behaviour is. . . .'

'No. . . .' Thanh had voiced his protest before he could stop himself. Seeing the look of surprise on his uncle's face, he attempted an apology. 'I'm sorry, Uncle. I didn't mean to interrupt you, but Nam is not responsible for my coming here.'

'Then perhaps you would like to explain to me who is?'

'The decision was mine. It's difficult. . . .' Thanh could have spoken of his failure to build a satisfactory relationship with Lan, but then that relationship was over and he didn't want to speak of it any more. He angled his knees so that he could grip Niki's hand without the others seeing. He knew he should speak of his feelings toward Niki and of how he did not want to repeat the same mistakes he'd made with Lan. In Hong Kong, although imprisoned in the detention centre, he'd felt more at ease in being able to express himself, but here, back in Vietnam with his uncle's clear eyes gazing steadily at him, he could feel again the social and family pressures engulfing him.

Thanh breathed in deeply. 'I know I don't have a future with Niki. And of course it is presumptuous of me to even speak of my love for her when I can offer her nothing.' Thanh hesitated. 'And I'm ashamed to say that I knew that you could have arranged her escape without my participation in it, but coming back here and rescuing Niki and Chinh gave me back a sense of my own worth. After so much time of doing nothing. . . .' Thanh could feel the sweat breaking out on his forehead. 'Any action was better than feeling impotent. Being in Whitehead year after year, day after day, is a living death. It eats a man up from inside out until he's not even human. I was a nameless economic migrant, camp number 1422, vrd:9/127/88.'

Uncle Chau looked from Thanh to Nam. 'So you don't even deny that this collusion between the two of you served more than just the needs of our motherland. Nam seals his relationship with his wife while you take risks that are unpardonable just to prove your manhood. There is a cause here that is greater than your individual egos.'

'I feel the same as you about our motherland. I'm not a traitor, but if we deny our individual morality, then from what base can we rebuild our country?' Thanh could feel himself trembling. He hadn't wanted to argue with his uncle, especially in front of Niki and the others, but he couldn't stop himself. For so many years he'd bitten back his tongue. 'It's only through listening to our conscience that we can ever have the courage and integrity to follow a just course. I agree that it's right to put the needs of the community before our own selfish desires and ambitions, but that doesn't mean we should let others tell us what to think. If we forget our humanity and place "the cause" above the individual rights of the people then what we are left with is empty dogma. . . .'

As Thanh spat the words out he could feel a rage building up inside him. 'Because in the end it's the dogma that becomes our master and when we bow our heads to it, we have totally given ourselves over to slavery. That's what happened in the Soviet Union and in China. Why did we follow them so blindly? Couldn't we learn something from their mistakes so we could forge our own path to socialism and. . . .' Thanh suddenly felt deflated. Leaving his sentence unfinished he let his voice drift into silence. He knew he'd already said more than he should. As he'd been speaking he'd seen the growing darkness cloud his uncle's face. He'd also been aware that the others in the room had fallen into a stunned silence where even the rhythm of their breathing had taken on an unnatural stillness. The filled tea cups sat untouched on the table.

Uncle Chau slowly rose from his chair and walked over to the port-hole. His breathing was heavy and he suddenly seemed to show his age. Gazing out of the port-hole into the gathering darkness it was several long moments before he turned back to address Thanh. 'Your words tear into my heart like a bullet.'

Thanh winced. He hadn't wanted to hurt or insult his uncle, but they were words that could not have been left unsaid. He gripped Niki's hand tighter as he watched his uncle reach toward a nearby bookcase to steady himself. When his uncle spoke his voice was hoarse. 'Many years ago, a young man about your age — full of the same passion for our people and for our beloved country — spoke in much the same way. I was taken aback to hear you echo his ideas.' Drawing his hand across his brow Uncle Chau heaved a sigh. 'I was several years younger than him and his destiny to become a great leader was only just beginning to take shape. Freedom and independence — independent thought does not run in contradiction to unity — it is a part of the whole. Although individualism holds many dangers for us — selfishness, ambition, greed and so forth, Uncle Ho repeatedly tried to impress upon us that the thoughts of the peasant were as important as the thoughts of the educated cadre. We must not become arrogant, he warned — filled with our own importance so that we assume the right to tell others what to think. All men must be free to think their own thoughts, to write their own words and to follow their own conscience so that they remain faithful not only to themselves, but also to the revolution. A genuinely free people committed body and soul to our revolutionary and socialist aims are stronger than slaves who, out of fear, bow their head to a powerful force.' He closed his eyes to press back the tears. 'Do you think I don't see the absurdity of what we have become? You think I am blind to the contradictions of our lives — to the ironies of this paradise we have created?'

Thanh muttered an apology. 'I'm sorry, Uncle. It was presumptuous of me to be so outspoken.'

Uncle Chau shook his head. 'No, no. Say what you must. It does an old man good to feel the passion of your beliefs. It's what I needed to hear again, loud and from the heart. For so long — the fleeting shadows of my dead comrades, the whispered voices of dissent that have been barely audible to my ears — all have left a bitterness on my tongue.'

He walked back to the table and slumped heavily into his seat. 'I'm sorry. It's of no consequence as to why or who brought you here; I have no right to interfere. Lan was not my first choice of a wife for either of you and her inclusion into our family was a source of irritation to me for many years, but as I mellow with age I have to admit to a growing fondness toward her and as for my grandson, he is a shining jewel for my dim eyes.'

Uncle Chau pulled himself forward. With steady fingers he poured away the cold untouched tea into a nearby bucket and refilled the cups. Then lifting his cup from the table he drank it back in one swift swallow. 'Let us deal with the matter at hand. I think you all understand that what has taken place here over the last few days must never be spoken of. If the Western press, and, of course, our own patriots within the government, were ever to hear of this, it would mean trouble for all of us.'

Thanh thought the word 'trouble' an understatement. A better word would have been disaster. His Uncle would be disgraced and imprisoned, never to emerge from the gloom of his cell. He watched pensively as his uncle fixed his gaze back on him. 'So . . . what about your future, Thanh? Where does this mess leave you and your young accomplice?'

Before speaking Thanh cleared his throat. 'For years it had been my intention to escape from the detention centre in Hong Kong and to make my way overland to India.' He shrugged. 'I kept putting the moment off although now I understand why. Firstly, I didn't want to leave Niki, but secondly, who's to say the Indian government is any more likely to want to take in refugees than any of the other governments around the world? They have their own problems. I could spend my whole life wandering aimlessly from one country to the next seeking sanctuary, yet never finding it.' He pursed his lips. 'That's not what I want; coming back here has helped me to realise that. I suspect I decided to allow Dung to accompany me because I recognised in him a kindred spirit.'

'If you come back here, it will be dangerous for you,' said Uncle Chau. 'You were tried in absentia, fifteen years, not to mention the fact that you escaped from prison in highly dramatic circumstances. That alone could carry the death penalty.' He sighed. 'Things are changing, but still, there will be consequences to your coming back.'

Thanh nodded. 'I know. Dung and I have discussed this. Dung's idea is to quietly disappear into the mountains and to live among the mountain people. While staying with them we all found a measure of happiness. I had considered that option myself.'

'And?'

'It would just mean more hiding. What I want Uncle is to travel back on the *Hy Vong* to Hong Kong with Niki and Chinh. I will separate from them before we come into contact with any of the authorities. I will then return to Whitehead. . . .' Thanh heard Niki gasp. 'The same way as I left. Many asylum-seekers escape to take on temporary jobs so they'll never know I have been here.'

'When you return to Whitehead what will happen?'

'There will be some punishment for my absence. I'll probably be sent to Upper Chi Ma Wan for six months but it's of no consequence. I will not volunteer for repatriation to Vietnam because I am a refugee, but I accept my fate to be returned here in their mandatory repatriation programme.'

'Things are slowly changing here and we have a policy of treating returnees with some leniency, but when you come back it will mean serving out some of your sentence. The minimum I could arrange would be two or three years in prison. I cannot prevent that.'

'I understand, Uncle.'

Uncle Chau shrugged. 'So be it.'

There was a long silence as everyone took in the full impact of Thanh's announcement. They all understood that in agreeing to Thanh's plan, Uncle Chau was willing to jeopardise his own security as well. Had it not been for the presence of Niki, Thanh would have assured his uncle that he would rather commit suicide than ever tell of his uncle's and cousin's unlawful activities. He had already faced torture and knew what had to be done if he ever found himself in such a situation again.

After the silence it was Chinh who eventually risked introducing further conversation. 'Sir, none of us would do anything to put Thanh in any additional danger. You have my word on that, but there is something I wanted to ask you.' He seemed hesitant to say what was on his mind.

'Please, nephew, ask me what you like.'

'There was a young man, Tang, whom we contacted. It was because of us the police arrested him.'

Nam turned toward Chinh. 'Tang is my brother-in-law. In the past I have been remiss in not watching out for his welfare but I promise you he'll be fine. He was questioned by both Public Security officials and members of the People's Committee. I've no doubt that was a troubling experience for him, but I have seen to it that the questioning and intimidation are over.'

Uncle Chau sat back in his chair. 'I imagine you also have concerns for your other friend, Binh.' Chinh lowered his eyes. 'Burning the flag, his outspoken remarks were all provocation. But we are intelligent; we do not have to be provoked. However, bringing explosives into the country with the eventual intent to bring down our government — that we cannot ignore.' Uncle Chau raised his brows. 'Binh will go to prison. In any country he would go to prison for his actions. But don't misunder-stand me, Binh is also our brother and in him we are reminded of our own youth. Many years ago I was like Binh, a young revolutionary with fire in my veins.'

Uncle Chau sighed. 'War is never a good choice. We chose it because we saw no other option. A third of our people died of starvation during the Japanese occupation. In the North the numbers were much higher. Whole families, villages were wiped out and when the French *"Mission Civilisatrice"* was to be restored . . . we vowed our country was never, never to be placed in bondage again. I'm sorry the American government failed to understand that. But now the war is over, and we must bury it along with our lost brothers and sisters. We must look forward to peaceful and happier times.' He shook his head. 'To go back when we have come so far . . . no, that's not the answer. Binh and others like him accuse us of restricting freedom, of suppressing the rights of the individual.' He gazed steadily at Thanh. 'Their criticisms have validity. The freedoms we fought for are only just coming into our grasp, but we still have enemies and cannot totally drop our guard.'

Uncle Chau poured out some water from the flask. 'Think of freedom as our blood or as this water.' He raised up his cup. 'It is precious only if it is protected and contained, otherwise it will drain wastefully into the ground. Enough blood has already been spilled so we move cautiously, slowly. We are writing new economic laws as we learn about international business and private enterprise. I want more freedom, more liberal attitudes toward our writers, artists and journalists, but so long as we are threatened by Binh, or anyone else for that matter, how can I reasonably convince the other leaders in our government that our people are ready for such freedom? Binh is the rod that torments me in my old age. He performs beautifully to the tune of the hard liners.'

Uncle Chau gave a half laugh before taking a sip of his tea. 'Maybe they even pay him to be their *agent provocateur*. Without him those of us who push for reforms would have an easier time. Security and reforms require a delicate balance. We take a stride forward, then panic and inch back, but the progress is there. After a disastrous economic policy we are correcting our mistakes.' Leaning toward Thanh, Uncle Chau gave a dejected smile. 'My son, our policy of *doi moi* is not so straightforward. With freedom comes the problem of prostitution, young girls thinking it is now acceptable to sell their bodies for profit. Getting rich is becoming the goal of many people and takes precedence over the real reforms. What we should be looking for is spiritual liberation and social reforms — better educational opportunities.'

As Uncle Chau spoke he looked exhausted. The lines in his face looked sharper. His shoulders sank forward and a heavy sadness seemed ready to consume him. 'Our children now go to school less than they did before the reforms. The rich become richer at the expense of the poor. We export large quantities of our quality food products which leave many of the population malnourished.'

Then, for just a brief moment, the old light blazed in his eyes as he glared at Thanh with all the passion Thanh remembered from their first meeting. 'Did you know that our children fill their empty tummies with cheap imported soda drinks instead of eating the fish and rice we send overseas? It's our old enemies — greed, exploitation of the masses for the few, who shadow us at every turn. Believe me, Thanh, I am for making money and reforms every bit as much as you are, but we need to move forward with wisdom. . . .'

Thanh wanted to say something but he wasn't sure how to respond. He was weighing up his thoughts when a knock on the door interrupted them. The captain's steward put his head round. 'The Captain asks me to inform you that the food is almost ready and will be laid out in the wardroom. There should be hot water and towels should any of you wish to avail yourself of them.'

Uncle Chau turned to Niki. 'Daughter, you look tired. I'm sure you would like to freshen up after your uncomfortable experiences. However, before you join us for dinner, there is something I wish to say.' He stood up and grasped Niki's hands. 'The only truly innocent in any war are the children and especially the children of mixed parentage. You were born into a situation where neither of your parents could claim you because of the intensity of our feelings toward the horrors we had just lived through. Please accept my most heartfelt apologies for all of the suffering we caused you.' He pursed his lips. 'Maybe we don't always see things as clearly as we should. What is important is, if having recognised our mistakes, we are willing to try to rectify them.' Gently, Uncle Chau lifted the dark hair, which had fallen across Niki's face, and tucked it over her shoulder. 'As I look into your face — your brilliant Western eyes, your soft Asian features — I am reminded of the beauty which can spring from the union of love between the people of two nations. It gives me hope that one day there will be real trust and friendship between people of all nations.'

When dinner was over and it was time for Uncle Chau and Nam to depart for the mainland, Uncle Chau turned to Thanh. 'Son, let us walk along the deck a minute.' Thanh stood up and stepped through the door Uncle Chau opened for him. 'There is still much for you and I to discuss.'

As they walked up the stairs, Thanh noticed that although Uncle Chau managed to keep his shoulders erect, he limped a little and had to struggle to maintain his balance. He must have sensed, rather than seen, Thanh's observation of his deformity, because at the top of the stairs he turned to Thanh. 'It is from spinal TB. It began during my detention in Poulo Condore, and then my lifestyle. . . . There is always a high price to pay for freedom, but no matter. I believe the worst is over.'

They walked along the deck and breathed in the fresh night air. Uncle Chau stopped, and resting his arms against the rails, turned to Thanh. 'Is it really your intention to come back here? Is there not some easier way for you? Maybe an American passport through marriage to Niki?'

'No, Uncle. Please don't make it harder. I can't deny that I am afraid, but it is my fate to return.' Thanh paused as he felt his throat tighten. He'd never spoken of his feelings about taking a man's life, although it was probably the most significant factor which lay behind all of his thoughts. 'I did what I had to do, but I can never totally justify having killed a man . . . and it wasn't one man; there were others — too many others. I feel the pain of each death as though it were my own.' He studied his hands as if it were they that were responsible for the deep pain within him. 'Killing, even in times of war, is still murder. It is like a black fog

that wraps itself around the soul. I shall never be free of it in this lifetime,
I know that, but if I were to take an easy route to America and not return
to Vietnam then these deaths and the deaths of my comrades, would
seem to me to be a mockery. Whatever the cost I must return.' He was
trembling inside, but it didn't matter if his uncle could see. His pain was
consuming and it seemed pointless to try to keep it hidden.

Uncle Chau nodded as Thanh continued. 'I know that my destiny
lies here. There's no dissuading me. But believe me, Uncle, I would kill
myself rather than betray you.'

'I know that and I will not throw obstacles in your way. But your young
friend, Niki, she will be hurt.'

Thanh breathed in deeply. How could he ever explain to Niki why he
must return, that his only road to freedom was back through Vietnam.
Their separation would be more painful to him than the deprivations of
prison life. 'Yes, Uncle, she will be hurt. I hope she can find it within her
to understand and to forgive me.'

'I know the massacre at Hue was the beginning of your disillusionment. You were so young and idealistic. I have always regretted sending
you there, but please don't judge us so harshly, my son. There was no
policy of killing innocent people. Discipline was seriously inadequate, so
local cadres like Khiem, seeking personal revenge, were able to execute
their villainy unchecked.'

'It took me a long time to understand that, but what happened in Hue
isn't the only reason for my disillusion. The day of liberation I was elated
— there was a lightness to my heart that reached ecstasy. I saw the floods
of refugees pouring into Saigon from the countryside, yet, I still couldn't
fully register what it was they were afraid of. But since the war ended. . . .'
Thanh's words faded to a halt. He turned and looked out toward the sea.
There were so many issues he'd struggled with that he didn't even know
where to begin to put his feelings in order.

'War brings terrible things,' said Uncle Chau, 'and the recovery of a
nation is always slow and painful. Communism was the only force strong
enough for us to win our freedom — it is only now that we can begin to
relax our hold. Believe me, I fully understand the reasons for your
disenchantment. During the war years President Ho skilfully juggled
China and the Soviet Union; we were dependent upon them for military
aid and given the choice between aligning ourselves with the Soviet
Union or China, our thinking was that it was better to select the ally
whose border is not on our doorstep.' Uncle Chau suddenly laughed. 'I
recall General Giap's remarks about our military strategy — Confuse the

enemy, keep them in the dark about our intentions. We used the same philosophy with our allies. The Soviets must have found us insufferable. But, having chosen to jump on the tiger's back did not mean we trusted him and there was always the dragon's stick to wield against the tiger if we feared he was becoming too assertive.'

'When our Soviet comrades took over the military facilities at Cam Ranh Bay, they didn't even allow us proper access,' interjected Thanh. 'Why did we give them so much power?'

'You of all people know that when Pol Pot challenged our border security we had no choice but to protect ourselves. There was no policy of expansionism toward Cambodia. All we wanted was to live in peace and security. We had hoped to gain normalization with the United States and even agreed to forgo the $4.7 billion in economic aid that Nixon had agreed upon as reparation. But it was not to be. Even under the Carter administration there was bitterness toward us in some circles and Brzezinski's policy toward Peking to use them in a military alliance against Moscow, took away our dragon's stick and pushed us into a deeper alliance with the Soviet Union. With the enormous costs of the war in Cambodia we were dependent upon Soviet goodwill more than ever. For my part I preferred the Soviet brand of revisionist communism to Mao Zedong's policy of destruction during the Cultural Revolution. We had wrongly thought that after the arrest of the gang of four Deng Xiaoping would look at us more generously, but it didn't happen. We were seen as the ungrateful little brother who had dared to challenge them. Dared to challenge them all,' repeated Uncle Chau with some pride. 'In any event, losing our independence was not what we desired. I suppose there were some American's who hated us so much they would have formed an alliance with the devil himself if it meant they could inflict more pain on us.'

'Perhaps more damaged pride than hatred.'

Uncle Chau laughed. 'Ah, that is progress indeed when the student speaks wiser than the master. Yes, damaged pride is perhaps a more accurate description. Hate burns with a fire which soon exhausts itself whereas damaged pride smolders.'

'Our treatment of our Southern brothers — the abuses, re-education. . . . That was a betrayal. We have to take full responsibility for that.'

'You are right, Thanh. Ho always spoke so eloquently of our being one nation — "Vietnam is one," he said. "The Vietnamese people are one. Rivers may dry up, mountains may crumble, but that truth will remain forever." I wonder how he would view our behaviour over the last eighteen years. We did indeed betray our Southern brothers, but we were an international outcast with far too many enemies to feel secure. The endless wars left our people exhausted and handling the enormous domestic problems proved to be more difficult than we had ever anticipated. There wasn't enough food. Perhaps there was jealousy, too. The South was far more prosperous than the North, so those who had profited during the war, or those we still felt threatened by, suffered the most.' Running his fingers through his hair, Uncle Chau glanced out over the sea as though the weight of it all was all too much. 'And the network of conspiracy and distrust we'd created to protect us during the time of war was impossible to step back from.'

'But some of those Southerners had fought alongside us. When we went hungry in the jungle, so did they.'

'I don't want to excuse what we did. I try simply to explain it.' Putting his arm around Thanh's shoulder Uncle Chau looked inquiringly into his eyes. 'I hope you can forgive us for the damage we have caused you, and especially my part in trying to take too much direction in your life. It was I that recommended you and Nam become Sappers. In order to prove that I was not like the other cadres who sent their children overseas to study, I was prepared to sacrifice you both for the revolution.' He sighed. 'Did I not become the tiger myself?'

Thanh gazed back at his uncle. 'I have loved you and cursed you, but you are as dear to me as my own father and mother. Forgive me for sometimes behaving like an ungrateful son. I was truly honoured by the opportunities you afforded me.'

Uncle Chau pulled Thanh into his arms. Thanh felt his love and his strength. It was as though the years of pain were truly drawing to an end. When he drew away Uncle Chau continued to look somberly into his eyes. 'And our country, Thanh? Can you forgive us?'

Thanh sighed. Tears came into his eyes. 'I have never stopped believing in our country and the Vietnamese people, but the suspicion and fear, the suffocating control of the people, our self congratulatory. . . . That wasn't what our patriots gave their lives for.'

Uncle Chau smiled sadly, 'Compared to running the country, fighting the war was easy. We are learning, Thanh, and there have been many obstacles for us to overcome. Tackling bureaucracy and corruption is just the beginning. We want to remain in power, we want to make money for the country, but above and beyond that we want a policy of socialism that will provide the people with all of their needs — healthcare, education, jobs and yes, happiness, happiness to be themselves. The breakup of the Soviet Union has been both a threat to us and a breath of fresh air. Give us time and one day we will be the great nation we have dreamed of.' Uncle Chau grasped Thanh's hands in his. 'That is why you are coming home, isn't it? To be a part of the struggle for that happy future?'

At the sound of approaching footsteps as Nam and the others came up onto the deck, Uncle Chau released Thanh's hands and turned. 'Ah, it is time for me to say goodbye to everyone. I am getting old now and my health is beginning to fail me, but I have a few years yet for us to see our dream realised. We will meet again soon, my son.'

As Uncle Chau and Nam said their goodbyes before climbing down into the launch Dung hung back a few moments. Drawing close to Thanh he clasped his hands over Thanh's. 'This is goodbye brother. I have no idea if or when we will ever meet, but I wanted you to know that you will always be in my thoughts. There are no words to express the gratitude I feel — the endless risks you took on my account, Cuong's and my brother's . . . how can I thank you for that?'

'It's me should thank you for inspiring me with the strength to face my own destiny.' Thanh gripped Dung's hands. 'What's your plan now?'

'Nam will drive me to Lao Cai, then I'll go by foot into the hills to join with our friends. Just to live in my homeland is enough and I know how to disappear. I'm a ghost remember. Neither you or your uncle need ever fear any harm from me.'

Thanh laughed. 'The Ghost Locust, I wonder at the meaning of it all. Our lives have intertwined throughout the past decade, you pushed by an outer chaos, me driven by some inner turmoil, yet we both find ourselves coming back to the same place. Good luck little brother, and as you ease your tormented soul, find some grace for me.'

As the boat started to pull away Chinh leaned over the rail to wave while Niki drew near to Thanh and held his hand. 'I don't want you to return to Hong Kong only to come back and be put in prison.'

'I know that, Niki, but I've thought about this for a long time and, really, it's the only way.'

'But it isn't. Why can't we leave here together for India? You had such good plans. Why has it all changed?'

'Niki, I would be dragging you down with me.'

'I don't care. At least we would be together.'

'I couldn't do that to you. We would be stateless, and in the end you would hate me.'

'I could never hate you Thanh.'

The Ghost Locust

'Then I would hate myself for putting a curse on your life.'

'We could get married and you could apply for a visa to the States as my husband.'

'That is the most tempting offer of all.' Thanh drew in his breath. 'Niki, you must never doubt that I love you. If fate determines our love is to be fulfilled, it will happen. I cannot denounce everything I have lived for and go to America. One day the trade embargo will be lifted, normalization will take place and our countries will truly be friends, but until then. . . .'

'I don't accept this idea of fate. If we want something, we have to make it happen. I want to be with you. That's all that is important to me.'

'Then we will make it happen, but first there is a price to pay. For anything worthwhile there is a price. When the time is right I will do everything in my power to find you again. Even if you were to meet someone else, it wouldn't change my love for you.'

'Don't say that. There is no one else, nor will there ever be. I will be as loyal as the woman who turned to stone waiting for her husband!'

'Her husband couldn't come back.'

'No, because of his damn, stupid principles.'

'I understand you being angry with me. Our future's uncertain, but loving you has given me the strength to go back to prison,' Thanh grinned, 'and we have the journey back to Hong Kong. Most people will never know such exultation as we shall know.'

Niki wiped the tears away from her eyes. 'Why did I ever fall in love with someone with so much integrity? It's what I love and hate most about you.'

'Forgive me, Niki. I know the pain I caused you.'

'What's to forgive? I knew from the beginning what you were like, but don't underestimate my strength. When the time is right I'll find a way to return here. You can't hide in prison forever.'

With his arm resting gently on Niki's shoulder, Thanh leaned against the railings and watched the small motor launch carrying Uncle Chau, Nam and Dung, skim across the water towards the misty outline of Haiphong. It was as though a heavy weight had been lifted from him. Freedom was more than being able to walk through an open gateway, it was something inside. It was the calm which warmed the heart when the struggle was nearly over. His path was different from Dung's, but he believed that in their own way they had each found their way home. The hope of meeting Niki again would carry him through his years of imprisonment. Three, five or even ten years — if that is what it took for the changes in Vietnam to fully come about — was not such a long time to wait.

Thanh returned the wave to his uncle. If there were others within the Vietnamese government who were as enlightened and visionary as Uncle Chau — and from the ease with which they had rescued Niki and Chinh, Thanh suspected that there were — then it would not be too long.

How terribly the rice suffers under the pestle!
But after polishing, it emerges white as cotton.
The same process tempers the human spirit:
Hard trials shape us into polished jade.
PRISON DIARY, HO CHI MINH

Author's note

As *Ghost Locust* was in its final preparations for printing I heard of the tragic suicide of Dung, a young Amerasian in the Philippines. No one can be absolutely sure why Dung committed suicide but several factors are likely to have played a major role.

From the beginning Dung's distinct Caucasian looks branded him an outcast. He never knew his American father, and at age five, on his mother's death, he was adopted by a Vietnamese family. However, when the US Consular Office in Vietnam refused his adopted family's application for settlement, on the grounds that his family 'did not meet the required relationship', Dung was forced to leave without them.

Life for a young man living in the Bataan Transit Centre was not easy. When he became involved in a fight after refusing to pay extortion money he was put in the 'monkey house' for one month. Deemed to be anti-social because of this event and some minor infractions involving the consumption of alcohol, Dung's case file was put on hold. (Dung had been told that he would be in the Philippines for only six months while he learned something about the way of life in the US, however, he remained in the Philippines for six years — from March 1992 until his suicide in November 1998.)

When Dung approached US officials for permission to go to the US he was advised to return to Vietnam, however, when he approached officials at the Vietnamese Embassy, he was told that he could not return to Vietnam because of his Amerasian status. Although he had temporary residence in the Philippines, he had no right to earn a living and so both he and his wife, Hanh, were forced to work illegally. Hanh worked as a street hawker while Dung worked on a fishing vessel. The realisation of his stateless existence may well have caused him to give up hope.

Dung's wife and two young children are left without support. Hanh is an orphan and has no family to support her if she is repatriated to Vietnam. It is my hope that in highlighting this case advocacy can be obtained for their acceptance into the US on humanitarian grounds and to also raise money for their support.

Many Amerasians find themselves in similar circumstances. They all left Vietnam legally under a US programme, and since it has become clear that the Vietnamese government will not take them back, these young people now find themselves stateless.

The royalties of *Ghost Locust* will be directed to Southeast Asia Recourse Action Center for the benefit of families such as Hanh's, who find themselves in such desperate circumstances.

Anyone wishing to make further inquiries or send donations, can contact:
Southeast Asia Resource Action Center (SEARAC)
1628 16th Street, NW, 3rd Floor, Washington DC 20009
Tel: (202) 667-4690, fax: (202) 667-6449, email: searacdc@aol.com

Acknowledgments

This novel would never have been written were it not for Lan, a young Vietnamese girl who trusted me enough to invite me into her world. It was Lan who first told me the story of Mrs Viet Ha. When Viet Ha died after giving birth to her son in the Fang Cheng Camp in China, the ploy of burying her with a banana plant cradled in her arms to prevent her young spirit from calling to her son failed, and the baby died a within a month of his mother. Three years after her death Viet Ha's husband escaped from Fang Cheng and took his wife's and son's bones back into Vietnam for burial. While crossing into Vietnam he was arrested by the Vietnamese boarder guards and charged with spying for China.

The story of Viet Ha, her son and her husband, haunts the pages of this novel as it haunted me during the years I spent working inside Hong Kong's detention centres. It was the driving force which motivated me to join with the ex-Dong Hung/Fang Cheng asylum-seekers in their quest for justice despite the more powerful voice of Hong Kong government that their claims for refugee status were invalid. Their freedom came painfully slowly after a decade of detention. Although the characters in this novel are fictitious it was from the personal courage and determination of the asylum-seekers that the pages of *Ghost Locust* drew its breath. I am grateful to them all.

I am especially indebted to my close friends on the editorial staff of *Freedom Magazine*. Even though their own future was insecure they painstakingly translated every word of the Fang Cheng case histories from Vietnamese to English. When I was banned from Whitehead Detention Centre by the UNHCR, for speaking on the radio they were confined to their sections and *Freedom Magazine* was temporarily closed down.

I wish to thank Adam Vosey of Garden Streams Art in the Camps and Hanh for their courage when, after returning from their honeymoon in Hawaii, they were immediately confronted with an ultimatum from the UNHCR that they dismiss me from their programme or risk closure.

I would like to acknowledge several journalists for their help in giving the asylum-seekers a voice. It was Adrian Edwards who provided the opportunity for Mrs Phuong to tell part of her story on the RTHK and the BBC. I thank Ron McMillan, a freelance photographer and journalist, Simon Winchester of *The Guardian,* Chris Dobson and Fiona Mac-

Mahon of the *South China Morning Post* and Jon Swain of *The Sunday Times,* who despite the risks were willing to write of the injustices that were not supposed to be spoken of. I thank Tony Budd for trusting his expensive video camera to the editors of *Freedom Magazine* and giving the asylum-seekers a voice in his film *Final Betrayal.* I thank Jo Gilhooly of AsiaTV for giving the Dong Hung/Fang Cheng group television exposure.

There are so many members of Refugee Concern HK and other NGO camp workers who took risks in speaking out on behalf of the asylum-seekers it is impossible for me to name all of them. To mention but a few, I give special thanks to Pam Baker and Michael Darwyn for their tireless energy, Robyn Kilpatrick of Amnesty International for her dedication to human rights, Chinh for his integrity and courage, and Martha Bourne for her quiet determination.

Thanks to Mike Hanson, Clinton Leeks and Brian Bresnihan, from Security Branch for letting me argue and drink tea with them even though I must have been a constant thorn in their sides. And thanks also for opening the gates to the detention centres even after others closed them. Thanks to Udo Janz and Rob Robinson of the UNHCR for defending my name and for their tireless work on behalf of the asylum-seekers. Thanks to Jahanshah Assadi, Chief of Mission UNHCR for recognising the last of the Dong Hung group.

I am grateful to Senator Paul Simon for honouring his promise to read the Dong Hung/Fang Cheng asylum-seeker seventy-page case histories that I thrust on him as he was leaving his hotel in Hong Kong for a dinner engagement. I especially thank him for speaking out on their behalf and for requesting publication of three case histories in the Congressional Record, Monday, May 20th 1991.

I am indebted to Quang and Thuy for their hospitality when I set out from London for Hong Kong, to Duyen for giving me a place to stay in Hanoi, Dao for being my travelling companion and The and Huong for their generosity. I thank my foster daughter, Lan Anh, for teaching me the Vietnamese culinary arts. I would like to thank all of my friends in Vietnam for their warm hospitality. Although they might prefer I do not mention their names I have not forgotten them and never will.

I give special thanks to my publisher, Mike Morrow for not turning me away when I arrived unannounced at Asia 2000's doorstep with the tattered, tiny print manuscript of *Ghost Locust* that I had carried with me around Vietnam for a month. Thanks also to Barbara Baker of Asia 2000 for being the kind of editor every writer hopes to work with.

I'd like to acknowledge the help of Fred Armentrout and Peter Stambler of Hong Kong PEN for taking time over my manuscript and for the opportunity to contribute to their anthology *Another Day in Paradise* of work from the camps. Thanks also to Laura Anschicks and Eddie Lucas for their editorial suggestions during the early stages of my writing and Ken Starks for getting my computer going.

Thanks to Kath and Richard Beacher for their hospitality in Hong Kong, and to Judy Von Ohlen, Mary Knepper, and Caroline Magruder for their help and encouragement.

Special thanks to my sister Loraine Tymons for being 'Mum' to my kids when I revisited Vietnam and Hong Kong. Last, but not least, to my husband Steve, for his love and support, and to my daughter, Kirsten, and son, Tristan, who put up with my adventures even when they rather I stayed home and behaved like a normal wife and mum.

About the author

Heather Stroud's strong desire to travel saw her leaving home in England at nineteen and taking up a job as an au pair in Turkey. She has since lived in the USA, the Soviet Union, Hong Kong and Brazil. With a degree in psychology and philosophy she has spent most of her working life in the human services professions.

In Hong Kong she worked in the Vietnamese Asylum-Seeker Detention Centres for *Freedom Magazine,* and was spokesperson for Refugee Concern HK. After six years of challenging the Hong Kong government and the UNHCR over the legitimate claims of a group of asylum-seekers, persecuted in both China and Vietnam, she succeeded in getting them recognised as refugees. She has travelled widely in Vietnam but, because of her advocacy of returnees, now finds herself unable to get a visa to make further visits.

She is presently working on a second novel, *October Chill,* which follows the story of an Estonian family who escaped from their homeland after the Russian invasion in 1940.

Best-selling fiction and non-fiction about Asia from Asia 2000

Cheung Chau Dog Fanciers' Society
by Alan B Pierce

'A rare read indeed. An accurate slice of Hong Kong life — touching on heroin smuggling, money laundering, corruption in the police force as well as in one of Hong Kong's most wealthy and powerful Chinese families — a thriller with a difference.' — *Hongkong Standard*

'One of the best Hong Kong novels ever written. It puts James Clavell to shame.' —*HK Magazine*

'Pierce [is] at his best when writing from the heart about the texture of life in a special place.' — *South China Morning Post*

Temutma
by Rebecca Bradley and John Stewart Sloan

Temutma, a *kuang-shi,* a monster similar to the vampire of European legend, is imprisoned beneath Kowloon Walled City in Hong Kong by his ancient keeper. Hungering for blood it begins a horrifying series of murders. . . .

'Page-turning . . . intelligent writing and suspense, suspense, suspense . . . thrilling' — *South China Morning Post*

Riding a Tiger
by Robert Abel

'Fisher is under house arrest and required to write his testimony as the result of the mysterious death of his friend Chen Tai-pan. . . . Characters richly populate Fisher's life. His observations are philosophical and heartfelt. A lively, upbeat and humorous look at Beijing life through the eyes of an unabashed Westerner.' — *South China Morning Post*

Shanghai
by Christopher New

The *New York Times* bestselling epic of five decades in the mighty city.

'*Shanghai* has all the ingredients: exotic location, epic sweep of time, strong characters, drugs, sex and violence. . . . New demonstrates a gift for putting the reader into a typhoon, a Chinese brothel or a tense Communist rally. The epic takes John Denton through British rule of Shanghai, Japanese invasion and Communist takeover.' — *United Press International*

Hong Kong Rose
by Xu Xi

From a crumbling perch with a view of the Statue of Liberty, Rose Kho, Hong Kong girl who made it, lost it, and may be about to make it or lose it again, reflects, scotch in hand, on a life that 'like an Indonesian mosquito disrupting my Chinese sleep' has controls of its own. Or, like a wounded fighter plane of the type her father used to fly, no controls at all. In *Hong Kong Rose,* petals metamorphose into scales that shine like mirror glass windows, reflecting equally the courage, cowardice and compromise of one of the world's great cities.

Chinese Walls
by Xu Xi

'Ai-Lin describes a Hong Kong childhood in the 1960s. That's before most of the skyscrapers had appeared, and when packs of foreign sailors sauntered down Nathan Road, eyeing the girls who hung around the entrance to Chungking Mansions, and when many of the buildings were still colonial, low-rise structures.'
— *Far Eastern Economic Review*

'Although simply written, *Chinese Walls* tells a complex and controversial story of a Chinese family. The author goes boldly where other, perhaps overly-sensitive, Asian authors fear to tread in tackling such subjects as sex, Aids, homosexuality, incest and adultery.

'Vividly, she describes the mother forcing the children into reciting Chinese dynasties in Mandarin, the little girl's curiosity about the prostitutes in Chungking Mansions and the night of incest between sister and brother — her only happy memory of family life.' — *Eastern Express*

Daughters of Hui
by Xu Xi

'Xu Xi is a Hong Kong writer who does not write like the typical 'Hong Kong writer' and speaks with more authority because of it.' — *Asiaweek*

'Their menfolk are arrogant, absent Chinese husbands who neglect their wives for even more arrogant parents. Their extended families are xenophobic, diaspora Chinese whose worst nightmare is the horror of their offspring assimilated with the loathsome *gweilo.*' — *South China Morning Post*

Best-selling fiction and non-fiction about Asia from Asia 2000

Chinese Opera
by Alex Kuo

'An American goes to his ancestral land, China, and confronts the strangenesses there. What life after revolution? After many revolutions? Alex Kuo helps us hear the music that strangers play to strangers, and a free individual plays to society.' — **Maxine Hong Kingston**

'Kuo gave himself an ambitious task, setting his story of an American-Chinese exploring his cultural roots against one of the most vivid historical backdrops of the century.' — ***South China Morning Post***

Getting to Lamma
by Jan Alexander

A young American woman carves out a place for herself in Hong Kong. To do so she must deal with an old flame, a handsome young Shanghainese, two babies and an elderly Chinese nurse.

Farewell My Colony
by Todd Crowell

A journal of the final two years of Hong Kong under British rule, by American writer and long-term Hong Kong resident Todd Crowell.

'An intelligent and illuminating book, the stylish writing is itself a source of pleasure.' — ***Asiaweek***

Cantonese Culture
by Shirley Ingram & Rebecca Ng

A guide to the etiquette and customs of Hong Kong and other Southeast Asian cities. The rituals of daily life — birth, death, marriage, and the many festivals that make up the Chinese calendar are described and explained.

Hong Kong, Macau and the Muddy Pearl
by Annabel Jackson

'A pleasure to read and an inspiration to learn more about a region that has a surprising amount to offer.' — ***Asiaweek***

Other titles
from
Asia 2000

Non-fiction

Cantonese Culture	Shirley Ingram & Rebecca Ng
Concise World Atlas	Maps International
Egg Woman's Daughter	Mary Chan
Farewell, My Colony	Todd Crowell
Getting Along With the Chinese	Fred Schneiter
The Great Red Hope	Jonathan Eley
Hong Kong, Macau and the Muddy Pearl	Annabel Jackson
Hong Kong Pathfinder	Martin Williams
Hyundai	Donald Kirk
Red Chips and the Globalisation of China's Enterprises	Charles de Trenck
The Rise & Decline of the Asian Century	Christopher Lingle
Walking to the Mountain	Wendy Teasdill

Fiction

Cheung Chau Dog Fanciers' Society	Alan B Pierce
Chinese Opera	Alex Kuo
Chinese Walls	Xu Xi
Daughters of Hui	Xu Xi
Getting to Lamma	Jan Alexander
Hong Kong Rose	Xu Xi
Riding a Tiger	Robert Abel
Shanghai	Christopher New
Temutma	Rebecca Bradley & Stewart Sloan

Poetry

An Amorphous Melody	Kavita
The Last Beach	Mani Rao
New Ends, Old Beginnings	Louise Ho
Round — Poems and Photographs of Asia	Madeleine Slavick & Barbara Baker
Travelling with a Bitter Melon	Leung Ping-kwan
Woman to Woman and other poems	Agnes Lam

Order from Asia 2000 Ltd
302 Seabird House, 22–28 Wyndham St, Central, Hong Kong
tel (852) 2530-1409; fax (852) 2526-1107
email sales@asia2000.com.hk; http://www.asia2000.com.hk/

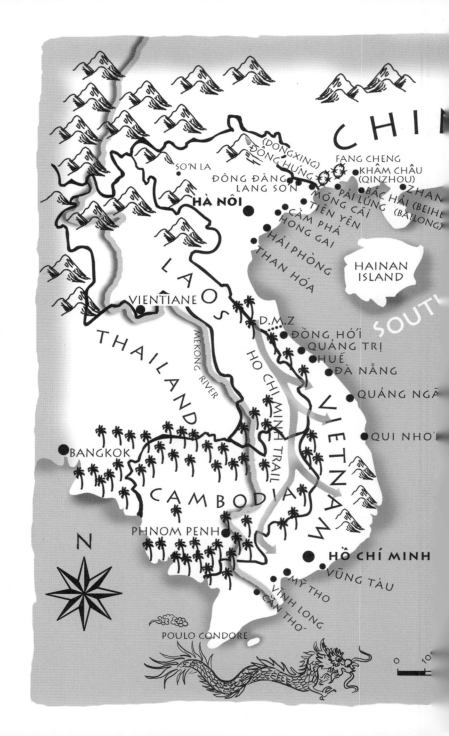

TAINAN•

KAOHSIUNG•

TAIWAN

●HONG KONG

●MACAU

NA SEA

≡≡≡ URBAN AREAS

✿ DETENTION CENTRES

0   5   10   15
KILOMETRES

NEW TERRITORIES

TOLO
HARBOUR

✿ Whitehead

●SHA TIN

HIGH ISLAND ✿

KOWLOON

MONG KOK● ✿ KAI TAK

GREEN ISLAND ✿

LANTAU
ISLAND

HONG KONG

CHI MA WAN ✿ CHEI LING CHAU

LAMMA ISLAND

PHILIPPINES

AIGON)

400   500

TANIA WILLIS